# Monkey Boy

# Monkey Boy

A Novel

## Francisco Goldman

Grove Press
*New York*

FIRST EDITION

*Published simultaneously in Canada*
*Printed in Canada*

First Grove Atlantic hardcover edition: May 2021

This book was set in 12 point Adobe Garamond Pro
by Alpha Design & Composition of Pittsfield, NH.

Library of Congress Cataloging-in-Publication data is available for this title.

ISBN 978-0-8021-5767-6
eISBN 978-0-8021-5769-0

Grove Press
an imprint of Grove Atlantic
154 West 14th Street
New York, NY 10011

Distributed by Publishers Group West

groveatlantic.com

21 22 23 24   10 9 8 7 6 5 4 3 2 1

*For Jovi and Azalea Panchita*

*For Binky Urban*
*&*
*In memory of my mother*

"Why you monkey," said a harpooner . . .
—Herman Melville, *Moby Dick*


"And now I want you to tell me," the woman suddenly said with a terrible force, "I want you to tell me where one could find another father like my father in all the world!"
—Isaac Babel, "Crossing the River Zbrucz,"
*Red Cavalry*


When someone goes on a trip, he has something to tell about . . .
—Walter Benjamin, *The Storyteller*

# Thursday

FIVE DAYS A WEEK and sometimes on Saturdays, too, my father used to get up at 5:45 a.m. to go to work at the Potashnik Tooth Corporation in an industrial pocket of Cambridge, a half hour or so drive from our town if you knew how to avoid the traffic. Moving around this apartment at that same predawn hour all these years later, hurriedly packing for my trip to Boston, I remember how his moving around the house always woke me before I had to get up for school: bathroom noises, heavy tread on the stairs, the garage door hauled up like a loud ripping in the house's flimsy walls. My father kept his Oldsmobile in the driveway but always came into the house through the garage. Late school-day afternoons and evenings, I especially dreaded that garage-door sound. Unless what I heard next was my mother's Duster coming inside, the flinching chug of her light nervous foot on the brake, it meant Bert was home and would soon be coming up the stairs. If I was listening to music on my little stereo I'd turn the volume way down or snap it off to be sure to hear his footsteps outside my door. Sometimes, if he was really angry at me over something or other, he'd burst into my room without knocking.

I remember no part of life inside the house on Wooded Hollow Road, which we moved into when I was in fifth grade, more vividly than my fear of my father. It seems now like years went by without a day when he wasn't angry. But that must not be true, not every day; it's not like there weren't things in his life that didn't bring my father joy or a kind of joy. Bringing home a new sapling or bush from Cerullo Farm and Nursery to plant in the yard on a weekend morning or winning his football bets and collecting from his bookie, joy.

But what a shitty start to the day, thinking about old Bert, feeling like his shadow is falling across the decades into my apartment as I get ready to head out the door doesn't seem to augur too well for the trip ahead. But I'm not like my father, am I. He'd let any little frustration enrage him. Right now he'd be stomping from room to room noisily seething: God damn it to hell, where's that goddamned Muriel Spark. Even in the most berserk moments of some pretty overwrought relationships, I've never even once screamed at another person the way he used to when he'd really lost it. Okay, here it is, on the sofa facing the TV, hiding underneath the Styrofoam tray last night's beef chow fun came in, *The Girls of Slender Means*. I left it out to read on the train, a bit of homework before I see my mother tomorrow. The novel, according to the back cover, is set in a London boardinghouse for single young working women right after World War II, and Mamita lived in one of those, though in Boston, and in the 1950s.

Five months ago, in October, after I'd moved back to New York from Mexico City, I rented this parlor-floor apartment in a brownstone in Carroll Gardens. I still had stuff in storage from when the city had last been my home, nearly ten years ago. But I've only visited since, coming up to New York once a year, sometimes staying as long as a few months. I didn't want to move back but felt forced to by a warning I received in Mexico that I probably could have ignored. But it didn't feel that way at the time, so I fled. The warning was the result of my journalism on the murder in Guatemala of a bishop, the country's greatest human rights leader, including the book I published less than two years ago. Maybe in some unacknowledged way I wanted to come back to New York. Thirty years ago, the first time I ever came here to live, I was also fleeing, looking for a refuge from humiliation, a new start. I don't buy that myth of New York City as a place to come and begin your ambitious climb. Better to arrive humbled, self-embarrassed, it kind of de-hierarchizes the city, spreads it out, offering you more places to hide and also more room to move, to discover yourself in obscure corners, inside shadows and murk. In the past, not wanting to miss out on the chance for some ever-elusive apotheosis, clinging to a relationship or some romantic delusion, I wouldn't have taken the time for all these trips home to Boston to see Mamita.

When I visit my mother tomorrow in Green Meadows, her nursing home, it will be for the fourth time since I moved back, this after a decade of sometimes seeing her only once a year. My sister, Lexi, visits a couple of times a week and speaks to her on the phone at least once a day. After all those years of living abroad when I often couldn't remember to phone her even once a month, I do try to talk to my mother every week now. She hasn't felt so present in my life since I left home for good at eighteen. It seems now like she's always just a quick thought away, and I like to picture her in her room at the nursing home with her patient rabbit smile, waiting to resume our conversations. I was a little puzzled when I noticed that I'm not in any of the framed photographs on her windowsill and wondered what the reason was; really, I should just bring her a picture now. Two photos of Mamita with her own mother are displayed there, one from when she was in her midtwenties and Abuelita came to Boston to help her move into that boardinghouse and get her settled; the other is from a few years before Abuelita died, when she looked quite a bit like my mother does now, puffy around the eyes, eyelids drooping. There's a photograph of Lexi from when she went to Guatemala during a college summer vacation: she's standing on the rough stone steps of the famous old church in Chichicastenango, smiling zestily, surrounded by the usual kneeling Maya shamans with their smoky incense censers, lighting candles, beseeching and casting spells for their clients. Another from about a decade later shows Lexi and our parents in a familial pose, standing close together, mother and sister in flowing dresses for who knows what occasion I wasn't at, my father in jacket and tie, but you can't see his face because of the piece of cardboard taped over it. Only Lexi could have decided to do that, though apparently without much opposition from our mom. When I asked Mamita about it, she looked blank for a moment, then there was a flicker of recognition in her eyes and she dismissively clucked her teeth like she does and said, Ach, no se, Frankie. I wonder if the nurses and other staff laugh to themselves over that photo, some even thinking: Oh yeah, I know about husbands and fathers like that.

Usually on these visits I spend at least a couple of nights in Boston hotels and sometimes a night at a highway hotel near the nursing home, located in a town nearly at the end of a commuter train line out to the southern suburbs. If I have to live up here again, for however long it turns out to be, this seems as good a time as any, when my mother has obviously started her mental and physical decline but for the most part is still lucid enough to have good conversations and giggles with. Ay, Mamita, we make each other laugh, anyway, don't we?


I head down the sidewalk in the cold March, just predawn dark, feeling half-awake and half-asleep, pulling a wheeled carry-on. I forgot to take the locker padlock I use at the gym out of the backpack hung over my shoulders, and the lock knocks against my back in rhythm with the fall of my boot soles on the pavement, a muffled clanking the quiet seems to amplify along with the suitcase's clacking wheels: *clackclack* clink *clackclack* clink.

The subway ride into Manhattan doesn't fully belong to the awoken world either. There are grim-faced, sleepy-eyed early commuters, some with heads heavily nodding down as they sit, and a few homeless men sleeping across the seats, blankets so blackened they look made of cast iron; it's like this train is transporting exhausted spirit miners out of a supernatural mine.

I still always call it going home to Boston, though I haven't lived in that city since I was an infant, back when my newlywed parents had an apartment somewhere on Beacon Street. But this year I didn't go home to Boston to spend any part of the Christmas holidays with my mother and sister. In early December I flew to Buenos Aires to report a magazine article on the search for the missing and stolen children of parents disappeared in the Dirty War years and stayed until just after the New Year. Then I'd only been there a few days when I got an email from my sister saying how happy she was that we'd be able to spend Christmas together for the first time in so many years. I hadn't told Lexi I'd be in Argentina for the holidays, though I had told our mom, but she'd probably forgotten to pass that on. Instead, I was invited for Christmas Eve dinner with one of the Abuelas de la Plaza de Mayo and her recently recovered grandson, the only son of her only daughter, who'd given birth while a secret prisoner of the military dictatorship twenty years before, after which she'd "disappeared" forever, most likely rolled from the bay of a plane into the South Atlantic. Her son's identity had been confirmed by DNA testing only a few months before. For my piece, I only had to try to describe that Christmas Eve just as it was in order to transmit an appropriate sense of the sacred, of the mystical presence of the missing mother-daughter—Paulina was her name—her blessing and love in the new bond between a grandson and grandmother who until recently had been strangers. Later, I got mail from readers who were moved by that scene especially, a few who had stories of their own to share about lost or missing mothers, even of ghostly visitations during holiday family gatherings and weddings.

In her email, Lexi wrote that we could hire a caregiver and take our mother, in her wheelchair, from the nursing home to have dinner in a restaurant, or else we could even have Christmas at her house in New Bedford. "I can't think of a better occasion for you to finally come to my house and see how I live here," she wrote. I've never been to the house Lexi bought a few years ago out in that old fishing port and now mostly defunct manufacturing city. She bought it as an investment, she says, with the money she got from our parents. An old gabled New England manse-looking place, originally built supposedly for a whaling captain back in the Melville time. There are plans to finally bring commuter rail service out to those South Coast communities that are a little closer to Providence than to Boston, and when they do, all those old Victorian sea captains' and textile magnates' houses are going to be coveted by yuppies who work in one or the other of those cities, and the house she bought is going to quintuple in value, so says Lexi. She's always considered herself a sharp businesswoman and has been waiting all these years to prove it. Regarding his daughter's self-proclaimed acumen, my father tended to be bluntly derisive. It's a shame Bert won't be around to get his comeuppance if Lexi's real estate gamble pays off. Our parents signed over all their savings and property, everything they had, to Lexi. During those last years when my father was constantly in and out of the hospital, they did need help keeping up with their bills and various other such obligations, and they both knew that after my father was gone, my mother would never be able to handle those tasks alone, so Bert had to teach Lexi how to do it. I know Mamita, especially, was worried about my sister's sometimes unstable employment and life situations and was determined to give Lexi some security but with responsibilities too. Those decisions freed me to be an aloof son and an even more aloof brother, almost always living far away, in Mexico, Central America, stints in Europe. Meanwhile Lexi has taken care of our parents, often a full-time job, first our father, whom she says she hated through his last years, and now our mother, whom she loves with what it's no exaggeration to describe as "total devotion." Look, Lexi deserves everything my parents have given her. I don't resent her for that, not even a little, possibly for some other things but not that. I wouldn't have traded the freedom with which I've been able to live my life for nearly anything.


As I emerge off the Penn Station elevator into a lightening gray dawn, the giant Corinthian colonnades of the post office building create the illusion of a grand boulevard, and an invigorated optimism floods me, like it's the first morning of a long-awaited trip to Paris. Even with the time I lost looking for the novel, I'm early enough to walk up Eighth Avenue a few blocks to the salumeria to get a hero sandwich for the train. The trip between New York and Boston is almost five hours long, as long as a flight from JFK to Benito Juárez, and traveling with a good sandwich makes all the difference. Hombre prevenido vale por dos, Gisela Palacios always liked to say. She loved those old-fashioned country grandma sayings, though she could barely cook a quesadilla. Whether it made him worth two men or not, planning ahead like this is just the sort of thing my father, both a scientist and a sandwich man, always did, though he would have found an old-style Jewish deli, corned beef on a bulkie or else tongue. Bert always drove, I can't even picture him sitting on a train or a subway. He only flew when he had no choice. The last time he made that end-of-winter drive from Florida back to Massachusetts, he was eighty-seven. He was passing through one of the Carolinas when, before pulling into a motel for the night, he stopped for dinner in one of those highway national chain steakhouses and only discovered the unpaid restaurant bill in his pocket when he got home. He mailed the bill with a check to the steakhouse along with a note of apology, explaining that the reason he'd left without paying was that he'd been tired from a long day of driving; he had to admit that at his age he no longer had the same stamina as when he was younger. Barely a week later a letter came in the mail from the restaurant's manager, who wrote that nowadays it was rare to encounter such an honest American traveler, and he included a certificate that would let Bert eat for free in that steakhouse in perpetuity. Free steak for the rest of his days! But he'd already sold his little Lake Worth condo so that he could live year-round on Wooded Hollow Road. My father would never drive through the Carolinas again. He wasn't always that honest, either, though he had a way of giving the impression that he was, with sort of an Abe Lincoln look of homely integrity, dangling rail-splitter arms. So Mamita took him back for that last time, and though she was nearly twenty years younger, the repercussions on her own health of those next six years of looking after and having to deal with Bert every day would be dire.

While the counterman prepares my sandwich, I sit at a table, quickly downing a small cup of coffee and a cup of yogurt, getting a healthy start to what's going to be a long day, and open the Muriel Spark novel to the first page: "Long ago in 1945 all the nice people in England were poor, allowing for exceptions."


Yesterday evening I thought it was already over with Lulú López. Even though we've only gone out a few times, it's the closest I've come to any kind of romantic relationship in five years, since things ended once and for all with Gisela. But then last night Lulú sent that maybe-it's-not-over text message: Hurry back, we'll ride bicycles, etcetera. I can't pretend I don't care what happens between us, but I do try to keep up a fatalistic interiority. But I'm excited about this trip to Boston, in fact, I've started out a day earlier than originally planned just so I can meet Marianne Lucas for dinner tonight in the South End. When she wrote to me out of the blue a couple of weeks ago on Facebook, we hadn't spoken, or had any kind of communication since tenth grade, thirty-four years ago. She's a family and divorce lawyer now and divorced herself. In one of her FB messages, Marianne wrote that she'd decided to try to contact me after hearing me on NPR. I was talking about José Martí and his years living in New York City, the focus of the novel I've just finished, which is not a strictly biographical novel. *The House of Pain* I'm calling it. No argument from me that it might make a suitable title for the biographies of so many of us out here on the sidewalk this morning coming out of and headed down into Penn Station, who've also spent consequential time in a house of pain. It's not a title anyone would ever use for an actual biography of José Martí, those always have to evoke heroism, martyrdom, literary and political genius, or strike the "Yo soy un hombre sincero" chord. But *The House of Pain* is a perfect title for my novel, the major part of which takes place inside a boardinghouse during a couple of the sixteen years Martí lived in New York City, back when he was a poor immigrant exile, tirelessly hustling freelance journalist, translator, private Spanish tutor, poet, and revolution plotter, all this over a decade before he finally found his martyr's death on his one-man, one-horse charge against Spanish troops on a beach in Cuba. I handed the novel in to my publisher just before I left for Argentina. It's only 182 double-spaced pages long, but it took five years to write. It required a lot of research, I even went to Havana and spent a few weeks in archives there. I needed to learn everything I possibly could about Martí in order to identify the gaps where there was no historical or written record, and let my imagination go to work inside those. One draft was 500 pages long. That was followed by another of 278 pages that I handed in, but it was a botch. My editor, Teresa Fijalkowski, was hard on it; that is, while she was fine with latter parts of it, she stuck it to me about the first third. So many voices and who's talking and whose thoughts? Look, Teresa, it's simple, I explained. The narrative spine of that opening section is Martí on a long walk through the city streets to his boardinghouse, where his wife, small son, and the boardinghouse owner's wife, secretly pregnant with Martí's child, are all waiting for him to come home. He's trying to work out in his thoughts how everything in his life has gotten so completely fucked up, and inside his head he's talking to his wife and to his lover and to other people, and he's even trying to imagine what they're saying about him. All of that trails after Martí on his walk back to the boardinghouse like clouds of consciousness that settle onto the page as if into wet cement as fragments of narrative and story. Teresa cracked a half smile, gave me one of her steady ice-cave stares, and finally, with perfect dry comedy, cracked: The dubious gift of consciousness, now I get what Blanchot meant. I said, And it's just my luck to have the only book editor in New York with a PhD from Oxford in critical theory. I wrote my thesis on Auden, said Teresa. But of course we read theory, so what? Frank, there's a lot of turmoil, a lot of pain in that boardinghouse, I get that, said Teresa. But I'd like to sense how they're experiencing it, one character at a time, right from the start. Martí was a hyperconsciousness, I argued, so voluble he was nicknamed Dr. Torrente, and he had more going on in his brain, in his life, than maybe anyone else living in New York City at that time. I spent another relatively monkish year in Mexico City working on the novel. I needed to fasten my prose not only to Martí's heartbreak and torment but also to his wife's, her life obscured by over a century of blame. You think Yoko Ono had it bad, imagine having Fidelista Communists and Miami Cuban right-wing fanatics all blaming *you* for the Cuban Apostle's failed marriage, separation from his son, and years of complicated private torment. It's my lost skinny ugly beautiful book that lived with me through my own most trying years and finally found its way home, my best book, *The House of Pain*. In about nine months maybe it will be displayed over there in the train station bookstore, facing out on the new-books table, ideally positioned between Zaro's bagels and the men's room. Maybe someone will buy it to read on a morning train to Boston a year or so from now, and I'll be taking that train again, and for the first time in my life I'll get to see someone reading a book of mine in public.

Call it Pain Station, too, I think, having just taken my Louis Kahn memorial pee at one of the urinals in here, can't think of a bleaker place to die of a heart attack like the great architect did than this always-stinking filthy men's room. I always picture his final collapse onto the floor like *Nude Descending a Staircase*, a paroxysmal grandeur but with a short, elderly Jewish man clutching his chest and falling, white shirt stained with airline salad dressing and coffee dribbles—he'd flown into JFK and come to the station to catch a train—his final breaths witnessed by drug addicts and the homeless psychotics who'd be in federal or state mental hospitals instead of sheltering in train station bathrooms if such hospitals still existed. Kahn was on his way home to Philadelphia from Bangladesh, where he'd just built his masterpiece, the Bangladeshi capital's National Assembly Building, ancient sacred monumental grandeur reformulated into rigorous vanguard modernist design. After creating one of the most beautiful, spiritually stirring public spaces of modern times, Kahn came home to die in one of the ugliest and most demoralizing.

Here in Pain Station, passengers wait to board their trains in a grimy plastic-and-linoleum arena enclosed by numbered east and west gates while heavily armed soldiers in camouflaged combat fatigues and bulletproof vests stand guard or patrol the floor, bomb-sniffing dogs, too, all of us jammed together as if into a ravine. As our train's scheduled departure time approaches, if we're Pain Station veterans who know how it works, our eyes fix on the clacking departure board, waiting for our gate to be posted, white numerals and letters, 7W, 11E, 13E, west on the left side, east on the right. Because these are posted several crucial seconds before they're announced over the station speakers, clued-in passengers get the jump and surge toward that gate; when it's obvious the train is going to be crowded, it's a stampede. There: *9W!* In this split second my eyes drop from the departure board to the back of the hand that my mole is on and I start moving. In my dyslexia I rely on this mole to tell me which way is left. Trapped inside that instant of panic—turn left!—I only have to look for the directional mole in the dead center of the back of my left hand to know which way to go. That Francisco can't tell his left from his right; oh, but he can, thanks to his directional mole.

"The 8:05 Northeastern Regional Amtrak train to Boston is now ready for boarding, please proceed to gate 9W and have your tickets out." But I'm already at the gate, near the front of the line.

Coming off the escalator I walk quickly ahead, passing passengers proceeding single file alongside the train, *clackclack*clink*clacking* all the way to the next to forwardmost train car. This cold March morning is probably not going to be a heavy travel day. Should have a seat to myself all the way to Boston.

\*   \*   \*

So Marianne wrote to me because she heard me talking about Martí on the radio. But why, really? When I discovered her message on the computer screen, my first reaction was that it couldn't really be from *that* Marianne or that it must be a hoax. Then I felt like I'd been waiting for a message from her practically forever. But we were only close for a few months back when we were fifteen. "It's funny," she wrote in her message, "what survives for more than thirty years." So what survives? She didn't say. What about those few months could still matter to her? Maybe I'm making too big a deal out of it, and this, my excited curiosity, is just phantom-limb nostalgia for the reciprocated first adolescent love I never experienced. Does Marianne still recognize herself in that long-ago girl, and does she think I am still anything like that boy? Sometimes I wonder if it would have made a difference in my life, to have had a high school love. Back in tenth grade, it was Ian Brown who provoked our not even speaking anymore. It was Ian, in middle school, who gave me the nickname Monkey Boy. Marianne is going to want to talk about Ian tonight, I know she saw him at the last reunion. "Same asshole as ever," she wrote. Just remembering Ian makes anger flare through me. I rock back in my train seat. Whatever, man, that was all more than thirty years ago. Like if it weren't for Ian Brown, you'd be happily married now, a dad even, instead of a man too ashamed to show up at a high school reunion because he doesn't want them to know that at nearly fifty he's a lonely grown-up Monkey Boy like they all would have predicted for Frankie Goldberg. A grown-up monkey on the cusp of fifty who hasn't had a lover of any kind since his relationship with Gisela Palacios ended some five years ago in Mexico City. A stretch of loneliness that was starting to feel fucking eternal. But things have unexpectedly picked up since I moved back to New York. As if change might really be in the offing. We'll see.

* * *

Out of the long tunnel, the train is passing through Queens, and the
pale morning light gives the monotonous if jumbled sprawl here the
look of something covered in grime being slowly hosed off, revealing
a submerged radiance like a soft, youthful glow in a face where you
wouldn't expect to see it, an old or sick person's face. I slowly finish my
coffee. The sandwich rests in my backpack.

It wasn't just Monkey Boy. I had another nickname before that one,
Gols, pronounced *gawls*. I wonder if Marianne remembers Monkey
Boy or Gols. Even though it was only inspired by a sixth-grade teacher
talking about the Franks and the Gauls as he stood in front of a map
of old Europe, it was a creepy-sounding name, it sounded like *crawls*
or *ghouls*. Even now, it's painful to consider why Gols struck kids as so
apt for me, but it's not really a mystery. When I was almost three, living
with Mamita in my grandparents' house in Guatemala City after she'd
left my father for the first time when I was around six months old, I'd
caught tuberculosis, and whether that was the cause, *something* grossly
impeded my physical development. In photographs from elementary
school, I'm an emaciated, sallow weakling, sunken eyes, wooly hair,
mouth dumbly hanging open, huge ears, a feeble boy raised in a damp,
dark cellar by spiders who feed him moths, a boy called Gols. Eventually
my limbs began to fill out; slowly I got stronger. By eighth grade I'd even
score a few match points for my middle school track team; a year after
I'd transform into a boy who won 440 races; in tenth grade, which is
when high school began in our town, I'd even try out for football. Yet
Gols stuck to me. I had other nicknames, too: Sleepless because I so
often looked sleepy, lost in a demoralized stupor, Chimp Face, Pablo,
but Gols was the one I really hated.

*    *    *

That snowy morning after Grandpa died, walking with my father through the town square to the bakery that sold bagels, rye bread, and challah, a snowball hit the back of my father's herringbone fedora in a burst of snow, the hat jumping up and landing almost jauntily tipped forward atop his head, gloved hands clapping falling eyeglasses to his chest. He shoved the glasses back onto his nose, pushed back his hat, and we turned and saw the boy who'd thrown the snowball, Ricky Rossi from my sixth-grade class, sneering baby face in a bomber hat with hanging earflaps. Pitching arm cocked as if about to hurl another as he lightly skipped backward on the snow-covered sidewalk, he shouted, Jew! The boy beside him, who I didn't even recognize—long, waxy, potato-nosed face under a wool cap pulled low—loudly screeched Gols, and they turned to each other to laugh as if in triumph and spun and ran away. A Norman Rockwell painting, quaint New England town square in prettily falling snow, rascally boys being boys. My father, a half snarl on his face, looked at me, and I tensed, certain he was about to ask, Gols? They call you Gols? What in hell does that mean, Gols? But he turned back toward the bakery into his composed silent grief. With his fedora, thick-framed eyeglasses, and weighty angular nose, he did look pretty Jewish. I'd hardly known my grandpa. He was pretty out of it in his last years and lived in a crowded multistoried Jewish nursing home that I so hated to visit I was only occasionally forced to, though my father went nearly every weekend, often accompanied by Lexi. Grandpa, born in czarist Russia nearly a century before, in the Ukraine, had grown up among Cossacks and pogroms. What must my father have made that morning of having a snowball thrown at his head by a punk kid shouting Jew?

My father liked to make emphatic statements about character. Things like: You can't hide not having any character, Sonny Boy. If you don't have any, it always shows. Like a hypochondriac trying to check his own pulse but unable to find it, I anxiously dwelled on this mystery and problem of character. Standing there in that pretty snowfall, those boys having just thrown that snowball and shouted "Jew" and "Gols" and my father looking at me like that, I felt that it was me who'd been exposed as lacking this thing called character, who couldn't even imagine, no matter how much I brooded afterward, what I could have said or done in that moment that would have demonstrated *character*, so that even remembering it now I feel frustrated by this sense of an insurmountable lack that seems to have a name; that name must be Gols.

"So why don't you ever come to any of our high school reunions?" Marianne asked in one of her messages. How long would it take me to answer *that*. Longer than it will take to eat my sandwich.

That year of eighth grade especially, Ian Brown used to invite me to his house, hectoring me on the phone to come right over, and I'd get on my bicycle or walk. If I cut across that side of town by walking on the railroad tracks, I could make it in about forty-five minutes. The Browns lived out by Fuzzi Motors and the House of Pancakes and the synagogue, in the same kind of split-level house that we did, common in the newer neighborhoods, plasterboard walls and doors, no basements, skeletons of wooden beams resting atop concrete foundations. Ian never came over to my house on Wooded Hollow Road, painted a bright tropical blue with black wrought iron Spanish grillwork underneath the front windows, my mother's touch. I was happy to have a friend who was as popular at school as Ian, it made me feel as if our destinies were auspiciously linked. That seemed even truer when our school system selected—or classified—both Ian and me as underachievers, meaning that if we didn't want to be held back, we would have to attend a special summer program.

Was there anything good about being an official underachiever? To my father, it was one more shaming of his son for his infuriatingly stubborn refusal to try to do better in school, one more signpost on the bad road he was always announcing in that lowing tone of doom and lament that I was ineluctably headed down: You're going down a bad road, headed for an ineluctable bad end, Sonny Boy. That's how I knew the word "ineluctable," surely no other eighth grader used it as much as I did. But if being an underachiever actually meant you were somehow a superior person, which according to Ian it did, you shared a bond with a fellow underachiever, you were like members of a secret club who understood the workings of the world in a way people outside it didn't. According to Ian, we didn't really have to worry about the future, high scores on our SATs would get us into college no matter what. When we took the exams our natural underachievers' intelligence would take over. I didn't really buy that theory. I was sure my low grades were going to count against me no matter how I did on the SATs, but I kept it to myself; even when you disagreed with Ian about something minor, he'd ridicule you until you took it back. Ian's elastic grin, the way it narrowed and stretched his greenish eyes, gave his face an ecstatically diabolical expression. But he was a handsome kid with a mop of sandy hair who could always create a circus around himself. On Halloween he came to school with his face dyed red with food coloring, carrying a jar of mayonnaise under his arm, and went around clapping his own cheeks to make the whitish goop squirt from his mouth into the paths of squealing girls and onto their clothes. Even the pretty young social studies teacher Miss Turowski came out into the hall to gape at Ian doing that, and I saw how she lifted her hands into her thick blonde hair and looked around appalled, then went back into her classroom shaking her head, sort of laughing. No one else but Ian could have come to school on Halloween as a perambulating phallus and gotten away with it like he did.

*   *   *

That's some goddamned friend you picked, that Brown kid, I remember
my father blurting as we drove somewhere in the Oldsmobile one day.
His father's in B'nai B'rith, I see him when he comes to meetings. He's
the one owns that toilet store out on Route 9, wears those pastel jackets and dyes his hair, a regular Liberace, that one. No wonder his kid's
a good-for-nothing, thinks it's a joke to be forced to go to a summer
program for lazy kids going goddamned nowhere, big joke that is, and
you running after him every time he snaps his fingers.

And me, running after Ian Brown every time he snapped his fingers. It
makes me feel sick to remember all this.

Ian's father did own a bathroom fixtures store in a small shopping plaza
on Route 9. Mrs. Brown worked as the personal secretary to the owner
of a Boston liquor distillery called Old Yeoman. There's one night that
I especially remember, when Ian must have snapped his fingers and I'd
gone running over, and Mrs. Brown came and sat with us at the kitchen
table after they'd all had dinner. She was wearing pajamas and a thick
quilted bathrobe, her hair a Phyllis Diller mess, cold cream spread like
cake frosting over her face, her nose like the carrot on a snowman. She
was smoking menthol cigarettes and sipping Old Yeoman mint-flavored
vodka straight on the rocks.

Gleefully grinning Ian proclaimed: Ethel says you're a sickly looking boy. He called his mother Ethel. A sickly little monkey boy. Come
on Ethel, don't deny it, and Ian rocked back in his chair as if propelled
by his inhaled wheezy laughter, slapping the tabletop with his big basketball player's hands.

Mrs. Brown wanly smirked at her son, thin eyebrow raised, opposite eye narrowed, and she exhaled a long plume of minty smoke.
Her chin was trembling.

Ethel knows you got tuberculosis down in banana land when you were a baby, said Ian. And you don't take the TB tests at school because they're going to be positive. So you don't even know for sure that you're cured.

Mrs. Brown's eyes fixed on me from inside her white mask in a way that suddenly sickened me. I should have heeded my mother's advice and never told anybody about having tuberculosis, but to have told Ian! The TB tests took place behind a curtain. Nobody even had to know I didn't take them because when the nurse looked at my medical record, it informed her that my skin would react with a positive.

Come on, show some character, I silently urged myself, then said as strongly as I could: I'm cured.

That made Ian laugh. I don't know, he said. Ethel thinks you're still sick and that it might be contagious, right Ethel?

Mrs. Brown laconically said, Oh Ian, stop that. Don't be such a jerk to your friend.

You're going to catch a sleeping illness from that sick little monkey boy. That's what you always say, Ethel, admit it, said Ian, even sounding somewhat accusing.

Alright, boys, Mrs. Brown slurred wearily. I've had enough of your joking around, what a couple of pranksters. I'm going to bed. She took a last drink of her vodka, stubbed out her cigarette, got up without saying goodnight, and headed down the hall, her big pink shaggy slippers, thin slumping shoulders, and wild hair making her look like a Dr. Seuss character.

So, really, it was Mrs. Brown who named me Monkey Boy.


What was Bert doing in B'nai B'rith anyway? He wasn't religious. Most years he'd go to synagogue for maybe one High Holiday service at most. I never heard him say a word, fond or disparaging, about his *Fiddler on the Roof* shtetl roots. Even his youngest sister, my aunt Milly, born in Dorchester, spoke some Yiddish, but if my father did, he never let on. Once as a boy when I asked him why he didn't love Russia the way my mother loved Guatemala, he answered with a wolfish snarl: Why the hell would I have any love for that goddamned country. They didn't want the Jews there, our family and all the others that got out alive were the lucky ones. He'd probably joined the local synagogue's B'nai B'rith to make some friends in our town, expecting to find other men he'd be able to talk to like an old-time Boston tough guy about horse racing, bookies, sports teams, forgotten local athletes, Democratic politics. Except the Jews in our town were of a younger generation and milder types than Bert: accountants, administrators, salesmen, a dentist or two, or else the owners of small businesses like Mr. Brown; dutiful dads, and Friday night synagogue goers, most of them; a few even with hippie-style affections, denim shirts and bell-bottoms, long bushy sideburns. Bert never put on a pair of blue jeans in his life. Most of my friends, from college years and after, got a kick out of Bert and his old Boston tough Jew ways, and some had a hard time believing the terrible stories I'd tell about him. Our neighbors, especially once we'd moved to Wooded Hollow Road, all seemed to like him well enough too. Anything they might have glimpsed of his violence with me, they probably thought I was getting what I deserved. It wasn't as if that argument couldn't sometimes be made.

The train slows, allowing passengers to linger, through the windows, over the ruin and splendor of Bridgeport: old factory buildings, many with bricked-in or gaping windows; tall smokestacks, some exuding black smoke; container cranes and storage tanks, a few berthed ships; the greasy sheen of canals and stagnant inlets under concrete highway overpasses; slummy apartment buildings and homes, plywood-covered windows gray with moisture or rot. Farther on, after we've left the station, a CasparDavidFriedrich graveyard with crooked gravestones, bare, black, twisted trees, enclosed by an old wall of stained, crumbled masonry and shriveled vines.

The Ways was what the rich-people part of our town was called, out near the Charles River and the border on that side, because it was only out there that the streets had names like Bay Colony Way and Duck Pond Way. Not many if any Jews lived out there. The various Ways turned off one or the other of a pair of sparsely settled avenues to loop past houses built on adjoining lots as in the town's other subdivided neighborhoods, except here the houses were much larger, none exactly alike, and some very unalike, and they stood far apart in yards that were like medium-size parks with their own stands of pines or islands of trees, with thick forest coming right up to the edge of backyards. But until the infamous Arlene Fertig night in the spring of eighth grade, I'd never seen any of those houses from behind, even though every morning before school I bicycled through the Ways on my paper route, riding at least part of the way up long driveways to snap tightly folded newspapers at front and side entrances, trying to make them fly end over end and land flat at the foot of doors, and keeping score, one side of the street against the other. The houses on the Ways had spatial depths I found it hard to imagine a house possessing. What was in those humongous basements? Movie theaters, indoor swimming pools, bowling alleys? Even the basement of our small ranch house on Sacco Road, where we'd lived before Wooded Hollow Road, had seemed kind of limitless to me, especially on the other side of the paneled bedroom that my father built for Feli when she came from Guatemala, sent by Abuelita to be our housekeeper and to help take care of Lexi and me, that area of raw cement where my father's massive pine carpentry table and the clothes washer and dryer were, pink fiber insulation wadded like cotton candy between two-by-four beams and into the ceiling, and the storage area at the back, a spooky tunnel of luggage and stacked cardboard boxes where when I was small I liked to hide for hours, and down at the basement's other end, a furnace like an iron dragon, a blaze roaring in its belly through the winters.

Arlene Fertig was the first girl I ever kissed. It comes back like this whenever I've been thinking about Ian Brown. In my memory they're linked, Ian and Arlene and later Marianne. Arlene was from the same neighborhood as Ian. Romance had been building between Arlene and me in the ways it does in the eighth grade, flirty smiles, cryptic comments from other girls, slow dancing with her to "House of the Rising Sun" at our middle school's afternoon dance, the warmth of her waist in my hands through her corduroy dress, her hands on my shoulders, her freshly shampooed hair that fell midway down her back, straight but not fine, tingling against my cheek. When the song was over she thanked me in her slightly hoarse voice and I speechlessly slunk away, stunned by the novel overload of sensations. Black bangs over darkly made-up eyes gave her a precocious look, and she was so slight that when she hurried through the halls at school she looked like a running marionette. Once, between classes, when we were trying to have a conversation, she said, My hair is too heavy. It's making my head ache. Do you think I should cut it all off? She seemed so sincere that I was too confused to say anything. In June, only a couple of weeks left in the school year, I was invited to Betty Nicholson's party on Duck Pond Way, the first and only time I ever saw a house out in the Ways from the back. Breathing in the early summer lusciousness, looking across the lawn toward the tree line at the fireflies hovering out there, hearing the yammering of tree frogs and crickets, I had the impression of visiting a plantation estate in Guatemala. Arlene and I danced to some slow songs on the torch-lit patio: "Crimson and clover over and over." One, two, three, go for it. I gave her a quick kiss on the warm flesh of her neck and turned into a trembling tree inside, and she lifted her head and stared into my eyes, an assertiveness like a tiny flame in each of her dark irises, and her small red mouth broke into a smile like a childishly happy and excited strawberry; that's how I described it to myself later that weekend, silently going over every detail of what had happened. Holding hands, we slipped away through a row of tall evergreen hedges into a neighbor's backyard where, in the nearly pitch-dark, we embraced and lowered ourselves, already kissing, down into the plush grass, me partly on top of her, and made out. I don't remember for how long; it could have been five minutes or twenty. The lawn's nutritious smell also held something stinky, a mix, I realized, of manure and moist soil that grew stronger the longer we lay there. There was just enough moonlight to see that her eyes were closed, her head turning side to side in tempo with the swirling of our tongues, her little hawk nose rubbing and bumping mine. I love you, Arlene, I whispered, I've loved you all this year. Arlene, with her lips against mine, murmured, Me too, me too, me too. A minute or so later she hoarsely whispered, We should go back. I remember how after we'd stood up, she reached behind her to rub her dress and brought her hand to her nose and sniffed it, but neither of us said anything about the fertilizer smell. We stepped back through the shrubbery, toward the torches and patio, and she stopped to put on her shoes. She laughed quietly and said, You have lipstick all over your face. She licked her fingers and rubbed them vigorously on my skin. You should go wash your face, she said. I obeyed, slipping quickly into the bathroom off the patio. At the sink I grinned in proud near disbelief at my reflection in the mirror, so smudged by lipstick that it looked smeared with red poppy petals.

Making out with Arlene meant I was going to have a girlfriend, I was sure of it. She was going away to camp soon, and I was headed into the underachiever program. We only had to make it through summer and by fall we'd be discovering love and sex together in the woods after school, over at each other's houses when no one else was home. We'd stand making out on street corners oblivious to passing traffic like the teenage couples you saw all over our town, talking and laughing with their foreheads touching. Maybe by Thanksgiving we'd even lose our virginity together, like only a few of our classmates, not including Ian Brown, supposedly already had. When I got to school that Monday morning, just before the homeroom bell rang, it seemed like everybody was waiting for me, though that really couldn't be true, there couldn't have been that many seventh and ninth graders waiting for me. What I do remember is stepping through the doors into the wide lobby by the cafeteria and hearing howls and shrieks of excitement, laughter and shouts about a monkey and a banana. I saw Arlene standing between Ian Brown and his best friend, Jake Rosen, our middle school's football star even as an eighth grader, and Ian was holding her by the bicep. Arlene's face was weirdly distorted, like a rubber mask of her own face hanging in a tree, her usual sweetly shy smile replaced by a grimace-grin, as if she were about to explosively sneeze. Her hands flew up as if to pull that mask off, and she turned and fled, Ian spinning to watch, her friend Betty Nicholson chasing after her.

Supposedly, Arlene had said that when she was making out with me, she'd felt like a banana being chomped on by a monkey. That joke electrified the school. But I've never believed it was Arlene's joke. It just didn't make any sense to me that she would have said that. I think it was Ian who came up with it and that he and Jake told everyone it was Arlene. In all the classes I went to that morning, I elicited snickers, sharp grins of malice, looks that mixed pity and hilarity, a few just pitying. Kids made banana-eating gestures when they saw me coming in the corridors or made screechy monkey sounds, some jouncing their hands under their armpits. In one class after the next, I sat stiffly in my seat as if trapped behind the steering wheel in an invisible car crash, that dazed sensation of wondering: Is this really happening? I felt as if I'd walked out of myself, leaving behind an eviscerated container. That horrible sensation of a vacated hollowness that follows one of those enormous disappointments that can seem to take over and permeate everything. Whenever I have a day like that, I remember my first kiss.

Two teenage girls who I noticed when they boarded at Bridgeport— both Latina looking, one a short-haired sprite, bright lipstick, the other long-haired in an oversized scarlet hoody—are sitting a few rows behind me and talking about, as far as I can tell, another girl whose name is Pabla, their giggles foaming over like a boiling pot of squiggly pasta. And now one sings out, with more hilarity than mockery: Pabla! Who names their daughter Pabla? The other girl says: It's her father who's Puerto Rican. Her mother's a white lady from here. And the first: But Pabla? So how stupid could her father be? Pabla! They laugh some more.

I'm grinning to myself too. Poor Pabla. I've never known anyone named Pabla. It sure is not the feminine version of Pablo, not in any common usage anyway. I once knew a Consuelo who told me that all her life in the United States people had been calling her Consuela. Consuelo literally means "consolation"—Consuela, "with shoe sole."

But I've just remembered another Pabla, in *Krazy Kat* I think it was. Krazy, for once distracted from his spurned love for Ignatz, meets a lively cat with amorous eyes named Pabla in a tree. They frolic like squirrels in the nearly bare boughs, but suddenly Pabla slips from a branch and instead of plummeting drifts down into a pile of raked leaves. Krazy follows, leaping into the pile, at first playfully searching it for Pabla but then more frantically, snatching up leaves one by one and flinging them aside until not a single leaf is left. No sign of Pabla. *Alone again,* wails Krazy, *natch-roo-lee.*


When I wasn't even a year old, my mother split from my father and took me back with her to live in her parents' house in Guatemala City. She's never told me a reason why. All my earliest memories are set in my abuelos' house, the same one Mamita and her brother, Memo, had grown up in, an old-fashioned Spanish colonial with a stone patio in the middle, dark cool rooms with polished tile floors, and usually shuttered, barred windows facing the street; heavy dark furniture in the living and dining rooms, the Virgin and saint statues in glass cases, the caged finches and canaries Abuelita kept in a small side patio; the thick, woven cloth huipiles always smelling of tortillas and soap that the servant women wore, the older one with a wrinkled face and the young one I spent most of my time with, the recollection of her ebony Rapunzel hair seemingly coterminous with her enveloping kindness and quiet giggles; the memory of sitting in my bedroom's window seat and passing my toy truck out through the bars to an Indian woman who took her baby boy out of her rebozo and set him down on the patterned old paving stones of the sidewalk so that he could play with the truck and my astonishment that he was naked. A memory like the broken-off half of a mysterious amulet that can only be made whole if that now-grown little boy remembers it, too, and we can somehow meet and put our pieces together. I don't even remember if I let him keep the truck or not, though I like to think I did. Not all that likely that he's even still alive, considering what the war years were like for young Maya men of our generation. Who knows, maybe he's up here somewhere and even has children who were born here.

Mamita must not have loved my father enough anymore, or must have convinced herself that she didn't, to want to live with him and raise a family. It's not like Bert was cheating on her and that's why we left. That seems like the kind of thing she would have told us or at least told my sister and Feli; they sure wouldn't have kept that a secret all these years. We were going to stay in Guatemala and make our lives there. But what misery and humiliation my father must have endured over those two years plus, a long time to be separated from his family; he couldn't really have been expecting us to come back. Then what large-hearted forgiveness he displayed when he found out that his truant wife and tubercular three-year-old son were returning to him after all. In Boston, I'd at least get better medical care; that was really why we came back, I understood later. My father rolled the dice and decided to move his shaky family out to that idyllic-seeming town off Route 128, where he purchased a ranch house in a neighborhood so brand-new it looked just unpacked from its box, set down between steep hills and ridges, and

comprised of only two intersecting streets, straight Sacco Road, where
we lived, and bending Enna Road, together running along three sides of
a large weedy-thistly rocky field called Down Back. That was the house,
already partly furnished, that my mother and I came to live in around
Christmas. My father must have met us at Logan Airport and driven
us to our new home, where he'd put up a Christmas tree down in the
basement, right in front of the furnace, a dangerously flammable spot,
instead of in the living room, as if he didn't want the neighbors to be
able to see it through the picture window, worried that at the last minute
we wouldn't come back after all, and the neighbors would wonder about
that solitary Jewish man who made false teeth for a living and had a
Christmas tree in his living room. His older sister, Aunt Hannah, married to a Russian Catholic, Uncle Vlad, had decorated it. Underneath
the tree, an orange toy steam shovel awaited me. But I was afraid of my
daddy and instinctively rebuffed him, this enthusiastic, grasping man
whose marriage and family I'd saved by getting sick. On a recent visit to
Green Meadows, my mother told me that. You didn't like your father,
she said. You were afraid of him. Really, Ma? I was afraid of him? And
you could tell? Because I don't remember any of it at all.

A hemorrhaging relapse while playing outside on a hot sunny afternoon that made me vomit sloshing wallops of blood onto the sidewalk—I
remember that—my father wrapping me in a blanket and rushing me
into his car and also that I got to stay in the Boston Children's Hospital.
Mr. Peabody and Sherman came to visit us in our ward, and my father
sat by my bed performing the magic tricks he'd bought at Little Jack
Horner on Tremont Street. One was a shiny black top encircled by white
flecks, but when my father made the top spin on its special stick, the
flecks became a rainbow blur before turning into a row of flying scarlet
birds that he said were called ibis.

That's how these visits with my mother go now, but her occasionally
blunt, unguarded way of speaking is a new trait. She's almost comically
the opposite of how she used to be, after all those years of keeping her

guard impermeably raised. This new heedless candor is a manifestation of the somewhat premature dementia that has been overtaking her in recent years, possibly the result, doctors now say, of a stroke that wasn't noticed, a commotion in her brain that caused a tremulous weakness in one leg that was misdiagnosed as a symptom of advancing age. But my sister and I also attributed her decline to the exhaustion brought on by having to tend to Bert during his unrelentingly demanding last years, when being repeatedly hospitalized for an array of health emergencies somehow only fueled his manic, cantankerous energies. By the end, it was Lexi who took over his care, moving home again, adamant that she was only doing it out of concern for our mother. Mamita's condition seemed related to another medical mystery, that being the most dreadful insomnia that overtook her, when it was as if the more Bert exhausted her, the harder it was for her to get any sleep, her often reddened eyes encircled by darkly puffed skin. It was only when she had to go from the nursing home to a hospital in Boston because of a nearly fatal case of pneumonia and an adverse reaction to her medications that doctors, studying her puzzling medical history, also hypothesized that prior stroke. On my mother's side of the family, there's no known history of strokes or heart disease or even of dementia; there are a few old family stories that along with the little bit I've found out on my own do suggest that Abuelito was manic-depressive and maybe even schizophrenic. In the nursing home, Mamita's doctors did finally straighten out her medications. She sleeps better now, though that fog she's often at least a little bit lost in and from which she does sharply emerge, nevertheless seems to be slowly, ineluctably deepening.

Soon after Bert Goldberg's beautiful young wife, Yolanda Montejo Hernández, came back from Guatemala with their sick little son, she became pregnant, with a girl this time, Alexandra. Husband, probably wife, too, must have felt blessed and redeemed, if not shocked, by this

successful fast work, which won them the right and even the responsibility to turn their long separation into a subject never to be spoken
of again, certainly not within hearing of the children. In the fall, living
in our neighborhood was like being snugly enclosed at the bottom of
a basket of flagrant fiery and more muted colors, replaced in winter by
hues of snowy slopes, pine crests nearly black in the distance, frigid gray
skies, flying flocks of crows, crimson-streaked Atlantic sunsets, followed
by successive seasons that wove into our little valley every shade of green
from sapling shoots to darkest boreal forest. How could my father even
have suspected the viciousness lurking all around us? The Saccos, related
to the contractors who'd founded and built our neighborhood, a brutal
clan, lived around the corner on Enna Road in a little ranch house like
our own. Whenever Gary Sacco called me dirty kike, I shouted back:
So are you. You're a dirty kike too!

Down Back, the weedy, stony field behind our houses, was where
me and my few friends from school, especially Peter Lammi, who at
school was called Lambi, used to stand shoulder to shoulder, throwing
rocks at Gary, who was a year older than us, and his brother, Chris, and
some of their friends, while they hurled and zinged them at us. We went
to Dwight, the public elementary school, and they went to St. Joe's. We
faced off far enough away that we could usually easily dodge the rocks
they threw. My rocks never even came close to reaching them, though
I left that part out when boasting at the dinner table about my daring
charges against the enemy and perfectly pitched throws. Peter Lammi
was much stronger than any of us on either side. Come on, Pete, split
a head open! He aimed his rocks relentlessly, one after another, but
always so they'd miss but be close enough to make our enemy pull back
and finally run away. He couldn't bring himself to intentionally hurt
even Gary Sacco. Peter launched those wild bombardments in part to
protect me but to protect himself, too, because he knew the Saccos and
their friends were desperate to see our faces covered in blood, if only
they could get close enough. I also wanted to see their faces covered in

blood, there was not a single thing in this world I wanted more. The serious problem of enemies, what to wish for your enemies.

We did have some nice neighbors, and Mamita even got along with Connie Sacco for a while. But then my mother decided we had to give Fritzie, our German shepherd, away and put an advertisement in the newspaper. Mamita couldn't take Fritzie anymore, such a rambunctious galoot that he didn't seem to even fit inside our little house, and he filled the yard with dog shit that it was my job to collect inside wads of newspaper and drop into the aluminum rubbish incinerator that resembled the robot in *Lost in Space*, a job I performed at best haphazardly. An elderly black couple came from Maine to see Fritzie. They drove an old-looking automobile and told us they lived on a small farm. They went into the yard to meet Fritzie, then sat in the living room with my parents over coffee and cookies, looking at vaccination and kennel papers. Two days later a petition was left in our mailbox, signed by our neighbors, maybe by every household on Sacco and Enna Roads, complaining that if we sold our house to Negroes, their property values would go down. No black families lived in our town, not one I'd ever seen anyway. "We, your neighbors, agree that we will take all necessary steps to prevent that," the letter said, which my father, astounded, read aloud in the kitchen, and then he mocked: What, they're going to burn our house down? They're in the Ku Klux Klan now, these goddamned wops and micks? Bert! exclaimed my mother. Don't talk like that in front of the children, you'll make them prejudiced. When Mamita suggested that all we had to do was tell our neighbors the truth—that we were only giving Fritzie away, not selling the house—my father exploded in indignant disbelief: Oh Jesus Christ Almighty, Yoli!

The next weekend, the couple came again to take Fritzie back to their farm in Maine, where he was going to be a happy dog with so much room to romp. I went with my father when he drove the dog shit incinerator to the town dump and on the way home sat turned away from him while sobbing like a German war widow: Fritzie, Fritzie, oh Fritzie.

*    *    *

Jesus Christ Almighty, *this*: I'm lying on my back among the weeds and pebbles of the apron at the top of Sacco Road, gasping for breath, unable to draw any air, in a rising frenzy of panic and terror because I'm suffocating to death. My recall is hazy, but I do know that Gary Sacco and some of the others had caught me alone, insults, shoves, a burst of boy punches, clumsy and savage, a hard punch to my throat. When they saw me on my back gasping for air, they ran away. There were no houses there on that side of Sacco Road where it ran alongside the steep hill that the old house of the Sacco family matriarch, Grandma Enna, sat atop, though there were houses on the opposite side. Panic, harshly gasping, unable to draw any air, that's what I most vividly remember, and that I was lying near a telephone pole, long slightly drooping strands of black wire high above me against the brilliantly azure sky. Soon enough my throat relaxed, opened, I gulped air, could breathe again. Then I must have gotten to my feet and walked home. How could I explain to my mother or Feli what had happened, describe the improbable punch that had caused my throat to close and how terrifying that had been, lying there unable to breathe. Whenever I go back to our town, usually by train, to spend some hours just walking around, I sometimes pass that way and see Grandma Enna's house up there, looking like something out of an old New England horror story or movie, with its always-curtained windows, two skinny chimneys, sagging porch, in winter the snow-blanketed wide downward incline of the lawn, crows waddling across it, pecking for pine nuts from the tall pines separating the property from the old part of the cemetery where the jagged, slate gravestones from colonial and Revolutionary times are. Peter Lammi and I once found in that part of the cemetery the ripped apart, hollowed carcass of an owl devoured by crows, eyes gone, its blackened mouth or throat lining partly pulled out through its pried-open beak.

One day a small round stone, hurled without warning from the Saccos' backyard in a missile arc over the Rizzitanos' yard and into ours, undoubtedly meant for me, struck Lexi in the middle of her forehead and laid her out flat. Though she didn't lose consciousness, the rock left a dark-blue welt. It wasn't long after, at the start of fifth grade, that we moved to a split-level house with mostly Jews for neighbors on Wooded Hollow Road, just on the other side of the hill, with the town cemetery atop it, between the two neighborhoods.

Not even my mother had ever given me the slightest indication of remembering or ever even having known about that time when I was punched in the neck, yet years later I found out that Lexi knew all about it. She told a girlfriend of mine when we'd come from New York on a visit. They had a conversation that I wasn't present for, just my sister and Camila. My sister was telling her how terribly I'd been bullied as a child and that in fact we'd had to move from our house because boys in our neighborhood had almost murdered me. They'd left me for dead, and I'd almost suffocated to death, she told Camila. You mean they strangled him? Camila asked. And Lexi said, No, but they hit him so hard in the neck his throat closed. Lexi said she'd witnessed it and that she'd run to my side to help me. I didn't want to let on what a disagreeable surprise it was to learn that my sister knew about that incident and to find out now, as an adult, in this way from Camila. Lexi had never been a part of my memory of what had happened. It felt like a too-intimate intrusion for her to be telling Camila about it now. At least that's what I decided later, when I tried to understand why it had so angered me. I wondered if that was a sort of trauma effect or if maybe it was the corrosive acid of humiliation that had wiped her and anyone else but those boys and myself from what I did remember. That memory should only belong to me, a terror and pain I couldn't or didn't want to share, especially not with someone who would later make such annoying use of it and who seemed to have a much clearer and more complete memory of what the episode had *looked like*, at least, than I did.

Almost murdered me? I scoffed. That's nonsense. I had enemies, but I don't remember anyone almost murdering me.

Well, that's what Lexi told me, said Camila. It sounded like something out of *Lord of the Flies*. I hated that book when I was a girl, because I used to imagine it was one of my own brothers those boys murdered.

Camila was half-English half-Cuban, and she'd grown up "posh" in England, daughter of a Tory politician. Her parents were long divorced, but she and her three brothers were incredibly close with each other and with their mother and also with their sometimes difficult Pa.

I've never asked Lexi what she knows or remembers about that episode. I didn't say a word to her about what she'd told Camila.

Lexi has blue-gray eyes and is pale and blondish, her hair the tint of rain-soaked straw. My mother used to love putting my sister's hair, when she was a little girl, in Heidi braids and coils and dressing her in frilly white smocks, like the girls from German coffee plantation families she remembered from childhood. She attributed Lexi's hair and complexion to her golden-haired Spanish rancher grandfather whom none of us had ever seen a picture of, though now I know that Mamita's abuelo was as far from a golden-haired gachupín as could be. Aunt Hannah had been blonde, too, but I only knew her after she'd gone gray; she was older than my father. Mamita's natural hair is orangish and curly, even kinky, though she'd been dyeing it black and straightening it, usually doing it herself at the kitchen sink, for as long as I'd been capable of noticing. Now that her hair is so sparse, she doesn't straighten it anymore but dyes it a soft maroon with a slight orange tinge, a sort of cranberry-orange English marmalade color. In photographs I've seen of her when she's young, most of them black and white, Mamita wears her hair like a forties movie star in thickly flowing waves over her shoulders.

Lexi was tall for her age, and as a little girl, when I was still in my infirm years, she was faster than me, could hit a rubber baseball harder and farther. She was a straight-A student, too, and played violin in a children's orchestra in Boston. All of this gave her the air of a favored child, even if her high-strung nature and explosive temper already hinted at some of the difficulties she'd have later on. Our father encouraged Lexi's athletic gifts but Mamita didn't at all, endlessly cajoling that a girl should always let the boy win in any sports competition, even bowling, as I recall still from a candlepin bowling birthday party when Lexi beat everybody and afterward was made to feel terrible. Mamita was still a captive back then of certain Latin American prejudices that hadn't changed since even before José Martí's epoch: a well-brought-up girl should have delicate, even coquettish manners and be dependent on the protection of men. Why should she be physically strong, was she being made to carry stacks of firewood or sacks of onions on her back or to till mountainside corn milpas? Later, to her lasting remorse and guilt, Mamita realized how horribly mistaken she'd been and dedicated herself to supporting her daughter in every way she could, even if it was too late now for her to become the college and Olympic softball star she probably could have been. Around when I was finally beginning to develop muscles and becoming more athletic, Lexi began having weight problems that seemed less attributable to genetic inheritance than to emotional states; in better times, at least into her thirties, she regained her youthful trimness, had romances and all that. But then would come the more difficult times, the causes of which she and my mother always kept secret from me.

Those girls sitting back there are going on about Pabla again and I don't know what else, their laughter rising to happy shrieks. Every Sunday morning throughout my childhood, *Boomtown* was on TV, with its opening routine of Rex Trailer, the Boston Wild West singing cowboy in the bunkhouse futilely trying to wake up his snoring Mexican sidekick, Pablo. Staged before a laughing and cheering live audience of New England children, the show even had a contest for TV audience members to write in suggesting new ways for Rex to try to get that lazy Mexican out of bed. Pablo was one of my nicknames too: Hey Pablo, wake the fuck up. In the kitchen at a house party, Fitzy flicking lit matches at me and taunting: Wake the fuck up, you fucking Pablo. His thug friends around him putting on Frito Bandito accents, slurring: Pablo, Pablo, Pablo. Remember that? Good times. No doubt Fitzy was only trying to provoke me into a fight so that he could massacre me. I just had to keep my mouth shut, not say a word, and get out of there, that's all. I slipped out of the kitchen, out of the house without saying goodbye to anyone, walked home in the cold dark.

My stomach just rumbled like wet pebbles inside a shaken bucket. I won't be able to resist that hero much longer. If I were traveling in the other direction and had bought the exact same sandwich in an Italian deli in Boston, same meats, cheese, and garnishes, same bread, it wouldn't be called a hero. It would be a submarine sandwich.

I know that some of the distance between Lexi and me, which I do regret, though apparently not enough to do much about it, is rooted in those childhood resentments and rivalries. My mother is always asking me to be a better brother to Lexi, and I'm always promising to try, but then nothing really changes. But when I suggest that I might possibly resent Lexi for other things apart from her having inherited all of our parents' money and property, what do I mean? What is it that I actually resent? Why should I resent Lexi at all? If it were only the other way around, wouldn't it be justified? That time when we were small, when Lexi took all the money out of our father's wallet and planted it around our yard because she thought money trees would grow, it kind of established a pattern. True, Bert was always complaining and ranting about money, and she wanted to help. He must have just collected in cash from his bookie or had a run of winning trifecta boxes at Suffolk Downs or something, because he went totally berserk. It took Lexi a couple of days to own up. They went out and dug in the yard, under the shrubbery, in the vegetable garden, in the dirt around the trees and bushes he'd planted, but they only recovered about half of it. So adorable, right? Something to make any good boy feel even fonder and more protective of his little sister than before. I dumped on Lexi about it like she'd done the stupidest thing in the history of humanity. What, you think if that was how to make money trees grow, you'd know about it and Daddy wouldn't? You think he wouldn't have already planted money in the yard? Now look what you did. You've made us poorer.

Then there was the incident when I snuck into Lexi's bedroom and stole the Indian arrowhead she'd found Down Back a few days before. I can still shut my eyes and perfectly recall her running up out of the field that evening, her strong thighs in short pants rising and falling, excitedly shouting, Look what I found! In the palm of her hand she held out a white quartz arrowhead, about three inches long, perfectly shaped, lethally sharp. I'd been desperately searching Down Back and our town's forests for an Indian arrowhead like that one since about forever. Jealousy rose inside me like a boiling magma that subsided into distilled malice and calculation. Then I played innocent for about a week, probably longer, waiting for the scandal of the missing arrowhead to blow over. If our parents never suspected me, that must be because it just seemed too cruel and far-fetched a thing for a boy to do to his little sister, steal her arrowhead and then do what with it, keep it hidden forever? (But, I'm remembering now, there was a girl I wanted to give it to, I think her name was Beth, though I only met her once, that Sunday afternoon when my father and his friend Herb, her uncle, took us to a Celtics game in the Garden, and to Durgin-Park for dinner after.) Because Lexi was always losing and misplacing things anyway, our parents tried to convince her that maybe she'd taken it to school and left it there and had just forgotten or had dropped it somewhere without noticing. After all she had so much else on her mind, with her violin recital imminent and Aunt Hannah coming twice a week now to give her lessons and coach her. Did she want Aunt Hannah to see her crying over the missing arrowhead instead of concentrating on her music? One evening a week or so later while my father was barbecuing in the backyard, Lexi sitting on the porch steps, I came running up out of Down Back excitedly shouting that I'd found an arrowhead, too, just like the one Lexi had found. Even now, sitting here on the train, I feel what a heavy sack of rotted flour would feel if it were infested and swarming with mealworms of shame. My father moving toward me, that look of revulsion on his face, uncinching his belt and knocking over the grill, the still-raw steaks falling like lopped-off faces to the grass. Those few whacks with a folded belt across the back of my thighs were nothing out of the ordinary, certainly when compared to what lay ahead in coming years. Hearing the commotion, my mother had rushed outside. The real punishment, as I lay there on the grass pretending to whimper from the sting of the belt lashing, was hearing my father explain to Mamita what I'd done and the way she looked at me, lips tightly closed, her narrowed gaze without pity, direct yet somehow absent, as if in reality she was staring inward, forced to face the truth about her life, trapped in a gringo suburb with this alien family, even this son who'd at least provided the reassurance of seemingly taking after her in temperament, who didn't scream or throw tantrums, whose cheerful disposition rebounded even after those savage boys tried to murder him, now exposed as a conniving little fool who'd just committed an incomprehensible perfidy against his little sister.

While I lay there on the lawn, curled up with my arms over my head, displaying my penitence, Lexi must have recovered her arrowhead and carried it back into her bedroom or wherever it was she took it. I never laid eyes on it again. Thankfully Feli wasn't with us anymore when that happened and didn't witness it. By then María Xum had succeeded her.

Feli had come to live with us right after Lexi was born. I'm meeting her for lunch the day after tomorrow. You really had two mothers, she always likes to say, meaning my mother and herself. Yet despite how close I've felt to Feli practically all my life, the last time I saw her was nearly two years ago, when I came through Boston promoting my little book on the bishop's murder and she drove in to meet me for lunch in Coolidge Corner. From when I was three until I was about nine and from when she was fourteen until she was twenty, Feli lived with us. I made up the name Feli, though only my sister and I and sometimes my father called her that. Her real name is Concepción Balbuena. Abuelita, who'd found her in a nuns' orphanage in Guatemala City, had sent her to help my mother but also to keep her company. All her life, my mother had only lived in cities where she'd always had lots of friends and a social life; now here she was isolated with a tubercular small boy and an infant in a little town outside Boston, in a two-road, mainly working-class neighborhood overlooked by a cemetery, amid rocky field and cold forest. The bedroom my father had built for Feli in the basement, with finished plywood-paneled walls and a smooth linoleum floor, was adjacent to our playroom, separated from it by a curtain of tiny metal rings hung from a brass rod. The first time I saw Feli she was wearing black-frame eyeglasses and a convent haircut, but a year later, she'd grown and fluffed her hair like Patty Duke's, wore loose sweaters and skinny slacks and eyeglasses with pink frames, and was always playing Top 40 music on the radio. Down in her basement room, Feli twisted, chachachá'd, frugged, and sang along to the radio, to forty-fives on her record player or to *Shindig!* on TV. Frankycello-Frankycello! she liked to call to me, like I was Annette Funicello's little brother. Swinging her hips side to side and holding out her hands for me to come and dance, she always smelled damply of detergent and Ajax. When I'd made up the name Feli, was I just mispronouncing feliz or making up a name only for her because she brought so much felicidad into our house? Feli was more fun than anybody I'd ever known. But when she'd get me to march around the basement with her loudly singing "estamos de fiesta hoy, la banda la banda," I suspect now that was her way of cheering me up, that I was, at least sometimes, a sadder boy than I remember being.

Feli didn't have parents. She had only one relative that she mentioned, her uncle Rodolfo Sprenger Balbuena, an army colonel fighting in the war against the Communists from Cuba and Russia. Feli and her uncle wrote to each other, his letters arriving in crisp airmail envelopes with red and blue stripes, and like all mail from Guatemala those envelopes had a distinct, stronger smell than American mail, something like a moldy raisin cake. Her uncle's letters came right from the battlefield, Feli told me; she'd read them out loud. In the mountains and jungles the soldiers ate wild animals, including opossums, iguanas, armadillos, tepezcuintles, jabalís, crocodiles, snakes, and even monkeys roasted over campfires.

About six years after she'd come to live with us, Feli left to marry Oscar, a handsome, languid, arrogant Cuban. We went to eat cake with them in Allston on their wedding day; their small apartment reminded me of the one in *The Honeymooners*. Oscar eventually became mixed up in small-time gangster dealings; their marriage only lasted a few years. After Feli left, our home was never a happy one again, not even in a fleeting or illusory way, I really think that's true. María Xum came next. Abuelita had sent her to do housework so that most days my mother could go into Boston, where now she was studying at Lesley College to become a Spanish teacher. She was probably about the same age as Feli. But neither Lexi nor I ever played with María Xum. Watching television she'd laugh uncontrollably at parts that weren't funny or stare in bewilderment or fright at the funniest parts. All that used to make me feel sorry for her and sometimes hostile. Her feet, coming out of her black slipper shoes to rub against each other, were rough and calloused, her face dark and flat, wide cheeks, a large fleshy mouth with something fishlike about it, and her black eyes shone with a disconcerting intensity. María never took me with her into Boston on her day off like Feli used to. Soon she left to get married, too—even María Xum could find a husband!—the way every girl Abuelita sent to us left to get married. She occasionally phoned my mother to say hello, but we eventually lost track of her. María Xum was replaced by the mysterious Hortensia. After only two weeks of being our housekeeper and living in that basement room, Hortensia left to get married. I have no idea to whom or how it happened so fast. What I do remember about Hortensia is her tight sweaters and voluptuous bust, her prominent Roman-looking nose. Yolandita from Nicaragua came next, so demure and pretty, always singing along like a happy novice nun to the radio while she ironed. She had her own room downstairs in the new house on Wooded Hollow Road and was my mother's favorite, though Mamita's relationship to Feli was emotionally deeper. Carlota Sánchez Motta, who was my age, was the last to come, but she wasn't a housekeeper. She was a foreign student who in exchange for living with us was supposed to help with the housework. During my senior year, Carlota went to high school with me.

More than forty years after Feli landed at Logan Airport with her little suitcase, the small settlement of Central American women founded by Abuelita in Greater Boston is in its third generation, Feli being a grandmother now, and maybe one or two of the others are too.


Mamita had married Bert because of his resemblance to her big brother, Guillermo, or Memo. That's what used to be said, though I don't remember by whom. Was it Feli or Abuelita who said that, or maybe Aunt Milly? They both had big noses, Bert's classically Jewish, Memo's a bit smaller, more triangular, classically Maya-mestizo. They both had black hair, Bert's wavy, Memo's tightly curly; they both wore eyeglasses and were forceful speakers. That was about it for what they had in common. Few things made my mother happier than my managing to impress Tío Memo the way I already had that day my father drove us to Fort Ticonderoga, with my energetic recounting of how on the night of May 9, 1775, Vermont's own Ethan Allen and a feisty rabble of his Green Mountain Boys, including the future traitor Benedict Arnold, had snuck into the fort and fought their way into the British soldiers' sleeping barracks, which used to be right over there, Tío. The redcoat commander jumped out of his bed just as the Green Mountain Boys burst in, and that's why, Tío, when he surrendered the fort to Ethan Allen, he was holding his breeches over his private parts like this. *Jajaja* went my uncle's booming laughter. I really was thrilled to be at Fort Ticonderoga, which I'd read about in Francis Parkman's *Montcalm and Wolfe,* checked out from the library, the actual place instead of just a historical re-creation like boring Plimoth Plantation, still-standing ramparts, cold redolent stones, even the same dirt the Green Mountain Boys had left their boot prints in. And Tío Memo *was* impressed by his nephew's knowledge and improbably extroverted outburst. He exclaimed, You'll be a professor someday, Frankie! Ay no, Memo, murmured my mother, crinkling her nose, because coming from her brother, a manly successful international businessman, she didn't consider that a great compliment. But from how she looked at me and smiled, fur coat hugged around her, rouged cheeks even more brightly fragrant in the cold, I could tell she was proud of me.

Tío Memo, during a business trip to New York from Guatemala, had come to Massachusetts by Greyhound to visit, and so Bert had taken us all on that weekend road trip up to Fort Ticonderoga, then across Lake Champlain on the car ferry and into Vermont, a state my uncle had never visited before. I sat in the back seat between Tío Memo and Feli, my mother and sister were up front, and Bert at the wheel, driving us to our motel through winter twilight and long rows of gray, white, and evergreen trees, past the occasional roadside farm stand selling maple syrup and cheddar cheese. Some of the souvenir shops we passed had teepees or big statues

of moose out front that made my father shout, Look at that, a moose!
the same way he shouted, Look at that, cows! whenever we passed milk
cows grazing in a mountainside pasture. Meanwhile my uncle and Feli
cheerfully bantered with Mamita, who sat partly turned around with her
arm hooked around my sister, their jokes and laughter, ala que alegre, and
púchica, and ala gran chucha, vos, Tío Memo regularly remembering to
switch to English for the sake of my father, a rare memory of snug well-
being, of happy pride in family. The way Tío Memo, at the start of every
sentence he addressed to my father, said, "Bert," in his deep, resounding
voice, sounding so manly and respectful. And my father would say, Well,
Memo, to be honest with you . . . Or, Frankly, Memo, let me tell you how
I see it. They spoke to each other the way leaders at the United Nations
spoke to each other, I imagined, men who understood power and how
things really were, their conversations meant to deepen mutual understanding and to clarify complex matters for the rest of us. That's why Mamita
always chirped along with utterances like: No me digás, or Así es, or Oh
no, they can't do that, or, Memo, is that true? Guatemala's improving but
precarious economic and political position in the world, always threatened
by powerful subversive enemies from without and within, always needing
to maneuver such treacherous geopolitical currents, gave Tío Memo an
urgent-sounding global outlook. My father was a serious Democrat with
thoughtfully calibrated positions on world affairs and how these were
complicated by US political pressures and rivalries, also from within and
without, subjects that he only ever got to talk about in such a seemingly
consequential way when he was with Tío Memo. In reality, considering that
my uncle was a fanatical right-wing anti-Communist, and my father was
just as fanatically against the Vietnam War and all right-wing warmongers,
it's amazing they never even came close to screaming at each other, the
way my father and Uncle Lenny, vociferously in favor of the Vietnam War,
used to scream at each other, even at one Passover dinner hurling plates
of food across the table. The one thing Tío Memo and my father agreed
on was that they both hated Russia.

Memo, who'd taken over and enlarged our family toy store business in Guatemala City, was a vigorous man who laughed a lot. Mamita
was always quick to laugh too. She had a wonderfully jolly, occasionally
silly laugh, but my father laughed less. Instead he sometimes hooted and
howled as if he were faking, imitating happy barnyard animals. I'm trying
to recall if he ever really genuinely laughed. Well, okay, yes, sometimes
he did, though not much at home, not with us; that afternoon in the
car driving into Vermont, he sort of did, with those hoots and howls it
feels so melancholy to conjure back now.


Lexi once told me about a memory she said still haunted her from another
of those family road trips. This was more than twenty years ago, when I'd
come for a visit during one of those periods when she was living at home
again on Wooded Hollow Road. It was just our parents, Lexi, and me
on this road trip, and we'd stopped for a picnic lunch at a highway rest
stop somewhere in Cape Cod. I was, as usual, off playing in the woods,
said Lexi, and she was sitting with our parents at a picnic table. They ate
their sandwiches in complete silence, she said. You could hear every bite.
Their chewing was the only sound except for some cars swooshing by
and a little breeze that came and went in the pine trees. I remember that
breeze because it was loud compared to our silence, said Lexi. It was the
most silent silence, Frank. It really started to scare me. Why don't you say
something? I thought. Mommy, Daddy, say something. Talk to each other
just a little. I tried to think of something to say just to break the silence,
said Lexi, but I couldn't get a sound out. It was like they were never going
to say anything again, and you were never going to come back from the
woods, and I was going to be trapped in their silence forever.


Because Aunt Hannah used to fill Lexi in and tell her stories when she
came to give her violin lessons, Lexi knew things about our father that I

didn't. Aunt Hannah would tell her about the family history, which is how
Lexi knew about our grandmother Rose, who'd died when my father was
a boy and whom he never talked about, just as he never told any stories
about his own growing-up years. Aunt Hannah, and Aunt Milly too,
were the keepers and upholders of the legend of the thwarted genius of
Bert, which supposedly explained why he was how he was. Once upon a
time, of course, some of the most prestigious universities and colleges of
the Northeast had had very restrictive Jewish quotas, and Harvard, locally
aspired to by Jewish immigrant children like no other school, was one
of the worst, accepting a secretly designated small number of Jews while
otherwise keeping qualified Jewish students out, especially those who
came from the Russian and Eastern European shtetl families of Boston's
most abhorred immigrant neighborhoods. Maybe Bert didn't even know
about the quotas, or if he did, had a faith that if it was indeed harder for
a Jewish student to be accepted into Harvard than it was for a Christian,
it must be by some small degree necessitated by the competitiveness of
the process and the unsurprising preference of Christian administrators
for Christians over Jews when having to choose, say, between two equally
qualified students for a last available place in the incoming class. But
Bert, gung ho Americanized as could be, one of the top students at Boston English, a football and baseball star, too, determined to become a
surgeon, had expected to be accepted into Harvard because everyone else
around him, teachers and coaches, were sure he was going to be too. The
ruthless Crimson quota crushed that dream. A year later, he was accepted
into Johns Hopkins in faraway Baltimore to study medicine, but it was
the Depression, and Grandpa Moe made him stay home and go to work
as a locksmith so that he could help support the family. That's why Bert
had to enroll in Boston University part-time, where he studied chemical
engineering, eventually leading to his long career in false teeth. I only
knew those stories from Lexi.

Aunt Hannah told Lexi that Bert had a boss at Potashnik Tooth
Company whom he hated, who'd been "picking on him" for years, Leslie

Potashnik, one of the sons of the company founder, Dr. Simon Potashnik. According to Aunt Hannah, whenever Bert would invent a new kind of false tooth, Leslie Potashnik would put his name on the patent. That jerk took credit for all the work Daddy did, Lexi told me. There are patents for false teeth? I asked. Back then I didn't know anything about it. Whenever you invent anything for any business, said Lexi, of course there are patents. Because of Leslie Potashnik, my father hated going to work. That's why, my sister said, so often when he got home in the evenings, she could hear him through the thin door of the downstairs bathroom in the shower cursing: You son of a bitch, you goddamned bastard you, get off my back. Lexi said that used to actually make her feel sorry for Bert.

During the years since, I've managed to learn quite a lot more about what my father used to do for living. Back when Bert was starting out, the manufacturing of porcelain dental prosthetics was rugged work. He used to travel to granite quarries in Canada to inspect and choose the veins in the rock he wanted for his source feldspar. At Potashnik, he worked in a Vulcan environment of furnaces and kilns, of grinders and iron mixers, pulverizing feldspar into powders. While the company never stopped producing the high-end porcelain teeth that were Bert's specialty, it also eventually became a major manufacturer of the acrylic teeth that came to dominate the market. The chemistry was completely different, but my father mastered it too.

A few years after I'd left for college, when the Potashniks sold the company to a pharmaceutical multinational, the new managers realized it was going to take a team of five to do what my father had been doing alone at the tooth plant for decades, seriously underpaid throughout. To convince him to postpone his retirement another five years, until he was seventy, so that he could personally train those apprentices to take over after he was gone, they more than tripled Bert's salary. He'd been resigned to a penurious retirement. Instead, he was able to buy his Florida condo.

\* \* \*

Here in New Haven, the train has to change from diesel to electric locomotives or vice versa. It takes about ten minutes. It's cold out here on the platform, but as the heat is always turned up so high inside the cars, I left my coat inside, on the rack over my seat. Back in the smoking days, this was always one of the great moments to light up. The locomotive, just disconnected, looking as if it's playing a juvenile prank, goes whizzing off all by itself, and now train-yard workers are huddled around the exposed front of the first passenger car, a few leaning over from the platform, the others down on the tracks doing whatever it is they do so that the second locomotive, when it comes rolling in reverse, will ram into that car, iron against iron, and latch on. If you've stayed inside in your seat, even though you know it's coming, it always delivers a disagreeable jolt, flinging coffee up out of your cup. That routine jarring collision of locomotive and car is a pleasing reminder that not everything is all high-tech, smooth, and quiet, the way the high-speed Acela is, which is almost three times as expensive as this regional train and usually doesn't even get you to Boston, New York, or DC that much more quickly, its velocity constrained by the archaic tracks and all the other traffic, including local commuter lines, sharing them. Though the Acela is a nice ride, with lobster rolls for sale in the café car and a certain elitist, briefcase-carrying Northeast Corridor glamour, if you're in the mood to spend some extra dosh just for that. I like to wait until the last moment to reboard, when the conductors, some leaning out the doors, are shouting to lingering passengers out on the platform, many of whom like soldiers returning to the front in an old movie take a last drag and toss down their cigarettes as they stride forward to hop back on the train just as it's starting to move.

Promise me you'll always be the happy one, said my mother. I can't have two unhappy children. If I can't remember when she first said that, I do remember thinking, She really means it—and feeling happy that she thought of me in this way and also pained for her. She said it more than once, though maybe not quite in those exact words. Still, having an inherently "happy-go-lucky" disposition, as Mamita liked to claim we both did, didn't necessarily make you kind to your little sister or even intuitively empathetic. If Lexi sometimes had a hard time as a child and adolescent, I was indifferent or pretended to be. Was it that she didn't have friends? But Lexi did have friends, more and better friends than I did. Maybe they weren't all nice enough to her, I don't know. She had an innocence that made her easy to confuse. When someone was mean, it hurt her, but it also confused her. When people were mean to me, it didn't confuse me. It didn't even hurt me that much. It was just the way things were.

Even into my thirties, even beyond that, I still felt a kind of internalized mandate to hide any unhappiness of my own from my mother—I would never have been tempted to share it with my father or sister anyway.

Eventually, over the years, I had a couple of girlfriends who got close enough to me to also observe my mother and how I was with her and to form opinions about it. I remember giving one of those girlfriends that whole spiel about my mother and me being so similar, happy by nature, smiling through misfortune, and I was so taken by surprise when she responded that it wasn't true. Yes, my mother might have a cheerful disposition, but she was sad inside. Camila said she could tell that in many ways Mamita had had a sad life, that she was a wounded woman. I, on the other hand, really did let things go. The bad things that happen to you, she said, it's weird, it's like you just shed them and go on to the next thing. A year or two later, Camila repeated those very words when she broke up with me. Sure, I was sad now, devastated even, but she knew I'd get over it, shed it, move on to the next thing like I always did. She reached out to actually stroke my nose as if saying goodbye to a dog, faithful and stupid, who'd miss her but would also soon forget all about her, happy to go off with a new master.

I did everything I could, tried everything for years, to get you to open up your heart, and nothing worked! That's what Camila exclaimed a few months ago as we sat in her kitchen in the Williamsburg loft that she shares with her partner, an Iranian German avant-garde theater director, having invited me for lunch. She shouted, Frank, are you laughing? You are such an asshole. You're laughing! But she was laughing, too, partly in disbelief, because it was me who'd just asked, all these years later, why she thought our relationship had failed, and she'd made the effort to answer honestly, I had some nerve to laugh! I don't know why I'd started to laugh, embarrassment probably.

Not long after that previous trip when Lexi had told Camila about how those boys had "almost murdered me," I'd come to Boston alone because my father was in the hospital to be operated on for a blocked artery maybe, though I'm not sure. Bert had so many emergencies and operations that I regard as minor only because he so robustly survived them all. Lexi, my mother, and I had met at the hospital to sit with Bert in his room for a while, and then my sister drove us in her car to the Chestnut Hill mall to have dinner at Legal Sea Foods, where, it turned out, my sister wanted to talk about her therapy sessions. I knew Lexi had been in therapy since her childhood, but this was the first time I'd ever heard her discuss it so openly. Of course one of the major problems she and her therapist had worked on was the harm my father had done to her, endlessly insulting her, demeaning her, making her feel like she was a huge disappointment to everybody, worthless. I know I'm not worthless now, Frank, she said in a tone of cheerful exhortation. But that took years of therapy, which helped me to find the confidence to prove my worth to others, yes, but mostly to myself. But, sadly, she said, trying to prove that to Bert is a waste of time. I know that now too. I was struck by how she'd pronounced "But, *sadly*," as if our father's cruelty was something she could now regard with a certain perhaps feigned detachment. Yes, darling, I know, my mother said, putting her thin, delicate hand on my sister's paler, more substantial, elegantly sculpted–looking one. Lexi really does have beautiful hands, as if shaped by all those years of violin and viola playing when she was a girl.

I hadn't been around many people who spoke in this earnestly self-disclosing way. Even Camila, who could be direct in expressing her emotions, possessed, I suppose, an innate British restraint. Starting in my twenties, I'd spent practically ten straight years in Central America, as a freelance journalist, covering the wars, trying to write my first novel, occasionally spending time in New York, but the focus of my life was always down there. The other journalists I knew never spoke like that, the way my sister did at dinner, nor did any of the Central Americans I knew. It would have raked stridently across almost anyone's nerves and sense of private equilibrium, would have sounded incredibly gauche, to hear someone going on about their therapy sessions or their personal emotional problems, "sharing" in this way. Obviously, violence, death, suffering were all around us. We were living through a terrible war, Central America in the 1980s, a war that many of us were dedicated to observing, to investigating in ways that practically required us to merge self and commitment to our jobs, emotionally, morally; it seemed the only way to rise to the horror of what we were witnessing. We couldn't help but try, at least. It's not like we didn't manage to have fun too. But I don't doubt that the experience was in some ways deforming. I can see now that it was. Of course some of us, maybe even most of us, also found partners to be close to, intimate with, even if discreetly. Not me, though. I didn't find anyone in all those years. It seemed fine, in the context of that time and place, to be the way I was. What a camouflage it was for me, I guess, to be down there in those years, emotional inarticulateness passing for stoical virtue.

So here was Lexi talking about her therapy, about what a bastard Bert was and how she'd worked through that with the help of her therapist. But my sister had a surprise. Her voice was now raised and flattened as if to focus our attention, or mine really, to this new level of seriousness. Recently, she and her therapist had been going deeper into her life's traumas, bringing those that hadn't seemed so obvious to the surface. I remember considering at that moment whether or not to order another bourbon on the rocks and deciding that one was enough; I've never let myself get even a little bit drunk around my sister or even my mother, afraid of what I might say, guarding against something, not sure what exactly. Lexi began to speak about what she'd suffered when we were children, watching me be bullied by the Saccos and other boys. Here we go with the almost murdered story again, I thought, and I got ready to scowl and say, Lexi, I wasn't *almost murdered.* Instead my sister said that even that had not emotionally hurt and damaged her the way, when we were a little older, watching my father beat me had. She explained that not only was it terrifying, just awful, Frank, to witness, but it also used to make her feel so helpless. It was her helplessness in the face of my father's violence, her inability to rescue me, to make him stop hitting me that had traumatized her. That's what her therapist had made her see.

Hah, yeah, I said, lightly scoffing, trying to turn it into a little joke. Back then there were all those protests against the violence of the Vietnam War, but I guess you couldn't just march up and down Wooded Hollow Road protesting against Daddy, could you?

Lexi pressed on as if she hadn't heard me. My mother was complicit in that helplessness, she was explaining, being helpless herself. I can't blame Mom, she said. She didn't know what to do either. We were both helpless. As she listened to Lexi go on in this way, my mother's expression became childishly blank, as if her dementia had chosen just that moment to seize control of her brain, which it hadn't, not at all. She was still teaching in those days.

I said coolly: So you pay money to talk about how Daddy hitting me used to make you feel. That's rich.

It was obvious I was going to be a dick about it. Inside I was seething. I was furious, as if she'd stolen something that was mine.

Lexi said, That's right, Frank. That's what I talk about with my therapist lately. Yes, it was traumatic for me. If you'd prefer, I won't talk about it anymore. It's private anyway. I thought maybe you'd be interested.

Así es, said my mother wanly. Tal cual, she added, a bit nonsensically. She was tired out from these long visits to my father in the hospital; soon she'd be putting up with Bert at home again. Just knowing that was coming was probably exhausting by itself.

Maybe I should go to a shrink, I said. I'll ask her to help me work through my trauma over hearing you talk about how seeing Daddy beat the crap out of me traumatized you.

I hope you're never a father, Lexi said. You're just like him.

I'm just like him, right, I said.

Yes, just like him, so condescending and nasty.

Without a doubt, the anger shooting up through me probably was like the anger that so often overtook Bert and made him go berserk, but it really was as if another chemistry operated inside me: I reached a boiling point, it peaked, and almost instantly subsided, just like that. I'd realized as a young journalist that in dangerous situations, when others were most frightened or most tense, I'd flatten out in a way that had nothing to do with bravery; sometimes I'd just fall asleep. I smiled at my sister and said, calmly as can be: I get it, Lexi. It's just that I've never been to a therapist. Maybe I will someday.

I'm sure it would help you a lot, she said, her voice now melodious, a little shrill.

Of course it traumatized her, the poor thing, said Camila, after I was back in our apartment in Brooklyn and had told her about it, playing up my own mocking indignation. And I understand completely, she said. If I'd ever seen my father beating up one of my brothers like that and couldn't do anything, I'd—She fisted her hands to her temples and let out a muffled little shriek.

Well, why not grab a baseball bat and hit him over the head? I said. My sister should have done that, if she wanted to help.

My oldest brother's cricket bat, you mean. I don't think it's so easy. Any hint of violence paralyzes me too.

Of course, I thought to myself. I'd finally answered Bert's violence with violence of my own, but I knew what Camila would say if I reminded her of that, that it was easier for a boy. Doubtlessly true, though I don't know that I'd call it easy.

Well, your own father could be pretty mean, you've told me, I said.

If you mean bashing you over the head with patronizing pomposity, yeah—that British two-syllable *yea-ah*. But he never would have laid a finger on any of us. I like your sister, said Camila. She's an emotional human, and she's brave enough to try to talk about what troubles her. She must have loved you a lot when you were children. Who knows, maybe she still does. Though I have to say, I don't see why she would.

Haha, I said.

Still my longest relationship, Camila Seabury. She and Gisela both for about five years, though with Camila, we were straight through to the end, whereas Gisela and I were off and on, probably more off than on, for all of it. And Camila was right, I did get over our breakup quickly. She kept the apartment, and I moved to Mexico City. I hadn't even been there two months when I met Gisela, and that's when something must have changed, because I'm probably still not over that. Would Camila really regard that as a change for the better?

Lexi and I are both unmarried. Neither of us has given our mother what she says she most wants, a grandchild. Just a coincidence, maybe? You can't just go around blaming your family, your town, for that kind of thing, not at our age. But somehow take away my upbringing, take away Gary Sacco, Ian Brown, Arlene Fertig, and even what happened with Marianne Lucas, take away Monkey Boy and Gols, and who would I be? Would it be as if I'd never walked the earth? But I have walked the earth, and it's been a long walk, and all of that is far in the past. Except I am seeing Marianne Lucas tonight. If nothing else, our dinner will be the only high school reunion I ever go to.

\*    \*    \*

So I did manage to resist until we left New Haven. I reach down into my backpack and lift out the sandwich, pull it from its bag, set it down on the lowered seat tray, unwrap the wax paper but only around its top half, and hoist it to my lips for that first bite of crunchy sesame-seeded bread, capicola, soppressata, fresh mozzarella, olive oil–soaked hot red peppers, and sit back, savoring those flavors and textures. Finally I open the little Muriel Spark novel, holding it up in one hand. And read this sentence:

"Their eyes gave out an eager-spirited light that resembled near genius, but was youth merely . . ."

It makes me think of Lulú, the sweet, eager light in her eyes that chimes in my heart like a silvery bell. Gisela's bottomlessly murky eyes were pretty much the opposite. Yet I've never in my life been so fixated—enthralled—by any gaze as by hers.


Besides journalists, all sorts of young foreign women, probably at least a slight majority of them gringas, were pouring into Central America during those war years: aid workers of every stripe, doctors and nurses without borders, solidarity activists, analysts and scholars of war and politics, spies, arms dealers, and even mercenaries. There were also those who would have been there even without the war: Peace Corps volunteers, embassy staff, grad students in every subject from anthropology to rain forest zoology, business types, eternal hippie backpackers; all manner of seekers seeking and scammers scamming, like those mixed up in the illegal adoption trade, fake orphanages filled with stolen and extorted babies.

Anyone might surprise. I knew a thirtyish British journalist, Cambridge grad, super suave fellow who was having a romance with a missionary nun from Indiana he'd met up in the Ixil. Sister Julia had

graduated from University of Chicago Divinity School, she read Pascal
and Simone Weil in French, and whenever she came down from the
mountains to meet him at the lake or in Antigua or in the city, she
traveled by bus with books of poetry in her knapsack. Rimbaud, Celan,
Denise Levertov, I remember were poets he named. The British journalist
and I weren't close friends. The reason he came over to sit with me in
Bar Quixote when I was drinking alone one night was because he was
excited to tell me about his love affair with the nun from Indiana, and
the reason he was so excited was because her last name was Goldberg,
too, though she was "half-Jewish" by birth. I'm only half-Jewish, too,
I told him. Do you think you might be related? he exclaimed. How
many half-Jewish Goldbergs could there be? That made us both guffaw.
Though she had a Catholic mother, she'd had to convert, because she'd
never been baptized. He told me about another writer Sister Julia was
into, Natalia Ginzburg, an Italian, half-Jewish and a Catholic convert
too. That was the first time I ever heard of Natalia Ginzburg, but I
didn't read her until a few years later when I found some of her books
in Spanish translation in a Mexico City bookstore. The British journalist told me he was in love with the missionary nun, but she refused to
abandon the religious life because the people she was serving so needed
her, the Ixil Maya being one of populations hardest hit by the war, the
army's now-notorious scorched-earth campaign of massacres, and its
other well-documented crimes and horrors. As long as Sister Julia was
living in a way that brought her closer to the meaning of Jesus Christ as
she understood it, she didn't care what other sins she was committing,
was how my friend explained it. He said, She likes to call herself a Jesuit
Anarchist. It's been something like fifteen years since I last spoke to the
British journalist, but I see him on TV quite a bit. He's become an expert
on the Taliban and Al Qaeda. I have no idea whatever became of Sister
Julia Goldberg, but I doubt she was killed. As far as I know, whenever
they murdered an American nun in Guatemala or El Salvador, and they
murdered more than a few, we heard about it.

\*    \*    \*

Of course there were millions of centroamericanas there, too, more or less my own age, born on the isthmus and still living there. Surely among them was the romantic companion I so longed to find. I even told myself that it would be a logical way to resolve my sometimes-confusing identity issues, to have a serious relationship with and eventually marry a centroamericana, as tritely prescriptive as that sounds now. But over the next decade, I only had a few one-nighters and brief involvements, which I was never able to keep going much longer than a week, with a mix of local and foreign women I can count on one hand. No real intimate connection or electricity, not smart or funny or political enough, that's the sort of thing I'd tell myself, whether she'd cut out first or I had. Instead, I'd carry around some absurdly far-fetched, unrequited crush or obsession, I could keep one of those going for years.


There were two bedrooms in the apartment, originally built for Abuelita's sister Nano, over my abuelos' house, and for a while Penny Moore lived in one of them. She was the most important human rights investigator in Guatemala, though she did that anonymously. Her cover was working as a stringer for one of the American newsweeklies, where not even her editor knew her secret. I accompanied her on a lot of her information-gathering trips up into the Quiché, Huehue, and Rabinal, and one time we crossed over from Mexico with an Ixil guide named Maria Saché, who led us to the camp of a nomadic Maya refugee group, one of the comunidades de población en resistencia, who'd fled into the mountains and forests to evade the army, living on wild plants and roots when they were on the run, sometimes able to settle long enough to harvest a season of corn, and improvise a little school. Even deep inside the rain forest, sometimes the only drinking water the refugees could find had to be squeezed or sucked from machete-hacked tree vines and roots that fathers held to the lips of their children, they'd even offer the chance to draw a few sips to a pair of thirsty journalists before taking any for themselves. I did my own reporting, too, in Guatemala and elsewhere in Central America, every year publishing three or so magazine pieces, and those occasional freelance checks were what I lived on. I saw a lot, but not as much as Penny and a full-time correspondent like my other closest friend, Geronimo Tripp, always rushing off to the latest hot combat zone. But in Guatemala City I stayed in my room a lot, too, trying to get my novel going, writing by hand on legal pads or pounding with two fingers my little Olivetti portable. Or I'd spend entire rainy season afternoons hidden away in the upstairs mezzanine of Pastelería Jensen, a café in the center, writing in my notebook or reading novels in those British paperback editions that I bought in the little foreign language bookshop one block over, owned by a young French-Guatemalan Jewish man. He had books in English, French, German, even Japanese, but he never stocked any title known to be politically left. I remember a young French backpacker type coming in and asking for Che Guevara's *Motorcyle Diaries*, and the bookstore owner looking like he was about to have a heart attack. He meticulously wrapped every purchased book with brown paper and tape, but if you tried to strike up even the smallest small talk with him while you patiently watched and waited across his counter, all you'd get back were terse nods, which must be why my memory of his very large head atop his small, slender body and his marzipan-pale, mole-splotched, sensitive face and thin, stricken lips remains so vivid. Sitting up on that café mezzanine with my little individual pot of coffee, I'd unwrap the brown paper around whatever black- (*The Sentimental Journey*), light-green- (Andre Gide's *Journals*), or orange-spined (*The Comedians*) Penguin I'd just bought, hold it to my nose, and riffle the pages to inhale that nutty mustiness possessed by any book steeped in a Guatemalan rainy season. Tío Memo used to come into Pastelería Jensen from the store every afternoon at five on the dot for his coffee and oatmeal cookies, always accompanied by at least one of my younger girl cousins. Usually I'd leave my table to go downstairs and sit with them for a bit.

Penny Moore strode into my bedroom holding a gardening hand rake and said, You should have this. But we didn't have a garden or anything like one. Her rake had five iron prongs, each filed or lathed to a sharp point. Someone had recently given it to her. She'd been keeping it by her bed, ready to use it as a weapon in an emergency. I'm trying to remember exactly what color its wooden handle was; a grayish shade, I think.

It was one of those times when Guatemalan G-2 Military Intelligence and the death squads seemed to be launching another of their sporadic killing frenzies. The dreaded intelligence unit known as the Archivo was then headed by Tito Cara de Culo, still just a colonel. What seemed different now was that they weren't only targeting Guatemalans. A junior diplomat from one of the Scandinavian countries had apparently spent several days in a guerrilla camp, not necessarily inconsistent with her information-gathering duties; in the middle of the night, intruders stealthily scaled the wall outside her rented home, climbed in through her bedroom window, repeatedly raped and stabbed her, and left her body for dead as a message that the people it was intended for would not misconstrue. Miraculously, she survived and was immediately evacuated by military air ambulance. There was a lot of nervous whispering going around about who was getting threats, who'd already fled, who might be next. Embassies and international aid organizations were all freaking, ordering staff living in apartments and homes conceivably vulnerable to wall-climbing agents of freedom to move into gated, multistory condominium complexes with good security.

Penny Moore, nonpareil information gatherer, also had a lot of contacts among the guerrillas. She'd received probably many more threats than she'd let on to me. It wouldn't be so hard for people with the required skills to reach our windows from the sidewalk or the roof. We knew that the "bad guys"—Military Intelligence, other Guat officials, the US embassy—must suspect that Penny wasn't just a magazine stringer, even if they didn't know for sure. Maybe they didn't think one person could be behind those voluminous human rights reports that were causing the Guatemalan military government and the Bonzo administration in Washington so many headaches. They didn't think one boyishly skinny, long-legged girl whose ears stuck out through her thin black hair, who had a laugh like a neighing donkey, who'd first come to Guatemala as a Fulbright scholar and college student to study bats in Mayan mythology could be doing all that by herself. One day she told me that until she let me know otherwise, we both had to stay away from every Guatemalan we knew; a deep source had told her that Military Intelligence had put a tail on us.

Our alarm system was beer and soda bottles stacked on the seats of chairs underneath all our windows, so that if they came in, bottles would fall to the floor and shatter. I'd developed a strange tic inside my cheek that twitched constantly. From that time on and even to this day, if I'm walking on the sidewalk and the door of a parked car suddenly opens just in front of me or a little way ahead, I jump out of my skin. Penny was in her black "Vietcong" jumpsuit that I liked to tease her about, a necklace of scarlet beads around her neck. Her extraordinary character amplified her awkward beauty, electrifyingly vital, with that touch of dark Azrael energy. I was trying to absorb that we were saying goodbye, for a long time at least, and would never be roommates again. She laid the garden rake down on my bed, her bequeathed going-away present. It was, indeed, a deadly weapon. She was flying to London, where she'd spend a week huddled with "Aunt Irene," as we were supposed to refer to Amnesty International whenever speaking of it over the phone, going over and preparing their next human rights report. She'd be briefing a parliamentary committee, flying to Geneva for secret meetings with UNHRC officials. Danielle Mitterrand had invited Penny to stay with her in Paris for a week or so, who knows what else. When she came back, she wasn't going to be my roommate in Tía Nano's old apartment anymore. We both understood it really was time for her to live somewhere more secure, people in London and elsewhere who knew her situation were pressuring her about it. I didn't pay any rent and had never charged Penny; we'd just split utilities. Besides her morning cup of yogurt, a banana, and coffee, she hardly ever ate there. I helped her carry her luggage down the long, narrow stairs to the metal door leading to the street. The drive to the airport was notoriously dangerous. If they didn't want people to leave the country but hadn't found a way to make them disappear beforehand, they'd sometimes ambush them there. A simple hatchback car with polarized windows, electrical tape over the cracks in one, was waiting for her, and a couple of sturdy muchachos got out, one to open the trunk, the other casting his eyes up and down the street, his hand thrust into the clearly weighed-down pocket of his baggy nylon windbreaker. Afterward, I went back up the stairs and could feel tears starting in my eyes. I almost never cried. When had I last cried? I had a terrible feeling of gloom, of foreboding, like my spirit was going away, too, another passenger on a long shadow train of the ghosts of the murdered or soon-to-be murdered, a train with shadow wheels on shadow tracks, its silent clacking echoing through blood and nerves, the rhythm of the flinching tremor in my cheek. When I went back into my bedroom, the sun was coming through the windows in a way I'd never noticed before, directly hitting the roughly surfaced, painted yellow wall over my bed, suffusing it with the deep golden yellows of ripe papaya skin, which contrasted with the large minty emerald squares rimmed in blue of the Momostenango wool blanket laid over my bed. Penny's hand rake propped atop the blanket somehow possessed the gravity of a compact heavy anchor plummeting into ocean depths despite being motionless, its glinting prongs like prehistoric fangs, with its painted whorled wood handle, the wet slurry seal color of just-laid sidewalk or maybe more a periwinkle gray, but that combination of colors and light, that unexpected tableau, as if inside a mysterious door opening in the air, suddenly struck me as unbearably beautiful and melancholy, and with a sob that came out of me like a punch, I fell to my knees, face against the scratchy wool of the blanket, hand clutching the rake by the handle, and wept like I never had before as an adult.

New London, the Thames harbor, docks, berthed sailboats, nothing out there today on the choppy grayish waters. The next stop, a short stretch of seascape away, is Mystic. Bert once brought us somewhere around here to see the submarine base, and to the seaport in Mystic to tour some of the old three-masted sailing vessels. I remember standing on the balcony of a motel early in the morning and looking down into the pool where Mamita was swimming laps in a light-blue bathing suit, her hair tucked under a bathing cap, how beautifully and swiftly she swam with her long, graceful crawl through the limpid water. Was that motel around here, in Mystic? Falmouth? Woods Hole? Wait, I think it was Boothbay Harbor.

I was on a quick book tour that I'd come up from Mexico for when Penny turned up by surprise at a reading I was giving at Politics and Prose and took me out for drinks and burgers afterward at the same bar good ol' Tip O'Neill and some of the Kennedys used to drink at, where she said she remembered the color of the killer rake's handle as fire-engine red. No, Penny, you're wrong. It was slurry seal, I said emphatically. Though I wasn't as sure as I'd sounded. Penny had spent years on the lecture circuit, traveling the country, talking about Guatemala, showing her slides, speaking in church and synagogue basements and public libraries, visiting colleges and universities. She wasn't making any money but was invited to sit with do-gooder fat cats on the boards of various human rights and foreign policy organizations; then she suddenly enrolled in the Wharton School of Business. Five years later, by 9/11, she'd made an immense fortune in big-time finance. Of course anything Penny turned her obsessive attention to she was going to excel at. That night in the bar, she confided after her third martini that she utterly loved being ruthless in her business dealings but only so long as she believed she was competing against the sorts of bastards who for decades had been dictating all the ways that Guatemala and the other Central American countries were to be fucked over. Not long after, Penny had some kind of breakdown, was diagnosed with severe PTSD and what they called "addiction to perfectionism," and spent two months in a treatment center in the Berkshires; then she went to live in Bali with her lover for a year; now she uses her wealth to found projects like the scholarship fund for Guatemalan Maya students whose advisory board she invited me to join, and she's promised a big donation to the "learning sanctuary" for immigrant kids in Bushwick that I volunteer at. Penny's back again on her relentless lecture circuit, too, paying her own travel expenses, traveling the United States speaking to ever-smaller audiences. She says she doesn't even care as long as at least a few people show up, and now and then she's nicely surprised, in California, say, by a college or even high school crowd that includes many students who came from Central America as small children, others born here, kids so eager to learn everything they can about what went on during the war decades in their ancestral countries that their parents fled, the most common complaint being that those same parents often refuse to talk about it. Penny always tells me she's writing a memoir, I hope she does.


Outside of my aunt and uncle and cousins, I couldn't deal, back then, with people who didn't get what was going on or didn't want to; people, both up here and down there, who weren't bothered by or were just passive consumers of all the lies endlessly poured over mass murder. The war and its politics made me judgmental in a vehement way I'm

likely to roll my eyes at now whenever I encounter it in others, less over
the judgments than over the vehemence, sometimes as embarrassing as
hearing a recording of my own much younger self. But a fundamental
truth of the war in Guatemala was always that those with the most
wealth and power to lose were *the most indifferent* to how many were
slaughtered: young mothers, babies, entire villages, whatever, it made
no difference to them. To this day they're sure they were on the correct
side of history, even if what they have to show for it are failed narco
states with starving populations and everybody trying to get the hell out,
and now here comes the next narco president, General Cara de Culo, "a
good muchacho," as the gringo ambassador called him in a newspaper
article the other day. Those trips back to New York in those years were
always incredibly isolating.

But by the end of the eighties I'd moved back anyway, where I shared
an apartment in Brooklyn with Gero Tripp. We still sometimes worked
in Central America, even went down together for the Panama invasion. But soon after, I decided I wasn't going to do that anymore. I
was at last finishing my first novel. Gero was on his way to becoming
an international war correspondent superstar. Bosnia, the West Bank,
and Gaza, with the Pashtuns who fought the Red Army in Afghanistan,
the Tamil Tigers, the Polisario Front in Western Sahara. He's in Iraq
right now. I was also venturing into risky territories I'd never been to
before. At thirty-three, I started having girlfriends and relationships,
one after the other, and that enormous change in my life consumed
me. It started the night I went to meet a younger friend, a Harvard
law student who'd been an intern reporter in Managua, for drinks in
the city, and she turned up at the bar with a friend of hers, Burmese
Belgian Pénèlope Myint, raised in Hong Kong and Brussels, a doctoral
student writing a dissertation on Italian feminist writers. At the end
of what turned into a long New York club-hopping night, we wound

up in a crowded taxi, Pénèlope sitting on my lap as we made out, the other people wedged into the back seat around us making cracks about how we were so fogging the windows the driver couldn't see. And so began that crazy incineration of a year, split between New York and Cambridge, the memory of which I treasure so much that often when I'm in Boston I walk down to the Esplanade only to gaze Gatsby-like across the river at that grad student high-rise against the sky and the white balcony from which, one winter night, Pénèlope threw her symbolic trinket engagement ring—I'd promised to replace it with a properly gemmed one when we made the engagement "official," that is, when I could afford one—down into the snow-covered playground eleven stories below. After Pénèlope came Camila in New York and Gisela Palacios in Mexico City, two long relationships, back-to-back, in a decade that lifted off when I was still a young man and dropped me back down in middle age.

But I hadn't done any journalism in years when, in 1998, the human rights bishop was murdered in his parish house garage in Guatemala City, just after presiding over the presentation of a church human rights report that exposed generals and colonels to possible future trials for war crimes. What I thought was going to be only one magazine article on the murder led to seven years of regularly returning to Guatemala to keep up with the investigations and trials and publishing occasional magazine pieces that I finally collected, along with some newer reporting, into my slender book. I thought, Now I can leave the case alone, and it will leave me alone. Fat chance of that.

Just this past weekend, General Cara de Culo, a former troop commander in the Ixil and later head of the Archivo and of the G-2, announced that he's running for president of Guatemala. He's suspected by some investigators of having been one of the masterminds of the bishop's murder, and when in my book I published some of the evidence against him, including allegations made by the Key Witness that had never been made public before, that did make some noise, though mostly down there. Of course, the general denies all, and because he's so powerful and people are so terrified of him, that was enough to make the issue go away—so much so that now he's running for president. On Monday morning, a Boston public radio station contacted me for an interview about Cara de Culo. They said I could do it from a New York studio, but when I told them I was coming up to Boston later in the week, we decided to do it there. I have to be at the radio station this afternoon, before I meet up with Marianne.

Seems they can never tear us apart, me and General Cara de Culo, also his main protégé, Capitán Psycho-Sadist, convicted for a role in the bishop's murder along with two other military men, the first Guatemalan military officers ever convicted of a state-sponsored political execution. Psycho-Sadist is a much more volatile and adroit figure than the other soldiers he went to jail with. Over the years the notorious capi has built a crime empire from prison: he runs the narcotics street trade in Guatemala City and also the city's most feared squad of assassins for hire. Supposedly Cara de Culo offered to protect and empower the capitán in his ambitions in exchange for his keeping quiet about others involved in the bishop's murder. In the meantime, several witnesses, a couple of Psycho-Sadist's losing defense attorneys, among others, have been mysteriously murdered. That was the first thing I thought of when I was urgently summoned to the US embassy in Mexico City last year to speak to a consul there who had information from Guatemala to pass on to me. Prosecutors there had been intercepting Capitán Psycho-Sadist's mobile phone conversations, some with General Cara de Culo, that revealed his ongoing obsession with everyone he thought had played a role in sending him to prison. All the people he named, among them a few journalists, including myself, were offered police protection if they were in Guatemala. That wasn't an option in Mexico. Cara de Culo and Psycho-Sadist have power, but it doesn't reach up to New York is what I thought when I decided to get out of Mexico for a while. Maybe the Key Witness came to a similar conclusion; the last time I'd spoken to the prosecutors they'd told me that the Key Witness, who had refugee status in Mexico, had gone missing, and they suggested that maybe he'd headed north, across the border.

Maybe Cara de Culo worries I've found more evidence about his role in the murder beyond what I included in the book. I know I'm still sometimes on his mind, because in an interview on CNN last year he accused me of being a liar in the pay of his political rivals and said he had proof, which of course he's never explained or revealed. Really, I don't have any more information than what I've already published, nor have I made the slightest effort to find out anything more. If the general somehow hears what I say about him on Boston Public Radio later today, he won't like it, but he also won't hear anything new, nothing that will be newsworthy down there. It's not going to be me who stops Cara de Culo from becoming president.

And yet if not for the murder of the human rights bishop and General Cara de Culo, and if not for the Key Witness, too, without whom the case would never have gone to trial, I would never even have met Lulú. That chain of circumstances is a little weird to think about—and to acknowledge.

Now, though, I think it's as if, without ever deciding to, I withdrew from life in some way during those five-plus years since things finally ended between Gisela and me. I can't really explain what happened. Often when I try, my inner voice stammers to a stop . . . Is it just that I reached age forty-four and told myself, Time to stop, take a break, in order to . . . so that before I ever try this again . . . need what in order to . . . and now I'm forty-nine, the sort of self-sufficient man people think must not really require or especially want anyone to be close to . . . he has his books, and an eventful past to ruminate on, just look at him, invited on the radio to talk about his enemy General Cara de Culo . . . to talk about José Marti, in order to . . . happy to be going home to visit his mother in her nursing home, to have dinner with Marianne, to see Feli, though probably he won't make the time to visit his sister, too, depends on . . . on how impatient he'll be by then to get back to New York . . . forty-nine, the perfect age at which to sit back on this train and gaze out this window in order to think that five years have passed and that it's all led exactly to . . . this, ready to try again . . . we'll see.

Lulú's stayed over at my apartment twice, though we only made love the first time, such raucous sweet bliss from deep within like I hadn't felt in years; not even with Gisela. It was all so different with Gisela, who possessed what Mexicans call morbo, a moody sultriness like human opium.

Lulú and I met a little less than two months ago, at the beginning of January, at that learning sanctuary for immigrant kids in Bushwick where I lead a Wednesday evening story-writing workshop. I have four students. Betzi writes stories about the adventures of a character she calls Sushiman. Ashley has been writing about her trip last summer to her abuelos' village in Zacatecas. Jazmery is obsessed with peregrine falcons, but her story has yet to get past its first line: "Peregrine falcons are the fastest birds alive." Marisela has been writing about her long trek north from her village in Veracruz with her mother and their pet pigeon in the back of a dark, smelly truck. Along the way a man in long white robes gave them a matchbox with a ladybug inside and said, This is Vaquita. She will get you over the wall. When they reached the wall, her mother opened the matchbox, set it down on the ground, and the ladybug turned into a small cow, red with black spots. The pigeon flew up to make sure it was all clear on the other side, and her mom, holding tiny Marisela in her arms, climbed onto Vaquita's back, and the cow jumped over the wall. Marisela always adds: Like the cow that jumped over the moon.

Those girls are often chatty and restless. It's a lot, after their long school days, to ask them to sit still into the evening, working on their stories, so sometimes not much writing gets done. Last night, they spent part of class passing my phone around, huddling over it, trying to crack the lock's four-digit code. That group giggling fit should have been a clue. Later, when I was home, waiting for my delivery beef chow fun, an email came in from Teresa Fijalkowski, my book's editor. A little nervously I opened it and found just a "?" I saw as I thumbed down that it was Teresa's response to a message sent from my email a few hours earlier: "Sushiman is coming to get you!"

One section of the long, green chalkboard in the one-room learn-ing sanctuary is covered with conjugations of Latin verbs: amō, amās, amat. Books piled everywhere, an upright piano, music stands. The kids, arriving from their various public and charter schools in midafternoon, get time and help for homework, but when I arrive, just before 4:30, when the writing workshops start, I usually find most of them, boys and girls, out on the sidewalk exuberantly kicking a soccer ball around, even in freezing cold. Other days they have classes and workshops in other subjects, including the Latin classes taught by Stephen, who founded and runs the learning sanctuary. He also has them reading Milton's *Paradise Lost* together. Stephen's a sort of saintly mad visionary genius, he even has the deep-set dramatic eyes and nearly platinum tousled hair. I know that if I had small children of my own there'd be no one better to entrust them to after school.

The Wednesday night workshops are led by volunteer writers, all on the young side; there's even an MFA student. The kids sit at separate tables crowded into that one square room, grouped by age and gender, from my four chamaquitas to sixteen-year-olds. Stephen has the three oldest boys, Mexicans, two with broad, thick shoulders seemingly set in perpetual wrestling hunches and young masculine faces so tender and apprehensive that sometimes when, as just now, their expressions come back to me, I feel a vague distress; the third is a brilliant boy from Michoacán, cheerfully aloof, tall, shock of hair falling into his eyes, in his first year at one of the city's top public high schools, a going-places boy. The older teenage girls, the largest group, sit at the table in the farthest corner, one girl at a time talking, moving her hands, the others listening, expressions deepening, lightening. Often they all break out in laughter or gaze with intense adoration as they listen to Angie, a Chicana writer who grew up in South Texas, whose memoir won a big literary award and who keeps her black leather jacket on inside while her Yamaha 450 waits by the curb outside.

Most of the mothers of the learning sanctuary kids work as housekeepers in Manhattan, the fathers at various blue-collar jobs in the boroughs and even Long Island or New Jersey. In the evenings when the classes end, the mothers, sometimes fathers, or other relatives, come to take the children home; only the older teens head out on their own. The mothers are mostly Mexican or Ecuadoran. There's one Guatemalan boy, a nine-year-old, diminutive even for his age, with close-cropped black hair and an owl-like face, who is always picked up by his grandmother, a husky Maya woman who wears a traditional corte under her winter coat and a gray cloth bomber hat with long furry earflaps.

The first time I saw the woman who came for Marisela I thought she might even be one of Angie's writing students. But no, her clothes seemed too refined, and she really didn't look like a teenager. That night it wasn't that cold and she was wearing a chic tan raincoat with black buttons. She was taller than most of the other mothers I saw come by that evening, slenderer, too, with a noticeably erect posture. Elongated teardrop black eyes in an oval face, high cheekbones, a pretty, pursed mouth, hair a very dark brown, a bit coarse and wavy, loose locks curled in over her cheeks, her complexion a shade lighter than her hair. When she turned her head sideways, I saw her classic Mesoamerican profile. It turned out she's Marisela's mother's cousin and lives with them. Marisela's mother, Stephen told me after they'd gone, works a night shift as a waitress, so it's always her cousin who comes for her. She works, too, he said, in Manhattan, as a daytime nanny.

The next time she came to pick up Marisela it was colder out, and she was in one of those puffy parkas and a thick, knitted blue wool cap and sneakers. I walked toward the door with Marisela, who said, Lulú, isn't it true that Mami and I crossed la frontera on a cow? I realized that Lulú had probably been in the country less time than Marisela had when she, with a bashful smile, answered in a low, accented voice I could barely hear: Oh yes, that is the true.

The next week I left the sanctuary when they did, falling into step beside Lulú and Marisela as we walked up the sidewalk past the Hindu temple with its mural of a blue-skinned goddess floating in the winter darkness, the street otherwise lined with plain three- and four-story walk-ups. Mostly Latino immigrants live on those streets, though gentrification, as Stephen often scornfully remarks, is underway all around there. Corner tiendas where neighbors like to gather to chat and gossip are being replaced with coffee bars where bearded blanquitos in eyeglasses sit on stools behind laptop computers at long front windows staring out at the street. With those words my seven- and eight-year-olds have described it to me; it seems to be the emblematic image of what's going on in their neighborhood. Staring out from behind their eyeglasses at the street that one day will be all theirs. What will Stephen do then, when all the children in the neighborhood are the sons and daughters of hipsters and young couples who've purchased their Bushwick starter homes with mommydaddy money? His educational vision is partly about erasing the privileges and advantages those kids are born with, not about helping them get even further ahead of poor and immigrant kids. I don't see Stephen keeping the learning sanctuary open for rich kids, motivating them to read *Paradise Lost* at age seven.

That first evening, as we walked up the sidewalk, Lulú and I made small talk about how crowded the subways are at this hour. The subways in Mexico City are faster than the New York trains and much quieter. They're chido. Yes, they're definitely chido, I agreed. You never have to wait so long between trains like here. And the Distrito Federal metro is not, she said carefully, a refuge for homeless people who have nowhere else to get out of the cold or heat and crazy and unstable scary people. Well they seem crazy to me. That's true, I said. But in New York there are plenty of crazy and unstable people aboveground, too, even riding around in limos. And the DF and New York subways both have gropers and perverts, but which do you think has more, I asked. And she said, Oh, definitely Mexico. In New York you worry about a terrorist attack on the subway, but in Mexico you worry about earthquakes, she exclaimed with widened eyes and a helpless shrug that made me laugh. At the L train stop on the corner of DeKalb I said goodbye and descended the station steps, headed back to Carroll Gardens. Lulú and Marisela live only two blocks ahead and one over, on Wyckoff.

We walked together again the next week and the one after. I learned that Lulú's given name is Lourdes, and she takes care of three-year-old

Tani for a Mexican couple who live on the Upper West Side. The father, el señor Juan Carlos, is an opera singer, un baritono, who sometimes has to go away for weeks or even months to perform in an opera somewhere else, and the mother, whom Lulú always refers to as Verena, is a financial analyst who advises rich Mexicans about where to invest their money and usually works from home or meets clients in their homes or for lunch. She sometimes travels, too, though on much briefer trips than her husband's. They have a dog called a Pomeranian, Lulú explained, and when the opera singer has to be away for more than a few days, he takes the dog with him. Last month the dog traveled to Vienna. As if she were sharing a remarkable piece of information, Lulú exclaimed in her characteristic way: When Verena was in university she studied linguistics! She speaks four languages *and* Spanish and English! Lulú's voice is ordinarily so gentle and quiet that sometimes to be sure I catch what she's saying I have to hold my breath, but I was taken with this funny way of talking, her voice climbing in a way that sounds almost like indignation until you realize it's how she expresses enthusiasm or amazement. It's a Mexican country-girl inflection.

I lived on the Upper West Side when I first came to New York, I told her. Infamous seventies New York. Hard to believe sometimes that this is still the same city. It's probably best not to go on too much about that time, call her attention to how long ago that was, I thought, though she'd like the part about seeing some of the famous punk bands at CBGB. When I'd asked what her favorite music is, she answered punk. Also cumbia, oh, Escorpion and Queen.

I wondered how old Lulú is and thought she could be anywhere between twenty and thirty. I wondered about that not just passingly but as if by concentrating hard enough, I could make her twenty-nine or thirty.

The sophisticated clothing Lulú sometimes wears are hand-me-downs from Verena. Her teeth are uneven, lusterless. Poverty teeth, bad childhood nutrition, rural Mexico in the post-village-agriculture economy. It doesn't make any difference to me; it's just that I noticed. My lower incisors are crooked but could easily have been fixed with braces. Considering my father's profession, I remember Gisela teasing me, his not having had my teeth fixed in childhood was comparable to a blacksmith having at home only a little wooden knife to carve his roasted turkey with. En casa de herrero, cuchillo de palo is how she said that.

The third week, a freezing evening at the end of January, as we headed up the sidewalk to the L train stop again and just as I was about to say goodbye and descend the stairs into the station, Lulú said that she was stopping into the Dunkin' Donuts on the next block for the hot chocolate she'd promised Marisela and asked if I wanted to come.

We sat for a long time, talking, switching back and forth between English and Spanish. Lulú is a determined English speaker. She makes mistakes but can get across most of what she seems to want to say. She ordered a hot chocolate for herself, too, and I had a coffee and ordered us each a donut. I'm mesmerized by the extraordinary hues and texture of Lulú's hair, a dark rich buffalo-pelt brown with faint coppery shadings, a whirly wild complexity like a Jackson Pollock painting but one in only those colors. She has a habit, I noticed for the first time that evening, when she's wearing her hair loose, of impulsively taking two long locks, one from each side, into her fingers to twirl the ends before pulling them around to the back of her head and then, holding her elbows out in the air, she twists a black elastic band around those two wound locks, knotting them together. Though it's something that can take a while to get right, her fingertips twiddling at the band, she keeps on calmly conversing and listening through the whole operation.

That evening I found out quite a bit more about her. She told me that she'd grown up in a village in Veracruz and that she and her mother had moved to Mexico State, Ecatepec, where she'd gone to high school. When was that? Oh, a long time ago, she said. Then with a friend from school in Mexico City she went to work in Puerto Vallarta for a few years; algunos añitos is how she said that. Not even three years ago, she came north, making the journey across the border with another old school friend. Is the friend living here in Brooklyn now, too? I asked. And she gave an abrupt shake of her head and said no.

I know not to ask what her border crossing was like, or if it was with a coyote or a pollero. When she wants to talk about it, if she ever does, she will. Hopefully, there's not much to tell. So many who've crossed never share what happened with anybody.

When Lulú told me that the family she works for is planning to relocate to Berlin for nearly a year so that el baritono can perform in an opera house season there and that they want to bring her along, I said, encouragingly: Well, that would be a wonderful experience, Lulú, you should do it. I'd only been to Berlin once, for a literary festival, I told her, but I left wanting to spend more time there. Everyone goes around on bicycles, I said. As I was talking about Berlin, her hands went to the back of her head to undo the tie holding her tresses together, which fell forward like two unraveling cords of tangled shadows. Aren't you excited to go? I asked her. She wrinkled her nose a little and shook her head no, and her eyes seemed to spark with disappointment or even resentment. I was a little taken aback. Marisela, who'd been listening to us the whole time and had finished her second hot chocolate, said, Don't go, Tía. Then Lulú's cousin phoned her from the restaurant she works at. After she hung up, Lulú told me that her cousin was surprised that she hadn't taken Marisela home yet. She had to make dinner and put Marisela to bed. Lulú's expression remained serene, even as she obediently told Marisela to put on her coat and rose to go, lifting her cup to her lips to finish the last bit of her hot chocolate.

All that week I wondered why what I'd said about Berlin had bothered Lulú. It must have to do with her immigration status, I decided, with Lulú of course not being able to fly to Europe and then fly back into the United States without at least a tourist visa. But wouldn't her employers have known that? Maybe they had a way of getting her a visa? Was there something about her employers—or one of them—that she didn't like and that I hadn't picked up on? Or did it have something to do with her being too attached to Marisela and her mother to be away from them for so long. Maybe she has a boyfriend here, I thought.

The next week, just moments after we'd sat down with our hot chocolates, coffee, and donuts, Lulú told me she wanted to go to college at one of the city colleges. In that instant I understood what had bothered her when I'd encouraged her to go to Berlin: it meant I assumed she was content to go on being a nanny.

In Mexico, Lulú explained, she'd taken the exams to be admitted into one of the public universities, but then she'd left home before even getting the results back. She said, Right after the exams, when I talked to my friends at school who'd also taken them, they all were complaining, Oh, I did so terrible. I'll never go to university. But I didn't feel like that.

You mean you thought you did good on the exam?

She nodded yes. It wasn't hard to answer the questions, she said.

Were you a good student? I asked. Did you like doing homework? I sure never did.

I was okay, she said. I could have studied more, but I never hated studying like some of my friends did. She said the reason she'd decided not to go to university was because she wanted to work, that's all.

And what finally made you decide to come to this country?

I don't know, she said in a tone of voice that sounded as if the question had almost put her to sleep.

It must have seemed like I was silently waiting for her to say something more, because she gave her head a willful little shake. I faked a short laugh that turned into a real one, of embarrassed relief, when she laughed a little too. Okay, she just wasn't going to tell me.

Instead she told me about her Mexican friend Brenda, so pretty and talented, who cleans houses in Manhattan. Brenda wants to be a designer, maybe work in fashion, and she met a Mexican boy here, but a fresa, a guero, here legally, who'd gone to college in New York, a math genius, and now he works in business in the city. He was in love with Brenda and was paying for her to go to Pratt. Though out of her own need for independence—Lulú mimed the Mexican gesture of clutching a stack of bills in her palm—she'd refused to give up all her housecleaning jobs, just enough to leave her time to attend classes. Lulú said that she would find a way to keep working through college too. She supposed she'd have to. Brenda is twenty-seven, two years older than her novio, so I think that is not too old for college here, she said. You're the same age as Brenda? I asked. Mmmm, yes, almost the same age, she said in a way that made us both grin. She comically rolled her eyes and said, One year older.

Meanwhile, Marisela sat upside down in her chair, face and torso hidden by the tabletop, legs and feet straight up in the air, the toes of her sneakers lightly bouncing off the wall behind her. Look, I'm a fallen angel, she shouted from under the table. I fell out of paradise and landed upside down! Lulú and I laughed, and I took a picture with my phone. I felt something like a foreshadowing, a sense that I was going to be doing this for years, sitting at tables with Lulú and Marisela, laughing at the girl's antics, taking their pictures.

We talked about mole de olla, and how good it would be to have a bowl of mole de olla on a cold winter day in New York. Do you miss Mexico? I asked her.

Claro que sí, she said. After a moment, she said, I don't want to go back until I have a profession. But if I study for a profession here, maybe this is where I'll have to stay, to work at that profession. I am good with that.

Have you thought of what profession you'd want to study?

I was good at math. I thought I wanted to be a civil engineer.

You mean build bridges and things?

Yes, she said. Or maybe be an architect.

All that following week, I thought about what Lulú had said about her desire to go to college and about her friend's story too. Now, on the train, I look at the digital picture on my phone of Marisela sitting upside down with her legs and feet in the air and wonder, What will this photo mean to me a month from now?

The next Wednesday night in our workshop, I couldn't help but listen and watch for clues and signs. Would Marisela say something that revealed that Lulú talked about me at home? Instead, as I sat in the ring of little girls at our table, Jazmery blurted at me: You're old. Why are you so old? We're the youngest children here, so how come we have to have the oldest teacher? I noticed Marisela looking at Jazmery as if this were new information she needed to pass on to Lulú. What about you, Jazmery, I thought. Why don't you try to get your damned peregrine into the air? Don't take your frustration out on me, chamaca. I felt hurt, as if a weakness of mine had been exposed and my stature with the girls had been toppled. You're overreacting, I told myself.

But we went back to the Dunkin' Donuts that evening and the next week too. We didn't linger quite as long as we had in previous weeks, as if Lulú were wary of upsetting her cousin. These conversations were a bit like we were auditioning for each other, a little careful and deliberate. I wanted to show that I could be a good and supportive listener and that she could trust me not to pry. Lulú told me more stories about how she grew up. Country-girl stories about stealing peaches from an orchard and getting caught by the farmer or about how during a certain time of year, you'd see coralillo snakes along all the paths, a dozen or so male snakes at a time trying to mount a female coralillo in heat, massing into writhing horrible mounds of snakes. The snakes weren't poisonous but she'd hurry past with a shudder, fuchi. Other stories were about her adolescence in Mexico State, when she wore her Ramones and Queen T-shirts practically every day, jeans with more holes than denim, and parts of her hair—she drew out the same long locks of hair that she now likes to fasten behind her head—were dyed peacock blue-green. She used to wear a metal stud in her tongue. You can't see anything there now, she said, and stuck out her bright-pink tongue. Lulú never mentions a father in any of her stories. She speaks of her mother with little affection. Obviously there are things in her past, probably in her present, too, that are off-limits. I sense a reserve in Lulú that's like her finely attuned twin, who steps smoothly to the fore whenever she needs her to.

Finally I asked Lulú out to dinner. It was the night of the snowstorm a couple of weeks ago, when Lulú decided to stay over, though she knew she might have to deal with her cousin's fury later. Even before we reached my apartment, on the walk from the pizza restaurant on Court Street—she'd never been to a pizza restaurant, either, as opposed to an ordinary pizza parlor—I knew I'd fallen a little in love with her. Clinton Street in the snow looked like a long, straight logging road through a frozen forest, snow-piled branches, blanketed parked cars and trash cans, the occasional taxi rumbling past like a Red Army tank; behind the trees, lamplight-filled brownstone windows; all this seen through a gossamer streetlight glare caused by snowflakes splashing into watering eyes, mine and surely Lulú's too. In both directions, men were riding bicycles, some with bike lamps, the clacking and clinking of pedals and chains, wheels softly hissing through snow, hoods up, stocking hats pulled low over dark eyes peering steadily ahead, scarves tied over faces, freezing cheeks exposed, leather pizza satchels balanced atop handle bars and other food containers and bags in the baskets, the deliverymen and boys of Brooklyn, mostly mexicanos, surely some chapines, guanacos, catrachos too, bringing dinners to the people living in all those warmly lit brownstones. Mira los pelícanos! Lulú exclaimed as we stopped on a corner, los pelícanos flying through the snow. She laughed as if delighted by her own wordplay. Pelícanos? I asked. She looked at me with a grin and said, They fly in straight lines through the snow, bringing food like pelícanos. Haven't you ever seen how pelícanos fly, Panchito? Lulú, I love that, los pelícanos. Bringing food, she went on, to the rich people in their warm houses. Imitating a baby pelican opening its beak wide for food, she looked straight up and opened her mouth to the snow. Within seconds, we were kissing.

In our shared lexicon mexicanos are now pelícanos. Marisela and the other girls in my workshop are pelicanitas. The next week, when I came out after class to meet her, she was standing on the sidewalk with her back to me and I overheard her saying into her phone: Le encantan sus elotes con mayonesa y queso, qué pelicanita es!

No matter what happens, I'll never forget los pelícanos or our lovemaking later that night, the most joyful I've felt in years. But the second time she slept over, Lulú discovered that her period was starting. We kissed, fondled, made each other come; that was lovemaking too. Burying my nose in her soft wild hair and neck, kissing her incredibly smooth skin, up and down her long country-girl legs, kissing her as if we were both young and passionate and hungry for each other's beauty—I know that she can't possibly find me beautiful in that way, but hopefully, maybe, in other ways—I felt that same incredulous joy that I had during our first time. While it's true that we're just getting to know each other, we've had meaningful conversations. We've revealed parts of ourselves that maybe we ordinarily don't share so easily, I know I don't. Yet that second morning, for no reason I could identify, I had the feeling she felt disappointed or was having second thoughts or was feeling ashamed, as if maybe our age difference had inevitably and viscerally kicked in. I even sensed I was like a stranger to her, as if she didn't give our "good conversations" the importance I did. I felt wounded and confused, guilty and worried. What did I do or say wrong? That was the weekend before last.

Last night we didn't go to the Dunkin' Donuts on Wyckoff near the L train stop like we've been doing every Wednesday night since January. She doesn't feel the same excitement and urgency to go to Dunkin' Donuts anymore, I thought glumly. After all, we're fucking now, so who needs Dunkin' Donuts, I told myself. Lulú said she was feeling tired and was worried she was coming down with something. The lower rims of her eyes were a little reddened. We kissed each other just on the cheeks, like we always do when Marisela is there, and I gave Marisela the usual vigorous handshake goodbye, bending forward like an old-fashioned gentleman.

A depressing subway ride on the L to the G. Already over with Lulú. Well, you knew that was going to happen. You promised that you'd feel grateful for what Lulú has already given you. I'm grateful. Finding true love, loving, and being truly loved back—dismissing for the moment questions about what that actually means—for the very first time at age forty-nine, can anybody believe in such a fairy tale? When I came out of the subway station on Smith Street and had internet service again, my phoned buzzed in my pocket, and I pulled it out and there was a message from Lulú, in English:

"Panchito, have fun but hurry back. We can ride bicycles in the park. Here comes the spring weather!"

I immediately thumbed back: "Yo más puesto que un calcetín," a saying that has always kind of annoyed me. But Lulú, like Gisela, loves those old abuelita sayings and expressions, too, and that was the one that came to mind. Not even sure what the equivalent of being más puesto que un calcetín would be in English: More pulled on than a sock, I'm so ready. My calcetín message she answered right away with a smiley face. Of course she did.

Right now I'm thinking that her hurry-back message didn't merit that surge of optimism. It could have just been a you-can-probably-tell-this-is-over-but-just-in-case-I-change-my-mind message. We'll go for a bike ride. Panchito. If the weather is good. Probably be a blizzard.

Right now, staring at my blank phone screen, I find myself marveling that any second incoming words might change my day, possibly even my life. That's what having even a little love in your life, after none for years, brings, so long as you own a mobile phone. But Lulú isn't a big texter. I'll go days and nights without hearing anything, then there'll be a flurry.

Proust wrote in his novel that a man, during the second half of his life, might become the reverse of who he was in the first. When I first read that a few years ago I liked the line so much I wrote it down on a piece of paper and put it into my wallet. Then I found a similar one in Simenon's *The Prison*: "Alain Poitaud, at the age of thirty-two, took only a few hours, perhaps only a few minutes, to stop being the man he had been up to that time and to become another." I decided to fill a notebook with quotes conveying that sense of the possibility of a seemingly magical personal metamorphosis, but then I didn't come across many more. But I did find this one by Nathaniel Hawthorne that's like the others but with an intriguing twist: "In Wakefield, the magic of a single night has wrought a similar transformation, because, in that brief period, a great moral change has been affected. But this is a secret from himself." Something, even overnight, has changed you for the better, but you're not even aware of it. But can't it be something that has been building for years and that finally gathers enough weight, even from one day to the next, to tip over from bad into better or even into good? How will you know? Because someone will love you who wouldn't have yesterday.

The train has just crossed from Rhode Island into Massachusetts. Along this stretch, it's been like watching our town out the window sliced into views and arrayed along the tracks: thick pine forest, sparse winter woods, low stone wall, cold dark pond, fen of gray-green water in which dead tree trunks stand like ancient stone columns, fallow farm fields, yellow-brown meadows. We're inland now, the land stretching away into the southeast corner of the state, toward Buzzards Bay and New Bedford, where Lexi lives. These are the old Wampanoag lands of King Philip's

War, and of Weetamoo, revered squaw sachem of Pocasset, entrusted by her brother-in-law, the warrior chief Metacom, aka King Philip, with the care and safekeeping of the famous captive Mary Rowlandson, who was taken along by Weetamoo when she led her tribal followers, mostly women, children, and elders, on a march deep into the wolf-infested forests to escape the Puritan colonial troops who would have killed or enslaved them. They were internal refugees, just like the Maya CPRs in the mountains and jungles of Guatemala. All around here there must be so many people who wouldn't exist today if it hadn't been for Weetamoo leading their ancestors to safety; maybe there are still descendants of Mary Rowlandson out there too. The Puritan soldiers finally captured Weetamoo a few years later, cut off her head, and stuck it on a pole for all to see.

Beginning around when Feli left to get married, day after day, from after school until dark, I used to disappear into our town's forest, woods, and swamps, roaming alone for hours. Alone out there in the forestland I could escape the ordinary self that seemed unable to do anything right. If I went slow, picking my way through thorny underbrush, I could imagine I was going fast, outrunning my pursuers. Hopping from hummock to hummock to cross a stretch of swamp, I could lose my balance, plunge a sneakered foot into ice-cold mud up to a knee, and still tell myself nobody was a nimbler hummock jumper than I was. The forests in our town were a remnant of the same vast unbroken evergreen and deciduous wilderness that had once covered all New England and in its deepest parts still seemed as majestically primeval. Those hours of freedom were often paid for when I got home, especially if I was late for dinner or if my clothes were muddy or torn or full of burrs, bloody scratches on my skin. Any of that could set my father off. But it was still mostly shouting or a cuff to the side of the head, the real beatings hadn't quite started yet; those were waiting just around the next bend.

They always come back though, making the muscles around my spine contract, forcing me to sit up straighter: my father shoving me down onto the floor with hand clamped around the back of my neck, my mother chirping: Bert! Bert! Not in the head! Don't hit him in the head! It happened so often, all the different times blend into one long memory like the loud blur of a fast train passing on the opposite track.

*HaHaHa*—that roared fake laughter of his that I hated. Is that what they call you, Monkey Boy? I can hear him snarling; his voice inside me always ready to mock, even though I don't remember him ever saying exactly those words.

Whenever I think about the one beating, when I was about ten, that must have shattered a barrier inside of him and led to all the others that came after, I remember the blind coin collector. It wasn't his fault, but the blind coin collector seems so intrinsic to how it happened, like in a fairy tale where an old hermit deep in the forest gives the young man passing through on his way to the king's castle something with magical powers that will later either help or doom him in the completion of his task. My father knew every corner of Boston and took me to neighborhoods as a boy that I haven't seen since. The one where the blind coin collector lived was a street of formidable but drab yellowish apartment buildings, no green growing anywhere, parked cars, windows giving off a gritty glare in the cold sunlight. That was during the early stages of my fixation with Matchbox toys. The minutia of detail in every small, painted die-cast car and truck entranced me; whenever I remember the detachable plastic ladder that came with the fire engine, its minute yellow rungs and rails, I still feel a pang of pleasure. The military ambulance with a Union Jack on top. All those diminutively armed and weaponized tanks, missile launchers, troop carriers. The trailer truck with its two dozen tiny cages holding minuscule white ducks with just perceptible orange beaks and, on its white cab door in green print you practically needed a magnifying glass to read: CAMPBELL CANARDS LTD. I have a sense now that certain kinds of personalities are drawn to small, intricate things, a smallness that focuses fantasies or that fantasies fit easily inside of, shutting out the world's terrors, even as, "playing," you reenact some of those terrors on a tiny scale.

At the Music Box in the town square a Matchbox toy cost forty-nine cents. In his bedroom closet my father kept cardboard banker boxes in which he stored tax and financial records, family home movies never watched by anybody, and in one box his coin collection, comprised of stacked rows of clear plastic-capped tubes, each tube filled to the top with silver John F. Kennedy half-dollar coins. The blind man was a professional coin collector who sold coins from all over the world out of his bare little apartment, coins he could identify by touch and kept catalogued by memory in cabinets. He was who'd advised my father to invest in newly minted JFK half-dollars. My father always had these local expert connections that only a veteran insider Boston guy like himself could have. But I've never heard or read anywhere that people who were astute enough to collect JFK coins made a killing.

Every JFK half-dollar coin, though, was worth one Matchbox toy. All I had to do was sneak into my parents' bedroom, pilfer a coin from one of those tubes inside the box in the closet, walk up Namoset Avenue to the square, and go into the Music Box. The Matchbox toys were displayed behind glass on two shelves beneath the cash register. I'd crouch down, choose the one I wanted, and slide a shiny JFK fifty-cent coin over the counter to the shop owner, who in return would hand me the boxed toy inside a crisp brown paper bag, and a penny in change. Over and over, for a few months, we repeated this transaction. The mind-his-own-business shop owner never asked why I always came into his store carrying exactly one JFK half-dollar. But my father finally made the connection between his disappearing coins and my growing fleet of Matchbox toys. One evening he burst into my bedroom, roared a couple of questions, then beat me up in a way he never had before. I retain a visceral memory of shock and terror, screaming while frantically crab walking and being kicked across the floor, my head swatted off and spinning in a corner.

Bert could get into trouble for some of those beatings now. The time I forgot we were supposed to go to Aunt Hannah's for Rosh Hashanah dinner and came home late from playing yard football is one. Just inside the front door, he kneed me so forcefully in the small of the back that my legs were left paralyzed—only temporarily it turned out later. The emergency room doctor, with a sharp look, tersely asked how I'd become injured, and when my father answered that I'd hurt myself playing football, his mouth tightened and his somber eyes settled on my face for a moment and looked away.

I was the only one Bert ever hit. With my mother and sister, it was insults, bullying, berating, derision. But he did more harm to them than to me. Oh yes he did, I think.

One snowy evening almost exactly three years ago now, after one of those rushed trips to visit Mamita when I was up from Mexico for a few weeks, I splurged on the Acela back to New York, hoping to arrive in time for a book presentation at NYU. José Borgini, a Mexican writer I knew, had invited me, along with a couple of other writers, to talk about his novel, now out in English translation. It was right around here, not that far past Route 128, that snow started to fall pretty heavily, but that wasn't why the train came to a halt. A teenage boy had committed suicide by throwing himself in front of the Acela's sleek locomotive. Soon I saw rescue workers and police and overheard a conductor standing on the platform between cars, snow blowing in around his legs, say into his walkie-talkie that it was going to be a long delay because the boy's jeans were stuck, or maybe he said frozen, to the iced-over nose of the locomotive. The police forensic unit had to get the jeans off in a way that preserved them as evidence, and a special fluid and applicator had been sent for. Flashing red lights suffused the snow and ice-laced window, turning it into a nearly translucent slice of intricately veined living tissue. An image from one of José Martí's New York City crónicas came to me: Martí standing under the elevated tracks after a blizzard as blood drizzles and drips down through the cindery air onto the snow around him, some onto his bowler hat and the shoulders of his overcoat, and he realizes that a man has thrown himself in front of the train that just roared past overhead. I used it in *The House of Pain*, that incident. Martí is walking along, musing on his miserable marriage, blaming his wife, and it happens, blood like red rain on snow. Outside the stopped train, as afternoon turned to evening, the snow kept falling, darkly tumbling past the lit-up windows of houses with backyards abutting the railroad tracks. I resigned myself to missing Borgini's book presentation. So many times when I was a boy I'd walked on the railroad tracks of my town, often long past nightfall, passing unnoticed behind the backyards of houses just like those. I could walk a long way on one rail, putting one foot in front of the other, without falling off. Had the boy who committed suicide lived in one of those houses, and when he heard the first still-far-off blast of the train's horn, had he crossed his backyard to the tracks? I remembered the couple of boys in my high school class who'd committed suicide and the three who'd died of heroin overdoses, but I especially found myself thinking about Brian Cavanaugh, whom we'd called Space. During a snowball fight alongside the railroad tracks, Space's little brother lost his footing and stumbled or slid into the path of an oncoming commuter train and was killed. Space, still in elementary school at St. Joe's, was there and witnessed it. Everyone in high school who'd previously gone to school with Space at St. Joseph's, including

Marianne, used to say that he'd drastically changed after his brother's death. That he went from being an A student altar boy to being the kind of kid who, like me, didn't try in school at all. But Space also became much more of a caustic rebel than I ever was. Even Ian Brown used to steer clear of his fearless kamikaze sarcasm.

Stepping out of South Station onto Atlantic Avenue, I head over, like I almost always do after arriving in Boston by train, to the Congress Street Bridge. My footsteps always lead me there. A cold wind is blowing in off the harbor, but it's only a couple blocks away. I'm thinking about Space and the friendship we had in the tenth grade. Space's father, George Cavanaugh, was a banker in Boston and supposedly when he was drunk at night he'd even say, It should have been you, trying to save your little brother, who fell in front of the train, but all you did was watch. Notoriously mean fathers, meaner than anybody else's, that's what linked me to Space, like a pact between us whose terms didn't need spelling out. Everyone knew about "George" and "Bert" and their distinct personalities, Space's father's clenched fury and disparaging, thin acid voice that his son was so good at imitating, mine with his snarling mockery, shouting, and violent rages. Our fathers hated us, and we publicly hated them back, flaunting our mix of martyrdom and heroism. Every day Space and I came to school with some new hilariously horrifying or just horrifying story to tell. On some school nights, in the a.m. hours, I used to get up from my bed, sneak out of the house, and run—how tirelessly and swiftly I could run!—through the silent dark streets to Space's house. Space always let me in through the back door, and we'd hang out in his basement, drinking beer he'd snitched from his father and chilled in their meat freezer. Sometimes we'd sip straight gin, smoke pot, and blow the smoke out a window, and we'd stretch out on the old sofas down there, hardly talking to each other, listening in our introspective complicit stupors to records with the volume low. *Father, Yes son, I want to kill you, mother . . . arrrrrRRRR!* Space leaning forward to lift the stylus and play that song again, over and over we listened to it, silently or just above a whisper mouthing Jim Morrison's words and anguished scream, grimacing and gesticulating. After two hours or so, I'd go home, sneak back into bed before my father woke for work.

THE CONGRESS STREET BRIDGE looks out on the Boston Tea Party ship wharf where, in the spring of my senior year of high school and into that first Boston Bicentennial summer, I had an unlikely job as a tour guide. Unlikely because out of all the local boys who would have given anything for that job, why me? But no one else had a Mamita like mine, always exhorting: Don't forget, you're Guatemalan too. Maybe not the most helpful advice for growing up in a town like ours, but I'd responded by becoming an obsessed American Revolution nerd. It was the best thing my mother could have done, I know now, all her reminding that I was "Guatemalan too" embedding in me the map of an escape route into my own future. Even back then, in my attempt to counter it, look what it led to, an ineluctable bad fate turned evitable, because I doubt I would have gotten into a respectable college without my job on the Boston Tea Party ship. The summer after junior year of high school I'd worked as a counselor at the YMCA day camp in our town, where Scott O'Donnell was head counselor; what none of us knew was that our boss, Scott, was also the weekend tour guide at the recently opened Boston Tea Party Ship and Museum, with its restored brig, the *Beaver II*. We thought he'd grown those muttonchop sideburns to look like John Lennon or in memory of Duane Allman, not to play the historical part of Captain Hezekiah Coffin, master of the original *Beaver*. One rainy day, for a screening of the Disney version of *Johnny Tremain*, I got to introduce the film and explain the Sons of Liberty to the campers. Later that fall, Scott picked me up at home in his car and we went to Friendly's for ice-cream sundaes. He told me the story of how some years before he'd befriended one of the *Beaver II*'s three businessman owners at a historical reenactment fair and been drafted into their enterprise as a Boston Tea Party expert, though he really wasn't one. In college he'd majored in psychology, and so he'd put in a lot of time in libraries and talking to historians, cramming to turn himself into Captain Hezekiah Coffin II. Now, with the first official Boston Bicentennial summer looming and the number of visitors picking up, he explained, he was going to be the on-site manager of the ship and museum, and his bosses had decided that by spring they'd need a full-time tour guide too. An outgoing and enthusiastic kid like you, Johnny Tremain, that was the first time he ever called me that. It was a perfect spring term senior year work-study project. I was even written up in the town newspaper: LOCAL TEEN IS BICENTENNIAL SON OF LIBERTY ON BOSTON TEA PARTY SHIP. Mamita and I drove into town and bought a dozen copies so that we could mail clippings to the admissions offices of every college I'd applied to.

But I didn't actually play a Son of Liberty tour guide. I wore the costume of one of Captain Coffin's seamen, an eighteenth-century Jack Tar, red-striped jersey, white canvas pants that fluttered loudly around my legs in harbor winds, a little waistcoat like organ-grinders dress their monkeys in, a funny black hat, too, square crown and narrow brim, that by the end of that summer I'd have to smoosh down hard over my wild bushy 'fro. Six days a week, I'd carry out my morning round of chores, mop the deck, set out the tea chests, shimmy out onto the bowsprit, and, holding on with legs clamped tight over the notoriously crappy harbor water, reach forward to undo the ties around the furled jib, then wriggle back down onto the foredeck to hoist the pointed sail. I'd climb the ship's rigging, hold on to a rung, and lean out, hand cupped to my mouth to shout: Thar she blow-ow-ow-ows! Down below on deck, tourists from all over the world would raise their cameras; if only I could see one of those pictures now. I especially liked to sit up on the crow's nest, gazing out past Fort Point Channel and the swing bridge. Deer Island was out there, where at the end of King Philip's War the colonists had imprisoned hundreds of Wampanoag, most of whom perished during that winter of 1675–76. The notorious disaster of the Deer Island sewage station, overflowing with untreated crap, was a prime reason the harbor was so polluted, Chief Metacom's revenge. From the Boston Harbor nautical map hanging in Captain Coffin's office I knew about Wreck Rock, Hull Gut, and Hangman Island, cool names, I thought, for rock bands.

So at the end of that summer, I was leaving home for good to start my freshman year at Broener College. What was that going to change? I was desperate for it to change *everything*. That's probably what I mostly thought and fantasized about, gazing out over the harbor.

Gentle, hulking Captain Hezekiah Coffin II, coming out on deck and seeing me up on the crow's nest again, would call up: You come down from there, now, Johnny Tremain. From the way he'd train his pale grey eyes on my hair, that anxious glitter, I could tell he couldn't bring himself to give me the order to cut it, that as much as he wanted to, he wanted also to respect his young employee's individual right to grow an ever-expanding bush atop his head.


There was always a small pile of false teeth on top of my father's bedroom bureau, loose nuggets in different ivory hues that he probably found in his pockets when he came home from work and that he'd take out and leave there. I'd never found a use for them until those weeks on the *Beaver II*, when I carried a handful of those teeth around in a pocket of my Jack Tar trousers, and some ketchup packets too. On his long Atlantic crossings, Jack Tar mostly ate hardtack, I'd inform the visitors jammed into the cramped area below deck during the shipboard tours I gave three, four, sometimes even more times a day. As much as Scott O'Donnell insisted on the ideal of historical authenticity, actual historical authenticity was in pretty short supply onboard the *Beaver II*. But I did always have tasteless hardtack to hand out to children. *Crunch-crunch*, they'd screw up their faces, going: Yuck! And I'd announce: History brought to life! Jack Tar sucked on lemons and limes to protect against the scurvy, but his shipboard supply—here, to bring a little drama to it, I'd pause and slowly look around before nearly shouting—always ran out! Describing the symptoms of scurvy, rotting bloody gums, falling teeth, I'd pantomime lifting my hands to my disintegrating mouth and with a gesture of tragic despair, hold out cupped handfuls of invisible oral gore. But what if I could find a way to furtively secrete some false teeth into my mouth along with some squirts of ketchup and at the climactic moment pretend to bloody-gummily exclaim, Shh-kahby! and spit the teeth and ketchup slurp into my hands? Just imagining it ignited mad giggling. Whenever I thought the moment had arrived for me to slip away, fists deep in my pockets clasping teeth and ketchup packets, to quickly prepare my performance, I could never bring myself to go through with it, I always chickened out. Through that hot, steamy bicentennial summer they came pouring down the ramp onto the *Beaver II*, for many tourists, especially patriotic pilgrims, the climactic stop of their forced Freedom Trail marches, the sacred site where the cadres of the American underground resistance had staged their destructive carnival riot, striking the revolution's first blow. All those usually-so-nice-seeming heartland moms and dads with sore Freedom Trail feet, exhausted, sweaty, thirsty, fed up with their bored, restless children, glad to be out of the sun as they crowded below deck into the briny mugginess to gather in front of the fo'c'sle, rousing themselves to listen to their rather exotic-looking teen-aged tour guide deliver his spiel. Except often there would be at least one person in the bunch, usually an ordinary-seeming Freedom Trail Dad, who even before I got started would launch into a full-throated speech about how what this country needs is another Tea Party, the tyranny of the federal government, unfair taxation, why should their own earnings pay for welfare mothers' vacations in Las Vegas and the Bahamas, that's not what the Sons of Liberty fought for, blah, blah, blah, at least some of the men and even women usually responding, boisterously even: Well said! Hear hear! Huzzah! in imitation of what they thought were colonial Boston accents. This seemed to happen more and more as the summer went on, as if this form of vehement, supposedly patriotic speech-giving was becoming a fad out there, like the "streaking" craze was among people my own age. Many had driven halfway across the continent or farther on long-awaited summer vacations to have a sweet spot moment like this aboard the Boston Tea Party ship. So it was hard to imagine them much appreciating a skinny, monkey-faced boy with a big wild 'fro shouting about scurvy and holding out his hands filled with teeth and red slime. That freak of a tour guide you have working, you know what he did, he . . . Even Scott O'Donnell, never mind the owners, would have considered that just too inexcusably weird and would have felt forced to fire me. The last thing I wanted was to be stuck at home the rest of the summer, waiting to leave for college. Instead, every day I dutifully chattered: Here's the fo'c'sle, folks. In stormy, icy seas, this is where the crew slept, jammed into these narrow bunks shoulder to shoulder like unwashed stinky, hairy human popsicles in a freezer tray! I hadn't found that description in any maritime history book, I'd made it up myself. The more alert children and teenage girls reliably responded: Ick, gross. I'd lead them back to the cushy, antique-furnished captain's quarters. Although Captain Hezekiah Coffin was a Nantucket Quaker, went this memorized speech, like the *Beaver*'s owners, too, the Rotches, who illegally snuck African slaves into their ship's crews to lower wage costs, Captain Coffin was most cool to the Sons of Liberty. Scott O'Donnell had taught me to derisively draw out those words: "most cool." Then I'd indignantly shout: Captain Coffin actually sympathized with the British Crown!

About fifteen years ago now, when my first novel was published, I came to Boston to give my first-ever bookstore reading, and the next morning I received a phone call from my book's publicist telling me that a reporter

from the *Globe* wanted to talk to me, in person. The novel had been
featured on the front page of the newspaper's Sunday Arts section. And
now, a newspaper profile, that was a first too. The publicist was excited
and I was too. I suggested that the reporter and I meet right here where
I'm standing now, on the Congress Street Bridge, that way I'd be able to
gesture at the Tea Party ship and say, During my senior year in high school
and on into that bicentennial summer, I worked here as a tour guide. I
used to especially like to sit up on that crow's nest. The publicist thought
it was a good promotional idea to stress my local roots. It was a chilly,
overcast April afternoon, and I walked over in my black jeans and leather
jacket, listening, I remember, to Jane's Addiction on my Walkman. Fred
Tarrell was the reporter's name. He arrived at the bridge before me and was
standing by the rail overlooking the ship. He looked around sixty, about
my height, and he was wearing a beige raincoat that accented the slump
of his shoulders, short curly white hair, small gray mustache, wide-apart
blue-gray eyes, large head, cetacean almost. Fred Tarrell said hello, spoke
my name without smiling, shook hands with a quick squeeze. The overcast sky, the reporter's unexpected lack of warmth, a premonition maybe,
made me think of spies in Cold War movies who arrange a rendezvous
on a bridge to exchange information after which they depart in opposite
directions, except one spy walks a few blocks and is murdered.

The reporter didn't congratulate me on my novel or attempt any
banter. He said, I'm sorry to put you on the spot like this, Francesco,
but it's best I get to the point. We received a fax at the newspaper that
makes a serious allegation we feel obligated to follow up on. Do you
know a woman named Lana Gatto?

Yes, we went to high school together, I answered, but I haven't
seen or heard from Lana in years. I felt apprehensive but also mystified.
Fred Tarrell spoke the name of the high school, and I said, That's right.
But what did Lana Gatto, the faded memory of that teenage girl, mean
to me? Here I was, having just published my first novel, reviewed on

the cover of Sunday's Arts section of Fred Tarrell's newspaper, the large photo of my face on that page now serving as birdcage liner and laid over floors for puppies to pee on all over New England, and now here was Mr. Fred Tarrell of the *Globe* asking about Lana Gatto, who I hadn't seen even once in seventeen years.

But the mention of Lana Gatto evoked what it always does, not primarily a memory of Lana herself but of an autumn Saturday afternoon of sophomore year when I found myself walking with Marianne Lucas and Lana across our high school football field after a varsity game toward the steep, grass-covered hill that our high school sat atop, looking out over the town. Marianne and Lana were singing "Come Together"—they knew all the words—in unison flipping their hands outward from the wrists and snapping their fingers to the abrupt beats. I felt incredibly happy to be there, included in their cool girlfriend intimacy as they sang that song, and I thought something like: This is what being a teenager is. Or: I can't believe this is me, walking across the football field with these two girls.

Marianne was half one thing and half another, like me. She was half-Irish and half-Portuguese. She had pale matte skin, slightly nutmeg hued, and ebony hair worn in a careless bob falling partly over one eye, and that she kept tucking behind the opposite ear. Neither tall nor short, she was skinny but so well proportioned that her skinniness, snugly adhered to by her jeans, was also ample, her floppy emerald-green sweater far from new, her breasts like emergent islets underneath. Dark brown eyes, elongated and a little slanted, flashing vivacity and humor, and from her upper lip's crest a thin scar, faint as a vein of milk, slanted toward a nostril, from when her cat had scratched her when she was a little girl. Lana was extroverted too, but Marianne was in a different way—chirpily sarcastic and sultry. Words poured out of Marianne in streaks of cheerful distress, and she had a robust laugh often directed at herself because she was her own favorite hapless comical character. She could talk on the phone for hours with me barely getting a word in, but

I loved that more than anything. I grew much closer to her voice than I ever did to her physically. I didn't have much choice.

Marianne and Lana were both junior varsity cheerleaders, and I was on the sophomore football team. In middle school, I'd never risen above third string. For years, though, I'd been playing yard football, those long afternoon three-against-one muddy backyard battles, often in the rain or snow or after darkness fell, when I'd carry the football on every play against Mark Milbauer, Matt Blum, and Leo Seltzer, Jewish kids from the Wooded Hollow Road neighborhood, relentlessly ramming my body into theirs for hours like some blind demented animal. At home, in the new house, I'd stomp up and down the stairs of our split-level, pumping my knees, or hopping up them one leg at a time, over and over, in a sweaty trance. During one of our first sophomore team practices, I made a perfect tackle on Joe Botto, though he seemed twice as big as me, thrusting my helmet into his solar plexus, driving forward with my legs. Joe got up wobbly and looking queasy, fixing me with a glance of perplexed resentment, and Coach Gomes shouted: That Frankie Goldberg, he's a tiger! There's a future Harvard University cornerback! Coach Gomes was under the impression that I got good grades, a studious Jewish boy who loved the violence of football. Goldberg's a ferocious little tiger, our coach repeated in that laconic rumble that we were always imitating. It changed my life a little, that one tackle in front of all those kids who heard Coach Gomes. I knew I'd get to play in our games. Our team went 0–8, but a few were close losses. In one game that we lost 14–8, I ran the ball across the goal line on a two-point conversion. Maybe I'd never been happier.

The JV cheerleading squad, including Marianne and Lana, cheered at our games, which were played on Thursday afternoons. Probably that had something to do with why I was walking with them across the football field that Saturday. But also, I remember now, Lana was in a couple of my classes, including English, taught by Mr. Brainerd, whose best friend in college had been one of John Steinbeck's sons. Mr. Brainerd had even stayed at John Steinbeck's house. When we read *Of Mice and Men*, Mr. Brainerd told us personal stories about the man who'd written it and what he'd heard John Steinbeck say, not all of it nice, about some of the other authors we read in our class, like J. D. Salinger, Ernest Hemingway, and Truman Capote. One thing I especially remember is when Mr. Brainerd told us that in high school Hemingway had been a D student, because my overall grade average was a D too. Some weeks, though, Mr. Brainerd had us write short stories for homework, the only assignments I always handed in, and he always gave my stories an A, with comments like: "Putting a grade on this is ridiculous. But why can't you write with margins and indented paragraphs like I always ask you to?"

Not everyone was as encouraging as Mr. Brainerd. The next year in a creative writing class taught by Mr. Gripper, I wrote a fifty-page story about a lumberjack during the French and Indian War and the magical powers of his axe. Mr. Gripper gave the story back to me with a grade of F and the written comment "Write what you know!" An F for a fifty-page story! That seemed unfair, and anyway I did *know* about the French and Indian War. But it was my strictest policy never to contest a grade.

Will you goddamned look at that, our future Hemingway gets a D in writing class! bellowed my father after I'd resignedly handed him my subsequent report card. *HaHaHa*, the boy genius writer, he cawed without laughing. I ran down the stairs to the front door to escape his horrible mockery, and he shouted down after me: Hey Hemingway, I've got news for you. You don't have the guts, you don't have the goddamned character to be a writer!

Now that I think of it, probably it was through Lana, who sat next to me in Mr. Brainerd's class, that I met Marianne.

Fred Tarrell said, Francesco, the reason I asked to meet with you today is that in her fax to us Lana Gatto alleges that you are not a Hispanic, err, or a Latino. She says that in high school your name was Frank and that you're Jewish. According to Ms. Gatto you had a nickname that everybody knew you by, and he glanced down at a notepad he'd pulled from the pocket of his raincoat, folded open to the page he wanted, and said, Gols. He pronounced it *goals* and looked at me as if silently willing himself: Show no facial expression.

I answered, Yes, Mr. Tarrell, I admit it. I am Jewish, and all these years I've been hiding my true identity behind the last name Goldberg.

It would have been great if Fred Tarrell had published our exchange in his newspaper, but he ended up not writing any story. Probably wanting to recover some dignity, which is sometimes impossible to do for a person who, after all, has just lost it, Fred Tarrell said, As you might know, recently there've been other cases of authors turning out not to be what and who they claim, so we do need to follow up when something like this crosses our desks.

He must have been referring to the case of the novel about a Chicano that turned out to have been written by a Jewish guy using the surname Suarez or Sanchez. Book and publicity-spurning author from the barrio were a sensation until he was outed, then book and author were nuked. That's what Fred Tarrell thought he was going to get to do to me, thanks to his Deep Throat source, Lana Gatto. But my answer landed like a clean punch to his puffy dwarf face.

You got me, man. My name's Goldberg, I reiterated with a shrug.

And Francesco? Fred Tarrell asked tensely, a mean little curl to his lip. Lana Gatto says that nobody called you by that name.

Francisco, I think you mean. You know, like in San Fran, the California city? Nope, they sure didn't, Mr. Tarrell. Growing up I always went by Frank, but I was named for my mother's father. Come on, man, you know what people are like around here. You think I was going to run around my high school waving a Guatemalan flag and insisting kids call me Francisco? At home I was called Frankie, not Panchito. See that ship, the Boston Tea Party ship? I worked as a tour guide on that ship. That's how American I was as a kid. Am.

Lana Gatto also wrote in her fax, said Fred Tarrell, speaking through visibly gritted teeth, that she was in your Spanish class and that you failed.

That's not true, I said. I got a C minus. Do you want me to say something to you in Spanish?

That's alright, said Fred Tarrell, slumping a little. Look, I'm sorry to have brought you out here only for this. He put his hands into his overcoat pockets and looked like he only wanted to go and get a drink.

It's damp and cold here on the bridge and getting windier. My bad knee is starting to ache. I might as well go check into my hotel. It's a pretty long walk, but it will do me good after the long sit of the train. I head back toward South Station, passing pedestrians in dark winter coats, confetti-colored parkas, scarves and hats. Bent into frigid harbor gusts or pushed forward by them, almost everybody resembles a clenched fist inside a mitten. Nevertheless, I keep an eye out for anyone who went to my high school, though probably not many can afford to live in our town anymore, not since the strip of suburbs outside Boston along Route 128 turned into Silicon Valley East. Lexi handled the selling of our house after my father died. I only know the house was sold to an MIT robotics engineer for about twenty times what Bert paid. Walking through this Boston gray winter gloom always brings back memories of coming into the city as a little boy with my mother to go shopping in downtown's cold cavern of department stores and bargain basements, and with Feli on her day off, once to see *Lady and the Tramp* at the Paramount and afterward to eat pizza in the North End, my first-ever pizza, the unforgettable surprise of tomato-soaked elastic strings of hot mozzarella.

I need to remember to buy a tin of butter cookies, Mamita's favorite, before I head there tomorrow, butter cookies from France, with a picture of the Eiffel Tower or some other Parisian scene on the tin. There should be a gourmet shop near the hotel.

One school night during that same autumn of tenth grade, Marianne and I were outside on her porch when she said, My mother says Jews are sexually perverted. *Portnoy's Complaint*, its notoriety as a dirty book, had something to do with her mother's opinion. My mom's a little worried because we've been hanging around so much, she said. In that same baggy green sweater, Marianne was hugging herself against the chill, her beautiful lips twisted into a teasing pucker. How I wanted to reach out my hand to stroke her silky black hair, a yearning so vivid it was like I could feel the winged soul of my hand weightlessly lifting toward her while my corporeal hand hung at my side at the end of a meat hook.

Marianne is the oldest of four sisters and one little brother. Her father seemed to be some kind of recluse though apparently there was nothing wrong with him physically. But it was Mrs. Lucas who especially watched over her children, and in these times, when any fifteen-year-old girl could so easily fall into miscreancy, she had to be extra hawkeyed with Marianne, who had no older sister to guide her. Mrs. Lucas, blue eyes soft with worry that could turn to stone, worked as a secretary for a medical technology business in the part of our town built over filled-in Charles River wetlands, now known as the Industrial Zone. I'd only glimpsed Mr. Lucas once, while standing at their front door one Saturday afternoon waiting for Marianne to come down their staircase after she'd run back up to her bedroom to get something. Looking down the hallway into the kitchen I saw a slender, angular man in a sweatshirt with sleeves rolled up over thin forearms, holding a cup of coffee and smoking a cigarette, jutting chin and longish nose, I remember thinking he looked Egyptian, though I knew his ancestry was Portuguese. When I waved and called a greeting, he slightly lifted a hand and stepped out of view. Lana Gatto had told me that Mr. Lucas was a veterinarian who'd lost his license to practice, she said she'd kill me if I let Marianne know that I knew. Did Mr. Lucas put down the wrong dog or cat? They lived in an old three-story house with a porch out front on McIntosh Avenue, which ran behind the high school. Out on the porch that evening I could hear one of the younger sisters practicing her clarinet upstairs.

Maybe I'm mistaken, and Marianne didn't actually say that her mother was worried about us hanging out so much, maybe my memory is tricking me with a fictionalizing finger on the scale. But I can hardly ask Marianne tonight, at our first reunion in over thirty years: Remember when your mother said that Jews are sexual perverts? Do you think the reason she said that was because she was worried that soon we were going to be fucking? What if she answered: But my mother knew I was never interested in fucking you, Frank.

Of course, I want it to be true that Marianne's mother did say that because she was worried about her daughter falling in love with me, not to express a literary opinion about *Portnoy's Complaint*. It must have been obvious to her that I was in love with Marianne. Whatever lay behind Mrs. Lucas's words, they told me that Marianne and her mother spoke about me, and that night out on her porch, that made me happy. Had I taken that thought a step further, I would have realized they only spoke about me because Mrs. Lucas was opposed to Marianne becoming my girlfriend no matter what. I hadn't realized yet that Marianne wasn't the type to defy her mother, at least not to go out with me, as she would a few months later with Ian Brown.

Autumn leaves were piled in the corners of the Lucas's porch and lay over the small front lawn. A classic autumn in New England night, cold, smoky smell in the air, glowing bursts of yellow and orange leaves in the streetlights, every tree a giant Gustav Klimt dress hung from a line running the length of the avenue, a zesty, gleaming night imprinting itself on memory even as it was happening, you'll never forget this conversation out on Marianne's porch, Frankie Gee, or these feelings, so weird, beautiful, and crippled. Does Marianne still remember?

There must be something I could have said that night, bold or funny, to turn things my way. Why couldn't I have at least joked: Hey, I'm only half a sex pervert, Marianne, and half of that pastrami sandwich is yours if you want it!

Toward the end of that walk from the Congress Street Bridge to the hotel, it feels like the temperature has dropped every block. Three hours, nearly, until I have to be at the radio station. I go into the bar off the hotel lobby and order a bowl of chili and a glass of red wine before even bringing my carry-on suitcase, knapsack, and the tin of French butter cookies up to my room. Gisela always had a thing for those cotton hotel room slippers you can take home, and whenever Gisela had a thing for anything, it was obsessive, so that now I always notice those slippers as if she's been here just before me and left them behind.

It was me who wrecked our relationship, but I don't think too many mortals, in love with Gisela, could have avoided committing a mistake even less reprehensible than mine that she wouldn't have forgiven anyway. If there were a perfect man for her, I used to wonder, what would he be like?

We had so much in common, and maybe it was one of my mistakes to believe it was good to have those particular things in common. She also had an extremely fucked-up relationship with her father. When Lazaro Palacios, up-from-the-bottom, high-priced Mexico City criminal defense lawyer, found out from a spying older daughter that his fourteen-year-old youngest daughter was apparently having sex with her boyfriend, the drummer in a Nezahualcóyotl punk band, he took her out to their garage, stripped her naked, and flailed at her with a bullwhip while she huddled on the cement floor determined not to cry. Ever since, she'd refused to acknowledge him as her father or to refer to him by any name other than Señor Palacios. Gisela's primly pretty mother, the daughter of Spanish Civil War refugees, seemed to fretfully long to be a close and supportive mom to her turbulent daughter but was constantly thwarted.

I met Gisela at a party within days of having moved to Mexico City. A love-at-first-sight thing, like I'd been torn open, gutted, and refilled with pure yearning I could hardly bear. Her Picasso harlequin girl expressiveness, the straight line between her lips that when bent downwards at the corners and pulling her face down with it could make her look so tragic and so childishly gleeful when stretched out, deepening her dimples. Her jittery overcaffeinated Audrey Hepburn lissomness and poise. Her rich-girl-gone-wrong haughty moodiness. Her aloof air of cool, of pertaining to a world I'd envied from afar while claiming to disdain it. I must have had a class fixation, one like a secret devotion, because my last two relationships (Pénèlope, Camila) had been with rich girls who came from other kinds of exclusive worlds, both, in different ways, essentially rebels against their upbringings. Gisela, my friend told me, was twenty-eight, a talented photographer, her work published in some of the Mexican art magazines, displayed in group shows. I didn't get to talk to her much that night. She left early with the young man my friend predicted she'd soon be breaking up with, and she did. Within a week she was dropping by my apartment nearly every afternoon. She used to tell me stories about her life in her funny breathless way, skipping over what seemed like the important and even crucial parts as if it bored her to have to slow down to describe them, so I always had to listen extra carefully, cast backward to fill in blanks, use my imagination a little, which I liked. Conversations like the scenes in a movie where the beautiful damaged ingénue discovers that she's found someone who truly listens to her instead of only lusting after her. Somehow I managed to be patient, didn't panic that I was being trapped into a "just friends" relationship. We were on my bed watching one of those Golden Age Mexican movies she adored the first time we kissed and within moments were having sex in what was like a secret language I hadn't even known I could speak and had been waiting to use all my life; it had a smaller vocabulary than Pénèlope's but struck deeper, the punctuation marks having a subtly startling poetry of their own, maybe love, the true experience of being deeply seized by love was what that was.

Gisela was extreme, hermetic, even strange in her individuality in a way that riveted me. She'd warned me: Soy una a niña perversa. One morning she threw me out of her apartment because she didn't like the way I'd hung up a towel in her bathroom, an obsessive-compulsive control freak to boot. Photography, the stillness it imposed, was one way she calmed her nerves and frenzies, as was any form of intricate beauty that drew her into its circuitry and patterns, absorbing and sustaining her attention: a fascination with Arab calligraphy, ceramics, and the hand tattoos of Berber women; with Mexican prison tattoos; with any unique object, the more eccentric the better, that she considered beautifully made. She fantasized about owning a shop that would consist of only one window in a narrow wall where she'd display and sell one object at a time, mostly lost and degraded treasures she'd buy in the Lagunilla flea market and carefully restore. She had a stray-cat knowledge of Mexico City, knew how to converse with all kinds of people, especially those others might callously overlook or be frightened by. Gisela was a master shoplifter too. She had tales of mind-boggling shoplifting feats, she'd been at it since she was about twelve and had never been caught. To this day the best kitchen knife I own is a Wüsthof that she stole for my birthday from the Palacio de Hierro on Avenida Durango, where the expensive kitchen knives are displayed in locked glass cabinets; whenever I move, I take it with me.

Any small disagreement or clumsy verbal slip could start a fight. We were always breaking up. All those hours spent phoning Gisela—it was still a few years before the masses started using cell phones—standing on Mexico City street corners even in the rain, sliding my phone card into payphones, the phone ringing and ringing or her answering machine coming on or else, finally, when she did pick up, she'd hear it was me and hang up.

I see now what I didn't then: back then, at least, I was some kind of emotional masochist, though not a sexual one, I've never been drawn to that kind of pain. Cruelty was something I didn't need to fetishize because I knew it too well, almost like a first language. He likes damaged girls, it could have been said about me. But is he himself too damaged to be able to help them or even to be loved by them?

During one of our breakups, one that lasted longer than usual, I did finally manage to tell Gisela on the phone that my birthday was coming up. She'd come out to dinner with me to celebrate my fortieth birthday, wouldn't she? My fortieth! I knew that would soften her. She was a good person at heart, sentimental in that way, she wouldn't want me to spend my fortieth birthday alone. I took her to Maxim's, in Polanco, the froufrouness of the place would be campy romantic fun. She wore the most beautiful vintage lacy white blouse and sat in the back of the taxi like Thumbelina going to the ball with her New Yorky toad. We drank a couple of bottles of champagne, had a fun night, and I suppose the several months that followed were our happiest, our least rocky.

The lie that would deform our relationship was exposed at Mexico City airport as we stood in the security line, our luggage already checked to Madrid, where the translation of my second novel was about to be published. Now it was Gisela's birthday coming up, and I'd promised to take her from Spain to Fez, Morocco. It was her dream to go there. She was fixated on the notion that she should get to ride on a camel on her birthday, and I'd promised her that too. She lightly lifted my passport out of my hands, opened it, her eyes intensely focusing on what she was reading there for a few seconds. She handed it back and said, Enjoy your trip to Spain, lying pinche cabrón, but if you come back without my suitcase, te la voy hacer de jamón. I'd never heard that phrase before, which I mistranslated as a threat to make me into a ham. I followed her out to the sidewalk near the taxis. We lit cigarettes. She smoked Faros, of course she did, carried them in an antique silver case. I smoked whatever, several in succession, shaking fingers shoving them into my lips.

What are you talking about, what lie? She told me, and I was flooded with shame. *That* lie. When I'd asked her out to dinner by telling her it was my fortieth birthday, it was really my forty-first. I'd said forty, I confessed, because I'd thought that if I told her I was turning forty-one that wouldn't have seemed a special enough occasion to get her to come out to dinner. Hadn't we made up that night? If I hadn't told that lie, would we be here now, at the airport, about to fly to Spain and Morocco? So long as we hurried back to airport security instead of arguing out on the sidewalk, we could still catch our plane. Hijo de la chingada, don't try to blackmail me. Martí called lies the despicable siblings of guilt, but what was I guilty of besides lying? Of stupidity, callow character, of not understanding that a silly lie wasn't just a silly lie. Sure, it wasn't like I'd tried to pass myself off as thirty, it hadn't been that kind of lie, but what did that absolve me of? I swear, I pleaded, I'll never lie to you again. We did manage to make our flight. And then throughout every day and night in Spain, she punished me. Anything that came out of my mouth was to be doubted, was worthless, because I was a liar. Even now, remembering it as I pace around in this hotel room, I feel sadness and regret weighing me down. You could argue that I ended up wasting a decade of my life because of that lie, unable to relinquish what I'd fatally ruined. We had almost three weeks before our return flight to Mexico. I'd told her it was going to be just a few days of publicity in Madrid, but I'd misunderstood or else nobody had remembered to tell me that the cultural section of the US embassy had decided to help sponsor my tour, sending me to Barcelona, Zaragoza, Bilbao, Toledo, Sevilla, press, bookstores, universities, even a high school. Gisela fought with me the whole way, was always going off to sulk, to wander the streets and have meals on her own. The book events she came to she walked out in the middle of. Later, back in Madrid, I learned from a Mexican writer friend who was living there that the chic Spanish publicist who'd accompanied us had begged the publisher to never publish me again. By the end of the tour and a couple of days resting up and exploring Madrid, we only

had a week left for Morocco. I'd promised two weeks, another lie. But
still, we did get to go. I was carrying all our luggage, several yards behind
her, through the Algeciras ferry port when a Spanish policeman stopped
her, gestured back at me and warned that a moro was following her.
That kind of thing has always happened to me in Spain. That's not a
moro, Gisela answered the ferry port cop, that's my boyfriend. She was
sure that was the funniest sentence she'd spoken in her life: not a moro,
my boyfriend, *jajaja*, it cheered her up. Thanks to that racist ferry port
cop, we crossed the Mediterranean to Africa in a pretty good mood.

I CAN'T BELIEVE what I just heard, here in this public radio station green room, listening to the piped-in interview with the guest who's gone on before me, a Buddhist monk who wrote a book called *Mindful Loving* about how to cultivate your ability to love through mindful living, meditation, yoga, healthy eating, don't you know bananas are a virility super food? Eat your banana, son! Then I heard the monk say, If our parents didn't love each other, if they didn't understand or care about each other or try to make each other feel loved, then how are we, their children, supposed to know what love is or looks like?

Really, what a coincidence. I, too, never once in my life saw my parents kiss, never saw one lightly caress the other in a loving or even passingly sensuous way. Radio interviewers never ask me to talk about such subjects; I wonder how that would go if they ever did. Welcome back to Hodgepodge Afternoon Radio. Our guest this afternoon is Francisco Goldberg, here to talk with us about his Guatemalan immigrant mother and some of the challenges she faced, devoutly Catholic herself yet married to a Jewish man and raising a family here in the Boston area. Sure, Hodge, like I was saying before the break, my mother grew up in a country with a strong German Nazi presence. No other country in the Western Hemisphere was so infested. Once I was shown an archival copy of a US intelligence map from the late 1930s that counted the number of coffee plantations, or fincas, owned by German Nazis in Guatemala, each finca marked with a tiny black swastika, so many swastikas that the central portion of that map, all

the way up to Mexico, looked covered by a thick swarm of flies. It's
a good example, I think, of the peculiar uniqueness any small country can possess. When my mother was a girl, German Guatemalan
National Socialists held marches in Guatemala City and vilified the
country's tiny Jewish community, including her piano teacher, Señorita
Rosenberg. Guatemala's military dictator unexpectedly took the side
of the Allies in World War II, which allowed him to deport Germans
and expropriate their coffee plantations, which were divided among
the dictator and his cronies. Ten years after the war ended, when
my mother's wedding to my father in Guatemala City was only days
away, Archbishop Rossell personally ruled that she couldn't marry a
Jew in a Catholic church in Guatemala. That belated gust from the
Nazi tornado was strong enough to expel my parents' wedding across
the border. In Mexico City they had a small wedding in a side chapel
of the cathedral, attended by half a dozen rented bridesmaids who
must have been genuinely nice, friendly young Mexico City women,
because Mamita forever after spoke fondly of them. My grandparents
came from Guatemala for the wedding. My mother's brother, her aunt
Nano, but none of my father's relatives or friends were there. Maybe
he rented a best man, but no one ever mentioned it if he did. Still,
my mother wore the splendid ivory wedding gown and almondine
French lace mantilla that she'd planned to wear in Guatemala, where
she was supposed to have had a religious wedding in the Church of
San Sebastián, followed by a party at the Club Guatemala. By rough
calculation I was conceived in the Hotel María Cristina in Mexico
City, where my parents stayed during that wedding week. Anyway,
fast-forwarding a bit, Hodge, when I was in the fourth grade, I checked
out *The Rise and Fall of Adolf Hitler* by William Shirer from the public
library, the abridged Landmark Books version published for children,
but my mother secretly returned it to the library, and when I went
and checked that book out again and hid it in my room, she found it
anyway and once more returned it to the library. That does seem funny

now, sweetly touching, yeah. But, seriously, what did she think she was shielding me from, not letting me read *The Rise and Fall of Adolf Hitler,* and did she really believe she could protect me from that? I did eventually read the adult version, years later, well, not all of it, to be honest. Back then my mother probably would have done better by not letting me read Landmark's *Remember the Alamo!,* written by none other than Robert Penn Warren. Of course I totally hero-worshipped Davy Crockett and all the rest who were massacred by General Santa Anna and the barbaric Mexicans.

Mr. Monk has just recommended his Meditation Mantra Number Three: What is it about sensual desire that we desire? During this break, public radio listeners across the land are meditating on what it is they desire about sensual desire. Yet shortly they'll be hearing about General Cara de Culo, who could douse even Walt Whitman's desire for desire. I was told my segment would be fifteen minutes. Maybe it won't even be that long, the monk seems to be getting on a roll.

On many Sundays, Mamita and Mrs. Lucas, little Marianne beside her in strap shoes and ankle socks, must have attended the same masses at the Church of St. Joseph. There's even a good chance the Lucases were there the Sunday that Father John Doyle gave his sermon that led to my mother's vow never to set foot in St. Joe's ever again. Father Doyle said that no Jews can go to heaven because from birth to death they are outside of the church. Jews are born in sin, and they die in sin. That's why it's a thousand times better, a million times better, INFINITELY better— Father Doyle, according to my mother, told his congregation—to be a bad Catholic than to be any Jew on earth, even the best Jew. That offended my mother. Father Doyle was baroquely bulky, with a ruler-straight part in his thin brown hair, narrow eyes that looked scribbled

in with a pencil, a long sloping nose, lips like jelly candy. It was the
Jews' fault, he went on, that there were now theaters in Boston showing pornography, just like in the heart of the most Jewish city on earth,
Times Square, New York. Father Doyle spoke as if what he was saying
couldn't be more obvious. The Jews hate that Boston is still a Catholic
city, said the priest. Boston is and will always be the most Catholic city
in the United States of America, the priest went on. But the Jews want
Boston to be a Communist city, especially all those immigrants from
Russia. That was sweetly funny, to see my mother's chagrined little smile
when she recounted that part, because she knew that my father's father,
Grandpa Moe, had been a dedicated Socialist and would have loved
nothing more than for Boston to become a Communist city. Grandpa
Moe had had the rotten luck to immigrate *before* the Bolshevik Revolution, and afterward he couldn't get over what a great time he was missing
out on. He was constantly threatening to take his family back there,
which infuriated his Americanized children, especially his son, already
a loyal citizen of baseball. Instead of going back to Russia to help build
Communism, Grandpa Moe became founding head and president of
the Boston Jewish Socialist Bakers and Pickle Makers Union, which at
its height had a membership of about five Red bakers and pickle makers.

When Mass was finally over, Father Doyle and his altar boys pro-
ceeded into the vestry. My mother went to the deacon and told him
that she urgently needed to speak with the priest. That scalding stare
Mamita gets when she's angry or frightened or both, her witchy beauty
exacerbated by the black lace mantilla she wore over her head, her chin
and spine lifted to help her draw strength from pride, both of her delicate hands clutching her purse in front of her waist, that's how I see my
mother waiting, in the post-Mass silence and shadows, rehearsing to
herself what she was going to say. The anti-Semitic priest reappeared,
still in his long, white vestments. My mother knew she had a chirpy,
accented voice that made some people not take her seriously, but her
English was nearly flawless. She launched right in and said, Father Doyle,

I come every Sunday to Mass in this church. Sometimes I bring my
children, but I am glad that today I didn't. My husband is Jewish, as
I think you know, and he is a good man. I prefer for the father of my
children to be a good man, not a bad man. Whatever is his religion is
not more important. Speaking as a mother I can tell you, Father Doyle,
you are wrong about that. I'm sorry to say this, Father, but it is wrong
to teach prejudice in church, to try to make people not like the Jews.
Father Doyle, I think you should apologize for what you said.

More than once I've asked my mother to repeat what she told the
priest, and her words always come out the same. This was one of the
bravest moments of her life, probably replayed in her memory countless
times. It happened during the years of Boston's Archbishop Cushing's
Jew-friendly, interfaith brotherhood initiative, but Father Doyle was
old-school, a former follower of the radio priest Father Coughlin and
a staunch ally of the Harvard-educated anti-Semitic madman Father
Feeney who until just a few years before had preached on Boston Common, drawing thousands.

The priest was totally unmoved by the tremolo-voiced, clearly tropical young parishioner Yolanda Montejo de Goldberg and the beseeching
sincerity of her speech. He gazed down on her and enunciating forcefully
and slowly, as if to somebody who barely understood English, though she
knew that the priest knew perfectly well that she did—*that* old trick—
he defended his sermon as "not prejudiced at all, Mrs. Goldberg." On
the contrary, what he'd said was established Catholic Church doctrine,
upheld by Vatican scholars, and so no, Mrs. Goldberg, I'm afraid that I
am unable to apologize for a word of it. In fact, Father Doyle went on,
his voice becoming choleric, it is *you* who should seek forgiveness, and
not from me, for scorning church teachings, and it is *you* who need to
look after your own soul and after the souls of your family. Don't you
consider it a duty, Mrs. Goldberg, to enroll your children in our Sunday
Bible classes, as all the other parents of this parish do? And don't you
ever try to convince your husband to seek salvation, Mrs. Goldberg?

I'm sure Father Doyle felt he'd crushed Mamita. But now she raised her chin and vowed with shaking voice: Father Doyle, I will never come to this church again. She turned and left, high heels clicking down the long stone aisle. From then on, my mother drove alone on Sundays into the much wealthier town next to ours to go to Mass at St. John the Evangelist. She didn't set foot in St. Joe's again for about another fifteen years, until Feli's oldest daughter had her First Communion there. By then Father Doyle was long gone, and the old blackened stone Gothic edifice of the first St. Joe's had been razed and replaced by a pristine, modern church that looked bought from IKEA, with brilliant new stained glass windows radiating restored brotherhood and love.

He is a good man, she says she said. Whatever is his religion is not more important than that. Well, this was still when we were small children. The thing is, no matter what, Mamita never really stopped believing that a part of Bert really was that good man. At least regarding any situation not directly involving me or my sister or their marriage, she trusted Bert's judgment, saw him as a kind of expert on moral principles she could count on to know right from wrong in any situation where she wasn't so sure herself. Bert, Bert, she'd chirp at him at the dinner table, trying to get his attention while he chewed like some ravenous Ukrainian peasant, as if the sound of his mucky gnashing in his own ears made it easier to ignore us and suppress the irritation we caused him. Bert, how should she vote at the faculty meeting? It's never wrong to stand up for yourself, Yoli, but what's just is not always fair. That's the kind of answer he gave. So she didn't want to vote in a way that was going to irritate the school president, he'd elaborate, no matter what tenured faculty wanted her to do, when she was only a Spanish instructor on a renewable contract. You mean, my mother said, if I lost my job, it would be unfair to me, whatever happens to the campus workers. She looked relieved to have understood. What? my father sneered incredulously. Oh no, *no*,

Yoli, that isn't what I meant. My sister and I would look at each other with expressions of: Huh? Later it would turn out that that was what he'd meant, but he'd been feeling too ungenerous to acknowledge my mother getting it right the first time, while also flinching against how baldly she'd exposed, without any nuance or irony, the perhaps amoral or pragmatic harshness of his reasoning, so he had to complicate it a little more.


I could always persuade my mother to repeat that story about how she'd stood up to the anti-Semitic priest. But I'd never heard Mamita complain about racism or prejudice against herself when I was growing up. She'd never given racism as the explanation for any unpleasant experience she'd had or blamed it for any other problem, though that doesn't mean she didn't regularly experience it. The Wooded Hollow Road housewives snubbed her; even Connie Sacco had been nicer. I knew that my mother resented being the object of comments or attitudes that people thought they were directing at a Puerto Rican or Cuban woman, but it wasn't as if being identified as a Guatemalan by a white citizen of the Commonwealth promised nicer treatment. I remember that traffic cop outside Shoppers World where she'd bumbled into an illegal turn grinning up from her driver's license and asking where she was from, and after she answered, he said, Oh yeah, Yolanda? So where's ya Chiquita Banana hat? And he emphatically winked. That was one historically literate cop, though, to make that connection between my mother's country and the originally Boston-based fruit company that gave birth to Chiquita and helped bring years of military dictatorship and slaughter to her country. But Mamita was always so proud of being Guatemalan, and I thought this pride was behind her refusal to become a US citizen too. She'd been eligible for citizenship for over four decades, but she'd always refused to take that step, insisting that she only wanted to be a citizen of the glorious republic of Guatemala. I'd always assumed, considering how much money she'd regularly taken and finally inherited from Abuelita, that there must be a tax reason behind her refusal too.

But even a Guatemalan can win a Nobel Prize, like Miguel Ángel Asturias did, or win the Boston Marathon like Doroteo Guamuch Flores, or become the Iraq invasion's first US casualty. Though the frontline combat death of Marine Lance Corporal José Gutiérrez, an undocumented immigrant raised like Feli in a Guatemala City orphanage, was still a few years in the future on that day, about twelve years ago now, when my mother and I were in Washington, DC, because even a book by the son of a Guatemalan immigrant can become a runner-up, like my first novel was, for a national literary prize of not exactly earthshaking significance unless you win it, which I didn't. That's the same novel that had brought newspaper reporter Fred Tarrell out to the Congress Street Bridge. My mother had come alone to DC. The event was held in an elegant old theater, guaranteed to impress the parents of the nominated finalists and make them feel proud, and afterward, as people were filing out into the wide lobby, the director of the prize organization, a gracious lady with friendly freckles all over her face, came over to greet us. That's when my mother, just like that, came out with probably the most surprising thing I've ever heard her say. The ceremony, she told the prize director, at which the judges had spoken so beautifully about all the finalist's books including her son's, had made her decide to finally become a US citizen. Mamita explained: Seeing my son honored here in the capital of this country made me feel that finally my family and I are accepted here, and that's why I decided that I can forgive this country and can become a citizen. It was almost as if it were the prize director my mother was forgiving. Mom, this is just *nuts*, I said, putting my arm around her and feeling my own weird mix of embarrassment, tender pride, and a little disappointment, because I liked boasting about my mother's stubborn refusal to become a citizen. It seemed totally unlike Mamita to have opened up like that to a stranger. That conversation in the lobby outside the theater exit was followed by cocktails and a fancy dinner in the wood-paneled hall where literary and New York publishing people mixed with the Washington, DC, political and media types for whom the prize ceremony was a springtime social event, and then it was off to get drunk in a nearby bar with the other nominated writers, including the winner, his big-clout agent, the jury, spouses, prize organizers, editors, publicists, and a critic or two all clumped around the bar on that sweltering night like glistening pork dumplings scooped from a roiling pot inside a big mesh strainer. After the dinner my mother had gone back to her hotel.

It was only late the next morning when, hungover, I met her for lunch in the coffee shop of the boutique hotel we'd been put up in that I asked, Forgive the US for what, Ma? She clucked her teeth as if she'd already changed her mind. Ay, Frankie, people like me, from Guatemala, Hispanic people, we aren't treated with respect in this country. But seeing my son honored, she said, her voice going dreamy again, by all those important people, I felt we are accepted now, so now I can become a US citizen.

I thought, You know what, Mamita? Even if I'd written *Don Quixote* and won that prize, that wouldn't have been enough to merit your monumental act of forgiveness. Originally my mother hadn't been so thrilled about my book. It featured a family that resembled ours in obvious ways, except the father was earthy, kind, and nurturing, and the mother character was brassily seductive and obliviously but comically assertive about her prejudices. Of course she's not you, Mamita, I'd explained countless times. I made her the opposite of you so that you couldn't say I'd written about you. But now people think I'm like that! my mother insisted. She photocopied the tiny paragraph in the book's copyright page that states: "This is a work of fiction, the product of the author's imagination, any resemblances to any actual person is entirely coincidental." Then she had it blown up and framed and hung it on the wall inside the front door so that it would be the first thing any visitor to our house saw.

That afternoon in DC my mother and I sat talking, in Spanish like we do when it's just the two of us, in the hotel coffee shop by a window with yellow daffodils growing outside, until it was time for her to take the train back to Boston. Do you think Boston has gotten better, Ma, in the way it treats people from Central America? No, she said curtly. Then she thought a moment and added, Maybe a little, because there are so many who come now and it seems like they all find work. Even our Stop and Shop, Frankie, has guatemaltecos working there now, fíjate, and all of Teddy Feinstein's yard workers are centroamericanos. He comes to talk to me about them sometimes. Some of his workers have been deported, Frankie, she said. Even when they have little children who get left behind. How can anyone do such a thing to those children, who depend on what their fathers earn to be able to eat?

Teddy Feinstein had been one of my father's most devoted yard work acolytes. I never showed the least interest in the horticultural mastery behind that annual abundance that allowed Farmer Bert to give away flowers and vegetables from his garden to the neighborhood wives all summer long. Many of the neighborhood children adored my father, who'd mastered the friendly old guy role before he was even old, and every few years a new boy would replace a suddenly grown-too-old predecessor as his special yard pal. The new boy, like the one before him, rang the doorbell on weekend mornings, and whenever anyone other than my father answered, he'd ask: Can Mr. Goldberg come outside? Of all those boys, the one my father had an especially big influence on was Teddy Feinstein, who had a learning disability. His father, a hospital accountant, fretted over his son's difficulties and what they portended without knowing what to do about it. But Bert got Teddy passionate about yard work, taught him about lawn care, trees, flowers, gardens, wormy loam piles, pesticides, and fertilizers, and eventually guided Teddy into going to a technical school instead of to our high school. Teddy, who I saw for the first time since he was a teenager at my father's funeral four years ago, was the most openly grieving person there, his reddened eyes pouring hot liquid candle wax. He now owns, Lexi told me, one of the most successful landscaping companies in Boston's western suburbs, his fleet of trucks filled with lawnmowers and Central Americans roaming from town to town.


I'm standing outside the radio studio-booth door after the interview, putting on my coat, when a young woman who works at the station comes walking rapidly toward me down the carpeted corridor, such an eager expression on her face that I automatically smile and get ready to sign a book, except she isn't carrying a book, only a neatly folded piece of yellow paper that she's holding out like a relay baton. When she reaches me she says, voice hardly above a whisper: Mr. Goldberg, a woman from Guatemala phoned and left her number. She says she lived with you when you were a boy and that it's urgent you phone her. From the way the radio station employee has her eyes trained on my face, I can tell she's curious to see my reaction to the name written on the piece of paper. This must happen at radio stations like this one all the time. A listener hears an old friend or lover or even the now-adult child she helped raise being interviewed and impulsively phones and leaves her name and number, believing, at least in the moment, that she really is eager to reestablish contact with this person from her distant past. But Feli has my telephone number and email, so why would she phone a radio station? Even before unfolding the note, I check my phone, but there's no missed call from Feli or any email from her. Though there's one from Marianne, she's running an hour late. "No problem," I thumb back. It must be Carlota Sánchez Motta—that causes a surge of excitement. I haven't seen Carlota or heard from her since the summer before I left for college, when I was working on the Boston Tea Party ship.

I unfold the piece of yellow paper and written in pen is the name María Xum, above a phone number with a 617 area code. I must silently

mouth: Wow, can you believe it, María Xum. The radio station employee's smile widens. I put the piece of paper into my pocket. Her
message is urgent. What could María urgently need to tell me now?
Maybe it's María Xum's opinion that Guatemala needs a president like
General Cara de Culo, with his law-and-order strong martial fist, and
she wants to argue with me.

I SIGNAL TO THE BARTENDER for a refill. When I came out of the station, I had over an hour to kill before meeting Marianne, so I ducked into this joint. On the TV over the bar, a local news report on high school hockey, the South of Boston tournament, a Catholic school team, the Coyle and Cassidy Warriors, in the finals, they're from Taunton, the very town where Weetamoo's decapitated head was put on display. It's just a forty-minute drive from here down I-93, not far from Mamita's nursing home and where Lexi lives. So many Massachusetts towns have old Native American names, as do bridges, state parks, rivers, beaches, and so on. There's a King Philip High School, but even in the town where she was martyred there's no Weetamoo High; instead there's a school named for the small-time Boston gangster played by Robert Mitchum in the movie based on the novel, *The Friends of Eddie Coyle*, and Hopalong Cassidy, for some good reason, I'm sure.

Wonder what Marianne's going to want to talk about after all these years. Besides Ian Brown, I mean. In reality, not much happened between us, hardly anything, during the short time in tenth grade we were close. Yet that very little was a lot. Does she remember our almost nightly telephone conversations, that last one especially? Later, when I beat up my father, did she ever hear about that? By then she was so deep into her relationship with Jimmy Gleason that Lana Gatto predicted they'd get married before graduation. Marianne and I had even stopped talking just before Christmas. Yet it was how I still felt about Marianne months later that triggered the horrible event that made what finally happened between me and Bert seem inevitable.

It must have been a springtime Friday, because the high school dance in the rich town next to ours would have happened on a Friday night. On my way to school that morning I walked past Sarah Hancock Pond and the small dirt lot overlooking Mulberry Cove and the benches for skaters to change into and out of their ice skates, and down on the shore, I saw Marianne making out with Jimmy Gleason. Dangling from her hand pressed to his broad back was a colorfully shiny piece of gift wrapping paper, and just like that I remembered it was her birthday. Back then, I knew the date of Marianne's birthday. April, it must have been, maybe early May. The world was wet, muddy, bright green, profuse with sweet pollens, inciting that adolescent hormonal buzzing under my skin that every spring made me feel like a walking Van Gogh painting, always breaking out in hives without warning or apparent cause. I don't think Marianne and Gleason even noticed me as I went past.

That night we drank beer in the swampy woods behind the brick rubber factory that was across the street from the pond. Bonks was the only one of us old enough for a driver's license because in elementary school he'd been held back, maybe even twice, and he could afford his own car because he worked, before and after school most days, for Hank Riggio and Sons, the contractors. You wouldn't think someone with the name Bonks would have a nickname, too, but he did. At work his morning chore was to pick up building-site trash and debris and carry it over to the dumpsters, and because one day Hank Riggio decided it would be funny to call him Mickey Dumps, the name stuck. Bonks used to drive us around in his car, but only whenever and wherever Joe "Hose" Botto, son of the master carpenter, wanted him to. We'll get Mickey Dumps to take us, Hose was always saying. That night in the swamp, Bonks was especially feeling his oats, showing off the new cobalt-blue suede jacket that he'd bought through some shady Hank Riggio connection. But he was especially excited because not only our usual crew was there but Paul Rizza, the varsity football star, was with us too. With his braying laughter, jerky gestures, and squinty grinning around, it was like Bonks thought this was his chance to really get in with the Sinatra Rat Pack now, but only if he could show Rizza he wasn't just Joe Botto's chauffeur. It all started when Joe said, What's a matter, Sleepless, no sleep last night? I suppose he'd noticed I was in a glum mood. Ordinarily even I wouldn't have been so stupid as to expose anything that personal in front of any of those kids, not even Joe, but I let down my guard and told them about seeing Marianne and Gleason making out that morning and that it was Marianne's birthday. Typically, I would have finished describing this scene with a fatalistic shrug, but it was still a sorry sad-sack story to have told, and Bonks, seizing the chance to shine at my expense, turned on me and said, Aww Monkey Boy, don't fucking get started with the Marianne Lucas bullshit again. And he made his idiotic crack about what she'd already done with Ian Brown's dick, was doing with Gleason's now, and was never going to do with mine. So just shut the fuck up and crack me open a brewski, he said, grinning around, practically strutting in place. Bonks was lowest on the totem pole among us but knew I was just above him, and this was obviously a ploy to reverse our positions. It being Bonks, I understood that if I didn't respond, my high school life was basically over, though the possibility of this sort of violence always made me feel nauseous with fear. I stepped toward Bonks with my fist cocked, and he reflexively lifted his arms in front of his face, and though I should have punched him anyway, I shoved him hard with both hands in the chest and he fell backward into the brush, where he thrashed around a bit. When he got back up, he made a show of carefully inspecting and brushing off the muddied sleeves of his suede jacket and said, Fucking Monkey Boy, can't take a joke. I said, You call me that again, I'll fucking kill you. Rizza made a sarcastic *oooh* sound. He couldn't have cared less about either Bonks or me. Bonks stepped past me toward the cooler and stooped to get a beer, and with his back turned to me, he stood up and opened it. It was a surrender. At least I'd shoved him, and in our unspoken rules and rites of aggression, a shove like that was a challenge to fight.

But Bonks drove us in his sedan anyway—there were five of us apart from Bonks—to crash that dance in the next town's high school, where in the men's room Rizza and Joe started a fight right away, Rizza with one of those rich boys in a headlock and pounding his face, splatter of blood on white enamel like a Catholic miracle and it was the sink that was bleeding. Everyone else, except for Bonks, was punching and grappling. Even I grabbed the shirt of a skinny blond boy who grabbed mine and we theatrically pushed and pulled on each other. Suddenly kids were shouting about police and we fled into the crowded gymnasium dance floor, where it seemed like everyone was drunk or drugged. I ran and dodged past couples holding each other up to keep from falling, saw a kid stumble forward with windmilling arms and land on his face; he lifted his head, blood sloshing from his nose as if from a tipped-over bottle. Rizza was tossing kids out of his way as he went for the exit, police charging in right past him. As far I was able to figure out later, the police must have grabbed hold of Bonks, slower than the rest of us, and warned him that we'd better go back to our town right away or else. I don't think any other of us knew that as we piled into the car, waiting for Bonks to catch up and get in, and when he did, we yelled go, go, go, and he peeled out of the parking lot like in a movie. Flashing blue lights, a police car zoomed up alongside us, Bonks hit the brakes. A policeman, not the one driving, got out of the cruiser and stalked over, shouting at Bonks through his lowered window that he'd cut us a break letting us go, but then someone yelled "fuck the pigs" and gave the finger. I couldn't see the policeman's face, only his wide uniformed torso, his knuckly hands grabbing the bottom of Bonks's window frame like he was about to lift the car over his head and hurl it as he shouted: So which one of you was it? Come on punk, own up, or I'm taking you all in! I hadn't shouted anything out the window or given the finger. I hadn't heard anyone else shout those words through the commotion inside the car, but if someone had shouted "fuck the pigs" and given the finger, it was probably Joe Botto, sitting up front. Did Bonks hold the cop's eye and slightly jerk his head back at me? I'd bet anything. The back door was yanked opened, and the policeman, face looking about to burst, roared at me to get out. It wasn't me, I pleaded. Don't make me tell you again, punk, get out of the car! I got out, body filling with the helium gas of terror and disbelief. The policeman took me by the arm and walked me through the glare of the cruiser's headlights, opened the back door, and guided me into the back seat with a firm shove. Another policeman was sitting at the wheel. But officers, I begged. It wasn't me. The policeman, now in the front passenger seat, barked, Shut up you little jerk! I saw you give us the finger. You think I'm blind? The policeman driving said, You stink like a brewery. You're stinking up the whole car. Don't even think about throwing up back there. If you wanna throw up we'll pull over and you get out and do it. You need to throw up? Punk, shouted the other policeman, you heard him. Are you going to puke? I had the idea of answering yes, getting out, staggering toward some bushes as if to vomit, and taking off running. No, I'm not going to puke, I said. The drive to the police station didn't even seem to take two minutes. It was the first time in my life I'd even been inside a police station. Gray, chocolate, and custard-yellow-hued floor. I'll never forget that floor, I feel like I even remember how it tasted. I answered questions, date of birth, address, home phone. Year after year, a policemen said, we have kids from your town coming over here to make trouble. It doesn't happen the other way around, said another policeman behind the main desk, an Asian man with a long, melancholy face. With an air of concerned curiosity, that policeman asked, What do you kids have against this town? Nothing, sir, I answered. You kids are jealous of this town, he said flatly. Your town is not so good as this town. I was put alone in a small room, a door with a wire mesh window, like a classroom for only one student. I sat on the edge of a high wooden bench that must also have been where I was supposed to sleep.

In the morning the door opened, and my father was in the doorway, his eyes fixed on me like a bad-tempered old dog's. Beside him was the same policeman who'd pulled me from the car. I told my father I'd been wrongly accused, that I hadn't shouted anything at the police or given anybody the finger. The policeman said with a loud weariness: We saw your hand come out the window. You were the one sitting by that window. He told my father that my friends and I had come to their town's high school dance to pick a fight. When they brought your son in, the policeman said in a disgusted tone, he smelled like a brewery. I was lucky they weren't charging me with disorderly conduct, he went on. That was only because they'd phoned the police in my town and there was no record of my having been in trouble before. The next thing I remember I was no longer in the detention room but outside its door, facedown on that grimy floor. There'd been other beatings in which my father had probably punched and kicked me as hard as he did in the police station, swatting at my head, hoisting me off the floor and slamming me down, kicking me in the side, under the ribs, against my thighs, though maybe he'd never done so with so much rage. The police stood and watched. I glimpsed some of their faces; I remember a pair of pale-blue eyes like soap bubbles. I'd never felt such shame, such a helpless rage of my own, had never experienced anything so sordid as being on that police station floor being beaten up by my father, had never felt such hatred as I did for my father and those police.

By the time I got home, that feeling of hatred had grown stronger and wilder, an uncontrollable combustion about to explode inside me. Yet I managed to stand in the kitchen telling my mother what had happened. The police had falsely accused me, but my own father had believed them and not me. He'd beaten me up while those lying policemen watched, I railed to my mother like a trial lawyer driven into frenzied indignation by the bewildered, passive stares of the jury, until my voice collapsed into sobs and I stood there horribly mewling. Yoli, the police said he stank like a brewery, shouted my father. He's lucky they decided not to charge him, this goddamned good-for-nothing. I went down the hall to my room. If someone had put a knife in my hand I swear I would have gone back and stabbed him and maybe my useless mother too.

Before that night, I merely thought I hated my father. Now it was like he'd been truly revealed. A father who could betray his own son like that, in front of those police. It almost stopped being personal. He deserved to be annihilated. Still, nothing happened right away. It wasn't until the next winter that it did. Even if it was inevitable, I was as surprised as he was when I finally did hit back.

Fists squeezed tight under the bar top and my eyes feel like there's a hot, dry wind blowing directly into them. The bartender gives me that glance, like he's wondering if there's something wrong with me and is about to ask, but I push my glass forward and say, Another refill, please.

About seven years passed between the first bad beating from my father and that last one, seven years of him pretty regularly beating the shit out of me. You can't put a similar time frame on his verbal violence—against my mother but especially directed at Lexi. What kind of father calls his twelve-year-old daughter *a fat fucking pig*? Even if it was the messiness of her bedroom that set him off, those words had no semantic credibility as punishment. They weren't going to make Lexi suddenly discover a yearning for a fulfilling tidiness. But what punishment reforms the father?

I don't even remember anymore what ignited it, only that it happened on a stingingly cold winter night out in the front yard, covered with frozen snow. I must have run out of the house barefoot, Bert chasing after me, and I was crouched by the hedges in my usual defensive posture, arms clasped over my head to fend off his barrage of hard cuffs and swats. From the bottom of that commotion, my eyes fastened on his chin, which somehow, miraculously, you could say, expanded like I was looking at it through a telescope. And next thing I knew, all the strength coiled in my legs was propelling me out of my crouch, up behind my fist and toward that chin, a jolt like an electric shock inside the bones of my hand, and as my father fell forward I hit him on the back of his head, driving him face-first into the crusty snow. I took off running, the ice in the road cracking under my feet. Bert was screaming behind me: I'm having a heart attack! Yoli! Yoli! He gave me a heart attack! I ran all the way to Space Cavanaugh's house and hid in his basement for three nights. Space brought me food and lent me a pair of too-large black rubber boots that I wore to school without socks. When I finally went home, Bert was wearing a bandage on his nose. He must have fallen on it, because I didn't hit him there. No word or sign of any heart attack.

He never hit me again, though. That sure counts for something. But remembering or even sometimes telling this story always makes me feel sick to my stomach, as if striking your father must inevitably result in a permanent ignominy. He was my tormentor and strong as a bull, but he was also sixty years old. I don't know what else I should finally have done. I've never thought I was wrong to have finally hit back. But I've always felt some shame and distress over it anyway, over that second punch especially, dangerous, as if driven by a lethal instinct to finish him off. If I'd only hit him just once, I might look back on it as a more cathartic event. It's the only father-son relationship I've ever participated in, and it was a failure in pretty much every way.

Late fall of freshman year in college, I was sitting in the cafeteria with friends on a gray afternoon when I looked up and recognized my father crossing the dun lawn of the quad, that driven trudge, the churning of his arms, fedora tilted down, raincoat flapping around his thighs. My first trimester grades had been straight A's. What could I have done wrong? He'd come all the way to my college in Upstate New York to punish me for *something*. Was it the money I'd been spending at the campus bar?

But I spent only what I'd earned through my job delivering newspapers around campus in the mornings. I hurried outside to meet him so that he couldn't make a violent scene inside the cafeteria. What must have been a look of terror on my face brought him up short. Sonny boy, he croaked, holding out his arms. He was driving up to Corning for a conference on ceramics that was related to making artificial teeth. He'd made a detour to take me to dinner.


Like all war stories, the ones you went through yourself, I mean, no matter how many times you tell it, you never feel like you get it quite right.

WELL, I NEVER GOT WHY you hung out with those guys anyway, Marianne is saying. Trapped in all that boy thuggery, pretending you belonged. Frank, that was never the real you.

Yes it *was*, Marianne, I answer. I was a thug too, come on.

She looks startled, until she gets it and laughs.

We're sitting at a small corner table in this restaurant Marianne chose. We've already ordered but are having a round of drinks first. She's been telling me about the reunion and my old sophomore football friends who, she claims, were all sorry I wasn't there. But Space Cavanaugh wasn't at the reunion. Seems nobody knows anything about what's become of him. Mike Bonks wasn't there either, though Joe Botto has kept up with him a little. Joe's a house builder who hit the jackpot during the suburban Boston housing boom. But Mike has had a hard time, Joe told her. He owned a company that cleaned up construction sites, but it went bankrupt. Bonks lost everything.

Unbelievable, I say. It's like his nickname held his future.

But Marianne didn't know he used to be called Mickey Dumps, so I tell her about that. Good thing high school nicknames don't always foretell destinies, I say, because that *would* be awful. She doesn't pick up on this bit of ironic metacommentary.

Oh, poor Mickey Dumps, she says with sincere-sounding sympathy.

So Joe is rich. Good for him, I say, not in the mood to feel even a little bit sorry for Bonks. Joe and I were in a lot of the same classes together. Because of my grades, I was mostly in lower-track classes, except for in English. School was never Joe's thing either. But *you*, you were always in top-track classes.

No big mystery, she says pleasantly. I just studied and did my homework.

Marianne's a family and divorce lawyer with her own practice here in Boston. I really am kind of thunderstruck by how good she looks, how fit and prosperous. She's dressed urban stylish, all in black, cashmere jacket, silk blouse, her legs as proportionally long and slender as ever in skinny pants. Only her leather ankle boots with slanted cowboy heels aren't all black but instead a gray-and-black zebra pattern. She wears her glossy black hair, no silver that I can see, pinned up in back. Just a little softer in the neck, around her eyes.

We ask after each other's moms. From our Facebook chats she knows that my father died a few years ago, at ninety-three, and I know her dad died around the same time, though in his midseventies. Our mothers are about the same age, Marianne's living on her own in a duplex in Swampscott.

Why not get right to it, the reason we're here, those few months when we were close during the autumn of tenth grade. Remember Space Cavanaugh's toolshed? I ask. Not the most direct prompt, but Marianne's expression lights up, because of course she remembers. It was there in that toolshed that I told her the *whole story*, she says, of *War and Peace*. Oh, Frank. Space and his toolshed, how could I forget? That was all so funny.

Among our classmates the Space and George Show was a much more popular show than mine and Bert's, we didn't offer comedy routines. In this week's episode, so as to no longer have to live under the same roof with his father, Space moves out to his backyard toolshed. It was like a miniature of the cocoa-brown neo-Colonial out front, one door, one window, standing in a small grove of birch trees and pines at the back of the yard. Joe Botto had done the carpentry, getting it ready for Space to move into. He even had a television that we'd stolen from the student union of the women's college in the next town, driving it back in Bonks's car. Space lived there until George padlocked it later that fall.

At first it was three of us in the toolshed that afternoon, drinking barely cool beer from a six-pack. Then Space said that he had to go and meet his pot dealer. We could hang out there as long as we wanted, he wouldn't be back until at least dinnertime. I hadn't asked Space to do that.

The girl who gets out of bed in the morning and her bare feet touch the cold floor and she says, Ohhh, it's going to be a cold winter, says Marianne. You said that foretold that all those French soldiers were going to freeze to death outside Moscow. I've still never read that book, but whenever I get out of bed and the floor is cold, I remember that girl and those poor French soldiers.

Natasha Rostova, I say. Effervescent, funny, impetuous, adorable Natasha. But young Natasha falls for Anatole Kuragin, the novel's Ian Brown.

We sat nearly shoulder to shoulder on the bottom mattress of the bunk bed that Hose had built. More beer for us, Marianne said cheerfully, pulling off a flip top with exaggerated exertion. She'd been doing almost all the talking, school gossip mostly. She lay back, knees up and poking through the thready spray of the rips in her jeans. Meanwhile I stiffly sat there, mentally rehearsing and visualizing lying back on the mattress, too, putting my head close hers, turning to kiss her.

I told her that she was like Natasha Rostova, and she asked, Who's that? That's when I'd started in on the story of *War and Peace*, which I'd read during the summer, the two-volume Penguin paperback edition Aunt Hannah had given me for my birthday. "And when Natasha set her bare feet down on the cold floor . . ." As if my not daring even to try to kiss her, going on with this story instead, was a charming show of quirky precocity and individuality. My hands were shaking so violently that I had to clench them into tight fists. That was the first time that ever happened to me, my hands shaking when it was the moment to kiss a girl, when I believed that the kiss was expected even though it probably wasn't, and that by bringing my lips close to hers I'd be changing everything, crossing over into the real deal. It's plagued me ever since, coming back like malaria, adrenalized terror and misery swarming through me, hands shaking. Two years before, with Arlene Fertig, the last and only other time I'd kissed a girl, I'd managed it fine.

We'd finished the beers. Marianne sat up cross-legged to smoke a cigarette, dropping the ashes into an empty beer can beside her. I could hear the ashes pattering down inside the can. She lay on her side with her back to me, knees drawn up in a way that pulled up her sweater, exposing a slim excerpt of waist, the curve of hip muscles down into her jeans.

But poor Prince Andrei, he was never going to get the chance because . . .

I could hear her soft, inside-a-seashell snore. I'd never felt so intimate with beauty, yet so far away. I'd do anything, risk anything for her, this is what love is, I told myself.

I take a drink of the wine Marianne ordered, an Oregon pinot noir. Her phone pings. My daughter, she says with a tight smile and excuses herself to type a response. I glance down at my phone: nope, no message from Lulú. The waiter arrives with our plates. Salt-crusted cod for her. Fried Ipswich clams for me, my favorite. Small talk about fried clams. She lives out there on the North Shore, yes, many hours invested in family clamming outings in the Essex marshlands. No, it's not that she's bored of them, it's just that one fried clam alone probably surpasses her allowed daily fat intake. Come on, just have one, I coax. Oh my God, that's so good, she moans. I'd almost forgotten. And I've never tasted coleslaw like this, so crunchy and fresh, and what are these flavors it has, fine New England dining indeed.

Marianne begins to tell me about her law practice. Right out of law school at BC, she went to work for a small prestigious Beacon Hill family firm. When, at twenty-eight, she decided to open her own practice, her former employers and associates couldn't have been more supportive. I was just so fortunate, Frank, right from the start. She had a little office near Government Center, and she and her husband, Derek, bought a townhouse right here in the South End before the neighborhood gentrified. When her son, Connor, was born, she brought him to work with her every day and into courthouses, breast-feeding him in judges' chambers conferences. When we had Maddy, says Marianne, we could afford a full-time nanny. We bought the house in Topsfield. It was a long commute, but it's a dream house with a pasture and woods near the river. The kids and I kept the house after the divorce.

The nanny? She seems surprised I'm curious about the nanny. The first one, Leena, was from Ireland. Later came Bonnie from Jamaica. Derek used to book rock shows here in Boston, she answers when I ask what he does for a living. When I met him in college, she says, he was a roadie for J. Geils. She makes a winsomely rueful expression. Then he became a booking agent for some of the Boston punk and new wave bands coming out of the Rat and other clubs. He did well for a while. I lived some of that life, Frank. Now Derek's trying to get back into it. When Maddy heard on NPR about Pluto being downgraded to a dwarf planet, she said, Just like poor Daddy, downgraded to a dwarf planet, too, and launching a comeback in his little punk rock rocket ship.

Ouch, I say. But she has a wit, doesn't she.

She sure does, says Marianne. Maddy is in her freshman year at Brown. Connor's a junior at Carleton.

Isn't there an Audubon sanctuary in Topsfield? I ask. My father used to take me bird-watching there. I rarely remember that when I was a little boy, Bert was at times a pretty devoted dad. Those better memories get buried by what came after.

It's called the Ipswich River Wildlife Sanctuary, says Marianne. Even though it's in Topsfield. If snowy white owls were called that because they deliver cocaine, then Derek would have taken our kids bird-watching too.

That comment hangs there in the air a moment. So many of the people I know in New York and Mexico City, I say, had pretty major coke habits. Some still do.

Something in her gaze looks ripped open. It closes. You're telling me, she says. That's not the only way Derek fucked up his life, but it's a long story.

We're forty-nine, I say. Life is a long story, don't you think.

Marianne recovers her smile with the aplomb of someone picking a hat off the floor and putting it back on without missing a beat, and says, Oh, you're telling me. Speaking of which, seems like you really get around, don't you. New York, Mexico, Cuba. The last time she heard me on the radio, she says, I was talking about that Cuban revolutionary poet who lived in New York City. José Martí, right? His name's everywhere in Miami, she says. But I never really knew anything about him. Something you said really struck me. A man should never do in the dark what he wouldn't do by daylight, you said Martí said. Right there I started making a list in my head of all the things I've done by day that I should only have done in the dark.

We laugh, and I say, That's in his diaries somewhere. Because of the mores of the time and his own sensitive position as the political and moral leader of the Cubans in exile, Martí had to keep so much of his life secret, and that hurt and humiliated him. I fill Marianne in a little bit, about the daughter, María, whom he'd had with his landlady, and whom he adored, and the situation in the boardinghouse and my book.

What's the title? she asks.

*The House of Pain.*

You mean like the guys who did "Jump Around"?

Yeah, I was already using that title before I ever heard about that group.

Sure sounds like it was a house of pain, she says. So you were talking about José Martí on the radio tonight?

No, I answer. They wanted to talk about General Cara de Culo. I explain a little about Cara de Culo, the bishop's murder, the general running for president. I don't tell Marianne that it was as a consequence of my writing on that case that I had to leave Mexico City. Now I've been exiled to New York City, too, in a sense, like Martí. I didn't want to leave Mexico, but I fled, there's no other word for it, heeding that warning from the consul. Then I vowed to try to live in the here and now of New York, and now Boston, USA. "What business have I in the woods, if I am thinking of something out of the woods." Thoreau wrote that. I've tried to think of it as a motto. Though my past isn't exactly a fantasy novel either. It's not like I can just pack it up in a cardboard box and leave it outside Housing Works.

We're into our second bottle of wine when Marianne begins to tell me about the last class reunion, about Ian Brown, why he's as much an asshole as ever. Ian's become a big deal contractor around Atlanta, building McMansions and shopping malls. According to Marianne, he got his start backed by his wife's family money. But Ian is a fellow alumni of our middle school underachiever program, why should his success surprise? Artie Kaplan, another of his old neighborhood friends, was at the reunion, says Marianne, and he sat at Ian's table. An early investor in some of those Route 128 tech start-ups, Artie is now a wealthy man too. Artie told Ian that his wife had left him for another woman, and Ian couldn't get over that. For the rest of the night he kept shouting: Artie, your wife left you for another woman, jabbing his finger at him and laughing until finally Artie would shout back: She did, that bitch! Same Ian as ever, says Marianne.

The Sandy Koufax of Jewish bullies, I say.

She responds with an uncertain grin. I don't think she gets the joke.

Ian gave me the name Monkey Boy, I say. Do you remember that? I do, she says. He's such a jerk.

I was called Gols too. Remember that one? I give her a fake smile.

Ian and his friend Jake used to call you Pablo too. Pablo, Monkey Boy, it was a racist thing, wasn't it. I didn't realize that back then. Now it seems too obvious.

You probably always thought of me as just another Jewish boy, I say.

Even a word like "halfie" wasn't around back then. You were categorized as the one thing you most obviously might be and that was that, not that it's changed so much since. Mexicans are always surprised that gringos have no word for or concept of "mestizaje."

I knew your mom was foreign, she says. But I remember being surprised when I walked down your street and all the windows had those electric menorahs, except your house. You had poinsettias in your picture window. Am I remembering right?

Plastic poinsettias.

She laughs. I told Lana that I didn't know poinsettias were a Chanukah flower too. I was a St. Joe's girl, what did I know?

Monkey Boy, Chimp Face, that all started back in middle school, I say. But what if I did look kind of like a monkey back then? You know how teenagers are.

Marianne gives me a skeptical look.

Seriously, I say. I've given this a lot of thought over the years, and I've concluded that probably nobody in middle school looked more like a monkey than I did.

Okay, she says. You have curly hair, your ears aren't small, but I really don't think you look like a monkey, and I didn't think so back then either.

I greatly resent that you consider curly hair a simian feature, I say. That's a totally false stereotype, Marianne. When was the last time you actually went to the zoo and looked at monkeys?

After a few seconds of near panic in her eyes, I mime a theatrical guffaw, and Marianne bursts into laughter, then shakes her head, an affectionate shine in her eyes. Abruptly, her expression goes still, her brows lift, and she says, But you went through all those years thinking that what Ian and those kids said was true, didn't you? Oh Frank.

I shrug and say, I guess. Well, who cares now.

A memory from high school of standing in front of the bathroom mirror and in a spasm of self-loathing punching my own face as hard as I could, blood from my lips smudging my cheeks, smearing it with fingers, punching myself in the face again, spitting at the mirror.

But as soon as you got away from our town, she says, did you stop thinking of yourself like that?

I take a drink and say, Pretty much. Then I ask, That day when you walked down my street and saw poinsettias, was I with you?

She looks like she's quickly calculating a sum. No, she says. But I wanted to talk to you. I walked over to your house, and I was trying to work up the courage to ring your doorbell, and at that exact moment, your father pulled into your driveway in his car. When he got out he looked at me like I must be a drug dealer, there to sell his son drugs. I was afraid of him, so I just kept walking.

You were afraid of my father?

Of course I was, she says. You used to tell me horrible things. He was abusive and violent with you, right?

Yeah, I really hated him.

You used to tell me that too.

But it's not like you had an easy time with your own dad, I say.

But I never thought I hated him, she says. He could be depressing to be around and vindictive with my mom, but he was terrified of her too, she could shut him up with a look. Did you forgive your father or at least make peace with him?

We got along better, I answer. A few years before he died, Bert tried to make a big apology for beating the shit out of me so much, but it was comically lame.

Well, at least he tried. That's good, right? She puts on a sort of sad smile.

So why did you come looking for me at my house that day?

To talk about Ian, she says. I wanted to tell you I was going on a date with him. I wanted you to hear it from me. Even if your father hadn't come home, I think I would have chickened out. One of the worse decisions of my life, going out with Ian. You remember what happened, don't you?

This must be what she wanted to talk to me about. This is why we're having dinner.

When I got to school that Monday morning, the idiotic horde was abuzz. Saturday night, Ian had picked up Marianne in his mother's car, and they must have ended up doing the usual things teenage couples do when they're not going all the way yet. But only Ian had ever come to school boasting about it in such an explicit manner, putting on an obscene show, provoking shrieks and blasts of laughter. I plotted routes through the corridors to avoid him, but I avoided Marianne too. It was all more about drawing attention to Ian than to Marianne, of course, but what he set loose took on a fiendish force of its own. Marianne was easily one of the most well-liked girls in our class, so friendly and kind to everyone, never a phony. Now they were calling her Piggy. Piggy Lucas they wrote in lipstick on bathroom mirrors. Marianne Lucas is a slutty pig! Someone even stole a fetal pig from the biology lab and put it inside Marianne's locker. Between classes, kids milled nearby, excited, waiting. Just before the lunch period Marianne stopped at her locker, opened it, and found herself face-to-face with the pig fetus, pink and glazed, oversized eyes, propped like a Play-Doh idol on the edge of the shelf. She lifted her hands to her face. Everybody watching was silent. She took her winter coat out of the locker, put it on, and turned to go. By then, Lana Gatto had reached her. Marianne calmly told her that she was going home. She walked down the corridor to the nearest exit in her red wool coat, pulling its hood up just before pushing out the door. Lana told me she started to cry, because suddenly she felt sure she was never going to see Marianne again. I remember that coat and its hood;

on its front Marianne had pinned a small wooden brooch of a red-eyed squirrel eating an acorn.

Of course I remember what happened, Marianne, I tell her. How could I forget?

I was cold to her, of course, avoided her, didn't phone. Meanwhile I waited for her to come to me for the sympathy and forgiveness she knew I wouldn't be able to hold back. But she didn't. She missed only a few days of school, but when she returned, it was like an inner light had been snuffed out, her gaze rowing through the fog in front of her feet. At lunch, she sat with her closest friends, all looking moribund, as if they didn't know what to say to her. I wished they would talk her into dumping a lunch tray on Ian's head the way that senior-class girl had done to that hockey star who was so obviously full of himself. If Marianne had done that to Ian, it might have provoked his downfall. The Christmas break came and when school started up again she was going out with Jimmy Gleason. I heard later from Lana Gatto that Marianne was out ice-skating with her little sisters on Sarah Hancock Pond when he skated over to join them, a scene out of *Little Women*. No wonder the pond was a special place to them.

Those first few months of tenth grade had been like a miracle for me, playing football, belonging to a group of friends, having Mr. Brainerd for a teacher, talking to Marianne on the telephone nearly every night. Everything had coalesced around her and was all part of the case I was making for why she should love me. When that was gone, the emptiness that replaced it stunned me.

We order a nightcap, a bourbon for me. Marianne says she really shouldn't but orders a Ketel One on the rocks, twist of lemon. After she's taken a sip she looks directly at me in a way that alerts me that something important is coming. She says:

Frank, I know all our high school memories aren't that great, and I don't deny that at fifteen I was confused and could be an idiot. But just that we're here together now shows how much our friendship really did mean to me.

A speech she'd prepared for tonight, that sounded like.

What seems hard to believe is that my hands, as if leading their own bewildering lives apart from me, have begun to shake. But I say it. Marianne, do you remember a telephone conversation we had one night, a long one, maybe the last time we ever spoke, just before what happened with Ian?

Marianne looks like she's thinking it over and finally says, Tell me more.

The part I remember is hard to describe, I answer, because I felt sure you wanted to tell me something but couldn't bring yourself to. You kept saying things like: Frank, why can't we—Then you'd stop. Or: Why can't I— Or: Frank, why can't they *be*— But you'd stop. Why can't you or we or they be what? Marianne is watching me intently. I tell her: You also kept repeating my name in a certain way. Oh Fraaank, you'd go, drawing it out, sort of sighing. Oh Fraaank. And then you'd be silent. That's not a very good imitation, but I remember it like it was yesterday, Marianne. I remember listening so hard to those silences, like I could almost hear in your breathing what you wanted to tell me. I've never forgotten that phone call, is all.

She says, And you think I might remember whatever it was I was trying to say?

I guess not, I answer. But here's the thing. Ever since, I've felt convinced that was the first time anyone ever told me they were in love with me. You didn't, I know. But that's what I heard in your stammering and in those silences, that really you wanted to tell me. Years passed until the next time a woman told me she loved me and meant it. Sad but true, Marianne. That must be one reason why I remember it the way I do.

Marianne's expression looks a little amused and moved too, maybe. She says, You think that what happened with Ian prevented something further from happening with us. Is that it?

I was really in love with you, I tell her. You knew, didn't you?

Yes, she says. I guess I did know that.

I wait a moment, in case she's about to say something more. But then I say, Even if it wasn't requited, at least I knew what love felt like. Except after that phone call I felt it *was* requited, that the feeling was there, anyway.

At least my hands have stopped shaking.

She looks at me through squinted eyes, her smile lopsided. I wish I could remember that phone call as well as you do, she says.

I've always thought that if we'd gone to school in another town, maybe things could have gone differently between us.

I've never thought of it that way, she says. Maybe you're right, in another town. She smiles at me in a way that reminds me of how she used to smile at me back then, both warmly and humorously, as if we were silently sharing a secret joke.

# Friday

GIVEN HOW MUCH we'd had to drink, I suggested to Marianne that maybe she should get a hotel room, or even stay on the extra bed in my room, instead of driving back to Topsfield. But she insisted she was fine. Plus she had her weekly tennis match in the morning. She promised to call when she got home, but once I was in my room, I fell fast asleep. When I woke this morning, there was a message on my phone from Marianne: "What a fun night, sweet Frank. We'll see how I play tennis with an ice pack on my head tomorrow morning, ha! Please, let's stay in touch. It's almost spring, let me take you canoeing on the Ipswich River."

No messages from Lulú, but it's still early, barely eleven. I'd meant to save half of this giant oatmeal and chocolate chip cookie for later in the day because I always get hungry at the nursing home and there's nothing I ever want to eat there, but I've just taken the last bite. I look around at the other customers in this techie-seeming café having their healthy breakfasts and coffees, so many fresh-faced, casually stylish young women, and, unusually for Boston, not all of them white, and doubtlessly all highly educated and knowledgeable about ways of life I don't have an inkling of.

I might as well get going. I'll walk all the way back to South Station, maybe swing past the Congress Street Bridge, too, pulling along my wheeled suitcase, knapsack over my shoulders, gym lock muffled inside a pair of socks, and carrying the tin of French butter cookies inside its pretty shop bag. The exercise and chilly Atlantic air will do me good, but my bad knee aches like it's a little hungover too. So what about last night? I think Marianne and I both got from it what we'd wanted. She was still hurt, after all these years, by what Ian and so many of our classmates had done to her, from one day to the next shattering everything she'd understood and trusted about her world and who she was in it. She'd wanted to talk to me because we'd been close back when it happened and she knew that I'd been hurt by it, too, and that at least I'd be interested. There are people who think, Oh come on, that was adolescence, how can you not be over it? They're like the people who say, Who cares what happened in faraway tiny Guatemala all those years ago now, why do you make such a big deal out of it? I don't like people like that. So why shouldn't Lexi talk to her shrink about what it did to her to watch Bert beating me up all those years, if that's what she thinks she needs? Who am I to dictate what should and shouldn't leave a mark? My walking pace actually quickens, I feel hyped up to tell Lexi and to apologize for having been nasty about it before.

Last night with Marianne I got to confess something I'd kept silent about for over three decades, and the way I'm feeling about it this morning, it's like I had a requited high school love after all. So I can go back in time and start my romantic life all over, fast-forwarding to now: a man confident since adolescence in his ability to inspire love, who knows what to do with it. Some people passing on the sidewalk glance suspiciously at a grown man laughing out loud to himself, like maybe he's about to pull an axe out from under his coat, but others genuinely smile, what is it that makes them react so differently?


Exactly out there, past the far side of Fort Point Channel, on a sunscorched field by Logan airport, at the start of my senior year of high school, trying out for varsity football, we had a late August preseason scrimmage against the East Boston High School Jets. Just a few plays after having been sent in as a sub at cornerback, I twisted my body to wave at a pass fluttering wide of its targeted Jet, my cleats caught in a withered clump of turf, and I fell. I got up, hopped around on one leg, limped to the sideline, and my football career was over. I've never understood how it was decided in the doctor's office to put me in a cast instead of operating, whether it was the decision of the doctor or my mother or both. The doctor who treated my knee and helped screw it up forever spoke in a heavy German accent. With one strong furry hand clamped around my thigh and the other grabbing my lower leg, he swiveled it side to side from the knee, and loudly singsonged in his cranky voice: Loosey Goosey, Loosey Goosey. Over the years, Herr Doktor said, he'd treated scores of mangled boys from our football team, and several times during the examination, as my mother looked on, he referred to Coach Tyree as a butcher, emphasizing the word "butcher" with such vehement contempt that he sounded like one of those comical Nazi commandants on television, Ach, ist a butcher! I had the impression the doctor was trying to impress my mother in some manly competitive way, cutting Coach Tyree down to size.

Having my leg in a cast that fall of senior year kept me at home after school, crucial in helping me earn the grades I needed to have a chance to get into a decent college. Practically from one day to the next, I learned to assert my will and use my brain in ways I never had before, paying attention in class, studying, doing homework. After Yolandita left to marry Richard the Vietnam War vet and Sears manager, Carlota Sánchez Motta, a Mormon girl from Guatemala who had a relative who was friendly with Abuelita, came to live with us and to go to our high school. Of course I never would have let anyone hear me speaking Spanish to Carlota at school, just as I never would have drawn that kind of attention to myself by speaking Spanish back in tenth-grade Spanish class. But at home, whenever Carlota spoke to me in her imperfect English, I insisted on answering in my imperfect Spanish, until finally one day she fell silent and looked at me with a hurt, flummoxed expression. You have a whole high school to practice your English with, I told her, but I can only practice Spanish here. Her eyes were like two full black moons of distress rising up from behind rounded, slightly pockmarked brown cheeks, and she exclaimed, Oh, Frankie, how did I not think of that? Here we will only speak Spanish, I promise! After that, when she spoke in Spanish, I answered in English. Ay, que malo eres, she said, turning and walking away. Carlota, I'm sorry, I piped after her, I was only kidding around, Carlota, perdón! Por favor, perdóname!

That same fall, after she'd been the Latin American Society of New England's most dutiful rank-and-file member for two decades, my mother was elected its treasurer. The society regularly hosted literary events in its philanthropic Boston Brahmin brownstone in the Back Bay, and it was Mamita who told me that Latin American literature had become such a big deal in the world that it was called a Boom. When Carlos Fuentes came to give a lecture at the society, she sat next to him at the luncheon, they talked about Jorge Negrete, and Fuentes even sang a snatch of the song that goes: qué lejos estoy del suelo donde he nacido, and Mamita joined in. She loved to sing despite her tuneless little voice; ever since she'd stood too close to exploding birthday firecrackers as a little girl, she'd been deaf in one ear. The urbanely affable Argentine MIT professor who was the Latin American Society's president and my mother's close friend was also a friend of Jorge Luis Borges and gave him science advice for his stories. That year it seemed like my mother was always carrying around a Carlos Castaneda book about Don Juan, the Yaqui Indian peyote shaman. *The Teachings of Don Juan* was a famous Boom book, too, I thought. The first Boom book I read was *No One Writes to the Colonel*, a bilingual paperback edition Mamita used in one of her Spanish classes. On the new-books shelf at the public library I found *Heartbreak Tango* by Manuel Puig, set in a small town in Argentina whose mean-spirited mediocrity, along with the secretive sexual misbehaving of its adolescent girls, resembled our town even more than the New England one in *Carrie* did. Mamita always said that Gabriel García Márquez's books brought back to her the sad pueblo our family was from on Abuelita's side, situated among the sugar and rubber plantations and ranch lands of the Costa Sur. That spring, the ophthalmologist whom Carlota met at my cousin Denise's wedding in Framingham told her she reminded him of his favorite female character in *One Hundred Years of Solitude.* He wouldn't say which one and challenged her to read the book and figure it out.

During those first weeks when Carlota was living with us, my father managed to keep his temper in check, but soon enough he was back to his ranting goddamned this, goddamned that along with his bawling: Yoli Jesus Christ Almighty get off my goddamned back. Sometimes Lexi had tantrums too. I wondered if Carlota was sorry she'd come to live with us.

That fall I discovered that I didn't really have friends anymore. Some had dropped me even before senior year or drifted away, or, like Space, they'd already disappeared into their own lonely disasters. Some had serious girlfriends or lovers. I hadn't even tried to kiss a girl since Arlene Fertig.

When Carlota had finished cleaning up after dinner, we'd sit at the Formica kitchen table doing homework after everyone else in the house had gone to sleep. She'd lean over whatever textbook she was studying or the notebook she was writing in, her concentration a plumb line, silky black hair curtaining her face, her smooth, brown forearm and hand, fingers loosely curled underneath, resting on the tabletop while the pencil in her other hand quickly slalomed down a page doing algebra. Sometimes she'd ask me how to say or spell this or that in English. She'd get up, go to the refrigerator, open it, and stand staring into it as if mesmerized, and I'd look at the shape of her thin shoulders under her black cardigan, and if she was wearing a skirt, at the backs of her knees and her calves like little owls poised atop the slender trunks rising from her socks. When she came back carrying a bowl of Jell-O or a tin of supermarket blueberry pie, setting down small plates, handing me a spoon or a fork, I'd say thank you and eat, hardly glancing at her. Now it was me who always felt flummoxed.

One night Carlota looked up and said, Our war in Guatemala is
going to become a bigger war than Vietnam, you know. You're Guatemalan, too, Frankie, she said. Which side will you be on? She was wearing
a striped cream-and-pink sweater, an elastic orange headband pushing
her hair back over her forehead; just minutes before I'd been about to
tease her that she looked like a Creamsicle, but now she looked like a boy
who wants to pick a fight. I can't go to war against the United States, I
said. That's because you're like all the other children at your school who
don't know anything, she said, lifting her chin, her nostrils flaring a little.
But you should know, because you're not just from here. I stared into a
corner of the floor, trying to grasp if this was serious. I'd thought that
war was over now, during those last summers in Guatemala, nobody
in my family had said much about any war, though you saw soldiers
everywhere, trimly muscular, stern-looking Maya youths riding by in
troop trucks or jeeps with machine guns mounted in back. Reverting
to her good-girl Minnie Mouse voice, she said, I am grateful to be in
this country, learning English, making new friends. In this town even a
mailman, like the father of Chip, owns a house, a car, and nobody ever
is hungry, and this country is a great maravilla, I know. But, Frankie, she
said, we have to be ready to fight for the people who don't have anything
but who are *our* people, God tells me this in my heart. I wanted to ask
who Chip was, but instead I blurted: You're wrong about me. I just don't
want to be some whiney hippie protester, I want to fight for real. And I
tried to make my eyes burn like hers. Before he became Comandante Che
Guevara, said Carlota, he was a doctor in Guatemala. Did you know that,
Frankie? She told me about how the young Che had come to Guatemala
to treat the poor but instead witnessed the United States overthrow of
our country's democratic revolution in 1954, the bombing raids over the
capital, the babies blown to bits in their exploded houses, and how the
president surrendered without arming the people who wanted to fight
back. After that, said Carlota, Che understood there is no peaceful way
to defend a revolution against the Yankees, just look what happened last

year to Chile. I remembered the photographs in *Life* magazine I'd seen as a boy of Che's half-naked speckled corpse stretched out on a wooden bench, soldiers standing around him, poking him, pulling on his hair. Carlota returned to her homework, and I tried to. A bit later, before we went to bed, she asked if she could sign my cast, which was smudged but still legible where I'd wiped off what kids had written there: "Eat lots of bananas, Gols!" and such. With a red marker she wrote HASTA LA VICTORIA SIEMPRE over her name, and she drew and colored in a red star. As I watched her leaning over my cast, listening to the squeak of her marker against the plaster, a warmth went through me like a wave, one that carried me all the way to that locked room where emotions are stored like bicycles that have never been ridden.

My social studies teacher, Miss Mahan, was kind and soft-spoken, with an out-the-side-of-her-mouth giggle punctuating anything lefty political she said. She'd dedicated some classes to César Chávez and the United Farm Workers and wore a UFW pin on the jean jacket she kept on in class. Once when I went to her desk to ask a question, her glazy eyes were bloodshot, and I smelled liquor mixed with breath mints. I was stumped about what to write my final fall term paper on for that class. Carlota suggested I write about Thanksgiving: A very interesting holiday that we don't have in Guatemala. Then I remembered what Jim Cerullo had said back in tenth-grade Spanish, the same class where Joe Botto got his name Hose-A, and Jim, whose father owned Cerullo Farm and Nursery, was Jaime. He told our teacher, Señora Hogan, that he was taking Spanish so that he could communicate with the migrant farm-workers who worked for his father. Not "communicate," he corrected, "boss around." If I went and interviewed those migrant farmworkers who were right here in our town and wrote my term paper about it, Miss Mahan would probably give me a good grade. Carlota wanted to come and translate, but I said I didn't need a translator. She said, Maybe they speak K'iche'; she could speak that Maya language because she'd grown up on a coffee finca. I'd never even asked Carlota about where she'd grown up, I didn't know why her family was Mormon or even what that meant. Your father picked coffee? I asked. No, he was the plantation's bookkeeper, she said. I pictured Bob Cratchit laboring over his ledger by candlelight in a hot, dark room filled with burlap sacks of coffee, mosquitos, and moths. Cerullo says the workers speak Spanish, I told her. I went alone to show her that I could. My cast had just been taken off and, gimpy leg swinging, I propelled myself down Parish Road on my crutches. A dirt road lined with tall pines on one side and browning thickets on the other led to a short row of brown wooden cabins. But I didn't see any farmworkers around and rested on my crutches, listening to the work sounds coming from the other side of the pines, iron sporadically striking or pinging. The air was spiced with scents of conifer, cold earth, withered leaves and brush, something like nutmeg or cloves, and a smokiness suggesting that winter was coming closer, as if on the far side of South Hill it might already be snowing. I'm never going to live in a city, I remember telling myself, always near forests. Eventually a group of men turned onto the road through the pines and came walking toward me. They wore jeans, baseball caps, sweatshirts. One, wearing a frayed corduroy trucker jacket, seemed to be their leader. He was the shortest, also the oldest, with a pepper-and-salt beard, skin like an old baseball mitt, deep eyes inside soft craters of rake-like wrinkles. I explained in Spanish why I was there, and when I told them I was a classmate of Jaime, they looked at me blankly. The son of the owner of the farm, I clarified. El joven Jeem? the older man asked gruffly. In our Spanish class his name is Jaime, I explained. The older man chortled and emphatically repeated Jaime, and the others laughed too. I pulled my notebook from my back pocket and started in with my questions, and to almost every one—Do you feel that you're being exploited? Does Mr. Cerullo steal your wages?—they answered no. But to a few—Do you miss your countries? Do you enjoy farmwork?—they answered yes. I asked, Do they give you enough to eat here? And the older man barked, Con una comida comen tres. I didn't know if he meant that one meal was so big it would feed three workers or that three had to share a meal big enough for one, but I nodded like I got it and a favorite phrase of Uncle Memo's came to me. I exclaimed, Ala gran chucha! and everyone exploded in laughter. The older man, whose name was Eugenio Pérez, was from Mexico. That first afternoon, I didn't meet the three women migrant workers because they were baking pumpkin pies in the farm store kitchen. Eugenio pronounced it *pum-keen*, the way my mother and Carlota did. The workers were headed down to farms in Florida soon for the winter. I spoke to Eugenio the most, especially during subsequent visits. He'd first come to the United States with some other Mexicans, driven in a truck in the middle of the night from Tijuana to a bell pepper farm in California. They arrived around three in the morning and by four, said Eugenio, they were already at work in the fields. After three more weeks of hard work, they were told that they'd paid off what they owed in transportation, room, and board, and a few days later, the pepper harvest ended and Eugenio found himself stranded in America with only a few days' wages in his pocket. "The green peppers on the sausage and pepper submarine sandwiches and pizzas at Dino's, in our town square, come from the farms in California that Eugenio worked at," I wrote in my term paper, and in the margin alongside Miss Mahan drew a row of exclamation points and a YES! If that insight, which I owed to Eugenio Pérez, is what hoisted my grade to my first-ever A+, it also directly helped me get into Broener College on the shores of Seneca Lake, in Wagosh, New York.

One night a month or so later, having forgotten her keys, Carlota rang the doorbell after everyone but me had gone to bed, and I opened the door and found her outside on the stoop with the boy who turned out to be Chip. Cold clouds of boozy breath puffed from their mouths, their freezing faces and smiles practically incandescent. Chip, on the short side, had long orange sideburns, and he held his ski-gloved hand out to me and, looking me in the eyes, smiled like a square-jawed Disney prince. I'd hardly noticed him at school. I think he was on the soccer team. I braced myself, waiting for Carlota's whisper that she was going to sneak Chip down into her bedroom. Instead they shared a quick kiss on the lips, she came inside, and I closed the door on Chip. She yanked her boots off, toes to heel like an expert New England girl, and with a bashful flash of a smile that made me feel like a stranger whispered, Buenas noches, and bounded down the stairs in her wool socks to her room.

That spring, my cousin Denise had her wedding in Framingham. In the parking lot of the restaurant and banquet hall where the wedding was happening, a fight erupted between my parents in the car that rapidly escalated into vicious mutual loathing. I was used to Bert's accusing shouts, his blame and complaints, but now they had a frantic, pleading edge. And my mother, who almost never raised her voice, was bleating her long-pent-up outrage and pain at my father in a way I hadn't heard before, that sounded both newborn and ancient at once. That was the year I first became aware of my mother's unhappiness, a gradual but disorientating recognition that would culminate months later during my freshman year at Broener on a December weekend just before our Christmas break when I came from Wagosh upstate to New York City to accompany my parents to some other distant relative's wedding out on Long Island. Lexi had started going to a private boarding school for girls that fall, one in the next town near the women's college, and she didn't want to spend any weekend away from there. I went out by bus to the horrible hotel by LaGuardia airport where my parents were staying, and when I let myself into the room I found my mother alone, sobbing facedown on the bed. Ma, what's wrong? I asked and then asked again. Finally her small smothered voice said into the pillow: Oh, Frankie, it's nothing. Her posture didn't shift. There was a cot at the foot of the bed, put there for me to sleep on. Where's Daddy? I asked. She didn't answer.

He was probably somewhere watching a football game he'd bet on. Ma, have you been drinking? I asked. Ay, Frankie, no seas baboso, she said into the pillow; she even made a weak attempt to laugh. Why didn't you call up first? she said a moment later. Frankie, leave me alone for a few minutes, please, so I can compose myself. She was crying softly again. Okay, Mami, compose yourself, I said and let myself out of the room. For a moment I stood out in the hallway wondering if I should go back in. I felt helpless but also hurt. I probably would have fled back to the city whether my mother had been crying or not, because there was no fucking way I was going to sleep on that cot like a dog at my father's feet.

I'd asked my mother if she'd been drinking because that same spring as my cousin Denise's wedding and the fight in the car, I'd come home one evening and found her passed out on the kitchen floor. Mamita had never been a drinker, though she liked her glass of sherry after dinner in the evenings with a bowl of salted peanuts as she sat with feet up in her reclining armchair to watch an *I Love Lucy* rerun or Carol Burnett on TV, Mary Tyler Moore too. Now she was drinking sherry before dinner. It took little to get her smashed; three small glasses were enough to put her on the floor, hands folded on her tummy.

Not long after my first year of college my parents would finally separate, as my sister had been urging my mother to do. My sister's world was opening up in a way it couldn't have if she were going to our high school. Mamita, determined to spare Lexi that ordeal—she'd had a rough enough time in middle school—had persuaded Abuelita to pay for her to go to the fancy private girls' school and even board there, though it was so close to home.

In the parking lot outside Cousin Denise's wedding that day, it was as if my sister and I felt obligated to remain in the back seat of the car while my parents rabidly bickered, as if we were keeping vigil in a hospital

they'd been taken to after an accident. Finally, as the fight began to sub-
side, the silences between agonized outbursts growing longer, Lexi and
I traded looks, and we got out of the car. We crossed the gravel parking
lot and went through an arched entrance in the faux old Colonial New
England brick wall into the tree- and tent-shaded yard where the wedding was being held. Carlota had come hours earlier to help with the
wedding preparations. Aunt Milly was paying her, of course. But what
if Carlota had said she didn't want to work that day? Would Aunt Milly
have invited her anyway? I spotted Carlota standing alone in a walled-in
corner by forsythia in frothy yellow bloom, arms crossed to clasp each
elbow, repeatedly lifting the cigarette held in one hand to her lips. I'd
never seen Carlota smoke before. Smoking, drinking, Communism,
maybe screwing Chip, she wasn't such a good Mormon girl anymore.
Eyeliner ran in dried dribbles down her cheeks. They're treating me
like a fucking maid, she answered when I asked what the matter was.
I'd never heard her say fuck before either. Who is? I asked. *Them*, she
said, your aunt, the people in charge, the flower lady, púchica, everyone.

How are they treating you like a maid?

The flower lady made me pluck thorns off roses, look. And Carlota held up her fingers, but her fingers looked normal. They were still
bleeding a few minutes ago, she said with a pout. They don't even know
my name, she said, taking a deeper draw from her cigarette and blink-
ing rapidly. *Mees*, Carlota mewed caustically, come here to iron these
tablecloths. She exhaled smoke again and said, But the flower lady's son
helped with the roses. At least he is nice.

She meant the ophthalmologist. He'd come early, too, to help
his mother, the florist, an old friend and neighbor of Aunt Milly. At
a table where the florist and her two assistants had done their work,
that love scandal's first course had been served. As they plucked thorns,
had he told Carlota that she reminded him of his favorite female
character in *One Hundred Years of Solitude*? I don't remember noticing

the ophthalmologist at the wedding, but he and Carlota started going out right after. He was in his late twenties, tall with long, muscular arms, a mop of soft black curls on his head, swarthy, and he drove a dark-green MG, often with a kayak strapped to the roof. As far as I know, the florist never forgave my aunt for having brought Carlota to the wedding, where that Guatemalan girl, surely described to her as Bert and Yoli's maid, had stolen her only child's heart. Because of the florist's opposition to the romance, I heard my mother say later, the ophthalmologist stopped talking to his mother too. True outlaws of love, Carlota and the ophthalmologist. Carlota was supposed to be going back to Guatemala at the end of the summer. One muggy evening, after walking home from the train stop after work, I found her in our backyard standing next to my father's twined tomato plants. She was in gym shorts, a T-shirt, and white socks, hair sweat-pasted to the side of her face. The back door to her bedroom, which she'd left ajar, opened almost directly onto the vegetable garden, and her sneakers were in the grass just outside it. Why are you standing out here staring at the tomatoes? I asked. She looked at me as if startled from a trance and said she'd been jogging. Jogging? Why? Because the ophthalmologist had told her she was out of shape and a little overweight. Come on, you're not overweight at all, I said. No, he's right, I'm a weakling blob, she said. Lips screwed in disgust, she held out her arm and pinched her fingers into her bicep to show me how flabby it was. It was unsettling that being in a serious love had made Carlota feel discouraged about herself like this; it was like one of those moments in a novel or movie when you understand a favorite character's childhood is over. She was saying: But it's not like when I go to college I want to be a rower on Charlie's Reever too. You're going to college up here? I asked. This year in school I had only A's and B's, she said. Her SATs hadn't been that bad, but her English was much better now, so she was going to retake them. The ophthalmologist was encouraging her to apply to colleges she could commute to. She said she couldn't decide if she wanted to study art history or premed. The ophthalmologist had taken her to art museums. Her visit to the Isabella Stewart Gardner, she said, had made her realize she would be happy to spend the rest of her life studying beautiful paintings. But if she went to college in Boston, I asked, where would she live? She responded with a listless shrug. Maybe my mother will let you stay here, I ventured. Three weeks later, Carlota announced that she was moving out the next day, she was going to live with the ophthalmologist. I was the only one from our family out on the sidewalk to see Carlota off. She gave me a peck on the cheek and a hug, promised to stay in touch, and the lovers got into the MG and drove away. I haven't seen or heard from Carlota since.

That same summer, often reading on the Boston Common in the mornings before I had to be at work on the Tea Party ship, and on the train home after, I finished *One Hundred Years of Solitude*, making my way through as if it were simultaneously a thronged maze and a picture illusion game where you try to find the hidden face, but none of the characters reminded me much of Carlota. When she'd left our house, Carlota still hadn't read the novel. Aunt Milly soon after moved with Uncle Lenny to Florida. In the coming years, if she ever had any news about Carlota and the son of the florist, she never mentioned it. One hot, soggy night in Managua a friend who'd been a teenage Sandinista fighter took me to a sanctuary house for wounded Guatemalan guerrillas because he was thinking of bringing his combat skills to Guate and wanted to talk to a comandante who was recuperating from a leg wound. The sanctuary was in practically the shell of a house among the earthquake and war ruins of the old center. The grizzled comandante was sitting in a chair just outside the doorway to get some air, and as he and my friend solemnly conversed, I saw a woman inside on a cot against the rear wall raise herself up on one elbow, gauze bandages wrapped around her head and over one eye, and peer at us with her other eye through the murk of that stifling room lit only by a few candles. It didn't even occur to me to wonder until later: Wait, could that wounded guerrilla have been Carlota?

For most of that spring on mornings when I had to be at the Tea Party ship, my father insisted I drive into Boston with him, detouring in his usual route to let me off by the Common. We'd leave the house just past dawn though I didn't need to be at my job until nine. He'd probably thought we were going to have conversations and repair our relationship a little before I went away to college but then realized he had no more to say to me than I did to him. He always had the car radio tuned to a Boston station with news and sports; on one of those mornings we heard about the fall of Saigon. Throughout my childhood, Bert had been in a rage over the Vietnam War, screaming at the TV: I spit on this country, I spit on this country! On weekend mornings in the Stop and Shop parking lot there used to always be middle-aged and old men in VFW hats, oddly mild yet mean mouthed, with their clipboard petitions to put Hanoi Jane in prison or demanding a new escalation or bombing campaign or a pardon for Lieutenant Calley or something about the MIAs, and my father would snarl at them: Get out of my way you warmonger you, and he'd stomp into the supermarket to buy his smoked mackerel and bagels. At the same time, he regarded hippies, even hippie war protestors, with rabid disgust and loathing. Now here I was sitting alongside him with a freaky bush growing atop my head.

In the evenings, doing my round of closing chores, I'd crawl out onto the jib to tie up and fasten the furled sail, and then I liked to sit there straddling it, legs dangling, looking out over the gleaming water rippling in from under the Northern Avenue Bridge, flashing blue chrome hues at that evening hour, gulls swooping. I was so fortunate to have had that job on the *Beaver II*. It was like "my first ship" in a Polish Joe tale, one that had taken me away from home to a distant port where I could now catch another ship headed anywhere. As the end of that summer loomed, whenever I had to squeeze my Jack Tar seaman's hat atop my ever-more-abundant 'fro, I'd be reminded of why I'd grown my hair like that, my rash secret plan, and feel a nervous tightening in my stomach.


A few days before I left for college, I went with my mother to a hair salon in the next town. The hairdresser applied a smelly heated paste that burned against my scalp, smeared and tamped it into my hair with a plastic palate knife, and massaged it in with rubber-gloved fingers, up to her wrists in gooey tangles. This is a big job! she exclaimed. I sat under the hairdryer for a long time, then the hairdresser went to work with her scissors. The whole operation took a couple of hours, and my mother patiently sat there, sometimes idly leafing through a women's magazine or staring primly at some apparently invisible point in space. When we left the salon, I had straight hair falling nearly to my shoulders, silky and thick. I remember how it tickled my collarbones and how thrilling that was. The hairdresser said I looked like a baby-faced George Harrison. I thought my hair was more like Todd Rundgren's, but when the Godard movie *Masculin Féminin* was screened at Broener College on a weekend night early that fall, I realized it was more like Chantal Goya's. After we came home from the hairdresser that afternoon my father's disgust didn't bother me because what did I expect? It didn't stop him, the day I left for college, from giving me a present, a meerschaum briar pipe, with a tin of tobacco and pipe cleaners, from Leavitt and Peirce in Harvard Square, where he bought his own pipes, tobacco, and cigars. A college man has to have a pipe, said Bert.


It's almost noon, South Station, and I'm looking up at the schedule board for the track number of the train to Mamita's nursing home when my phone vibrates, a text message from Lulú. It's in English: "Tani want to know. More windows in the world or more children? So cute. I tell her that my friend know the answer! More windows or more children? Besitos." I walk out onto the long platform with a bounce in my step. Pelícanos and now this. Is Lulú a poet? In little more than an hour I'll be in Green Meadows, walking into the overheated dayroom on my mother's floor, where I usually find her sitting in her wheelchair, often dozing like a dormouse, and I imagine myself shouting with such overflowing ebullience "Mamita, I'm in love!" that all other dementia- and Alzheimer's-afflicted old folks in there, faces pale as frozen pie crusts, lift their heads to smile at me. Frankie, what good news, Mamita will say. Does that mean that soon you'll give me a grandchild?

More windows than children in the world or more children? As we pull out of the station, through a sunny concrete ravine, this commuter train, its grimy steel floor and scarred, brown leather seats, reminds me of a troop carrier, maybe an East German IFA truck like the Sandinistas used. I'd hitched rides in the back of a few, sitting squeezed on a bench between young soldiers and their AKs, smell of metal and grease, overheated bodies inside fatigues of heavy green cloth, overripe sweat and always a slight but pervasive odor of shit, a result of what constant fear does to churning adolescent stomachs already infected with jungle parasites. My hands, fingers intertwined, dangle between my knees. Really, you spend much more time looking at your own hands than you do at your own face. My hands probably resemble me more than my face does. I unclasp them and look at the mole in the middle of the left one. At Wamblán, a Sandinista special forces outpost by the Honduran border, the young commanding officer, Jacinto, was convinced it was a stigmata scar and wasn't sure if that presaged good or bad. But for this mole to be credible as a stigmata, you have to imagine people worshipping a Christ who dangles from the Cross by only one arm. These are also the knuckles that crashed into the side of my father's head, the second punch landing harder than the first as he fell forward, the appalling sensation of bone and skin through hair, a criminal punch in a way the first wasn't. I can never recall it without a queasy lurch in my stomach. Could that first punch alone have been enough to make him never hit me again or was it the follow-up that put the fear in him.

In a town like ours there were easily more windows than children. The house on Wooded Hollow Road, for example, had, let's see, five downstairs windows, seven upstairs, plus the sliding glass doors onto the porch. The overwhelming numerical advantage of windows over children in Boston, New York, probably in any Western city, any city in China or Japan too. But what about Lagos, Mexico City, Rio, childless skyscrapers versus ever-spreading child-teeming misery belts, more children than windows—or close to a tie? Traditional Maya village houses of one room with mud walls or built from mud packed with grass and sticks might not even have one window, just a door, often a half-dozen children or more living inside; the rural poor's residences all over the world, in Mexico for sure, the Amazon, too, in every jungle environment I've been to, way more children than windows. "Every child represents infinite windows, querida Lulú. So does love. Questions open windows." I thumb these words into my phone, hit Send, sit back. Jesus fucking Christ, did I just write that corniness? Did I just tell Lulú that I love her? I quickly type: "80 percent of the world's children live in poverty, so more children than windows. Though really, not sure." And: "Miss you." Send.


Phone María Xum, I remind myself, here on the station platform where I've just gotten off. Find out what's so urgent. In the middle of the first ring, she answers: Hello? Hello? I resist the urge to hang up. María, it's Frankie. How silly yet automatic it feels to identify myself by my boyhood name to this woman I haven't seen since I was about twelve. Frankeeee! María Xum responds. I'm so happy you phoned. I was worried you didn't receive my message. I'm a little surprised that María's accent isn't so strong. Sure, she's lived in the Boston area some forty years, but Feli has been here longer and doesn't sound as fluent. I am at work in the laundry, she says. We listened to you on the radio last night, and oh, it was so interesting, Frankie. That's why I had to phone the radio station. Frankie, do you want to come to my laundromat? We can speak there. It is in East Boston. Yes, I want to tell you something. I know you will be interested. Frankie, how is Doña Yoli? And Mr. Goldberg? I tell her: María, my father left us four years ago, but he had a long life. I'm meeting Feli tomorrow, so I agree to see her Sunday, in her laundromat. I'm the only person on the platform. A small redbrick station, which seems to have been locked up for years. Approaching on the train, you see old factories like bombed castles among the dead-looking swamplands on the outskirts of this town. Though it's about thirty miles inland, this is the closest commuter train stop to where Lexi lives. There are no taxis waiting, but it's only a half hour or so walk to my mother's nursing home.

Last night, at the restaurant, I told Marianne about Lexi buying that old ship captain's house in New Bedford as an investment. Marianne thought it was eccentric of my sister to have bought a house there, even an old ship captain's house; her impression was that it was a depressed postindustrial city, even its seafood business in distress. I told her that I didn't know much about it, only that supposedly the commuter train is finally coming there and that yuppies who work in Boston and Providence are going to want to buy up the beautiful old houses.

Grander houses, I imagine, than these I'm walking past on the uneven sidewalk of this long avenue into town, pulling my wheeled suitcase and carrying a tin of French butter cookies.

So, doing that to my hair, did it really change my life? I have to say that it did. Having long, straight hair really suited me. Suddenly I was at least a little bit good-looking, and that was confusing, partly because it was a lie, partly because I was still me. It was the first weekend at Broener

College after the orientation week, our first football home game, the
only one I ever went to. I was sitting in the stands that weren't any bigger than those at my high school, though these, on the home side of
the field, were packed with students. The stadium was located behind
the hill where the girls' dormitories were. The boys' dorms, including
mine, were on the other side of campus around the quad. A pretty
girl, fairly petite, with a head of shimmery blonde ringlets and nearly
sapphire-blue eyes sitting in the next section of the stands seemed to
be keeping her gaze fixed on me, and every time I glanced her way her
smile widened. Needless to say, I could hardly believe this was happening. Her father was an executive at Bloomingdale's, and she was from
Syosset, Long Island, a classic JAP, Frecky Papperman from my dorm
told me. He'd already scoped Abbie Schneider out, thought she was one
of the prettiest girls in the freshman class. What do you mean a classic
JAP? I asked. Frecky explained about Jewish American princesses. I'd
never heard Jewish girls called that in my town. Broener was known as
a JAP school, Frecky told me. By that night, Abbie was my girlfriend.
For the first time since Arlene Fertig I made out with a girl—on a lawn
and in the dark again—on the quad. Abbie was sweet natured and fairly
reticent, a conventional suburban teenager of the sort I would have
stood no chance with in my town. She had a strong Long Island accent
and was a chain-smoker too. I filled many of our silences with made-up
stories, total lies, about what I'd been like in high school.

   We'd been going out a little more than a month on the afternoon
when her roommate, a WASP preppie, a severe beauty with a flinty stare,
intercepted me on the autumn-foliage-carpeted lawn outside their dorm
and told me that Abbie didn't want to see me anymore. She asked me
to tell you, said the roommate, and also to please just leave her alone.
Her Clint Eastwood squint, flickering with disdainful comprehension,
had fastened on my straightened hair, which was beginning to lift at the
sides like desiccated wings, pushed out by the not-yet-quite-visible new
growth of curls underneath. Imagine the conversations Abbie and her

roommate must have had about me: How's the sex going? Is he good in bed? Well, no. He hasn't even tried to touch me . . . my . . . Oh God, please stop, I promise to dig a deep hole in a shit yard, bury myself, and never come out again. Our campus suffered from the usual horrendous American segregation, the small number of black students as defiantly isolated as a survivalist group except for a few athletes in frats. There was also a pair of scholarship Puerto Ricans brought to Broener, both probably from somewhere in the Northeast megalopolis. They became inseparable, he with a big afro and she with straight, glossy black hair, ash-brown skin, large eyes like shadowed ponds. They'd sit together on a hill behind a dorm while he played his bongos for hours. I used to spy on them from afar, longing to go up, say hello, and speak in Spanish, of course I didn't dare. In my dorm there was a boy who lived down the hall, a lacrosse and basketball star, the classic Adonis. He took ten showers a day, briskly parading his muscular alabaster physique back and forth from the shower room with a towel wrapped around his nar-row swivel waist. Within weeks he was Abbie's new boyfriend. In our dorm we could hear her cries of ecstasy up and down the hall. They sure seemed happy; for all I know they're married now.

But it wasn't as if my classes weren't interesting or as if getting good grades wasn't a novelty, auguring that I'd be able to transfer to another college, one where nobody knew me, and start over. I took a lecture course taught by a fortyish gentle genius who spoke like a hypereducated five-year-old, in which we studied Egyptian hieroglyphics, *The Epic of Gilgamesh,* the pre-Socratics, Bach's fugues, and *Alice in Wonderland*, and wrote essays in Egyptian hieroglyphs with colored pencils, all to help us recover the amplitude of our lost mythopoetic brains. In Modern Day Prophets, taught by an old Scottish Marxist, we read *The Autobiography of Malcolm X, Pedagogy of the Oppressed,* Marcuse. Instead of an academic final paper, students could do a participatory project, and the one most students chose, arranged by the professor through his friendship with a comrade infiltrator of the police state, was to spend a weekend in a prison cell in Buffalo, though you had to pay room and board. I decided for my project to become a modern-day prophet, jumping freight trains and riding them to Finger Lake towns to turn up in supermarket parking lots handing out leaflets on behalf of the United Farm Workers. My reputation would spread, the skinny, long-haired boy with a Dolores Huerta button on the front of his black watch cap who hands out UFW leaflets, then vanishes! Knapsack stuffed with mimeographed leaflets, I descended the steep bluff at the edge of our campus to the railroad tracks by the lakeside and, running alongside one of the boxcars of a slow-moving freight train, hauled myself up through its open side doors. I got off in Penn Yan, handed out my leaflets in an A&P parking lot, and after—whoosh!—vanishing, took a bus back to Broener, heart drumming with honest pride.

Mamita shares her room with a long-widowed and retired school-teacher from Worcester named Susan Cornwall, who lies perpetually like a log cake under her beige blanket, mannish wax-pink nose and myopic-seeming eyes aimed up at the ceiling, her silver hair like a wrung mop on the pillow behind her. She only seems catatonic, because she hears everything and does in fact speak. One morning soon after my mother came to live there Susan Cornwall interrupted my mother's friendly chatter to shout at her: Will you shut up, please just shut up. I cannot stand the sound of your voice one more second, shut up!

My mother has never forgiven her roommate for that outburst, hasn't spoken one word to her since, not a single "good morning" or "good night" or "bless you," responding to her rare utterances with silence.

So far as I've noticed, anyway, Mamita is Green Meadows' only resident who isn't a white person. But the staff seems to be mostly Caribbean, Brazilian, and Asian, and many of those people seem genuinely fond of my mother. They recognize the tropical gentility of her manners; a few speak to her in Spanish. Lexi insists Green Meadows isn't merely the best place she could find for our mother on "our" budget. She's sure people pay much more elsewhere without getting the kind of personal care that Mamita gets here. We really lucked out. Plus, it's a relatively easy drive from New Bedford. Mamita does stay busy enough. She likes the Bingo games and sing-alongs, she has her physical rehab sessions, and a Catholic priest comes once a month to celebrate Mass in the chapel; otherwise a church layperson leads the Sunday prayer service and also a midweek Bible-reading group my mother has joined. In the downstairs dining room, Mamita used to have to sit at the same table for every meal with three other women, one a Boston policeman's widow with a florid, knobby face and eyes like violet marbles. During one of my first visits, I was sitting next to Mamita at dinner when the policeman's widow, aiming her vitreous stare across the table, snapped: It's rude that you don't speak in English. It *distracts* us. She was always bullying my mother, Lexi told me, but finally my sister took care of the matter, and Mamita was moved to a table with nicer ladies.

The door to the stairwell off the entrance lobby is kept locked, so I ride the elevator up one floor to the dementia and Alzheimer's patient wing, called Golden Meadows, and head down the hall to my mother's room. The first thing I notice is that Susan Cornwall's bed, the one closest to the door, is empty. I step back to check the name tag over the door frame. Susan Cornwall still there over Yolanda Goldberg. Danielle, the Haitian nurse, is in the room; she must have come in just before me to take my mother to the bathroom. Mamita is next to her, in her wheelchair, smiling at me with her lips together, making her cute axolotl face. She always gets her hair done when she knows I'm coming, and it's arrayed over her head in ringlets that resemble threadbare reddish-orange Christmas ribbons. I bend to kiss her pale cheek and show her the tin of cookies and ask about Susan Cornwall. Danielle says that she was taken to the hospital for some routine tests. I set the cookies down on the sill by Mamita's window, alongside the framed photographs there; that one with my mother and sister and Bert with cardboard taped over his face, I remember now, was taken at Yolandita's wedding with Richard the Vietnam vet and Sears manager. When we speak over the telephone, does Mamita visualize me as I am now or as I was when I was a boy? Leaving the bathroom door open to give herself room to maneuver, Danielle expertly lifts Mamita from her wheelchair onto the toilet, and I step out into the corridor to wait. The day will come when either my mother or Susan Cornwall will outlive her nemesis and find herself sharing a room with an empty bed and a cleaned-out closet, until a new roommate is moved in and a new name tag is put up. The survivor won't feel a twinge of grief but instead will feel like a soldier numbed by a long war. Lexi once told me that Susan Cornwall never receives visitors, that her only son lives in Wisconsin and hasn't come to see her in five years.

Mamita, I ask her, what was the name of that boardinghouse you and Dolores Ojito lived in? It's like restarting the same conversation we had last visit. She'd told me the name. I'd even written it down, but I lost that notebook; so often they fall from my pocket. She must have moved into the boardinghouse during the spring of 1952, because that's when Doroteo Guamuch Flores won the Boston marathon, and I know Abuelita was up here with Mamita, because she always liked telling about how together from somewhere along the course they'd cheered their compatriot on.

My mother's gaze withdraws back in time, her rust-hued lashes quiveringly lowered. Our Lady Gih . . . gih . . . she stammers, Ay no, Frankie, no se. Then she quietly pronounces as if under a spell: Our Lady's Guild House. That's it, I've looked it up before, a rooming house attached to a convent of cloistered nuns, the Daughters of the Immaculate Heart of Mary, still in operation, a brick-and-granite building on an exposed corner of Charlesgate Road and the Pike, only blocks from the Berklee College of Music, where my mother would spend the last fifteen years or so of her working life.

Mamita, isn't it true that you were distinguished professor of marimba at Berklee.

Ay, hijo, and laughter trills out of her, her soft body shaking in her wheelchair. As a son, I have countless failings, but I've always been good at making Mamita laugh.

Back when she was a Guatemalan working girl in Boston, a bilingual secretary, in her twenties, boarding at Our Lady's, what would she have thought if she could have glimpsed her future, a professor at Berklee, teaching Spanish, not marimba, to some of the world's most gifted student musicians? Would it have seemed the fulfillment of a dream or did she dream of something else? Now, even mundane questions can seem to task her mind the way a perplexing riddle might, and her eyes flood with anxiety.

You don't remember what your dream for the future was back then, Mami?

No, Frankie, she says firmly, I don't. I've also noticed how her anxiety eases whenever she can respond to a question with an answer she feels sure of.

You were just happy to be in Boston, probably, I say. Having fun, you and Dolores Ojito going out on dates with those Harvard foreign grad school muchachos, Zbiggy Brzezinski, no less, right Mami?

That makes her smile. One evening when I was home from college and we were watching the news on the portable TV in the kitchen, President Carter introducing new members of his cabinet, my mother's eyes went wide and she exclaimed, Zbiggy! She knew him from her single working-girl days in Boston, it turned out, when she used to get invited to foreign grad student parties. After one of those parties, Zbigniew Brzezinski had carried her in his arms across a muddy Harvard yard. I asked her what he was like and she responded: Zbiggy was like a lion! *Liiii-yun,* she pronounced it.

Ay, Mamita, how did a niña bien from the tropics like you ever end up in a joint like this? That's another of our routines. Whenever I visit her at Green Meadows, I ask her that, and she always answers the same way: Ay, no sé, hijo, and that deep giggle that rolls on into helpless yelps of laughter.

From grade school through high school, Mamita attended Guatemala's first bilingual school, the all-girl Colegio Inglés Americano.

At home she had a pet spider monkey named Coco whom she spoke to only in English, so that by the time she was ten she could translate for American customers who came into her parents' stores. One morning Mamita found Coco curled up in a corner of the patio, his head slumped forward with a coffee cup wedged over it. Coco, awaken! she commanded in her Inglés Americano English. This is not amusing! Her monkey's accidental death by suffocation so affected her that even a year later, whenever anyone asked, What's new, Yoli? she'd respond, Coco died. He no longer exists. That's why, she told Lexi and me, she never allowed herself to become attached to our pets. It's true my mother never liked our pets. Fritzie was sent away to live in Maine, and within days of our having moved into the new house on Wooded Hollow Road, furnished with brand-new furniture and powder-blue carpeting, Beaker, half-beagle, half-cocker spaniel, somehow escaped his backyard leash while Lexi and I were at school, and he never came home. It's practically a game of ours now. I tease my mother that I've always suspected she gave my dog away so that no muddy paw would besmirch her new sofa and carpets, she always denies it, and we end up laughing, Mamita in her helpless hilarity mode. The possibility that her denial really is a lie that she's forced herself to keep up all these years, as if she fears I'd be as devastated now to learn the truth as that ten-year-old boy would have been, is what cracks me up, but I don't get what my mother finds so funny. After her graduation from the Colegio Inglés Americano, Mamita went to college in California, at San Jose State, so that she could be near her brother, who was in his third year at UC Berkeley. Memo had been sent there by my abuelos to study business administration so that when he got out he'd be ready to capitalize on the money-making opportunities that the booming postwar US economy was bringing even to Guatemala. When her brother graduated, Mamita went home too. A year or so later, Abuelita again whisked her out of the country, this time to New Orleans, the US city most accessible to Guatemala during the decades when the

Great White Fleet of the United Fruit Company was plying the Gulf between New Orleans and Puerto Barrios, carrying passengers as well as bananas. Even during our childhoods, Lexi and I had somehow picked up on the fact that in her youth Mamita had had a tragic love, which had something to do with how she'd ended up living in Boston, where she became our mother. I don't recall our having any idea what exactly made it so tragic. All we knew was that this suitor, or novio, was a handsome Italian with no money and Abuelita wasn't going to let my mother marry someone who was poor no matter what. Then she married my father, who was far from rich.

During one of those earlier visits to Green Meadows, when my mother had surprised me with her new candor, she said, Abuelita saved me from throwing my life away. When talking to me and my sister, Mamita always refers to her own mother as Abuelita. That was the first time I ever heard the name Lucio Grassi, though I'm sure Lexi has long known it. Ay no, Frankie, the way he took advantage of me, he lied and stole my savings! my mother exclaimed, her voice girlishly welling with disbelief. I knew that in Guatemala and California she'd been friendly with plenty of young men, that she'd had boyfriends, yet here she was almost sixty years later, feeling it as a fresh shock that somebody who professed to love her could have treated her with such calculated dishonesty.

Lucio Grassi had turned up in Guatemala one day and talked his way into certain youthful social circles. Blondish, green eyed, freckled, strong and graceful as a circus horse, Mamita's friends said he was the handsomest man they'd ever seen. One day Lucio Grassi told her it was his ambition to open a European-style hotel on Lake Atitlán, back then still considered an unexploited paradise. He'd found partners eager to invest but needed money for his own share. His grandfather had managed a seafront hotel in Genoa that had been destroyed by bombing in the war; the hotel business was in his blood. Mamita lent Lucio Grassi all her savings. Then she found out there was no planned hotel, no partners. He just needed money to live on, even to lavish on her and not only on her; it turned out she wasn't the only damita he'd borrowed money from. Of course, after that, she was done with Lucio. But I was afraid he was going to keep chasing me, Frankie, she told me. I've seen photographs of my mother from back then, her witchy eyes and girlish smile in lipstick, the effulgent fall of her then-wavy hair, the off-the-shoulder dresses and blouses she wore. In a different society or time her relationship with Lucio Grassi could probably have run its enthralling course without life-altering consequences until she woke up: But you don't have any money, mi amor. I can't marry you. What was I thinking?

Considering that she came from a family of fairly prosperous shopkeepers, not of coffee plantation owners or magnates like the family that produces all the country's cement or the one that makes all the beer, Mamita really wasn't great fortune-hunter prey. She must have been the one feeling pressure to convert her beauty and respectable upbringing into a fortune. And Lucio Grassi did keep chasing her, full of apologetic justifications and arguments. He even wept at her feet. That's what my mother blurted out in Green Meadows during my last visit, seeming dazed by the memory. Like the overwrought leading men of so many Italian movies, like Giovanni groveling before his callow gringo lover, Lucio put on his show. He couldn't live without her; he tore at his hair. But he never paid her back the money. Sitting there in the nursing home I was suddenly so sure that my mother cherished this memory of the grand passion she'd inspired that I felt like getting up from my chair and shouting at Lucio Grassi: Ridiculous fool, get off your fucking knees and leave my mother alone!

No one has ever accused *me* of being a cool cucumber, that's for sure, but I've never wept over a woman like that. I can only imagine Gisela savoring the spectacle of me weeping at her feet and tearing my hair, I can see her pitilessly amused smile.

When Mamita said that Abuelita, by spiriting her out of Guatemala, saved her from "throwing my life away," I understood that to mean "in the nick of time." A few years later Lucio Grassi married an old school friend of my mother's, "not a beauty pero siempre bien simpática," Beatriz Oiza, from one of those extremely wealthy coffee plantation families. Lucio and Beatriz had seven children and raised them in Vista Hermosa, then a fashionable neighborhood, where they led quiet lives; they bought property in Italy, too, and stayed there during the worst of the war years because their wealth made the family obvious targets for kidnapping. But Lucio and his wife, even before the 1996 peace accords, began spending a few months every year in Guatemala because it wasn't wise to always be so far from their coffee farms, and not one of their now-grown children, studying, marrying, settling down in Italy, still asking for money, wanted any of that responsibility. I doubt my mother ever envied Beatriz Oiza. She'd never wanted the idle Latin American rich wife life that might have been hers. As attached to her family as Mamita was, she never envisioned herself working in the toy and baby clothing store that was the family mainstay. Instead, she took the path she did, Boston, Sacco Road, a nearly forty-year career as a Spanish teacher, now Green Meadows.

But first Mamita went to New Orleans, where maybe the Italian sprang a banana boat visit, because something sent Abuelita up there in a hurry, on a Pan Am flight, to escort Mamita to Boston and into Our Lady's Guild House. Abuelita, or Doña Hercilia as she was widely known, always had good government connections, whether during the Ubico dictatorship or after the October Revolution brought democracy, because politicians and bureaucrats of every party needed to buy toys for children or grandchildren during Christmas and Tres Reyes. Abuelita's connections most likely had something to do with Mamita so quickly landing a job as a bilingual secretary to the Guatemalan consul in Boston. Dolores Ojito, from Guatemala City, too, though they hadn't known each other there, was my mother's roommate at Our Lady's. Dolores, or Lolita, worked as a bilingual secretary, too, at the United Fruit Company's headquarters on State Street. But I'd never heard, or registered it if I had, anything about my mother's friendship with Dolores Ojito and their respective places of employment until after my mother went to live at Green Meadows. When she told me, it seemed too good to be true: a John le Carré Cold War spy novel mixed with a Latin American version of Muriel Spark's novel about women living in a London rooming house after World War II. Mamita and Lolita, two young secretaries from Guatemala City, who'd come to find their futures in the so-called Hub of the Universe, though if not really of the universe, indisputably of the global banana trade. Before the overthrow of President Jacobo Árbenz in June 1954, Mamita, working at the Guatemalan consulate in Boston, was essentially in the employ of his government, while her best friend and roommate, Lolita Ojito, worked for the United Fruit Company; though the CIA organized and carried out the coup against Arbenz, the Boston-based banana company was notoriously its instigator.

But what does that have to do with Mamita and me, half a century later, sitting down here in the visitors' nook at Green Meadows, playing Scrabble and talking? I brought her down in her wheelchair. The air is fresher here, wafting in through the pneumatic doors that open off the lobby onto a pine-lined parking lot. The well-lit, drably pleasant dining room, where Mamita still usually has her evening meals, is situated between the visitors' nook and Lilac Meadows, the tranquil assisted living wing where she lived during her first year. When the weather is warmer, I take her outside to the garden in the middle of the complex and sometimes wheel her out onto the sidewalk and into the adjoining neighborhood, down Codman Road, so like Sacco Road with its small ranch houses and yards. Pushing her along, I'll break into a run, singing out "Georgy Girl" or some other song I remember Mamita liking, though instead of singing along or laughing she just widens her eyes.

The Scrabble board on the table between us, Mamita sits in her wheelchair, maroon quilted jacket worn over her shoulders like a cape, pink fleece cardigan zipped up to her neck. By our rules, she can form words in either Spanish or English, but I'm only allowed to use Spanish, despite the absence of ñ tiles. Two years ago, Mamita was better at

Scrabble. Now her arthritic fingers tremble as she nudges a tile into place, spelling out words like "si" or "no" or "que," maybe even a "mama" or a "casa." A year ago she could still manage a word like "maestra."

If the coup had never happened, if her country had still been a democracy instead of a right-wing military dictatorship, might my mother's life have taken another direction? After a few years of being a single, foreign working girl in Boston, would the novelty have worn off, and with her and Abuelita no longer needing to be on guard against Lucio Grassi, might she have gone home? Or would she have stayed and married Bert Goldberg anyway?

A few days ago, when I phoned to let Mamita know I was coming to visit, she said, in English: I miss the sun in Guatemala, the sunheat, you know? Here they won't let me go outside. I couldn't remember her ever complaining on her own behalf before, not in recent years, certainly not about Green Meadows, guarding against saying anything I might construe as a criticism of Lexi, who makes every decision regarding our mother's care. Sunheat as one word, lovely. No, Mami, I said, you can't go outside. It's still winter, I know it's been a long one. Would you like to go back to Guatemala, at least for a visit? That's something else she never admits to wanting. But she answered, Yes, but I can't. Something happened to my legs. I'm in a wheelchair. Lately she often tells me about her wheelchair as if it's a recent development. I played along: Oh no, Ma, how'd that happen? I don't know, she said. Lexi doesn't want to live in Guatemala, said my mother. She's happy here, she has her life here.

Well, I said into the phone, maybe we can find a way to go back for a visit soon.

You know, Frankie, says my mother across the Scrabble board, Lexi is an important person in New Bedford.

Really, Ma? I ask. Important how?

She's married to a policeman, says my mother. And she has children.

But wouldn't Lexi have told me, I wonder. When I last saw her two years ago she didn't mention a husband or children, she didn't seem like a woman married to a policeman, much less a woman with children. Are Lexi and I estranged? I know I'm a distant, neglectful brother, but we're not *estranged*, are we? She wrote me those emails before Christmas, inviting to me to her house.

I ask, Do you mean the policeman's children from an earlier marriage?

Now my mother's expression seems both blank and consternated.

That's great, Ma, that things have worked out so well for Lexi, I decide to say. It was a brave thing she did, buying that house in New Bedford. How many children does she have, anyway?

Memo, says my mother, and she wanly sighs. I don't remember how many children.

I'm Frankie, I tell her, not Memo. Even before, Mamita had a propensity for mixing up names in what seems like a verbal echoing of a mental stutter, so that when she means to address me she says, BertMemoLexi-*Frankie* . . . To my sister she might say, FrankieConyYolandita*Lexi* . . . But more recently she really does seem sometimes to mix me up with her brother. Well, people have always said there's a resemblance, that when I was young I supposedly looked like Tío Memo when he was young. Maybe when I'm old I will too. Memo's a handsome old gent, a dapper dresser.

Lexi went to see a brujo, says my mother.

A brujo? I repeat. You mean like a Maya shaman?

I don't know, she answers, her laugh mixing mischief and embarrassment.

Even if she was once a reader of the Carlos Castaneda books about the Yaqui shaman Don Juan, my mother has never believed in that sort of witchcraft, probably not even when she was a girl, and I ask, Ma, what are you talking about? Why did Lexi go to a brujo?

Frankie, Lexi asked the brujo to help you find a wife so that I can have a grandchild, she says. Don't you think that was thoughtful of her? She grins expectantly at me.

But Ma, I say, you just told me that you're already a grandmother. You said that Lexi has children.

They're not Lexi's children, she responds, so they're not my grand-children. Oh, Frankie, I don't know, she says plaintively. Lexi told me she asked a brujo to help you, pues, ojalá, verdad?

Mami, I say, I hope you'll find yourself becoming a grandmother one of these days or years, but if that kid is mine, it won't be because Lexi went to a brujo.

What I was thinking was, if Lulú and I somehow end up married, Marisela will become my mother's granddaughter. But she won't, of course. Marisela is Lulú's second cousin.

Above the *i* in my mother's "si" on the Scrabble board, I set down a *p* tile and an *s* and below it, a *c*, an *o*, an *s*, another *i*, another *s*, "psicosis." Pretty nifty, though we don't keep score. I choose seven new tiles and say: Psicosis, Mamita. Your turn.

In front of that last *s*, my mother drops another *i*.

I say, "Is" instead of another "si," muy interesante, Mami.

During that year or so leading up to the coup, what did Yoli and Lolita, one working for her country's consulate, the other for the power-ful banana company, know or notice? Did one pass along information, whisper an overheard secret, or carry a sheaf of pilfered documents or an intercepted telegram to the other? Wouldn't they have at least known that something was up? I've tried to excavate whatever connection my mother and Dolores Ojito could have had to the coup or whatever memories she might still have about it. And I've forced myself to read at least part of every book I can find on the coup—which I first learned about in high school from Carlota Sánchez Motta, who didn't have all her facts right but whose indignation was on the mark—searching for a reference to any even minor or accidental role my mother and Dolores Ojito could have played or to their proximity to the men helping to scheme the calamity or maybe trying to prevent it, hoping always for at least a glimpse in printed words of their shadows in wasp-waisted dresses or skirts passing through a Boston murk of boardrooms, offices, private gentlemen's clubs, and cocktail lounges.

In case bananas should someday be wiped from the earth by an ineradicable plague, forcing the Boston Banana Brahmins to find another fruit to grow down there or even to develop a new one like the grapefruit more or less was, the United Fruit Company had prudently kept much of the land it owned in Guatemala fallow. The land expropriations of President Árbenz's agrarian reform included those fallow acres. Something like one out of every six Guatemalans got some land. The DC wise men asked, What if every other government in Latin America does what Árbenz did? Those peasant farmers will clamor for more and more land, and next thing you know . . . One of the venerable Boston Banana Brahmins who'd founded the Latin American Society of New England was also the US ambassador to the United Nations, and Mamita got to meet him. Mr. Ambassador, I imagine someone saying, this is Señorita Yolanda Montejo, a secretary at the Guatemalan consulate. She comes to every one of our events. Wouldn't Yolanda's place of employment have made her kind of suspicious to the ambassador? Or else maybe Yolanda's boss, the consul, was in fact known to the ambassador as a reliable secret collaborator. Don't have a clue which, if either. The ambassador's speeches in polished Yankee dudgeon attacking Árbenz's Moscow puppet regime were a recurring high point of the era's UN sessions, like Cold War Shakespeare. But it wasn't true that Árbenz was hiding Eastern Bloc weapons of mass destruction inside volcanoes. "Such lies are not lies, rather they should be understood semiotically as seraphic incantations for doing good" is how the United Fruit Company's famous Vienna-born public relations man, who happened also to be Sigmund Freud's nephew, explained this new form of propaganda in one of his pioneering books. The coup plotters perceived that in so pious and backward a country as Guatemala, the most powerful force for good they could wield would be the archbishop, who did begin to energetically preach against the Communist atheist president. This was the same archbishop who two years later would prohibit Mamita from marrying a Jew in Guatemala, forcing her at the last moment to move her wedding to Mexico City. Though bananas had nothing to do with that decision, it can at least be said that Mamita was directly connected to the coup by marriage.

Did the United Fruit bilingual secretary, Lolita Ojito, ever filch a note or diary page in which Freud's nephew had scribbled something like "if this is gonna work, boys, we gotta get that archbishop on board, and pronto" and bring it to her best friend in Our Lady's Guild House, so that she could give it to the consul, who would pass it directly to President Árbenz, maybe in time to save the day? Doesn't seem so. At any rate, the day was never saved. Questioning Mamita about the coup has turned out to be pretty futile. If only I'd thought to ask her about it years ago. If only.


Mamita, that consul you worked for, I ask, what was his name? She confidently answers, I don't remember, Frankie. She never remembers that guy's name. The Guatemalan consulate was located at 72 Liberty Street, an old office building no longer standing, I found the address on my last overnight visit when I spent the morning in the Boston Public Library scrolling through blurry microfilm of 1950s Boston telephone books with a librarian-lent magnifying glass held to the smudgy columns of print on the screen. It took hours to find. I ended up having to hobble-run to Back Bay Station to catch my train back to New York and didn't have time to stop into the Italian deli to get the submarine sandwich I'd been thinking about all morning. But at least now I can say, Seventy-Two Liberty Street, that's where you worked. Does that ring a bell, Ma?

While my mother gazes sleepily at the Scrabble board, I pull out my phone. Lulú hasn't answered my message about children and windows. Might it have gone missing? Should I resend it? No, better wait.

Mami, I say, I know the consul was allowed to run his own business out of the consulate. He imported shoes from Italy, didn't he?

As if she had this answer ready and was just waiting to give it, my mother says, No, not shoes, Frankie. Heels and soles.

Tacones y suelas in Spanish, such pretty words, it could be a song title. The consul only imported tacones y suelas, Ma?

Yes, she says, in one room at the consulate, he kept cardboard boxes full of tacones y suelas.

Whenever we talk about her years at the consulate, my mother never alludes to the coup, yet she never fails to mention that room and the cardboard boxes packed with heels and soles. What is it about that room that keeps it so present in her memory when so much else has faded? Maybe it was the daily drudgery of filling out invoices and other forms for the importation of heels and soles from Italy and their shipment to shoe factories and cobblers elsewhere in the United States that imprinted an inky stamp in her memory. When I'm very old and someone says pelícano and I brighten with recognition, will I remember why I do?

On the Scrabble board I've just spelled out "chumpa," a word only used in Central America. Do you remember what a chumpa is, Ma? I ask.

A jacket, she answers with a note of resentment, as if she's thinking: You think I'm so far gone that I don't remember what a chumpa is?

Can you make a word with an *a* in it? Calamidád? Calambre? Cat?

No, no puedo, she says.

How about the *p*? Chompipe.

With quivering gnarled hand she slowly slides the *a* under the *p*.

See? You can do it, Mamita. "Pa" is a perfectly good word.

After the overthrow in Guatemala, didn't Yolanda Montejo and Lolita Ojito realize what they'd been perhaps uncomprehending witnesses to? Growing up, I never heard my mother say anything that would have made me think she didn't share her family's politics, regarding Guatemala, I mean, though she never expressed those opinions with the usual family vehemence. The year after I was born, after she'd left my father and taken me to live with her in my abuelos' house, Eisenhower's veep came to show support for the postcoup dictatorship, and Mamita got to meet him—or at least see him close up—at a reception at the Club Guatemala. Ay, no, that Nixon, she'd say, recounting it years later, and she'd stick out her lower lip, crunch her eyebrows together, hunch her shoulders, and say, Que hombre más feo.

If I'm remembering right, Madame Chiang Kai Shek, who'd studied at the women's college in the next town, was her favorite political figure. Ma, I ask, who did you admire more, Madame Chiang Kai Shek or Jackie O?

Madame Chiang Kai Shek, she says without hesitation. She warned the world about the Communists.

My expression must be a bit surprised, because she smiles as if embarrassed and lets out one of her little yelping laughs. I feel a start of tears in my eyes and forcefully blink to make it go away.


When Lexi was in the fifth or sixth grade, she had a friend at school, Caroline Biddle, who lived out near Riverbend Street, in a remote corner of town even more exclusive than the Ways. Caroline, like my sister, was tall, with wide shoulders, heavyset. Her ginger hair dangled in springy curls to her shoulders, and her blue eyes had a teasing shine that could quickly turn querulous. My sister's other friend, Bonnie, even taller, long hair, strikingly pretty, played the guitar. All three girls would shut themselves into my sister's bedroom and sing along to records by the Cowsills and the Troggs. Through the closed bedroom door, their voices sounded as if they were emanating from frail children. They were going to form a rock group, they said, Bonnie on guitar, my sister, who had easily learned some guitar, too, and Caroline, who would play tambourine and be lead singer. Lexi invited Caroline and Bonnie to sleep over one Saturday night so that they could practice during the weekend. Caroline said that she wanted to but that her mother had to give permission, and for that to happen, her mother would first have to come to our house and meet my mother.

Mrs. Biddle, a housewife, with Caroline, must have come to Wooded Hollow Road on an afternoon when my mother didn't have to teach. She wouldn't have canceled a class just to receive Mrs. Biddle. The two women had coffee or tea and lemon cream–filled cookies, sitting on the sofa in the living room, facing the oil paint portrait in an ornate white frame with gilded trim on the opposite wall of my young mother in a silvery-blue evening gown, her shoulders bare, an orchid on one side of her cleavage, against a cerulean backdrop; my father's boyhood friend, Herb, who became a Boston portrait artist, had painted it. Mamita would have brought out her best silver and china, put on a nice dress, arranged her unruly hair into the usual dyed black loaf. Lexi and Caroline sat in some chairs eating cookies, too. During that tête-à-tête, as years later Lexi recalled it, Mrs. Biddle pointed more than once at one or another of the Guatemalan folk objects displayed among Hummel and porcelain ornaments on the side tables and said something like: That's an interesting piece, Yolanda. To which my mother would respond: That is a wood carving of a Mayan Indian man carrying a load of firewood on his back. Or: That clay figurine is of a Mayan woman selling her wares at the market. Often when people who didn't know anything about Guatemala came to our house, Mamita would launch into the same speech that she surely gave Mrs. Biddle, about how the country was famous for the native Maya who lived in the mountains, keeping their ancient traditions, so picturesque, but also, you know, backward. The capital, Guatemala City, where she was raised, was a modern city, with tall buildings and shopping centers, like Miami. She would also have told Mrs. Biddle about the family stores, especially the flagship toy store on Sexta Avenida downtown, and her brother's weekend morning children's show on Guatemalan television, which featured Jingle Hop, yo-yo, and Hula-Hoop contests. He'd even made a television commercial with children and teenagers Hula-Hooping on the steps of an ancient Maya pyramid at Tikal. Those were the same spectacular ruins that Ambassador Henry Cabot Lodge had visited. The ambassador had been so impressed by Guatemala. She knew the ambassador and some of the other Cabot Lodges and Boston Brahmins from the Latin American Society of New England. Of course, she also would have told Mrs. Biddle about how she'd become a college Spanish teacher, about her studies in Boston and abroad, and also, with pride, about how the women's junior college in Brookline where she was on the faculty sent her on trips to South America, to Buenos Aires, Bogotá, Santiago, to recruit students. She must also have told Mrs. Biddle that her husband, Bert, a chemical engineer, was in charge of dental prosthetic tooth production at the Potashnik Tooth Company in Cambridge.

Mrs. Biddle seemed satisfied with what she'd heard. Why wouldn't she have been, said Lexi, recounting the story years later. Mom was warm and gracious, and Mrs. Biddle must have realized how exceptional she was, a woman from Guatemala who'd made herself into a college Spanish teacher and the treasurer of the Latin American Society of New England.

So, Caroline can sleep over then? asked my mother, posing the question as a polite formality.

No, I'm afraid not, Yolanda, Mrs. Biddle answered. I'm sorry.

Mamita gaped at Mrs. Biddle, truly at a loss for words. After an agonizing moment, Mrs. Biddle said, Well, I guess there isn't anything else for us to talk about, Yolanda, so Caroline and I had better be going. My mother remained rigidly seated, still speechless, as Mrs. Biddle got to her feet. Lexi has told me she has never forgotten the look on my mother's face, that it has troubled her ever since. Caroline and my sister never spoke again. Years later, Lexi found out, Mrs. Biddle had a nervous breakdown. So the incident wasn't what it seemed. Mrs. Biddle was "unstable." *Sure.*

As the Latin American Society of New England left its 1950s Cold War heyday behind, the surnames of philanthropic banana cronies resonated less and less, until there was hardly any reason to name-drop them anymore. By the time Mamita was elected the society's treasurer, the new president was Bruno Irigoyen, the MIT astrophysicist and telescope expert from Argentina who was a friend of Borges. Now the society invited people of opposing viewpoints to speak, and they furiously argued over such issues as the coup and military dictatorships in Chile and Argentina, and there was almost always weeping in the audience, or, afterward, glasses of wine contemptuously tossed on shirtfronts or even folding chairs hurled, Bruno threatening to summon the police and insulting people for being "incivil stupids." My mother and her friends were always describing this or that event as "eye-opening." Around that time Mamita was also going around quoting Yaqui peyote shaman wisdom from *The Teachings of Don Juan.* "I am a controlled warrior" is the one I especially remember.

My mother, like so many other immigrants, has lived her life between two cultures and countries; after enough years had passed, she may have felt that she didn't quite fit in either, never the United States, no longer Guatemala. One of the strangest things I've done with my own life has been to follow her path, in a sense willfully divesting in order to pour myself into that mold of divided, not quite belonging anywhere.

Mamita's last trip to Guatemala was seven years ago. I was there. I took her to San Sebastián, her girlhood parish church, where she'd been baptized and had planned to get married, where my sister and I were baptized, too, and where, on a Sunday night one year before our visit, the human rights bishop had been bludgeoned to death in the parish house garage. The still traumatized sacristan, Toño, and I gave my mother a little tour: Monseñor was found right here, Señora, in a pool of blood. They'd folded his hands over his chest like this and crossed his feet at the ankles. To which I added: Thirty-six fractures in his skull, Ma. He was hit so hard with, probably, a metal pipe, his jawbone was driven back into his trachea. Ay no, Frankie, que feo, murmured my mom.

Lexi's last visit was one summer when she was a year or two out of high school. Over the years I've heard conflicting, partial versions

of what happened during those months, mostly from my mother and
Feli, some from our relatives, not much directly from Lexi. She did
tell me how she used to like to walk to the Hotel Camino Real before
nightfall, the cypresses lining the Avenida Reforma thick with chatter-
ing grackles at that hour, to buy the *New York Times* that always arrived
at the hotel in the afternoon a day late. She'd sit alone with a glass of
wine at the bar reading it, just like I'd regularly done when I'd lived in
Tío Memo's house a few years before, though I drank beer. Tía Meche
was scandalized. She accused my sister of going to the hotel to try to
pick up men. There were other such incidents, the inevitable results of a
lonely gringa college student abroad asserting her own individual rights
and clashing with my aunt's rigidly old-fashioned sense of how a single
young woman was supposed to behave. My aunt's insinuations grew
uglier; horrible words were exchanged. One night, after Tía Meche had
sent our alcoholic cousin Fernando to fetch Lexi from a disco, where he
found her sitting at a table conversing and having drinks with a Lebanese
cardamom importer, he called Lexi a puta as soon as they were back
home, in front of our aunt. My mother has never forgiven Meche for
how my sister was treated that summer, it's the one thing she's never
hidden her anger over. That's probably part of the reason, at least, that
Lexi seems to regard herself as only American and also, despite her
closeness to my mother and her poisoned feelings toward my father,
as a Jew, never blurring her identifications in the way I've done since
childhood. I dash down to Guate every chance I get, never just to visit
our family, but I do always at least stop in to the toy store downtown,
family headquarters, to say hello.

Anger flashes in my mother's eyes. What? I respond.

Memo, she says, why didn't you come to my wedding?

Memo didn't come to your wedding?

She gapes at me and after a moment she says, No, he didn't, Frankie.

But he did, I think. I've seen photographs of the wedding and
Mexico, and Memo was there. Or am I wrong, and I'm confusing those

with photos of my mother at Memo and Meche's wedding, that's probably it. Jesus, both our memories suck.

Mamita closes her eyes again like she's meditating.

So often when my mother asks me to try to get along better with my sister, she weighs her pleas by reminding me what a good brother Memo has always been to her. Yet here Mamita is now, convinced that Memo didn't come to her wedding. If he didn't, why didn't he?

She's awake, looking at me crossly. She says, Frankie, péinate.

Si, Mami, I say, and lift crooked fingers to my head and swipe at some curls. Not a visit passes without my mother scolding me to comb my hair.

Her eyes close. Soon I hear her soft snore.


I know Lexi has had some hard times in the past, but it does seem like she's doing much better now, an important person in New Bedford, according to my mother, married to a policeman, a woman who can go to a Maya shaman to ask him to cast a spell to help her brother find a wife—


Lourdes López, at the moment, being the only possible known candidate for that. In Dunkin' Donuts and during that morning after we made love for the first time, she told me stories from her childhood, like the one about the old man who used to arrive in her village to sell ice cream on weekends and holidays and how because her mother would let him stow his wooden cart behind their small house while he went off to get drunk and sleep somewhere, Lulú was allowed to scrape ice-cream scraps off the bottom of the cart with a spoon; happy memories, the only times in her childhood she tasted ice cream. But when she was an adolescent, she and her mother moved from Veracruz to gritty, polluted Ecatepec, in Mexico State, where Lulú's uncle had a job working for the railroad. There, she said, they lived in a small concrete house like all the others on their street. Their next-door neighbor brought stray dogs home and kept them on his rooftop, feeding the dogs to fatten them up so that later he could mix their meat with lamb into the birria he sold from a sidewalk stand. He kept his sheep in a little pen in his backyard. At night Lulú could hear the dogs innocently barking, excited to be fed.

Those were the years when Lulú only wore rock band T-shirts, ripped jeans, and a steel bead in her tongue. Her best friend, Janeth, talked her into trying crack when they were fifteen. They rented a room in a cheap by-the-hour pension, Janeth showing Lulú how to cook the drug in a spoon. She and Janeth met to smoke crack four or five times, as if they were rehearsing to become crack addicts, but Lulú didn't like it. Crack made her feel nauseous and paranoid, and since then, she says, she hasn't even tried pot again.

So then what is this message that has just come from Lulú now resolute: "A gringo boy invite me to a party for ayahuasca. He move into house where my friend and her family live before. I am sad because now my friend they move to Yonker. Drugs scare me, so I think maybe no. But he seems like a good muchacho. Panchito, you ever take that drug?"

She's asking me to give an opinion on whether she should accept this apparent housewarming party invitation from this good gringo muchacho or if she should go and take ayahuasca. She thinks no, maybe. When did she meet Ayahuasca Bro? I saw Lulú only the night before last.

I had better think about what I'm going to answer. I feel a little sick.

During one of our first conversations in Dunkin' Donuts about her friend Brenda, the college student housekeeper with the boyfriend who pays her tuition, Lulú said that Brenda had decided to try to have a New York gringo-type relationship instead of a Mexican one. How are they different? I'd asked. Here in New York, she explained, the couples give each other freedom, but they have to be honest and talk about everything. In Mexico, she said—she slid her lips sideways, narrowed an eye—at least one part of the couple, the man, probably lies. It's impossible, she said, to have an open relationship in Mexico because the man, almost always but probably the woman too, would become so jealous and angry. But the men, too many are violent too. You know how people say: He hit her, but it's understandable because he was jealous. To be jealous is so stupid, said Lulú. I totally agree, I said. So, your friend is having an open relationship then. Yes, she said, Brenda's boyfriend believes in open relationships. But that doesn't mean he wants to sleep with other women, she said her friend had explained. He says he doesn't want to because he loves Brenda. But if it happens that he has sex with another woman, or if Brenda does with another man, it is permitted, but only as long as they don't hide it, they have to tell each other everything. My friend says that's the way young people here have relationships.

Tell each other everything, sure, I repeated. Here in New York. Then I thought, Maybe that is how they have relationships now; what do I know about what the young couples are doing?

She said with a gentle firmness: Educated people, I think Brenda means.

DURING MY FRESHMAN YEAR of college, after I'd taken off into the city from that hotel out by LaGuardia instead of going home with my parents for the nearly monthlong Christmas vacation like I was supposed to, I stayed on in Manhattan, first at the family apartment of a friend from my dorm. When that college friend's flight from Rochester, the nearest airport to Wagosh, was canceled because of a snowstorm, his parents sent a limousine to bring him all the way from Broener to the city, and knowing I planned to take a bus there in a couple of days to meet my parents, he invited me to come along and stay at his place. I'd never ridden in a limo before. It steadily ploughed through the blizzard and blowing snow like a coast guard cutter down the endless thruway all the way to New York City. This is real money, I realized for maybe the first time in my life. Here is what real money does. My friend's family apartment was on Park Avenue, but he had his own little apartment attached to theirs with a private entrance. I never got to go upstairs where his parents and sisters lived, though once I saw his mother, looking like Cleopatra in a shiny black-and-gold dress, a long fur coat draped over her shoulders, coming down the stairs from that main apartment to the lobby.

I didn't want to go back to Broener after the Christmas break. I couldn't face being in my dorm, living on the same floor as the Adonis, where Abbie Schneider had practically moved into his room. The Adonis must have known that all I'd done with Abbie during our more than a month as a couple was make out until our lips were like chewed-on balloons, feel her up outside her bra, and JesusHChristdryfuckinghump. They must have shared some sweet laughs over that, mixing ridicule, bafflement, and hilarity as they cuddled in intimate bliss, she even faking pity and affectionately scolding him for having too much fun with his cruel mockery. Who else had they told? I was sure that if I had to go back to Broener again I could die from the humiliation of it. The city represented the chance for a new start, and though I really didn't know how I was going to survive, I felt different to myself just walking out onto the city sidewalks. By the end of that initial week in New York, I'd found a job at a florist shop on Broadway on the Upper West Side, where during those first several days, I must have tied thousands of pine cones onto Christmas wreaths with bits of wire. Soon I was renting a tiny bedroom in a nearby apartment too. After Christmas, six days a week, I was up at dawn to drive the florist's van down to the wholesale flower market on Twenty-Eighth Street in Chelsea to pick up the flower orders. Most of these came packed inside long cartons, wrapped in wet newspapers from all over the world: Colombia, South Africa, the Netherlands, Ecuador, South Korea, Costa Rica, Haiti. Occasionally the tropical flowers, birds-of-paradise, heart-shaped red anthuriums with long yellow stamens, heliconia, voluptuously fragrant tuberoses, came wrapped in Guatemalan newspapers, and some of the orchids, packed inside crates with moist mossy jungle earth, were from Guatemala too. Down in the basement workroom, I'd spend the rest of the morning sorting flowers and snapping thorns off rose stems, while constantly enduring raunchy homosexual teasing from the owner, Steve, a diminutive, hirsute Jewish Buddhist horticulturalist with pointy elf ears, and Howie, the Cheerful Fat Slob Master Flower Arranger, as I'd privately nicknamed him. They weren't a couple, but they gave the impression that in the past they'd had a thing. Sweetie Pie, Howie used to call me. Upstairs, the ferny, earthy, nutrient-enriched smells of deep forest rot, sweet blossoms, and photosynthetic saturation of the flower shop's misty air made it like being inside a cloud forest. Everyone kept their jackets or sweaters on except for Howie, who always worked in an old flannel shirt, usually wildly unbuttoned, sliding off and baring his blotchy ham-hock shoulder or exposing hairless belly blubber, the maw of his navel hanging out over his belt like a screaming Edvard Munch face. Downstairs in the workroom he'd lewdly tease me: Is Sweetie Pie a cherry pie or a blue-ball pie? and Steve would cackle. Shut the fuck up, I was always shouting at them. Leave me alone! Shut the fuck up! I'm not a fag! I'd pretend to menace them with flower-cutting shears. They'd run into corners as if to hide, laughing. They made me laugh, but I made them laugh more. I regarded their harassing antics as part of the "New York experience."

Around noon, I'd go back out in the van again until nearly evening, delivering flowers and plants. Often, after apartment building doormen put down their intercom phones and waved me in, I brought flowers up in elevators that opened directly into vestibules that provided peeks into some of the most opulent homes in Manhattan. One elevator man gruffly advised me to show some respect and remove the Red Sox baseball cap I was wearing because the apartment I was bringing flowers to had once belonged to Babe Ruth. Usually I handed the deliveries over to servants but sometimes to women, mostly older, who came out to receive them and who looked so mesmerizingly stylish, artificial, glamorous, women who went outside in winter wearing Russian novel fur hats, long mink coats, hands plunged into muffs, uncanny faces glowing like glasses of neon milk, intense red lips. One afternoon, Yoko Ono, arm in arm with John Lennon, came walking toward me up Broadway, she looking so magnificently leonine with her streaming black hair and darkly lustrous midthigh fur coat, her powerful tread pulling John nearly weightlessly along, pale and waifish in his skimpy black leather jacket and little black cap, my face went red hot, as if I'd been caught spying on their intimacy. I delivered bouquets to young women barely older than myself who lived in apartment buildings without doormen and buzzed me in or came down to the grimy, small lobby in sweatpants to open the door, usually delighted to be getting flowers, lifting the paper cones to their noses and happily exclaiming, some even blushing. Those were the girls who'd earnestly apologize for not being able to give a bigger tip or sometimes any tip at all. But some received their flowers with a smirk or a fed-up roll of the eyes, carrying their bouquet back to the elevator like a dead rabbit by the hind feet.

I was out making deliveries, stuck in clogged traffic near Lincoln Center that February afternoon, when I heard on the van's radio that a massive earthquake had struck Guatemala. Tears blurred my eyes; I had to find somewhere to pull over. Abuelita, the rest of my family, my cousins, had they survived? I hadn't seen Abuelita since the summer after seventh grade, when we'd gone down for the last time with my mother. That was the summer of Abuelita's eightieth birthday party, held in her house and to which all the shopgirls were invited, and there was a marimba band and some traditional Guatemalan dancing. Watching Mamita dance like the village Maya girls, hands clasped behind her back, doing those hopping steps, one heel lifted back at a time, was always a little embarrassing. Whenever I go back to Guatemala and stop into Juguetelandia, I say hello to Amalia, who has worked in the store for at least half a century, so withered and stooped in her blue store smock, her smile like a twist of lipsticked yarn; she always first asks about my mother and then enthuses over that party of thirty years ago like it was the single most festive night of her long life: Ay, Frankie, it was so alegre. Do you remember how even Abuelita danced? It was at that party, in front of everybody, that Abuelita reached up to pinch my cheek and pronounced me the most Montejo of the Montejos, and that made me so happy.

The quake had hit the capital hard, but in the provinces the situation was catastrophic: avalanches, roads and villages buried. In Guatemala City, homes and buildings had collapsed, including a hotel blocks from our family stores . . . thousands feared dead . . . still too early to know. I had to phone home, but I made more in tips than in salary and had to finish my deliveries first. I twisted the radio dial, searching for more news. Over the next few hours, assessments of the disaster were becoming graver and there were urgent pleas for rescue teams and international donations. As soon as I returned to the store, I stood in the middle of the floor telling everyone about the earthquake in Guatemala and my family, repeating the news I'd heard on the radio, my voice rising with emotion and even panic. Why this public display? I suppose I wanted Steve and Howie and also Megan, who worked the cash register and the shop floor, to realize that I was also from this other place, the same country that some of our exotic flowers came from, where now an earthquake had snuffed out thousands of human lives in seconds, maybe including some from my family. But I also wanted to prove to myself that this forceful emotional connection I'd felt to Guatemala and my family in the van hadn't been spurious, that it was real, and so I didn't try to hold back the tears spurting from my eyes and rolling down my cheeks.

Of course Steve said I could phone home, even though it was long distance. My mother answered and said that she'd gotten a telegram from Tío Memo that our family was safe and that she was more worried about me than about Guatemala. I'm doing great, I told her. I have a job, maybe I'll go back to school, I don't know yet. But, Frankie, you got A's on your report card, she pleaded. Yeah, they're not called report cards in college, Ma, just trimester grades. She said, Frankie, we're so proud of you. Daddy wanted to take you out to a good restaurant in New York City and celebrate your *wonderful* grades. Listening to her go on, I felt angry. I wished she'd accuse me of being an ungrateful brat for having left school after my father had paid for it, then I could speak the words I had ready: I'm not going to cost him another cent ever again. I have to go, I said curtly, I'm at work. I remember the expressions of apprehension on Steve and Howie and Megan as they waited for me to finish my call and their smiles of relief when I told them my family was okay. What good, kind people they were. Years later, during one of my returns from Central America, I would drop in to the store and learn that Steve had died of AIDS and that Howie had gone to live in Hawaii.

Down in the basement in the mornings, while I sat on a tall bucket turned upside down, snapping thorns off rose stems, Howie would often tell stories about his extreme nighttime fun in the gay bars, such as offering himself through a hole in the wall to the room full of anonymous men on the other side. If Steve was there, he'd smile sadly with what seemed a Buddhist resignation meant to suggest, I think, that he'd done that, too, and mostly hoped he wouldn't again. Gross, you guys are so fucking disgusting, I'd exclaim, which, of course, made them laugh uproariously. It struck me as a mystery of human temperament how Howie could seem almost always so robustly cheerful, until I decided it was his bravery that fueled the joy he took in his dementedly horny, brazen sexuality, however inconceivable it seemed to someone like me, who until just a few months before had still been sleeping every night in his boyhood bed. Who was more admirable? Howie or Ian Brown, the most brashly sexually individuated person I'd known until Howie? Howie, by a long shot. Steve and Howie may once have been lovers, but now they were good friends. Girls who went out with Ian ended up despising him. I'd decided that Howie the Cheerful Fat Slob Master Flower Arranger, even among the heaped blossoms and plants of his basement worktable, sat atop a kind of Sex Mount Olympus; like a novice monk setting out on a long apostolic journey, all I had to do in order to experience the lowest lowlands was walk around Times Square and stop into any of those peep show or live-sex places. I'd take my place in the daytime parade filing briskly in and out, mostly men in business suits and ties—"fake rich," I'd heard black teenagers taunting some of those business guys out on the sidewalk, mocking their cheap suits and overcoats, even their shoes—but all sorts of other types, too, once inside rarely acknowledging each other's existence for even a split second while at the same time casting hungry eyes all around. Put a quarter in a slot, a window or shutter would open, and you could watch a man and a woman doing sixty-nine or a woman eating out another woman; after about ten seconds the window would close, then you could put in another quarter and the window would open and now the woman's midriff would be quaking in orgasm. Some of the window portals let you poke your hands through, and I got to touch the pale breasts and pebble-like nipples of a girl about my own age, such a nice smile; she told me she was from Honduras and that she liked the way I touched her. I bet you make your girlfriend happy, she said. Even if she'd said that only to get me to drop more quarters in the slot, I left walking on air and also trying to remember exactly how I'd touched her so that I'd be able to do that again. I wondered what would happen if I dared to ask the Honduran girl out on a date. It's not like I went to those places every day, every couple of weeks seems more like it, and while I probably did try to find her, all I remember for sure is that I never saw her again.

During that call from the florist shop, I'd given my mother the phone number of the apartment I was living in. The young couple who lived there, Gail and Blake, had rented me a tiny bedroom with one window that opened on a narrow airshaft. Gail had two mongrel dogs she'd found abandoned on the city streets that were always fighting each other. I hated walking those dogs that always wanted to attack every other dog and old person walking with a cane they passed. She also had a hyper-active orange cat she'd gotten from a shelter. Blake had a late-night jazz show on an obscure radio station and dealt pills. Once, when my father phoned, I managed to hang up after a few words and left the phone off the hook intentionally and then forgot, which infuriated Gail, who'd been trying to reach the apartment for hours from the restaurant where she worked. She was bad-tempered anyway, at least partly because of all the speed she took for her waitress double shifts and because she and Blake were always broke. He was always shouting: Well, if you weren't spending so much on dog food!

Tío Memo phoned me there that same February. He'd come up to New York City like he did every year for the American International Toy

Fair, and he took me to an Italian restaurant in Greenwich Village, where we had a long talk, by far the longest we'd ever had. When I'd come into the restaurant with straightened hair down to my shoulders, my uncle had watched me walk to our table with an expression of hawk-like stern astonishment. Two weeks had passed since the earthquake; the death toll was over twenty thousand. No one in our family had come to harm, and while the stores' employees had all survived, some of their homes had collapsed; relatives had been killed or badly hurt. On the night after the quake, while the aftershocks continued, Abuelita and Tía Nano had slept in their car after their chauffeur, Chepe, had backed it out of the garage and into the empty lot across the street. Chepe, elderly himself and armed with a pistol, had stood guard. We didn't know yet that Abuelita had cancer and was only going to live less than two more years. When the end was near, poor Mamita would cancel her last week of classes leading into the Christmas break to be able to spend more time with her in Guate; when she had to fly back home in late January to start the new semester, Abuelita was still alive. One evening a month later, after her separation from Bert, all alone in the house, Mamita got the telephone call from her brother that she'd been dreading.

In the Italian restaurant, I was still taking bites out of the bread sticks before anything else had been served when I told Tío Memo about having found my mother sobbing in the hotel room. I could see I'd instantly made him uncomfortable. My father makes her really miserable, I said heatedly, the way he makes everyone miserable, but my mother has gotten the worst of it by far, and because she never complains, nobody notices or does anything.

Ahh la gran, sighed my uncle, stretching out the sides of his lips and inhaling through his teeth the way he does. Qué pena, pobre la Yoli. I don't like to hear this. He paused and said, Maybe it was just a bad day. All women are emotional, Frankie.

Rather than give a direct opinion on his sister's marriage, Tío Memo started in on a story about my mother in her youth, as if hiding a clue inside of what initially seemed a tale of affectionate reminiscence. But to this day, I'm confused about the story Tío Memo told me that night. As a rule, we avoid discussing unpleasant topics in the Montejo Hernández family. My uncle especially is always looking for the next chance to say "ala, qué alegre" or "qué alegre, vos," nice words to pronounce. I like saying them, too, in irony or sarcasm but also in goofy joy: Oh, what happiness! But what else is a lifetime of selling toys devoted to, if not getting people to exclaim, Qué alegre!

In their adolescence, said Tío Memo, he and Mamita used to share the same friends, a group of high-spirited ala, qué alegre youths. They'd go out to our family's little chalet on the small lake near the city, Amatitlán, to waterski, or to their friends' coffee fincas for horse-back riding and picnics, and it was always so alegre. But my mother became especially close to one joven, said Tío Memo, who was a good student, an intellectual even—I sensed that my uncle calling him an intellectual was like that Chekhov rule about introducing a pistol in the first act—from a good family, a good family that employed the joven's mother as a servant. Because the boy was so clever and had inherited his father's light complexion, he'd always been allowed to live in that household and was eventually recognized by the father and given his surname. The joven's mother went on working in the house and living in the maids' quarters with her little son during his preschool years, then the father bought her a small home in the rough working-class barrio of La Limonada and gave her a monthly pension. The joven liked spending weekends and school vacations with his mother in La Limonada, where he was the only boy around with fair skin and hair. Tío Memo said that was probably the source of the joven's societal resentments, feeling so torn between opposite worlds. The mother died when the joven was still in adolescence. My uncle and mother attended the funeral, where the coffin was carried to the grave atop a small wooden cart painted yellow, piled with flowers, and pulled by a donkey.

That night in the Greenwich Village Italian restaurant, when Tío Memo was telling me about the intellectual joven and my mother, he must have told me his name. Later I vaguely recalled it being either René, Ramón, or Raul, though I always mix up those names, often to my own embarrassment; whenever I'm introduced to a René, I'm bound to call him Ramón or Raul the next time we meet. That's why I always think of him as el joven. As adolescents, Tío Memo and this youth, el joven, had participated in the student movement—Chiquilines de la Revolución the young people were called—that sparked the peaceful 1944 October Revolution. Everyone was so excited and proud that Guatemala was going to be a democracy. Even my mother, at twelve or thirteen, stood in front of the store handing out campaign leaflets for Arévalo. A couple of years later, Tío Memo went off to college in California and two years after that, my mother followed; the youth went to San Carlos, the public university in Guatemala City. After we came back from California, said my uncle, we didn't see him again. My uncle said that el joven was the type who likes to stay in school forever. A few years later I would learn that people like my uncle liked to describe leftist militants as perpetual students, meaning that the universities were where they could sit around plotting the coming of the workers' and peasants' revolution instead of having to work.

Now I know, though I didn't then, that it was after California and before she went to Boston that Lucio Grassi came into my mother's life, but Tío Memo didn't even mention the Italian. The restaurant was an old-fashioned Venetian trattoria, with white tablecloths and older male waiters in bow ties, most with mustaches. It was a favorite of my uncle's. Over the next twenty years, when Tío Memo came up for the toy fair as he did every February, if I was in the city, too, we'd go back to that restaurant. I always ordered the Venetian-style spaghetti Bolognese.

Yoli always had so many friends, said Tío Memo cheerfully. She was the soul of any party. He let out a blast of laughter and said, But the family never thought her friendship with that joven was good for her. Do you understand what I mean, Frankie, when I say that he was not even good for himself? After a pause, I said, You mean he was self-destructive? Yes, Frankie, self-destructive *and* destructive, said my uncle. That patojo always did what he wanted and never considered how his actions could affect other people. Now I get it, I thought. Tío Memo was pushing the conversation in a direction meant to be instructive for me, who was also behaving, he must have thought, in a self-destructive way, doing whatever I wanted, not taking into consideration how my actions affected my parents.

Suddenly Tío Memo jumped ahead in his story. My mother had already been in Boston for a year or two, the coup happened, and the joven destructivo was one of the hundreds of Guatemalans who fled to the Mexican embassy. Three months would pass before the new government would allow those refugees to go into exile, most to Mexico.

You mean he was in the Árbenz government, I said.

Not that I know of, said my uncle. He was more what they call a fellow traveler. Do you know that term?

I've heard it, I said. People were always being smeared with it back in the fifties, right? Okay, so this self-destructive lefty guy was friends with my mother. But what do you mean, Tío? How friendly were they? Was my mother a fellow traveler too?

My uncle seemed to find that genuinely funny; he sat back and enjoyed a hearty laugh. No, Frankie. Yoli wasn't interested in things like that, he finally said. They were just good friends, you know, the way young people are, joking and laughing about any silly thing.

What kinds of silly things, I asked. Do you remember an example, Tío?

My uncle did seem to think that over for a while, which I assumed was for show. But then he said, One time three of us went to the movies together, and maybe because the joven was hungry or had indigestion, his stomach kept growling, loudly enough so that if you were sitting nearby you heard it. And Yoli leaned her head close to his stomach and said, Shhhh, naughty stomach, we're trying to watch the movie! Well,

that joven's stomach answered her with its loudest growl yet! I don't
know how he did it, like a ventriloquist. Now they did have to leave the
theater, because they couldn't stop laughing. Ala, qué alegre, Frankie.

My uncle's story made me laugh, too, even though it didn't seem
to have anything to do with the subject of my mother's unhappiness.
But Mamita wasn't all we talked about in the restaurant that night.
Tío Memo had his mission, to find out what was really going on with
me and convince me to go back to college. Wasn't it true, he asked,
that I'd gotten all A's for grades? That was true, I admitted. Then why
didn't I want to go back? Was college too easy? There's a jovencita
behind this, verdad, Frankie? My uncle leaned forward, like now we
were getting down to the truth. No, really, there isn't, Tío, I said. I
wish, but no, no girl. I saw alarm in my uncle's eyes. Maybe he was
thinking, Frankie ran away from college because he was upset about
Yoli? And now here he is, with his girlish straightened hair. What a
strange boy my nephew is.

Even before I'd started working in the flower shop, with some of
the money my college friend had lent me I'd had my hair straightened
again by a super cute, chatty boricua lesbian with hair dyed glossy
pink at a unisex hair salon up on Amsterdam, who when I was leaving
said, If you were a girl, I'd go out with you, and she kissed me, leaving a pink cloudlet of lipstick on my cheek. My hair was now longer
than ever, tangled and viny like I'd dreamed it could be, something
like how Jim Morrison's hair must have looked at the end of his life
or even like Chantal Goya's hair after wild sex. Everywhere I went in
the city girls smiled at me, though nothing had happened with any
of them. I'd developed a crush on Gail, who seemed to want to break
up with her boyfriend who was never home anyway. Every evening
I faithfully walked her horrible dogs in Riverside Park. Gail was an
inch or two over five feet, with a fey prettiness and slanted sleepy eyes
and wavy black hair that snaked to her bony hips, and like most New
York waitresses, she wanted to be an actress. The other night I'd gone

to meet her in the Dublin House after her waitressing shift. We were both a little drunk when she gestured toward another young woman in a red leather jacket and a so-called little black dress leaning against the back wall and said, I want to fuck her. I said, I want to be a lesbian. Gail laughed, put her small hands in my hair, and said, Too bad you're not one, then. I'm ridiculous and pathetic, I thought, sitting opposite my uncle. My face felt hot and prickly. I lifted a cloth napkin over my face and pretended to sneeze. Frankie, estás bien? my uncle asked. I excused myself and went to the men's room, where in the mirror I saw that my skin had slightly broken out in hives. I leaned over the sink splashing cold water over my face.

Over dessert, a sticky dark chocolate-and-cherry roll called Vampire Cake, I asked my uncle if I could come to Guatemala and stay in his house. What I was telling myself was that New York City is fucking me up, I should go to Guatemala to help the earthquake victims. He said, You know you are always welcome, Frankie, but I think it would be better if you went back to college first.

My uncle did know how to tell a story in a way that made you sense, in the nonsense cake he was baking, darker layers of frosting, which as soon as you tried to taste them with your finger turned to air. All I wanted my uncle to say was that I've always known Bert was an hijo de la gran puta, and my sister ruined her life by marrying him.

Ay Yoli, Tío Memo suddenly blurted. Pobrecita, la Yoli.

Sí, Tío, pobrecita, I practically cried out. Allowing myself that exclamation was like squeezing a sponge, and my eyes filled with tears that probably weren't only for my mother.

A few weeks later I'd go to a barber, cut my hair short, and head back to Broener for the spring trimester. But by the next January I'd be back in New York, transferring into a special program at the New School.

As we were finishing our coffees, Tío Memo said something that took me by surprise. He said, That joven, not so joven anymore, turned up in Boston and found Yoli there.

Maybe because I'd been silently dwelling on my own problems, it didn't occur to me to ask if this muchacho's coming to Boston had happened before or after I was born.

When my uncle said a moment later that my mother had sent el joven away and told him not to bother her anymore, I sensed he was improvising. Who knows where he is now, said Tío Memo. Cuba, probably, and he guffawed at the idea of el joven ending up in Communist Cuba instead of Guatemala, the Little Land of the Free.

On some of those previous visits to Green Meadows, I'd asked my mother if she remembered her old friend who came to look for her in Boston. Every time I asked, she really did seem to think it over before shaking her head no or saying, Frankie, I don't remember. Well, I'd said across the Scrabble board during our last visit, I don't know if his name was René, Ramón, or Raul. Maybe his name was Rodrigo or Roberto. Maybe it was Juan, Tomás, Diego, Gonzalo, Miguel—

Miguel? she pronounced softly. What do you mean, Miguel? There was a quiet note of defiance in my mother's voice.

Before I leave today, I'm going to ask my mother who Miguel was.


Mami, that tooth Daddy made for you? I ask. You still have it, right?

She doesn't respond. She looks back at me as if she didn't hear me and is waiting for me to resume our conversation.

One evening, when I was about eleven, when Bert had taken the family out to dinner, he presented Mamita with a velvet ring box. When she opened it, instead of a ring with a radiant gem, she found a radiant artificial tooth. But my mother seemed happy with her gift and laughed gaily with her napkin held over her mouth. She'd been going around with an Alfred E. Neuman smile for months, a gummy gap where a central incisor had been pulled. My father must have put all of his expertise into that tooth, trying to achieve perfection as his craft defined it.

You do remember that Daddy made a tooth for you, I ask, don't you?
Yes, I do, Frankie, she says.

Smile, I say, and she smiles. Her front teeth all look pretty much
the same, healthy considering her age. I can't tell which one is the im-
plant, though.

My father hated the words "false teeth." What's false about them?
he'd growl at anyone who called them that. When you don't get it right,
that's when it looks *fake*, I remember him shouting. A false tooth is a
badly made tooth. I can spot one of those in somebody's mouth from
ten feet away!

Artificial tooth, prosthetic tooth, those were the correct terms. "A
mix of science and art," once you start doing some research into the field
you repeatedly come across that description. Bert was a chemical engineer
but also a color scientist or a color chemist. I've also learned from the
scientific histories that modern ceramic artificial tooth production has
its origins in the methods and discoveries of the European alchemists
and Kabbalists. So does the story behind Mary Shelley's *Frankenstein*.
(How did Frankenstein get his "pearly white teeth"?) Bert the alchemist,
a contemporary practitioner of that ancient sacred craft of the Kabbalists. I only need to slide my laptop out of my backpack like this, set it
on my lap, and open the desktop file titled (sorry Dad) FalseTeeth to
find these notes copied from a journal:

"Light passes through porcelain in a manner that makes it seem
both luminous and internally lit. An artificial tooth formed from porcelain materials, containing finely divided opacifying particles, including
refracting pigment particles, can refract and transmit light in a manner
exactly resembling the opalescence of a natural tooth."

Mamita, smile again, please, I say. Just hold that smile a sec. I pull
my phone from my pocket and take a picture of my mother's smile.

* * *

I was a year out of college when I did go to live in Tío Memo's house in Guatemala City. Most days I holed up in my cousin's bedroom—Freddy was studying at Texas Tech—on the side of the garden opposite the main house, trying to write the three short stories required for my MFA school applications, and spent most of my free time hanging out with the primas, my two teenage girl cousins, and their friends. On a whim, I also submitted those stories to the fiction editor of a magazine in New York whose name, whenever my primas tried to pronounce it, came out sounding like *Er-squirrel.* A few months later I was back in New York, living in a rented loft over a vacuum cleaner shop on Fourteenth Street with three roommates, including Frecky Papperman, and was still half-asleep the morning that he brought the phone with the long cord into my little plywood alcove down at the loft's noisy street end: A Mr. Rust, said Frecky, is on the line. It turned out that *Er-squirrel's* venerable fiction editor was phoning to tell me that he wanted to publish two of the three short stories I'd sent to the magazine. One of those stories was inspired by Space Cavanaugh's toolshed, the other was partly about Gail and her dogs and the flower shop. Afterward, I lingered in bed trying to absorb that news and finally chose a book from the pile next to my mattress that seemed appropriate to this life-changing moment, a paperback of the Carlos Baker biography of Ernest Hemingway, and opened it at the index, found my name, and turned to the page where I read that on a November morning in 1981, Francisco Goldberg learned that he'd become a published writer too. *HaHaHa, our Hemingway here, you don't have the character, the guts . . .*

The young editorial assistant in charge of the slush pile told me later that it was the anomaly of receiving a manila envelope covered with Guatemalan airmail stamps that made her curious to read what was inside. Thanks to that stroke of luck, I was earning my living as a writer—I'd sold my stories for a thousand dollars each—and so I decided not to accept the offer of a scholarship to an MFA program and spend the next few years in the middle of cornfields working on *In the Toolshed and Other Stories*. Instead, I wrote my first "war correspondent" article for *Er-squirrel*—its new owners said they wanted to bring "new blood" into the magazine's journalism—about what was going on in Guatemala, as depicted, mostly, through the eyes of my primas and their friends. "My father says that every morning now when he goes for his jog he runs past at least one dead body flung onto the side of the road." "People are saying it's going to be a Black November, that the Mayas are going to come down from the mountains into the city with their machetes and slaughter us all!" When Bonzo was elected president, Tío Memo and Tía Meche were ecstatic, they scorned the previous US president as Jimmy Castro. Human rights only meant rights for Communists. In my article I didn't only describe life inside those upper-middle-class high walls that shut out so much of the annihilation going on beyond them, but I also tried to portray my own guilt and confusion over being trapped behind them too. A striking thing is that Tío Memo never said a negative word about my article, at least not to me, even though so much of it drew on what I'd observed while living in his house.

One evening during that year in Guatemala City, my aunt and uncle had thrown a cocktail party, which is where I'd met Ursula, who'd come with her parents. She was around my age, maybe a year or two younger, a skinny girl in an unfashionable yellow dress that I guessed her parents had made her wear since she seemed so uncomfortable in it. Her father was a lot older than Tío Memo yet seemed to defer to him. It turned out that Ursula was a medical student at the public university, San Carlos. Holding our weak scotch and sodas, served in glasses neatly swaddled in paper napkins, as is the genteel custom down there so that your fingers won't get cold, we began our obligatory conversation. Whatever we were making small talk about was swiftly subsumed by the urgency in her pale-brown eyes, magnified by her eyeglass lenses, and her determined voice. Once a week, Ursula told me, she had a forensic medicine class in the Hospital Roosevelt morgue. Some days, when she got there, there were so many bodies they had to be stacked like firewood on the floor. I remember her exact words: And you should see the condition they arrive in.

*I should see.* Well, probably, I should, but . . . In a small staff nook in that hospital a few days later, I pulled on, over my clothes, the doctor's robe Ursula had handed me. She tucked a pair of examination gloves into its pocket and hung a stethoscope around my neck, an odd instrument for where we were going. We went into the morgue. There weren't bodies stacked like firewood that day, but there were corpses laid out on three of the concrete autopsy tables. The cement floor had a wet sheen, as if just hosed. Up until that day, the only dead person I'd seen, a peek into the open coffin, was shrunken Grandpa Moe in a suit and tie and white yarmulke. On the autopsy table closest to us lay the corpse of a young man with a trimly muscular body, a handsome face with Amerindian features, eyes serenely closed, skin youthfully toned and damp, a black mustache, soft-looking instead of bristly, and wisps of chin hair. His torso and arms were speckled with brownish dots. Ursula whispered, Those are cigarette burns. What looked like a popped blister, circular and pink, was where his penis should have been. His smooth feet were unblemished and melancholy looking, pointing up as if gazing back at his face. What we were doing was risky, and I suppose other things besides risky, and we quickly left. As soon as we got into her car, one of those little hatchbacks, she asked if I'd noticed that his throat had been slit. I hadn't. They'd already cleaned him, she said, and washed away the blood.

Afterward we went to a restaurant in la Zona Viva, owned by a Belgian, where we ordered quiche and salad and tried to have a normal conversation. Over the years, I've often described that visit to the morgue as "the day I became a journalist." As if just asking the inevitable questions—who was he, who did this to him, and why?—sent me tumbling down a rabbit hole that I came out the other end of changed into a journalist. Probably all of Guatemala knew who was doing that, to young men and women especially, and why. Then what difference could it make to see it for yourself? Because to witness something like that implicates you, it allows that reality to go on living inside you, growing darker, more impenetrable, unless you accept the challenge of living with it and trying to make it clearer instead of ever darker and more confusing. Though, of course, you can also try to run from it. But could even the most astute and veteran journalist explain to me how the murdered torture victim in the morgue and having quiche for lunch in the Belgian's restaurant fit coherently together inside the same hour—or even inside the same life? I remember our lunch, the quiche and salad, as vividly as I do the morgue. We didn't eat in complete silence, but I don't remember anything we said, just an impression of Ursula's eyes like small wet leaves stuck to the inside of her eyeglass lenses. I wondered what came next. It didn't seem possible that all that was going to happen after lunch was that she was going drive me back to my uncle's house, but that was all that happened.

I left that story about the morgue out of that first magazine journalism piece so as not to expose Ursula to any danger. Later I heard that her parents had sent her to live in California.

Before I leave the nursing home today, I'm going to show my mother that photograph of her maternal grandfather posing with her mother, Abuelita, when she was young. I have the photo in my backpack. I brought it last visit, too, though that time I didn't take it out in the end. I didn't want to upset her, even though I do think it's only right that she see it. Like el joven, my mother's father was an illegitimate child, but that was never a secret. My mother always told us about her grandfather Colonel Montejo, who'd recognized Abuelito as his son. My mother knows the names of both her grandfathers, but she's never been able to tell me who her grandmothers were.

Mami, I'd insist, it's impossible that your father never spoke to you about his own mother. He never did, she'd respond, like that was normal.

The few times I'd asked Tío Memo, he'd answered pretty much the same: Ay Frankie, a saber, who knows. Maybe my abuelo's mother was a prostitute or a beautiful concubine. Maybe she was a servant, like el joven's mother.

Abuelita's father, Luis Hernández, emigrated from Spain and became a rancher, Mamita always had stories to tell about her maternal grandfather. His true calling as a cattle rancher came to him late in life, after years of failing to strike it rich, that's how that gachupín-in-the-tropics legend went. In some versions, he started out as a cattle rustler, riding with his outlaw cowboys into El Salvador to steal his first herds. In Guatemala, those herds prospered and multiplied, as did the number of his ranches. He became mayor of his pueblo and married the prettiest niña living there. In the family history that my mother and uncle shared, that girl, their grandmother, was always an adolescent, and Luis Hernández was always around fifty. She gave him six children, four boys and two girls, but she died giving birth to Tía Nano, Abuelita's little sister whom Mamita always loved like a second mother. What was the name of that prettiest girl in the pueblo, Mamita, who gave birth to the Spanish rancher's six children, including your own mother and aunt? My mother didn't know her name or anything else about her.

You mean you don't know the names of either of your grandmothers, and that doesn't bother you. You were never even curious? I'd often pester her. No, it didn't bother her. She was never even curious.

After my great-grandfather the Spanish rancher died, his four sons inherited ranches, and his two daughters, Abuelita and Tía Nano, came to the capital with their dowry trunks to live in a boardinghouse, a finishing school–type place run by twin sisters from France. Abuelito managed one of the big general stores on Séptima Avenida in the center, and on weekends he sold imported toys from Germany and France from a pushcart in the city's Parque Central, in front of the cathedral. On one of those Sundays in the park, he met Abuelita.

Two nameless great-grandmothers, like two holes in the head. The missing identity of the Spanish rancher patriarch's wife, my great-grandmother, was the most perplexing family mystery. Until, about a year ago, when a letter from Guatemala arrived for me at my publisher's in New York by regular post. How easily that envelope could have been mislaid had that young editorial assistant who opened it, recognizing its potential importance to me, not express mailed it to Mexico City. Inside that envelope was a private letter and a photograph. The letter was from a woman named Sandra Hernández, who wrote that we were related through the Hernández family. We must be close in age. She'd been meaning to write to me since reading an interview in a Guatemalan newspaper in which I'd mentioned not knowing anything about either of my two great-grandmothers. "First of all, I can tell you that our great-grandparents hailed from Los Esclavos, Santa Rosa, on the Costa Sur," Sandra wrote. "Our great-grandfather's name was Luis Hernández, by profession a farmer and cattle rancher, and our great-grandmother was named Francisca García. Everyone called her Panchita. As the color of her skin demonstrated, she was of African origin. Your great-grandmother Panchita was beloved by all for her lively personality, the strength of her character, and for her kindness. She died in childbirth, to her infant daughter, María, who became known as Nano. That, Francisco, was what was passed down from my abuelo to my father and to us, about our great-grandmother." That's the part of the letter I know by heart now, though it was several pages long, telling the whole story of the Hernández rancher clan, generation by generation, down to Sandra and her own children. When Luis Hernández died, his ranches were left to his oldest son; orphaned Abuelita, exiled by her brothers to the city with her baby sister and their meager, landless inheritances, severed relations with the family forever after. Sandra Hernández is now a professor of women's studies and feminism at the Universidad de San Carlos in Guatemala City. "About your family on the Montejo side," she wrote, "all I know is that your grandfather committed suicide."

Abuelita's mother was black, so that was the big family secret. On the Costa Sur, mostly to work the sugar plantations in the lowland heat that so many highland Maya couldn't endure, the Spaniards had brought in African slaves from the Caribbean plantations. That Abuelita was a mulatta, with her flat nose and wide nostrils, her broad cheeks, even her heavy-lidded eyes, now seemed obvious in her photographs, though that had never occurred to me before. Mamita, with her orange kinky hair, was what used to be called, in a city like New Orleans, a quadroon. What Sandra wrote about Abuelito having committed suicide was also new to me. I assumed he must have been bipolar, maybe schizophrenic, but I'd always understood that it was being struck by a bus in downtown Guatemala City that had killed him. After all, Don Paco was known to be always in a hurry, speeding along the sidewalks with the shiny dome of his bald head lowered while pedestrians parted to make way. It seemed believable that he'd accidentally collided with a bus, I still consider that the likeliest version. But I also understand that if Abuelito did commit suicide, even by intentionally ramming his head into an oncoming bus, it would have been kept secret from my sister and me and our cousins. When I was a boy, my mother had let slip some stories about her father's "colorful" manic episodes, really bouts of full-throttle madness. On random mornings, inexplicably singing Verdi arias at the top of his lungs, Abuelito would bolt from the house out into the city, inevitably ending up in a brothel and giving away family money and properties to whores. He only sang Verdi arias during his attacks of madness. Abuelita managed to get all their banking accounts and properties put solely under her own name, an unprecedented maneuver for a woman in those days, but the rough cattle rancher's mulatta daughter with the French finishing school polish, if that wasn't a fiction, too, always had friends where it counted. Tío Memo used to have to chase his father down and get him into a straitjacket. Then they'd take the slow United Fruit Company train with its open-air wooden carriages that ran through the heart of the banana plantations, a tunnel of emerald green with stops named for Ivy League colleges, to Puerto Barrios, where they'd book a cabin on a banana boat—some of the human passengers were also bananas!—to New Orleans so that Abuelito could receive electric shock therapy. After I included some of those stories in my first novel, my mother reacted as if from now on everywhere she went people were going to say, There's that poor woman, insanity runs in her family. Nobody should risk marrying her children. Whether anyone ever reacted in the way my mother feared isn't the point, I'd violated her ingrained discretion and decorum. From then on, she hardly ever passed up a chance to say to her Guatemalan relatives and friends: Don't tell Frankie anything. He'll put it in a book.

The photograph that my distant cousin Sandra Hernández sent with her letter was a copy of an old-fashioned studio portrait of great-grandfather Luis posing with his adolescent daughter, Abuelita. With his wrinkled dark suit, dusty shoes, thick double-buckle belt, splendid white mane, self-assured posture, and hard-ass expression, though I sense an underlying sadness, too, he did look like a ruthless cattle rustler who became a prosperous, no less ruthless rancher and mayor. But no way was he a Spaniard.

Now I take the photograph out of my backpack, pull it from its envelope, and lay it down atop the Scrabble board for my mother to see. I tell her about the letter from her distant relative, Sandra Hernández, a professor at San Carlos. Your abuela's name was Francisca, I say, but everyone called her Panchita. Panchita had African ancestry, I say lightly. She was black.

My mother giggles and clucks her tongue, says, Ay Frankie, that's not true.

But your abuelito looks like an intimidating rascal, I cheerfully press on. Doesn't he? Ma, really, what an impressive-looking man. You should be proud. I can't help adding: But he sure wasn't a Spaniard.

My mother stares down at the photograph, white scalp showing through her orangey curls. This is too much for her to process now. All those years that my mother stood over the sink straightening her hair and dyeing it from orange to black, was she fully aware of what she was hiding and why? Did my father even know, suspect, or have any opinion about it?

Though my abuelos aren't here to explain themselves, it seems obvious they made their own mothers disappear in order to protect their children from knowing the truth about their own forebears and from the social repercussions of others finding out. In the case of great-grandma Panchita, at least, it was racial shame.

Abuelita looks so lovely, I say. Doesn't she? Isn't it wonderful to have this photo of Abuelita when she was so young?

A slight smile forms on my mother's lips, and her expression is rheumy-dreamy. My heart clenches. Mamita so loved her mother. I put the photograph away. It's not as if some major injustice has been righted, not even the injustice committed inside one family. But I'm glad to have this photograph. I'm happy to have found out that my great-grandfather Luis Hernández looked like such a Don Cabrón and that he wasn't a Spaniard. I'm even happier to have an idea of who my great-grandmother was. I love that she was named Panchita. If I ever have a daughter, I'll name her Panchita.

Yolandita was an angel, exclaims Mamita. She was like a little doll! I told her I'm seeing Feli tomorrow, and she started going on about Yolandita like she always does whenever I mention Feli. She holds her hands out imploringly and says, Did you know that two days after Yolandita passed away, her husband, Richard, went jogging and had a heart attack and died? Frankie, he died of a broken heart.

My mother's feelings toward Feli are more complicated than her feelings toward Yolandita, deeper, harder for her to express. Feli's second marriage has been happy and solid, and she has raised daughters who went to university and have their own careers, both married to successful husbands too. Feli studied the stock market and made smart investments with her husband's earnings. She is also a straight talker whose directness at times must have offended my mother or punctured illusions.

I'm going to see María Xum, too, I tell my mother. Remember María Xum, Mamita? She barely spoke Spanish when she came to live with us. K'iche' or Kaqchikel or one of those was her first language, remember? My mother seems to be trying to recall María Xum but not succeeding. Remember that time you caught María eating a stick of butter with a knife and fork in the middle of the night? I ask. You had to explain to her that it wasn't that kind of food.

My mother is staring down at the Scrabble board, and with what seems a slightly effortful lifting of her hands, she plucks up two tiles and pushes them into place beneath the *m* in MUSA.

M

U

X

Mux, I say. Qué bueno, Ma. Xum backward. Or is that a Maya word?

My mother looks back at me. She even looks a little guilty, and I have to squeeze the muscles inside my cheeks not to laugh.


Soon after the coup, but before my mother met my father, Dolores Ojito's parents sailed with friends on a yacht from Izabál and the Río Dulce to Miami, from where they were going to fly to Boston to visit her. But the yacht disappeared in a storm, no survivors. Lolita changed overnight, said Mamita that time when she first told me the story. She retreated into her relationship with a Boston College grad student in philosophy and within months they were married. He became a professor and later an administrator at the college. Though Dolores used to occasionally come to events at the Latin American Society of New England, it's been years since my mother last saw or heard from her.

Maybe the Guatemalan consul in Boston was replaced by a new consul after the coup, and maybe Mamita was replaced, too, or else decided to leave on her own. But her next job was as a bilingual secretary at the Potashnik Tooth Company, and the way she always told the story of how she met my father is that she was habitually late for work, something the consul must have tolerated but that her new boss didn't. The day she was fired, Bert Goldberg, head of Potashnik's artificial teeth lab, found her weeping by a drinking fountain in a corridor and asked her to dinner. Despite his unglamorous-sounding job and his being almost twenty years older, he was an athletic bachelor about town with colorful friends: rakish sportswriters, crusty gamblers, wisecracking World War II veterans from his boyhood Dorchester neighborhood, including one who was now a Boston portrait painter, even a blind coin collector. In his forties, Bert Goldberg, playing for the University Club, had been state Class B squash champion, and he invited the young bilingual secretary to some of his matches. Sitting in the spectator seats elevated above that cramped, white box, Mamita watched my father and his rival scuttling around in short white pants, swatting at the speedy black pea ricocheting off the walls and corners. Bert had once played Cape Cod League baseball, not that that meant anything to my mother. He eventually let Mamita know about some of the immigrant hardships he'd endured as a boy, how his father had made him sell potatoes from a pushcart after school when he was only eight and how his mother, Rose, had died when he was in early adolescence.

When he met my mother, Bert was living with Uncle Lenny and Aunt Milly at their house in Waban. At my father's funeral, Cousin Denise affectionately recalled that when she was a girl her uncle Bert used to sneak into her bedroom to hide presents inside her shoes. Lexi once told me, that our father, during his courtship of Mamita, used to take her to the most fashionable restaurants and nightclubs in Boston. When those Zbiggy Brzezinski grad student types also invited her out, she delighted in knowingly name-dropping restaurants and clubs she knew those muchachos usually couldn't afford to take her to. Lexi said that Mamita thought that was part of the fun of going out with an older man. Jewish, no less. What did that matter? Lucio Grassi, who claimed to be a devout Catholic, had stolen from her and lied. Maybe by taking Mamita to those expensive places, Bert gave her a misleading impression of wealth.

*   *   *

I've wheeled Mamita upstairs to her room again. She sits on her bed
with her back to Susan Cornwall, who's returned from her hospital out-
ing. I'm in the chair in the corner facing my mother, the tin of French
butter cookies on my lap. We've each just eaten a cookie. I offered one
to Susan Cornwall, too, who now, on her back under her blanket, is
eating her cookie in slow, savoring nibbles. Since we returned to her
room, Mamita's been answering my questions without even the usual
hesitation. I offer her another cookie, take one for myself, and, sensing
that there's not going to be a better moment than this one, I ask, Mami,
in all the years you were with Daddy, did you ever have an affair?

She's just taken a bite of her cookie, and as if stimulated by baked
French butter and sugar and a humming "afternoon tea" lucidity, Mamita
answers, Yes, I did.

You did, Ma, really?

Yes, she says. She smiles wanly and says, Just one, Frankie.

Was his name Miguel? I ask.

But Frankie, how do you know that? Yes, Miguel, she says, slightly
widening her eyes. He was from Mexico City. He worked for Honeywell.
But Honeywell brought him to Boston for a year to learn about their
new computers.

It's so obvious that they must have met at the Latin American
Society of New England that I don't even ask. Mamita, I say, I'm really
happy to hear this. I'm so happy for you that you had a love affair. She
sits back, her expression girlishly complacent. My words are heartfelt,
but I also feel a little bad. Still, I can't stop myself and ask, Mamita,
when you and Miguel wanted to be alone together, where did you go?

Sometimes we used to meet at the Hilltop Sheraton, she answers.

The Hilltop Sheraton, really? It's as if the French butter cookies
have drugged my mother like a truth serum. The Hilltop Sheraton is
in our town, out by Route 128. On summer nights in high school we'd

sometimes sneak into the swimming pool there. I ask, This was around when I was in high school, right?

She thinks this over and says, Yes, it was.

So what happened?

What happened? Well, he had to go back to Mexico, Frankie.

Ay, Mami, I say, I'm so sorry. Were you very sad?

Yes, I was sad, she says.

Did you love him, Ma?

And with that tone of voice and enunciation that reminds me of a polite contestant in a 1950s quiz show who masters her composure even as she knows she is providing the winning answer, Mamita says, Yes, I did love him, Frankie.

And this Miguel, he's the one who gave you *The Teachings of Don Juan* and those other Carlos Castaneda books?

She laughs quietly. Oh, I don't remember, she says. But he did like to read.

"I am a controlled warrior," I say. Do you remember that one, Ma, your favorite Don Juan quote?

Recognition like two tiny fragile bubbles of light float up into her eyes, is that what that is? Do you remember, Ma? I repeat. "I am a controlled warrior."

She giggles a little. Yes, she says. I do. Now she's smiling to herself.

Was he kind of a hippie type?

He had long hair, she says and laughs again. But not as long as yours used to be! But, yes, Frankie, he enjoyed life.

He enjoyed life, I repeat. But, you mean, in a laid-back way.

In a what way? she asks.

He wasn't a drinker or a big party guy, I say.

Oh no, she says. He had a tranquil personality.

A tranquil personality, not like Daddy.

Ay no, she says.

Do you still think about Miguel?

It was only a year, you know, she says. And only in Boston. But I have some good memories of Miguel, yes, and she smiles with closed lips.

After he left, did you ever see him again, Ma?

I was going to take a summer course on Mexican writers in Cuernavaca, on Juan Rulfo and some others, she says. She pauses, seems to be holding herself as still as she can as if that will help her remember, though suddenly her eyelashes rapidly blink. But, no, she says, I didn't go, Frankie. We never saw each other again. She sits with her hands folded in her lap, staring off, but when she shifts her gaze to me, she lifts one hand over the end of her chair's arm, raises her chin, a look like calm satisfaction in her eyes and an avid glint behind, like the very tip of a new memory rising. Something in her posture and poise reminds me of that oil portrait of her in her evening gown that hung in our living room. Now she looks down at the floor.

Well, I'm proud of you, Mami, I say. That you were brave enough to do that, to have your love affair.

Yes, Frankie, she says. She looks up again, slightly furrows her brow for a moment, then reaches her hand out for another cookie, and I hold the tin out to her.


I feel like a burglar who's broken into her memory. But I also have this thought, which doesn't exculpate me: Besides that warning, this is another reason that I came back from Mexico, to visit my mother at Green Meadows and ask all the questions that finally led to this one. It's as if I've been slowly making my way through the dark narrow streets of her fading memories to finally discover this one room of light and calm where she keeps, instead of cardboard boxes filled with heels and soles, her most precious secret.

Where was my mother sitting within herself, what did she see around her, as she spoke to me? Maybe the past or a dream state or a fantasy had displaced the present. Was she really aware of what she was

sharing with me? By tomorrow she might not even remember we had
that conversation. But I also sense that she won't have forgotten Miguel,
that even if she sometimes loses her way trying to get back to the room,
she goes there regularly.


Mamita didn't go to Cuernavaca that summer. Someone, Mamita or
Miguel or maybe both together, decided that she shouldn't. But during
several summers when we were small children, into at least our middle
school years, she did sometimes go abroad to take courses of at least a
few weeks' duration. The courses qualified her to teach rudimentary
literature classes rather than only give language instruction. She went
to Mexico City, to the UNAM, more than once to Spain. In Madrid
one summer, she studied golden age literature in a program also attended by students from the University of Havana and came home
from it with an adamant dislike of Cuban men. Los Cubanos son
muy groseros, no son caballeros, son tremendos, she was always saying
things like that and also that they were loud. At first I thought it was
that they were loyal Fidelistas and Communists who'd mocked her
for being from Guatemala, a servile, humiliated American colony, the
country that had let its territory be used to train the soldiers who went
on to take part in the Bay of Pigs invasion, where they were soundly
routed. Only a few years ago, it dawned on me that there was probably another reason Mamita always looked so perturbed whenever I
brought up Cuba and Cubans, whether telling her about my own trips
to the island or even asking her again to tell me about those Cubans
she'd studied with years ago in Madrid. Son tan groseros, Frankie. No
tienen respeto. In what ways, Mamita? I asked, and she twisted her
face into a grimace, clucked her teeth, and said, You know, they're so
aggressive and rude. How, you mean about politics? Ay no, Frankie,
ya. Mami, I said, laughing, I know what it is. They used to come on to
you and openly flirt with you, right? I bet they teased you about what

a prude you are. What did you expect, I said. A beautiful chapina all by herself in Madrid, and everyone knows what Cuban men are like. And she tightly pursed her lips and turned away, and I could tell she didn't want me to see the amusement in her eyes or even that she was stifling a laugh. But that's also how I knew that it wasn't anything truly horrible that had happened to her with those Communist literature student Cubanos in Madrid.

I get it, Mamá. Geeky hippie-ish romantic intelligent Miguel, something of a free spirit, his enthusiasm for those peyote mysticism books, his gentle Mexican manners and awkwardly seductive, yet gently forthright ways, after two decades of dealing with Bert, it's easy to imagine what you found so attractive about him. When you're in Cuernavaca, Yolanda, we'll escape to San Luis Potosí for a few days and with a shaman to guide us, we'll take magic mushrooms or peyote. Yolanda, your life will never be the same. Mamita's fantasies of what that will be like, God knows, make her eyes glow. She laughs with excitement. Yes, Miguel, we will, yes.

I've booked a room in a chain hotel out on the highway. Waiting out in the Green Meadows parking lot for a taxi, I think, How you answer Lulú's message about Ayahuasca Bro and his hipster housewarming party could turn out to be really important, Frankie Gee, even decisive. But answer her later, at the hotel. Have a drink at the bar and think it over. You don't want to mess this up.

But at the hotel, after I've checked in and gone into the lobby bar that I don't want to spend another minute at, crowded with boisterous lower-level corporate types, "artistic" prints of iconic Boston athletes on the Irish green walls, I shout to the bartender through heads and shoulders for a double Maker's on the rocks, then carry it up to my room with my luggage. From room service, I order a French onion soup and a Salisbury steak with mushroom gravy and another bourbon, this one straight. When I'm ready to drink it, I'll get ice from the machine down the hall. I used to like Salisbury steak TV dinners when I was a child, this one will probably be no worse than those.


That first morning with Lulú in my apartment, fresh snow coating the tree branches outside the window, the scraping sound of snow shoveling coming from outside, the old steam radiator hissing and gurgling, when we woke in my bed, kissing and touching, that soft chain of delicious sensual shocks, didn't we also begin to confide in each other? Lulú did in me. She lay on her belly, her arms crossed over the pillows, looked at me over her bare shoulder with her dolphin eye and said:

If I had a father, a father who cared about me, he would say you are too old, and he would not let us be together. Maybe he would do anything to stop it, even kidnap me and lock me in a room, you know? Her smile, I guess, was ambiguous. But I don't have a father, she said. Or else, well, I don't know where he is. I only have a mother I don't really speak to anymore and whose advice I would ignore anyway. There's nobody I have to listen to. My cousin doesn't interfere in my life. The only one responsible for my life is me.

A few moments later, Lulú said, I've done things I'm not proud of, Panchito.

Yeah? I said and waited a moment. Well, there's so much that I'm not proud of, too, Lulú, I said. I could write an encyclopedia of all those things.

So many? she asked.

I've been around a lot longer than you have. I've accumulated my share of mistakes, believe me.

I want to be finished making my mistakes, she said. But if you're planning to make some more, don't make them with me. She playfully punched my bicep, then lightly bit it.

Lulú has the most lovely bare feet. Her toes rows of nearly identical delicate peanuts inside smooth shells and her high perfect inner arches.

Alright now, be honest but not too honest; better yet, don't be dishonest.

I answer Lulú's text: "Ayahuasca gives you diarrhea and makes you throw up. I don't enjoy either of those, that's why I've never done it. But don't let that stop you. ☺ Have fun. Miss you xo"

Now I have to wait for her to answer. I carry the small Styrofoam ice container out into the hall.

# Saturday

But no message from Lulú this morning. In the taxi to the train station, a horrifying vision of walking into a Brooklyn café and there, having breakfast, are Lulú and Ayahuasca Bro and a baby in one of those carriages that looks like a Mars rover and a girl who could be Lulú's little sister but whom she introduces as the nanny. But Lulú wouldn't introduce her like that. She'd say something like: This is my husband, Sam, and this is Susana. And I'd think to myself: The nanny. Then she'd turn to Ayahuasca Bro and Susana and say, Francisco was Marisela's story-writing teacher at the learning sanctuary.

I'll ride this commuter train to the closest town and take a taxi from there. I'm meeting Feli at one of those chain sandwich-bakery cafés in the Industrial Zone.

Now we're taking the Route 128 exit that passes right underneath the steep hill overlooking the highway, dark pines marching up its slope that the Hilltop Sheraton stands upon. A sterile traveling-businessman hotel where she'd be extremely unlikely to run into a neighbor but from where she could easily get home in time for dinner with her children and Bert. Ay, Mamá. We take the avenue that leads past the neighborhood that Ian Brown and Arlene Fertig lived in and turn into the expanse of former Charles River wetlands, filled in to make way for the Industrial Zone. High-tech and online media companies, the distribution hub warehouses of box stores and online marketers, the Boston television studios of a national network are located here now. Feli asked me to meet her out there, instead of in the square, where Dino's Pizza and Subs, formerly our town's best and almost only place to eat, is long gone, replaced now by half a dozen healthy-food family restaurants with play areas for toddlers.

The place is nearly empty. Separate or together? asks the young woman working the counter.

Together?

Oh my God, she exclaims, clapping a hand over her mouth. I could have sworn you were with a woman! She's college-age, friendly button-nosed Irish face, hedge of curly hair down the middle of her head, shorn closely at the sides.

I look over each of my shoulders and back at her and pretend to look spooked. It's just me, I say. I'll have a cup of coffee, please. Black.

Believe me, sir, she says with a giggle. I'm not on drugs. I know this sounds weird, but the woman I thought I saw standing next to you looked like the French actress in that movie *Amélie*. You know who I mean?

I've seen the posters, I say. Well, I wouldn't complain.

No, you sure wouldn't, she says cheerfully, going to pour my cup of coffee.

I sit by a window with my coffee. Feli's, what, sixty-one now. Whenever I tell anyone about Feli and the life she's made with her husband here, the respect I feel makes me reluctant to pronounce "American Dream" with overt irony. But I do anyway, partly because I think the only part of anybody's life that's a dream happens when they're asleep. Feli's second husband, Giorgio Montolivo, is Argentine, from an Italian family that emigrated there after World War II. He's the head mechanic at a garage that specializes in repairing European luxury cars in Brookline. He and Feli bought a small house in our town, at one edge of the wooded swamp that we lived on the other side of, near the pond and where the rubber factory used to be. Their two daughters, both taller than their parents, went to high school in our town and to good colleges. Clara is a business technology analyst for a company in Waltham, and married a young man from a prosperous family that owns several locally famous seafood restaurants. Younger Jenny became an investment banker married to an investment banker; they live in Dover. They've given Feli and Giorgio five grandchildren so far.

Through the window, I see Feli drive into the parking lot in her blood-orange Jaguar, a late-1970s model that Giorgio rescued at his garage and beautifully restored, using all his expertise. She crosses the parking lot, spritely as ever, pixie hairdo dyed a dark reddish hue, big sunglasses of a coppery tint, magenta lipstick, tight maroon corduroys, a waist-length leopard-print jacket. When she comes in through the front door and sees me, she puts her fists out by her sides and sways her hips like she's inviting me to dance and exclaims: Frankie! Her caramel features are a bit sharper, more drawn, but she's the same. When we go up to order, the counter girl's grin is rakish as she says, Separate or together, sir? She thinks Feli is my wife or partner. I give a wink, answer: Together, and I order the meatloaf sandwich special and a bottle of Snapple. Feli has an apple spice muffin and a chamomile tea. Back at the table, Feli explains that she wanted to meet out here instead of in the square because she's fed up with the way even the young mothers in our town stare at her. The other day she was in Walgreens and speaking on her cell phone when, as she approached the checkout, she was so provoked by a woman's stare that she erupted, Excuse me, do you know me? Have we met? Then why you look at me like that? It bother you that I am speaking Spanish? It's not illegal, right? Because Feli laughs, I do too. Ay no, Frankie, she goes on. Every year this town get richer, and the people get worse, and she puts two fingers under her nose and lifts it. I don't doubt the truth of that or that the town is as white as ever, but I also think that those young mothers mostly see other adults who resemble themselves day after day and never encounter anyone like Feli, driving around in her magnificent old Jaguar. She clearly isn't somebody's nanny.

We've been talking about her family, how proud she is that her eight-year-old grandson, Colum, is fluent in Spanish as well as English.

She says that she never hears from Lexi in a tone meant to let me know she's a little hurt by that. But they were never as close as Feli and I were. Lexi was a newborn when Feli came, whereas Feli and I immediately, in our shared solitudes down there in the basement, bonded. I've finished my sandwich, but Feli has only eaten some pinched morsels of her muffin. I ask her about my parents' marriage, back during those first years when she was living with us. Did they at least get along a little better than they did later? You know, just doing some research for *The Newlywed Game*'s special fifty-year anniversary show, I joke, but Feli doesn't even seem to hear me. Her expression, the way she takes off her sunglasses, brings me to a stop.

Her smallish amber eyes, rimmed in black, shift inside a second from unsettled to resolved. With a surge of emotion, she says, Oh Frankie, no child should ever have to see and hear what you and your sister did in that house. Lexi was too little to understand, but you were so frightened. You were always crying, *ay no*.

I don't know what she's talking about. I don't remember being frightened in the way she's suggested. I remember during that first winter in our town when I was recovering from tuberculosis standing on my green sofa by the picture window to look out at the other neighborhood children who came into our snowy yard in their snowsuits and hats to look at me on the other side of the pane. I remember raucous crows streaming across the gray winter sky like the flying monkeys in *The Wizard of Oz*. I remember wrists seared by ice-stiffened mitten cuffs and how icicles dangled from the eaves of the house and over the doorstep, silvery and transparent, narrowing into long sharp points that as I stood ringing the doorbell, desperate to come inside to pee, might break off and stab through my skull, down into my brain. I could sit back if I wanted to and immerse myself in a kaleidoscope of childhood memories. But I have no memory of what Feli begins to tell me about my parents.

Twice your mother tried to leave your father in those years, she says.

Twice Mamita had her luggage packed and set out in the living room, ready to flee back to Guatemala again and to her parents' house. The first time she packed for my infant sister and me, too, but if I understand Feli correctly, that second time she was going to flee without us. Both times, Aunt Milly, summoned by my father, rushed to our house to tell my mother that she wouldn't allow her to abandon her husband, wouldn't allow her to destroy her brother's family and ruin his life.

Feli says, Mr. Goldberg sat in his chair doing this with his hands, and she puts out her hands, wringing them. But ohhh, she says, Aunt Milly scolded Mr. Goldberg too. She told him that he had to change or he was going to lose his wife and family. Doña Yoli was all packed and ready to go to the airport, but Aunt Milly convinced her to stay. Two times I saw that, Frankie. At your father's funeral, says Feli, Aunt Milly came from Florida in her wheelchair, so old now, and she apologized to Doña Yoli. I heard your aunt say, I am sorry, Yolanda, for how you suffered with Bert all those years. I feel responsible, because I forced you to stay.

Your tío Memo didn't like to visit your mother here, says Feli. That's why when he came, he would stay at the Holiday Inn in Dedham. Memo knows how your father treated Yoli; he always knew. Because of that he couldn't stand to be with Bert.

I didn't notice that conversation between Aunt Milly and my mother at the funeral. As a boy, I wasn't aware of Tío Memo's hostility toward my father. I was deaf to the icy notes in the forced bonhomie with which Tío Memo spoke to his brother-in-law.

My mother sobbing in bed with her nightgown ripped off her shoulder, her skin scratched and bruised, scratch marks that bled, Feli seems to think I saw that too. Bloody claw marks on my mother's soft bare shoulder, how could I not remember? My father, Feli tells me, sat on the edge of the bed, face in his hands, then got up shouting at my mother and went into the bathroom, slamming the door. That didn't happen just once, Frankie, she says. Maybe I saw it or maybe hearing the commotion, I ran to the bedroom door, but if I did, I don't remember. When Mr. Goldberg tried to make love to Doña Yoli, says Feli, he couldn't. Then he would be enraged and that's when he would hit her. Mr. Goldberg was impotent, she says. My mother would tell Feli to take me downstairs. Your mother, she told me everything, says Feli. Because in those days, Frankie, she had no one else.

Her uncle, by whom she meant Rodolfo Sprenger Balbuena, the Guatemalan army colonel who eventually rose to general, who she always says was like a father to her, told Feli that she should leave our house. She had no obligation to us or to anyone to endure such ugliness and sadness, her powerful military relative said. She was young and had to look for her own happiness. But I couldn't leave your mother alone with your father, she says. Or abandon you and Lexi. I couldn't, Frankie.

Feli tells me that Tía Meche used to phone from Guatemala to thank her for taking care of my mother and of me and Lexi. Tía Meche was right to thank Feli, I think. Because of Feli I was happy, shut away, as much as was possible, in our own world in the basement, out playing Down Back, walking with her to the town square to buy penny candy, sometimes even going into Boston with her on her day off to see a matinee movie and eat pizza in the North End.

I used to find your mother shaking, Frankie, shaking like this. And Feli puts out her hands and makes them shake. He was brutal with her, Mr. Goldberg was, says Feli. Oh, she suffered, Frankie. Your mother suffered and she couldn't talk to her family. Your abuelita was such a strict Catholic. You could never divorce. You were supposed to accept your fate. Doña Yoli was always telling her mother that everything was fine so she wouldn't worry. I felt like I was responsible for your mother, says Feli. I wasn't afraid of your father. God gave me strength to stand up to him. I would get between them and say, I'm going to tell them in Guatemala what's happening, and that would scare Mr. Goldberg. That's when he'd turn and go away. Doña Yoli used to call me her salvation. Cony, tu eres mi salvación, she'd say. Her studies and then her teaching, that saved her, too, says Feli. That was your mother's escape. Her Latin American Society too.

I do remember being left at home with Feli almost every day because my mother would drive off in her car, whatever car it was that came before her Rambler. Some adults remember the terrible things they saw as small children and can be powerful witnesses at war atrocity trials; others forget or block it all out. But war atrocities, come on, that's a bit much. Lexi's memories of incidents like that one when I was "almost murdered" are much better than mine; it seems she even remembers Bert's beating me more vividly than I do. Yet my memories are detailed, even pristine, of so many other long-ago things. It sure doesn't seem like Feli is making all this up.

The Jaguar's door shuts with a neat *click*, and I slouch down into the seat's plush red leather, and the engine ignites with a smooth purr. This is *class*, I say, as if it's what you're required to say when getting a ride in an old Jaguar. Feli drives me to the Newton Highlands T stop. So Mamita used to tell Feli: Cony, tu eres mi salvación. But she was my salvation too. Feli has always loved to talk and gossip about my mother, about our whole family, but she's never before told me what she did today about my parents, about my mother wanting to leave again, about my father becoming violent with her, about his *problemita*. Why now? Maybe she's wanted to tell me for years and today sensed or decided it was time. Sometimes people like to hear family horror stories from their own distant past because they can seem to excuse and explain so much. But I would never have wished to be told what Feli just told me about my father. I concentrate on this new knowledge of my mother as a woman who suffered that violence, a young woman alone in this country, trapped with him, and a kind of panic fills me. I practically need to restrain myself from throwing my arms around Feli like a frightened boy. We're parked by the T stop now, near where the sidewalk leads down to the tracks. I have my hand on the door handle, and I'm about to say goodbye and get out, but instead I turn to Feli and ask, Why did you decide to tell me what you did about my parents today, Feli? Why now and not years ago?

Feli, both her hands high on the wooden rim of the wheel, looks a little frightened. Maybe I seem too agitated. I try to compose my face and as calmly as I can say, I mean, I'm really glad you told me. I'm just wondering why today.

Frankie, Doña Yoli made me promise to her that I would never tell you or Alexandra about this, says Feli in a firm tone that suggests that as we both know my mother, that should be obvious. And yes, she says, so many years have passed since your mother has talked about this with me. But the last time I saw you, Doña Yoli had not been in her nursing home for very long. Her memory is going to get worse. Maybe there is not so much time left for you to talk to her. I don't know if you ever will or not. But I decided it is not right, Frankie, that you don't know anything about what your mother had to go through, after she came back to Mr. Goldberg.

You mean Lexi doesn't know about this? I ask.

I did not tell her, Frankie, she says. You know, Lexi never calls me.

Do you think that's why my mother left Bert that first time, after I was born and we went back to Guatemala? I ask.

I wasn't living with you yet, so I don't know, says Feli. But Doña Yoli told me a little about it. Your father was who he was, Frankie. But he got worse after you came back, after Lexi was born. Abuelita made Doña Yoli come back because of her religious beliefs. Also, when you got sick, she made your mother feel too guilty over that. It wasn't because your mother left Mr. Goldberg that you got sick, it wasn't right that Abuelita made her feel to blame. But to your mother, Abuelita could never do anything wrong.


On the way into Boston, the subway stops at Longwood. Out the window I see the massive brick edifice of Longwood Towers, the familiar green awning outside the entrance of the former luxury residential hotel,

by now pricey apartments or condos. The bridge club my father belonged to was in the basement, down at one far end. I went there a few
times, once with my sister to caddy at a weekend bridge tournament:
we brought new racks of cards to the tables and collected the played
ones and scorecards. Lexi was better at it than I was, arriving promptly
at each table when she was supposed to—one cardplayer crabbily asked
me why I looked so sleepy—and at the end of the tournament, Lexi
was given more in tips than I was. The atmosphere at the bridge club
was a mix of library-like concentration and cantankerous outbursts
inside a constant cloud of cigarette and cigar smoke, of complaints,
wisecracks, howls of histrionic disillusion and defeat. So that I could
repeat it at school, I memorized this exchange between two men playing as partners for the first time. Player One: Stop calling me Fuck, my
name's Fuch [*fewk*]. Player Two, later that afternoon, angrily throwing
down his cards: Aww go *fewk* yourself. Most of the bridge players were
middle-aged Jewish men, though some were young, students from the
Boston-area universities, unshaven chain-smokers, shirts pulled taut by
rolls of flab. My father wasn't particularly funny, but he laughed at the
bridge club like he never did at home. A grand master, a onetime New
England champ, Bert was a revered figure there. Your father is good at
games, any game, my mother used to say.

Will I ever talk to my mother about what Feli told me? I don't know. I
need to think about how I'd bring it up or under what circumstances.
Does Lexi really not know about it? I mean, if it's something she and
Lexi have already talked about, I'd like to know that. I've been away
for so many years. I'm an outsider, at least regarding Lexi and Mamita's
shared secret world.

   I wish I could remember every single second of my entire life so
far, in full 3-D Technicolor and surround sound, and at every past scene
reinhabit myself exactly as I was.

*   *   *

I check back in to the same hotel I stayed in the night I had dinner with Marianne. No messages on my phone. Maybe I should go out and get a cheeseburger at a nice bar somewhere, but no, the Saturday night Boston bar crowds, forget that. I order an individual pepperoni pizza and what the room service menu calls the Healthy Kale Caesar and a bottle of red wine. I turn on the TV to SportsCenter. Have to admit, I'm feeling just incredibly desolate.

So what is loneliness, really? Doesn't it have to ache night and day, to weigh you down at least like a ceaseless low-grade sorrow, to be the real thing? Otherwise how could it be true, like I read in the newspaper, that loneliness is a marker for early death as much as high cholesterol. I'm not depressed, I don't even think I'm all that lonely. I've just been alone longer than I would have liked.

And I'm on that filthy Tangiers beach yet again, struggling along under the weight of our bags, which are laden with all the beautiful objects, fabrics, and bags of spices and tea Gisela bought in the stalls and cave-like shops of the Fez medina and trying to see as far as I can down the length of the beach, into the blue seaside fog into which she's disappeared, chasing the receding silhouette of a camel that she'd spotted far ahead or maybe two camels close together. At the ferry office, after Gisela had shared her disappointment to be leaving Morocco after only six days—and on her birthday no less—without even getting to ride a camel, the sympathetic ticket clerk told her that she could get a camel ride at the beach. There was still time if she hurried over there; our ferry to Spain was leaving in two hours. The tide is out but just beginning to come back in, and the wide beach is crowded, mostly with men and boys in their long djellabas, sitting in the sand, playing soccer, standing in small groups talking, smoking, walking with companions or alone. The many stray dogs mimic the humans, sitting in the sand, scampering after the soccer players, milling in groups or loping along alone. If she gets her camel ride, she'll forgive me; my lie will be erased. She'll never cut me any slack but she won't for anyone else either. She's a hydra of explosive nerves; the key to being with her is learning how to avoid lighting those fuses. I want to explain to her how well I understand her, but I know it's impossible, she doesn't really know how to assimilate and respond to what I usually don't know how to express anyway, not on the spot, when it's the moment such things need to be expressed. You can't make Gisela feel loved without also making her feel that you're trying to change her in some unacceptable way, and somehow I'm the same; we're *unlovable*. Nevertheless, that hasn't stopped her from letting me try to love her and even hoping I'll succeed. I say to her: Trust me, I'll protect you. But she answers: And who's going to protect me from you? We still have a little more than an hour. The air is warm, sticky, and fetid with smells of fish rot, garbage, excrement. What seem like sewage pipes abruptly emerge here and there from the sand, releasing fluids that run through shallow narrow ditches to the sea. I can't leap or skip over them the way Gisela must have, I'm too weighed down with luggage, so I take zigzagging detours. The light is darkening; our ferry is leaving in an hour and ten minutes. I keep my eyes fixed on the mist-blurred horizon for some sign of a camel or of the bright white of her blouse. Now it's an hour. If we miss the ferry, we'll have to stay the night in Tangier, and we'll lose our flight home from Madrid too. Tangier's cosmopolitan bohemian glamour seems far in the past, though the old tourist guidebook she once bought in a Mexico City used bookstore says to keep an eye out for Jean Genet. On the avenue separated from the beach by a long wall, streetlights have come on, and I can see the tops of illuminated busses passing. Evening is falling fast now; people are streaming off the beach. Forty-five minutes. If we run all the way, we can make it to the ferry

dock in ten. She must have been unable to catch up to her camel and
will soon come walking back alone, crestfallen. I strain my eyes for any
white speck that might be her blouse. Reality, to Gisela, is a symbolic
tapestry that unspools in time, the image of a girl walking alone on a
dark beach to be interpreted by herself like a tarot card just flipped over.
Her not getting her camel ride today, on her birthday, will be the fatal
last judgment on our relationship.

But I can stop worrying about that because here she comes, yay.
Even through the fog I can make out the distinct shape of a camel, its
Q-tip risen head and neck. And isn't that a rider? If I can't see the white
of her blouse, that's because it's too dark now, the mist too thick, and
they're probably still too far away. The camel's owner must be on foot,
leading it by a halter or leash. I'm so relieved, so happy that she got her
camel ride that I don't care if we miss our ferry. Maybe there's a night
flight from Tangiers to Madrid. But wait, why is the camel diagonally
crossing the beach, toward the city side, seemingly headed toward an exit
in the wall? I can make out the camel's undulating neck and bobbing
head as it mounts the balustraded tiled steps leading off the beach, and
even though I'm loudly shouting Gisela, the camel proceeds through the
gate into the city and its noise, out of sight. Are they taking a shortcut
to the ferry port? Does she think I'm waiting for her there? Twenty-five
minutes. Under the weight of the loaded backpack, a heavy bag in each
hand, I run through the sand toward those steps. A squalid moat of rank
water separates the bottom step from the beach. The people leaving the
beach splash through, some hiking the hems of their djellabas. I roll
up my pants and wade through in my boots, holding our bags high,
and scramble up the steps to the well-lit sidewalk and look both ways
up and down the avenue at busses, cars, taxis, pedestrians—no sign of
a camel. I frantically ask passersby in Spanish and English if they've
seen a woman in a white blouse atop a camel. Nobody has. From the
sidewalk the beach below is a vast blackness. I carry our bags back down
to the bottom step. From there you can still see across the beach to the

silver-flashing waves, moonlight and the streetlamps above infusing the fog with a nearly purplish glow. Twenty minutes. I go back up the steps, back down. Less than fifteen minutes now. Coming toward me through the fog, swiftly as if in speeded-up film, are three camels. They look covered in gold dust. She sits atop her camel, grinning ear to ear, looking so happy and proud. The owner of the camels dismounts, lifts our luggage onto the back of his camel, and helps me seat myself atop the third camel, and we go galloping over the sand to the ferry port and back into our scheduled future.

About three years ago in the Condesa, in El Centenario, on a night when the cantina was booming with drunks, a friend of Gisela's spotted me from her table and gestured for us to step outside for a smoke. Did you know that Gisela is in Iran? she asked me, out on the sidewalk. Her new boyfriend, a Spanish photojournalist and war correspondent, had invited her on a long reporting trip to Iran, Iraq, and Afghanistan. Her friend said, Gisela's always dreamed of a trip like that. It's just what she needs. It will be life changing for her . . . If she survives! Oh, she'll survive, I said. She's like a lobster that can live in boiling water. That's true, it's the Spaniard who might not survive Gisela, she said, and we both laughed. A knowing laugh, I thought. Though I told myself to be happy for Gisela, it hurt to be reminded that she hadn't found the partner she wanted or needed in me, like she must have with this Spaniard.

About two months later I ran into Gisela's friend again, this time in the Superama by Calle Amsterdam. When she saw me, she let go of her shopping cart and came practically bounding over to me, an excited look on her face, and she exclaimed, Weyyyyy, you're not going to believe what's going on with Gisela in Iran. In Tehran, she told me, where Gisela and her boyfriend's trip began, the Spanish photojournalist and war correspondent had been too terrified to even leave his hotel room. That gachupín turned out to be a fraud. He'd never covered a war in his life. He sometimes took pictures of beach resorts for Spanish travel magazines and lived on family money. He literally wouldn't leave their hotel room! Wey, he was afraid of los iraníes, that's what Gisela wrote in her email. Ay no, poor Gisela, her friend went on, she's always had the worst luck with men. But you know what she's like when she's angry. Gisela and the Spaniard almost got thrown out of their hotel; the owner threatened to call the police. Gisela went off by herself with her camera and a knapsack but not just to go and walk around until she calmed down. Her email had been sent from some holy city, weeks after she'd left Tehran. The friend said, Gisela is traveling around Iran by herself, wearing a chador! Neta, wey, Gisela in a chador. That girl is crazier than a goat, but she says she's never been happier. I decided to write to Gisela, too, just to ask if she was okay. I still wrote to her every year on her birthday. Geronimo Tripp was continuously in and out of that region, and I passed on his email address and urged her to write to him. He'd be happy to hear from her and would lend a hand however he could. Around three weeks later, when she answered, I opened her email and it was empty. I wrote back and told her that her email had arrived empty and to please resend it, and about three weeks after that, I got another one from her. She wrote, "Why did that email arrive empty? It took me a long time to write. It was a very long email." That very long, very lost email haunted me for years. Typical of her to accept the loss of those words as a sign of fate that it would be impious to defy by trying to re-create them. In this new email, which I read over hundreds of times, she wrote that she'd spent six weeks in a city called Isfahan, going around covered head to toe in black, but it didn't matter. All the men were dogs. She'd never been anywhere else with so much sexual harassment. They shouted out gross things to her in the streets, followed her on foot and on motorbikes, spied on her. She was having just the best time anyway; she had lots of stories. Now she was in Yazd and was "in love" with it, one of the oldest cities in the world, super cosmopolitan but with afghanis, paquistanis, and nomads, a ferocious place. Yazd was like some of the towns we'd been to in Morocco, she wrote, but with no one out walking in the streets; the heat was insupportable. She was looking for a place to rent. She wanted to lose herself in the desert.

More than a year after that, Geronimo Tripp one night in Baghdad heard some journalists talking about a Mexican woman living in Kabul, on Flower Street, in a house shared by foreign aid workers. When she was described as beautiful but difficult, he had a hunch they were referring to Gisela. One of the journalists, an Italian, seemed badly hung up on her. Gero had lost all track of her since. A year ago I ran into her friend again, who told me Gisela was back in Mexico, living in the Sierra Tarahumara with her husband, a Bulgarian doctor without borders she'd met somewhere in Afghanistan, and their children, twin boys. Her friend had had lunch with Gisela when she was in Mexico City for the day to catch a flight to Paris later that same night. I'd run into the friend not even a week later. Gisela was having a show at a gallery in Paris of photographs she'd made during her first year in Iran, when she was living alone in some desert town.

We can leave what made us unlovable behind. We can grow or evolve or determinedly slog our way out and become lovable.

The clock reads 4:03 a.m. I just woke again wondering: Could Lexi actually be el joven's daughter? Tío Memo gave the impression el joven was blond, didn't he? That's preposterous, don't be preposterous.

Aunt Hannah was at least blondish too. Lexi even resembles Aunt Hannah, doesn't she? Aunt Hannah who passed away something like twenty-five years ago. I reach for my phone, maybe a message from Lulú came in and I didn't hear the buzz . . . Zip, nada.

# Sunday

A FEW YEARS AGO, during a time when I was researching the science and history of artificial teeth, thinking it would help me to understand Bert better should I ever want to write about him, I came across a few technical publications in which Leslie Potashnik and the Potashnik lab were cited in footnotes and knew that was the lab my father had run. Finally I did find what I'd hoped against hope to find, a mention of my father by name. In a prosthetic dentistry journal article titled "Sourceless Illumination and Color Measurement," by Dr. Rishi Kamble of the University of Connecticut School of Dental Medicine, there were several sentences dedicated to Bert Goldberg's work and expertise. I wrote to Dr. Kamble, and he invited me to Storrs. It turned out Rishi had been one of Bert's five apprentices during those five years when he was kept on by Potashnik's new management to train his own replacements; he was only a few years older than me. Introducing me to the grad students in his lab, Rishi said, This is Bert Goldberg's son. Bert made the porcelains at Potashnik, remember? Your father's teeth, Francisco, had a very recognizable style.

We were having lunch later in an Italian restaurant not far from the dental school campus when Rishi said, Bert Goldberg was a scientist, but he was an artist too. He compared the techniques pioneered by my father and a handful of his contemporaries around the world to those used to produce the famous glass flowers at Harvard, though, of course, within a much narrower range of colors. Between the brownest feasible tooth and the pearly whitest, Rishi explained, exists an infinity of hues and shadings, and that's where Bert worked his mastery.

I said, You mean a bound in a nutshell but king of infinite space kind of thing. And Rishi said, Exactly, and we laughed nerdily.

But, gotta say, Daddy-O, not really buying that whole artist thing.

Sure, Bert suffered, but he always had the consolations of his art. No, it was his fate to suffer on account of who he was, and though he got away with a lot, it was never art that provided his escapes.

Is it true that the son is the father and the father is the son? People like to say that, but is it true? People say that daughters turn into their mothers, but is that true? I don't think any of that is true. Not *necessarily* true.

I was eighteen when I got out of that house and out of that town, so don't feel sorry for me, I tell myself, sitting here in this Starbucks on a corner by the Common. But my mother and her devoted daughter never did escape, or whenever either did it was never for long enough or far enough away.

Walking over here from the hotel, I crossed the Common. Frozen crunchy grass, hard scraps of snow, a late-winter cold deadness in the air, everything tired of being dead. A squirrel hopping across the frozen ground with a scrap of snow in her mouth; no, it's a piece of plastic spoon. I remember coming here once when I was about six with my mother to feed peanuts to the squirrels. It was one of those weekend afternoons when she would bring me into the city to see a Cantinflas movie in the basement of an old Boston church, Lexi, still a toddler, left at home with Feli. Mamita had been summoned into our elementary school and told to speak only English with me at home, and once a week I was taken out of the classroom for pronunciation tutoring in order to rid me of my stubbornly persistent un-American accent. Maybe the Cantinflas movies had something to do with it, but we spoke Spanish on those Sunday afternoons in Boston, and I loved how that made me feel so close to Mamita, like we were alone in a foreign city. Near us on the Common, an old woman in a long, dark fur coat, with a pale, round face was feeding walnuts to squirrels, walnuts as large as the squirrels' heads. The woman smiled at me and said, Well, young fellow, you don't think a squirrel can eat a whole walnut? She spoke in what I thought of as a public television voice, like that woman in *The French Chef.* Her underhanded toss made it look like the walnut was as heavy as a bowling ball, but it rolled into the proximity of a fat squirrel. Spanish for squirrel is ardilla, a feminine noun. The squirrel plucked the walnut up in her front claws, transferred it to her mouth, and ran with it up a tree trunk where she hung upside down, hind talons sunk like iron hooks into the bark, splayed legs elastically stretched, and turned the walnut over and over in her hands, gnawing on it. When her teeth broke through the hard shell, we heard it. The old woman smiled at us and said, Isn't that marvelous? Oh yes, it is, said Mamita. We were all smiling at each other.

In a little while I'll take the subway to East Boston to see María Xum in her laundromat. She has something urgent she wants to tell me. Not expecting any Feli-like revelations about my parents from María, though. She wasn't with us that long, for one thing, and didn't have nearly that degree of emotional closeness with us.

At Bert's funeral, held at graveside in a cemetery in a town near ours, with an officiating rabbi who despite his benign huff and prattle clearly didn't know anything about my father—a member of the Greatest Generation, the rabbi called him, that's a good one—I read the eulogy I'd written in a notebook on the flight up from Mexico. It was a story about visiting Bert in Florida. We'd gone to one of those offtrack horse-betting places where mostly retired people sat in a room at tables and folding chairs watching the Hialeah or Gulfstream races on a closed-circuit television screen. At a counter in an adjoining room, you placed your bets. My father was a superb horse better, and as he sat studying the racing form, other old people, men and women, would come and stand behind him, trying to peek over his shoulder to decipher which horses he was circling with his stub of a pencil on his racing form or marking on the betting tickets. I don't recall him ever having a losing day, but, at least in front of me, he bet only small amounts. That day in the offtrack betting place there was a guy there, hulking and glowering, tousled black hair, swarthy cheeks and chin, older than me but young for that place, who I assumed must be visiting family in Florida too. During every race, he shouted and flung his arms around and kept getting up and blocking everybody's view of the screen. He looked like Bluto. The old people there were too passive or polite to reprimand someone else's misbehaving son, but a few times I'd shouted at him to sit down, and he'd shot threatening looks back at me. As four tightly bunched horses, including the one my father and I had bet on, rounded the last bend, he stood up in front of the screen again, waving his arms and screaming his horse's name, and I shouted out: Sit down! We want to see the race, not your fat ass! During my eulogy, I shouted out those words just as I had in Florida: Not your fat ass! When he heard me—though he'd probably heard me all along, this was just the first time I'd mentioned his fat ass—Bluto turned and charged through the tables, meaty fist raised and elbow cocked, with a speed that stunned me. He was massive. I rose from my chair and put my hands out to ward him off and just as he was about to throw a punch that was going to split open my face, eighty-something Bert was standing between us, shouting: Go back to your chair, you goddamned bully. Leave my son alone. You've been asking for trouble all day. Go back to your chair, and sit there so we can watch the races, you bully, you!

I finished my eulogy blubbering away: Oh Daddy, Daddy, best Daddy. Yes, I did. My sister, standing next to me, read the eulogy she'd written next but couldn't even get through its first paragraph. She stood there sobbing and bouncing her sheaf of printed papers off her thigh like a tambourine, and I put my arm around her. There were times he'd loved us as we'd wished he always would have; maybe it took the shock of death to remind us. I haven't been back to that cemetery since and wouldn't know how to find it, don't know its name or even what town it's in—Norwood, Canton, Dedham—though my sister must. That last time we saw each other, a couple of years ago, when we took my mother out to dinner, we'd talked about how none of us had been out to my father's grave since he'd died. Reap what you sow, said Lexi.

Teddy Feinstein, whom my father guided into a landscaping career, spoke at the funeral too. He told how when he was growing up his own father used to work all the time, even Saturdays, but Bert always had time for him. He was only three when he began spending time with my father in our yard, nearly every day and weekends when the weather was warm, helping with the rosebushes, the vegetable garden, the lawn. Bert had even taken him to Sarah Hancock Pond and taught him to skip rocks. Teddy started to cry then and, embarrassed, finished by saying that he only wanted to thank my father for everything, and he went and sat down.

Bert never took me to the pond to skip stones. Your father likes everyone's else's children more than his own, I remember my mother saying. I remember lying awake in bed the night after the funeral, asking myself what I could have done as a boy to make my father like me as much as he did Teddy.

During those first years that my parents were separated, when he had his own condo in Walpole and was still working at the tooth factory, Bert was always returning to mill around the yard and would even come inside to sit in his armchair. Mamita, having trouble handling the responsibilities for the house all alone, summoned him home more and more. After he retired, Bert spent his winters in Florida, but when he came north in the spring, driving himself in his Oldsmobile, eventually it was Wooded Hollow Road he returned to. Finally, he sold his Florida condo.

A couple of years before he died, Bert tried to apologize for beating me up so much when I was young. He blamed our neighbor, Phil Ferrini. When Phil Ferrini, who lived up the block on Blue Jay Road, had fallen on hard times, my father helped get him a job at Potashnik in the sales department. On their drives into work together, they liked to talk about their problematic children. Phil Ferrini had a temperamental, beautiful daughter, Michelle, and one of the boys she went out with for a bit was Ian Brown. After she stopped coming to school, there were whispers about a secret late-term abortion. On their drives to work, Phil Ferrini advised Bert that the only way to handle kids today is to beat the crap out of them. Beat the crap out of them, that's how to get their attention! brayed my father that Sunday afternoon years later, reclining against stacked pillows on his bed like an old-man emperor. That goddamned Phil Ferrini, I wish I'd never listened to that goddamned son of a bitch! Gisela used to enjoy even the most violent of my Bert stories, but the uniquely Gisela place inside her where cruelty, empathy, and comedy merged especially relished the story of my father's apology. Whenever she needed an excuse for anything, she loved saying: But Phil Ferrini told me to do it!

Years later, when I was in my thirties, a published novelist and journalist, when even Bert was proud of me, I came home on a visit to introduce my parents to my then-serious girlfriend, Camila Seabury. Bert took Camila out into the yard on the pretense of showing her his rosebushes but really so that he could get her alone. Frankie always gets hurt by his girlfriends, he told her. Promise me that you're not going to hurt him, too, or else end it now, before it goes too far. I'm begging you, dear. That conversation so freaked her out she kept it secret from me for years, until long after our relationship had ended and we were friends again.

But I'm not like you, Daddy-O. Oh no I am not. If there's one thing I'm especially sure of right now, it's that I'm not like you, at least not in the way that, after what Feli told me, seems most crucially definitive. In Pénèlope Myint's grad student penthouse apartment in Cambridge, only a couple of months into our relationship, she did something so uninhibitedly and joyously erotic that my dick wilted in terror. *Too much woman for me.* Futilely flopping against her, soaked in anxiety sweat, the scarlet fish fin of shame rising from my spine. It lasted a couple of weeks, frantic failure repeated over and over, but impossible to give up, to creep away and curl up in some dark corner forever; the terror of going for it again every night and day, though, was like a virus of anguish and humiliation digging down into every part of me, infecting every organ, vein, and nerve ending. But Pénèlope was incredibly patient. Ohh, *no fun,* she'd pout, never anything harsher. So, Pops, here we can draw the significant distinction. Never felt a flash of anger toward Pénèlope, instead took it out on myself, getting out of bed and punching the wall until my knuckles throbbed and bled. Finally something happens to unblock the cognitive processing of sexual stimuli and hush the horrible, panicked inner voices, letting the divine spark fly: lying in bed one evening, she casually lifted a knee up through the opening of her white bathrobe, revealing a glide of inner thigh so supple and soft it looked never before exposed to light or air, spontaneously drawing my lips to it, and I was cured.

You see, Daddy. Not like you. Was never even close to tempted to hit her. I, despite my humiliation, the nonstop hurt and disappointment of it, the fear that I was being revealed not just to her but to myself as a ruined man, instead went forward, kept trying, trusted the love I had inside me, not only for Pénèlope but for what I wanted life to be and desperately believed it could still.

No. Not ever like you. If I can feel sorry for you, it's because you weren't more like your own son. Well, that's been clear to me since I don't even remember when, maybe from that moment when I socked you in the face, left you on the ground squealing Yoli Yoli. What's unforgivable is what you did to your young foreign wife, your captive, my mother. Though I know it's really for her to forgive you, not for me.

A TATTERED CRIMSON AWNING over the door, ALEPH LAUNDRY in faded but legible white letters in the front fabric. Aleph, really, like in the Borges story? María Xum comes out from behind her counter to greet me between the rows of washing machines and dryers. Her obvious excitement makes me think she must not have thought I was really going to show up. She's a smaller woman than I remember, but I recognize her unguarded smile, her plump lips, though if she were sitting directly across from me in the subway, I wouldn't have known it was her. With gray-streaked black hair falling loosely to her shoulders, wire-rimmed glasses, and jeans and a thickly knit comfortable gray sweater, she could be a long-tenured professor of Marxist theory. After we've embraced, with a proud sweep of her hand, she says, This is my laundromat. The machines are old but they are still good. You mean you're the owner? I ask. Yes, she is the owner. Careful not to sound too surprised, I say, That's wonderful, María. Her smile widens, evidently she agrees. She says, Yes, thank you. But now her expression has turned solemn. She looks at me and says, Of course, in this story there are reasons to cry too, Frankie. She holds my gaze, until I respond, I'm sure there are, María, and she says, Pues sí, with a sad little half-smile. She turns to step back behind her counter. I stand a little awkwardly, hands shoved down into my pockets, across the counter from her, as María begins to tell me the story, her English animated by the energetic pronunciations of her native Mayan language. She'd been working here for sixteen years when the original owner, el señor Alberto Markowitz, an Argentine, committed

suicide. With her savings, she bought a half share from the widow; the
other half was bought by Alberto's younger cousin, Alicia. The widow
returned to Argentina with the twelve-year-old son. Two years ago,
María bought Alicia's half, so now she's sole owner. María tells me she
raised her own son, Harry, alone. Her first marriage to the Mexican,
Juan Camacho, was brief, and she never remarried. Harry is an Afghan
war vet who lives out on the West Coast now, but she doesn't live alone.
For years, through her church she's been involved with the local Central
American community. Several times, she says, she's taken people in who
needed help getting settled in Boston. But Rebeca has been with her
five years now; she's from Quiché, like María herself. She's graduating
from high school in the spring. Rebeca comes in on Sundays to help
out, María tells me. But I think she had too much fun with her friends
last night. Pues, that's how the teenagers are, fiesta, fiesta, says María,
making loose pom-poms of her fists. You know, Frankie, she says with
a wry little smile, for the churches and laundromats, Sundays are the
busiest days. I can tell by the shine in her eyes that she's delighted
that I laughed out loud over that nearly aphoristic remark. Of course
I'm eager to hear what she has to say about all kinds of things, about
her life since leaving our house and about her son who was a soldier
in Afghanistan, but I especially want to find out why she said it was
urgent that we speak. María leads me over to one of the long tables for
folding clothes, gestures up at a lone shelf on the wall above. It holds
a small collection of books that belonged, she explains, to el señor
Alberto, who loved to read. Cortázar's *Rayuela,* a book of his short
stories; a Borges anthology, too, undoubtedly including "El Aleph";
Sabato's *El túnel*; a non-Argentine book *De perfil,* by José Agustín,
the Mexican "La Onda" writer from the sixties; Manuel Puig's *El beso
de la mujer araña.* Damn, there's my first novel, an orange remainder
Band-Aid across the spine. My face flushes with embarrassment, so
this is why she led me over here. María brings it down, says, I always
take books from the library, but I bought this one. Oh yes, Frankie,

I liked it very much. Please sign it for me? The book does look as if it's been read, the spine creased. I can't help but ask, María, did the mother in the book remind you of my mother?

Doña Yoli? she says, with a surprised expression. Oh no, she says. I never thought that.

Thank you, María, I say. Because my mother has always worried that people do think it's a portrait of her.

Doña Yoli is much more nice, pues, she says. In your book, the father is the kind man, and María looks at me knowingly, her eyebrows skeptically hiked.

This María Xum really is kind of a gas. Who would have suspected? And I say, You're a good reader, María.

I do enjoy to read, Frankie, she says.

After signing the book and handing it back, I ask how old Señor Alberto was when he took his own life and she says, He was forty-three, six years ago. He'd be my age. Then María, in a new tone of seriousness, says, *Death Comes for the Bishop* I also liked very much. We read it in our church reading club, and I think we all did learn many things about Guatemala, but oh, it is so terrible what happens in our country.

Yes, of course, terrible, but thank you, I answer. And before I can think of what to say next, María has to return to her counter, where a short line of customers, some looking back at us with expressions of annoyance, are waiting. She takes payment from one and laundry to be washed from another, hoisting a duffel nearly twice her size onto the weighing scale. In the tip jar on the counter, there is a sole five-dollar bill curled up on a smattering of coins. The door opens twice in quick succession, more customers entering. It really is growing busy, about half a dozen people doing their own laundry, sitting in plastic chairs waiting for their cycles to finish or standing and folding at the tables, others dropping laundry off, picking it up. To most of her mostly female customers, speaking in Spanish and English, María tries to sell Tupperware, pulling out catalogs and samples from under her counter. But she doesn't offer Tupperware

to the few scruffy young men who've come in to do their own laundry,
every one of them, actually, looking badly hungover.

I glance up at the clock. It's 12:20 and I'm hungry. I probably
should have had more than coffee back at the Starbucks. Should I ask
María if she wants a pizza or takeout Chinese? I can go and get some for
both of us. Or maybe I should tell her I'll be right back, find someplace
around here to scarf down a burger. I'm standing here in quandariness
about what to do when I hear María say my name, and she's standing
right in front of me, and before she can say anything else, out pop the
words I'd rehearsed only minutes ago: María, you need to correct your
gender prejudices. I bet some of those guys need Tupperware more than
the women do, to help them keep their clam chowdah fresh. María
looks confused, until her lips part, releasing a tiny cackle like a muffled
cough. Ay, Frankie, you never change, she says, smiling. Always joking
and teasing! Well, I do like to tell a corny or intentionally weird little
joke and get a laugh, though I'm always meeting people who don't like
these kinds of jokes at all. Some even experience them as aggression,
yet for others the very same words and delivery ignite at least a small
burst of hilarity. Mamita, who loves to laugh, married Bert, who almost
never told jokes.

There's a teenage girl standing alongside María, taller, smiling at
me, her cheeks soft slabs. She's wearing a blue-and-gold East Boston
High School Jets hoodie, the very school I wrecked my knee against.
María says, This is Rebeca. The girl who lives with her and has come
to help in the laundromat after all. Rebeca hoists a brimming plastic
laundry basket atop a folding table and for a split second seems terribly
flummoxed over what to do or say next. She thrusts out her hand to
shake mine, her fingers are icy cold, and she's saying, even as her eyes,
a little bloodshot, shift to María: Nice to meet you. We heard you on
the radio. She softly claps María on the shoulder, says, Okay, I'll go get
to work and leave you alone. She turns and hurries back to the counter.
What a nice girl, I say to María, who now has her face tilted up to me,

her expression almost distraught. She says, Frankie, when I said I had to tell you something important, it was because I spoke to a woman. Her name is Zoila, who escaped Guatemala before the bad people could kill her. I think it is a terrible story, yes, there are too many. But when I heard you on the radio, I thought, I have to speak to Frankie. Zoila's story will be a new chapter in his book about the murder of our monseñor. If you can write it before the elections, I know you can stop this general Puño de Piedra from being president.

Puño de Piedra is General Cara de Culo's new campaign nickname, for his rock-hard law-and-order fist. But María, I say, the elections are only a couple of months away. I'm not sure I even want to hear what she's about to tell me. But of course I do. This trepidation is probably in anticipation of what María might expect me to do about it.

María is explaining that in her church there is a basement office where help is provided to immigrants. Help with the immigration laws, taxes, or a mortgage, all those things, she says, and even to find a lawyer. An elderly priest, Padre Lorenzo, had run the office for years, but he has gone now to the home for very old priests. Padre Rolando, a very young priest, Uruguayan, has taken over. Rolando is the son of a Tupamaro guerrilla who was killed when he was a small boy, María explains. And his mother was imprisoned for many years; he was raised by his abuela. But the padrecito does not know so much about Guatemala, she says. That's why when Zoila went to tell him her story, he was not sure what to think. So he asked me: María, can you come and speak to your paisana and tell me your opinion?

So on a very cold day in February, just weeks ago, María went to meet with her in the church early in the morning before she had to open the laundromat. Zoila, she says, is young but not so, so young. But you can see the suffering has made her older, she says. Her black hair is filled with silver, and she is so delicada, Frankie, and her eyes so full of fright and sadness, how did she ever survive such terrible things? How did she make it alone through Mexico and all the way to Boston, where she came to live with her cousin? I am a small woman, too, says María. I am a K'iche'. Zoila is mestiza, but we small women from Guatemala are always much stronger than the men think. Isn't that true, Frankie? But when Zoila began to tell her story, María says she was confused, because she thought it must be a story from my book about the bishop's murder that she'd somehow forgotten, because she mentioned so many people who are in the book. María says, Even that friend of the capitán, Ulíses, who near the end is found murdered in the trunk of a car, he was in Zoila's story, too.

Ulíses was probably Capitán Psycho-Sadist's closest friend at the time of the bishop's murder and later his top lieutenant in the narcotics street trade. It was just assumed that Psycho-Sadist had ordered his murder from prison because of how much Ulíses knew or because he'd run afoul of the dreaded capi in some way or for both reasons. It was one of those murders that barely gets investigated, if at all, because they seem so inevitable, and I'd felt frustrated to be unable to find out more about it. Now María is saying that Zoila had a novio, in whose desk at home she found several receipts for weapons purchases, signed by Ulíses. Arms to bring into the prison for the capitán, she was sure. Zoila's boyfriend was a warden of the prison where the three military men convicted for their roles in the bishop's murder had been sent. And now María is saying that Zoila overheard the warden and the capitán talking about and planning a murder in the prison on the orders of General Cara de Culo.

Whoa, what? I interrupt. María, what do you mean Zoila overheard that? How? Who?

We're sitting in plastic chairs now, facing each other. In her seat, María turns her head and torso, first one way and then around the other, as if to make sure that no one is eavesdropping on us or maybe just to affirm to herself that she is still here in her laundromat, where everything is running smoothly on a busy Sunday.

The warden worked at the prison in two-week shifts, she explains. Two weeks there, two weeks at home. Zoila stayed with the warden when he was at home, and though she'd kept her room in a little house she shared with a friend in another part of the city, he'd recently asked her to live in his house when he wasn't there too. Zoila assumed that before long they'd be married; for a while it was what she wanted. In the days, Zoila worked in a day care nursery. But when the warden was in the prison, she'd go there almost daily, bringing him food, usually some Pollo Campero, which he'd be happy to eat every day of the week, and she'd pick up his laundry too. That's what she was doing in the warden's bedroom at the prison, gathering his dirty clothes, when she heard the capitán come into the warden's office in the adjacent room. From there in the bedroom, Zoila could hear the capitán and the warden in the office discussing and planning a murder. Several times in the conversation, General Cara de Culo was mentioned too. She decided to stay in the bedroom without making any noise until the capitán left and then to pretend she hadn't heard anything.

Ever since Capitán Psycho-Sadist had become an inmate in his prison, the warden had changed. He had much more money, and was driving a new jeep, one of those like the narcos drive, with bulletproof dark windows. He bought geese to keep in his yard, which in Guatemala City some people prefer to watchdogs and not just because they respond to a nighttime intruder with an eruption of frenzied honking. It's easy to kill two or three watchdogs. But try to kill a dozen geese with one pistol or machete, María says the warden had told Zoila.

Zoila was already disturbed by these changes in the warden even before she heard about the murder. But after the murder happened, she broke up with him. She didn't want the father of her future children to be one more corrupt official involved in murders and who knew what other crimes.

Wait, I interrupt. What murder? I think I maybe know the prison murder she's referring to, one there'd been rumors about, connecting it to Cara de Culo and the men imprisoned for the bishop's murder. But María says she doesn't know which murder, because Zoila didn't tell her. There are so many murders in Guatemala, she says. Look how many murders of witnesses are just in your book, she says. Yes, that's true, I say. Because María had to be at her laundromat in time to open it, that morning their conversation was a little hurried. She thought she and Zoila would have many other chances to speak. Also, she has to admit, Zoila frightened her. María says, I think Zoila was worried she'd told me too much already, because before I left, she asked me: Please don't even tell Padre Rolando that I said the general was involved, I only told the padre about the warden and the capitán. But Zoila must have told the lawyers, says María. Because if she needs to argue for asylum, of course she should tell about the general.

Lawyers here in Boston, I assume you mean. Did Zoila come up here right after she broke up with the warden?

No, after she broke up with the warden, Zoila went back to the house she shared with her friend, says María. A few days later, Zoila was going to work when she was kidnapped and taken back to the warden's house, and locked in a storage room with just a little foam mattress on the floor. The story María now begins to almost race through is horrifying but familiar, even inevitable. Two men wearing ski masks came regularly into the storage room to demand that Zoila tell them what she'd overheard Capitán Psycho-Sadist and the warden discussing and also everything else she knew about the capitán's prison dealings and about Cara de Culo's role. They also demanded to know who she'd spoken to about it. They were sure she'd at least told her friend she'd shared the house with. Zoila insisted she'd only overheard that one conversation and that of course she hadn't told anybody. The men didn't believe her. They came into the room every day to shout at her. They beat her and called her a liar. The geese were always noisy in the mornings. Whenever Zoila heard their uproar after hours of quiet, says María, she thought another morning had arrived and that soon the daily torture sessions would begin again. The warden came into the storage room too. By then she was too weak even to sit up, but he kneeled by the mattress and begged her to tell the masked men what they wanted to know so they could be left alone. He promised he would stop being a warden. They would go live somewhere far away and peaceful, maybe Switzerland, and they would be married and he would love her forever. Zoila's friend, her housemate, was murdered; the masked men showed her a newspaper clipping. Now María draws a deep breath, exhales, and says gravely: They did the worst things bad men can do to Zoila, and she became ill and almost died. She woke up in a clinic. By her bed was standing the warden, the warden's mother, and some men she didn't know. Do you know who the warden's mother is, Frankie?

No, María, I don't, I say.

She is Matilda Ercolano Garay.

The woman Cara de Culo picked to be his vice president. I say, Ah, now I'm beginning to see. Though really, I'm looking into a tunnel of fog. I've heard Matilda Ercolano is the married general's lover. I've heard but don't mention now that her late father, the owner of a construction company and a former congressman from the Petén, had a hand in many of the country's dirtiest businesses and that his family still does.

Yes, the future vice president, says María. But this was three years ago, when this happened in the clinic. Nobody had heard of that woman yet. The warden's mother said to Zoila: You are alive because of me, because I intervened, and she told Zoila that if she promised to keep everything she knew a secret and went home with her son the warden and let him take care of her, and if he was good to her and she was good to him, then nothing would happen to them. Zoila obeyed, or pretended to obey, but a few weeks later, she somehow escaped. She came here to Boston, to Chelsea, to live with her cousin and to work as a housekeeper. Last year her cousin's husband, a puertorriqueño, tried again to molest her, Frankie. Do you understand? Yes, many times, he wanted to, but this time was different. Zoila was so angry and frightened she told her cousin about it, and the husband, for revenge, called ICE, and she was put in deportation proceedings with an electric bracelet on her ankle. This is when she came to speak with Padre Rolando. I told the padre that of course I believed Zoila's story and that the church should help her. Now with her lawyer, Padre Rolando told me, Zoila is asking for a stay of deportation and asylum. So good, now Zoila will be safe, I thought. But, then, only a week and some days ago, who do you think came to Boston to corner Zoila in the parking lot outside the supermarket where she went to shop? Came to tell her that in Guatemala they know that she is talking to lawyers. Who do you think, Frankie?

I don't know, I said.

This is what Padre Rolando told me. It is very confidential, okay. I know you understand, Frankie. They showed Zoila pictures on a phone of her two sisters, her parents, her sister's children. They said, Now you know we can get you and your family, Zoila, so of course you will not tell any lawyer about the general, the captain, or the warden. When you have your asylum hearing, we will have someone there in the courtroom to listen to what you say.

In a supermarket parking lot here in Boston? Who was it?

Matilda Ercolano Garay. And some men from Guatemala. This is what she told Padre Rolando.

Wow, they really don't want any of this to get out, do they?

The lawyer took Zoila away; she is hiding. I don't know when I will see her again. But Frankie, you have to write about this.

María, I would need to speak to Zoila or at least to her lawyer. And verify as much of the story as I could. And I would need Zoila's permission.

Please, Frankie, I think you can help stop this criminal general from being president. María puts her hands out as if to take hold of mine, but then pulls them back.

I'll try, María. I promise. Could you tell Padre Rolando I want to speak to him? Maybe he can put me in touch with Zoila's lawyer. That's really the only way.


So much for the notion that being up here puts you beyond the reach of General Cara de Culo and Capitán Psycho-Sadist.

\*    \*    \*

Back when she left our house to marry Juan Camacho, María is telling me now, she was already pregnant. But Juan abandoned her, left her alone in their Boston apartment, which she couldn't afford by herself. She worked as a daytime housecleaner for various families in the suburbs, taking long commutes by train and bus, with an infant, and that was so difficult. When el señor Alberto opened, she says, I was lucky that he hired me. Her son, Harry, graduated from East Boston High too. Then he joined the army and stayed in the service for twenty years. Harry was in a transport battalion in Afghanistan—he did three tours—and now he is out in San Diego and has his own trucking company. He does not like to come to Boston anymore, says María. But someday I will go out there to visit. I have never been to California, she says. Oh, I think you'll love it out there, I tell her. But the truth is, I've never been to San Diego either, though I've been to Tijuana. I do like LA.

I'm standing beside María at a folding table as she sorts through heaped laundry. She says, One day el señor Alberto brought me the magazine with your article about our monseñor and the murder, and he said, María, isn't this the boy you took care of? Could there be more than one Francisco Goldberg from Massachusetts and Guatemala? I was so surprised! Meanwhile María has formed two piles of socks, male and female, it looks like, and with deft snatches she's bringing matching socks together, smoothing each out with a quick stroke of her hand, her fingers plucking dryer lint like feathers from baby chickens. She lays one sock over its pair to make a cross, folds, tucks, folds, the result is a perfect little sock package. She does this over and over, conversing all the time. There's something uncanny valley about her hand movements, a true soft machine.

The last time I see Doña Yoli, she says, was I think ten years ago.

You saw her ten years ago?

A little more, I think. María tells me that it was at the Arlington Street Church, when she went to hear Penny Moore give a talk in the basement there. It was full, Frankie. So many people wanted to learn about Guatemala from this woman who is so brave, who knows so much.

Penny sure is exceptional, I say. She's still a very dear friend of mine. You're saying my mother was there?

Oh yes, Doña Yoli gave the introduction talk. She did not ever tell you this? She said, I am so proud to introduce my son's friend Penny Moore.

I never knew about that. If my mother or Penny ever told me, I thought, it must have gone in one ear and out the other; the most likely explanation, I'm ashamed to admit, being that back then all I ever thought about was Gisela Palacios. Those years must all be a blur to Penny now, when that was what she did, traveling the country giving those talks night after night, day after day. But my mother, introducing Penny? Of course, in those years, Mamita was changing, evolving. She heard what people said about the wars in Central America in the college settings she worked in and at the Latin American Society, she read everything I published and she probably read beyond that, too, and she knew about Penny and her work. Mamita, you really did step up, didn't you. But I didn't know even the half of it, always nursing my resentment that it was only Lexi who absorbed all your attention. Yet there you were, without me even paying attention, showing your love in this devoted motherly way. Who would have foreseen then that in less than a decade you'd be in a nursing home?

My attention is snapped back to María, who is talking about her church book club. It is a small group, she says, five of us from our countries in Centroamérica, a señora from Peru. It was my suggestion we read *Death Comes for the Bishop*, she says. Our three guatemaltecas wanted to read your book to learn more about the murder of monseñor, our martyr for justice. Then Padre Blackett asked us what we think about a Jewish man writing this book about a Catholic bishop. Frankie, I was so surprised I had to speak. I said, But Padre, in the book Frankie wrote that he is Catholic, too, and was baptized in the same church where

Monseñor was murdered. Father Blackett didn't know this. Frankie, he hadn't even read your book. And, imagine, he was leading the book club discussion and saying those things.

Well, even if I was only Jewish, María, I say as kindly as I can, that wouldn't disqualify me from writing a book like that. Though María's wrong. In the book I didn't write that I'm "Catholic too," only about having been baptized in that same church. Half-Catholic, does anyone ever call themselves that, does it even make any sense? I am half-Catholic. I *half* believe in Jesus Christ, our *half* savior. Thus this stigmata in only one hand.

Sometimes people are just surprised or jarred by a name like Goldberg in a Latin American context, I tell María.

You know, Frankie, María responds, when I came here, I didn't know that Goldberg and Markowitz are Jewish names. I thought they are just names that are not like ours, American names like Smith and Brady. In our towns and villages, we never meet Jewish people, you know, and many people have ignorant ideas. So I was disappointed in Father Blackett.

Blackett. He's Irish? I ask.

Yes, she says. But he is from Boston. But in our church we have priests who are latinoamericano too, like Padre Rolando.

He's probably just very old-school Boston then, I say. Is he old?

I think around forty, she says.

Well, like I said, it happens all the time, people reacting like that, I tell María. But especially Americans, for some reason. One time in Mexico, after a book presentation, I was standing around talking to a couple of Mexican writers, Federico Campbell and my friend Martín when a gringa, a college student, I think, came and joined our conversation, a pretty girl in a T-shirt and skirt, long skinny legs stuck into a pair of clunky Doc Martens. She'd come to Mexico to take some literature courses, and she knew Martín. Everyone turned toward her, and Martín introduced us. This is Federico Campbell. Oh, mucho gusto, how do you do? And this is Francisco Goldberg. *Goldberg*!? this gringa squawked right into my face. That isn't a Mexican name! Like she was accusing me of . . . accusing me of what, right? Why didn't she react to Federico Campbell like that? Did she think Campbell is a Mexican name? Federico's a lot whiter than me, by the way. He looks like Santa Claus without the beard. Oh well, so what. Like I said, I got wise to that sort of thing a long time ago. I try not to let it bother me.

María looks a little disconcerted, she probably hadn't intended for her remark to set me off like that. Not that I'm even done thinking about it. So why wasn't that girl's idea of Mexicanness similarly offended or at least surprised by Federico's surname? Because to someone like her, Campbell is a *white*-sounding name and white is the template. White can pass through walls. A Mexican with the surname Campbell won't be suspected, in what seems a practically instinctual way, of trying to pull something off, of a dishonest or opportunistic appropriation. What could he possibly have to gain? But if my surname had been Olajuwon or even Mohammed, that girl would still have been taken aback, though not in that particular way. Maybe she would have thought Martín was making fun of her gringa gullibility. Oh yeah, Francisco Mohammed, sure, tell me another one. Father Blackett, on the other hand, was calling out what he saw as possibly an unscrupulous infringement. Good for María, standing up to him, almost like Mamita so long ago with Father Doyle.

María suddenly asks, What is Alexandra doing now, Frankie? Is she married? I tell her that Lexi is not married—no reason to mention the policeman—and that she's living in New Bedford in a big Victorian house that she bought there.

Suddenly María looks alarmed, and she whispers, as if to herself: I almost forgot, and she gets up and walks back behind her counter again. I see Rebeca saying something to her, and María nods, sinks out of view, a moment later straightens up, and now she's walking toward me with a big smile. When she reaches me, she holds out her hand, and in her palm there's an arrowhead. It's that arrowhead, isn't it? Alright, what is this? What the hell is María doing with it? She puts the arrowhead in my hand. White quartz, flinted, lethally sharp. Of course it would seem a little smaller to me now than when I last held it, relinquishing it as I fell to the ground with my enraged father standing over me, lashing at my thighs with his belt. Well, Bert, it's hard to hold that one against you, anyway.

A smile flickers at the corner of María's lips. I say, That's Lexi's arrowhead, right? María nods, says, You recognize it. But now she has a slight look of worry, as if she'd expected me to whoop in overjoyed surprise, and she explains that Lexi had asked her to keep it safe, and so she'd put it into her bag where she kept spare buttons and other chunches, and that when she left our house, so distracted and worried, knowing she was already pregnant with Harry, she'd forgotten to give it back. Díos mio, she says, so many years have passed. Please, when you give this to Lexi, tell her I am sorry to not return it until now. But isn't it nice, Frankie, that it is you who gives this to Lexi? Oh, I'm sure you and Lexi will laugh about it now. The sweetly hopeful look in María's eyes so moves me that all my breath flutters out and I slump, but I rouse myself, smile, and say, Oh María, she is going to be so surprised.

Rebeca is going out for a soda and snack break, so María has to tend to customers again. I should have said goodbye to her when she left. Now it's only polite that I wait until I can say goodbye to both. The first time I saw this arrowhead in Lexi's hand, I'd immediately remembered reading about an arrow fired by a Wampanoag warrior from a distance of two hundred yards that went all the way through a Puritan militiaman and the woman he was out walking with, pinning both to the trunk of a tree, and I'd thought to myself, That arrowhead must have been just like this one. That's what especially inflamed my covetousness, I think. I put it into my pocket and sit down to wait. The midafternoon sun, weakly breaking through the clouded-over sky, now seems to infuse the stucco façade across the street, making it glow tomatillo green. If María succeeds in helping me get in touch with Zoila, will I write something about her case? We'll see. If she gives me permission, along with enough information so that I can dig into it a little bit more, sure I will. How could I refuse?

ALL MY LIFE, I've been answering some version of the inevitable question: But aren't you Jewish? (Weren't you just introduced to me as Frank Goldberg? Then what do you mean that you were baptized in that church?) I'm half-Jewish, I've always answered. Usually adding: My mother is Catholic. (I'm half-Jewish and half-Catholic, I'm sure I used to say as a boy.) Those questions always felt threatening to me; to some degree, they still do. When I answered like I did, did people think I was saying that I was or wasn't Jewish? That's what I'm thinking about, sitting here in this sleek hipster pub that I stopped into after saying goodbye to María and Rebeca at the laundromat and walking around the neighborhood a bit, fuming about Father Blackett, Lexi's arrowhead in my pocket.

When I was a kid, I never would have dared to say out loud: I want to be just one thing, like a normal person is, though I thought it all the time. Having a mother from Guatemala is weird enough, but at least she's Catholic. I'd rather be Catholic because that's more normal. I did know there was some sort of rabbinical law that if the mother isn't Jewish then her children aren't either, but it wasn't a law I ever saw enforced in any way, or that anyone else seemed to know or care about. As a child I did ask my mother to let me go to Sunday School at St. Joe's. But Bert said, Yoli, they'll slaughter him. He can't defend himself against one Gary Sacco, what's going to happen when every goddamned kid is Gary Sacco? Instead, I was put into after-school Hebrew classes. I don't know how Bert didn't foresee what a disaster that was going to be. When two weeks later I just stopped going, not a mote of dust was stirred by query or protest from any quarter.

I want to be nothing. Why can't I just be nothing? What if I'd said that? But what can a fourteen-year-old really know about being nothing?

Nada us our nada as we nada our nadas. But there's no Nada IPA on the menu, so I tentatively order the Spaceman IPA. The waitress, tall and trim in all black, reassures me that I've made a good choice. I order a grilled fontina and guanciale sandwich, too. She brings the beer, and I silently toast and drink to nada.

Up to fifth grade, Mamita always took us back to Guatemala City for the summers, and even though they were supposed to be our vacation months, we were always put in schools. For a few of those summers I was enrolled in the Colegio Ann Hunt. Ann Hunt was an expat from Alabama, and her husband, Scobie, owned travel agencies and tourist hotels. It was at the Colegio Ann Hunt that I encountered for the first time, in the school library, the phenomenon of strictly classifying writers by ethnicity and race. The shelves labeled "American" held books by writers from Alcott to Wolfe. The bottom shelves, inches above the floor, of two adjoining bookcases were labeled "Negro," Baldwin to Wright, and "Jewish," Bellow to Wouk, the lower parts of those book spines scuzzy with the dust of broom sweepings. Latino/Latina, or Hispanic, or however Ann Hunt might have labeled it, wasn't on her map yet, and neither were Asian, Native American, etcetera. What would Ann Hunt's library be like now, if she were still alive and her mania for disaggregating and classification had never slackened? Ever-expanding, infinitely bifurcating? Now I know that Ann Hunt was a pioneer of the American multicultural book business, however inadvertently. She should have gotten a medal.

"In a hypercapitalist society like this one, this commodification of ethnicity and race is both inevitable and good business, much better than just dispersing these writers like multi-colored sprinkles into our more established commercial batters, but you do have to be clear about what you're selling. Somebody buying a novel in our coveted Guatemalan-American niche doesn't want to be surprised to find a bunch of Jews and half-Jews in there." I didn't foresee, when I published my first short stories, how easy I could have made things for myself by publishing under my mother's maiden name, Montejo, as other writers in situations like mine have done. Then I thought that as I'd already published under Goldberg, altering it would be shameful, as if admitting it bothered me to be thought of as only Jewish. I was jealous of Jewish writers and half Jews whose last names didn't sound Jewish, all those Millers and Bakers, Mailer, Salinger, and Proust. Or writers who simply changed their name and paid no price in shame or ridicule, James Horowitz to James Salter, who said he hadn't wanted to be typecast as "another Jewish writer from New York." Could it really be possible that Frank Gehry would have had fewer important architectural commissions if he'd kept his name, Frank Goldberg?

It was only about a year ago, when I read an essay about Natalia Ginzburg and her youth as an Italian girl in Turin with a Jewish last name and Catholic mother, a girl from a stalwartly anti-Fascist family, longing to fit in with her Catholic schoolmates, almost all from Fascist families, that I understood my own longing to fit in was normal enough, as was the loneliness of not fitting anywhere. Natalia wrestled with that kind of sadness and exclusion, which she privately referred to as "pathos ebraico." Whenever I read her I'm reminded that it's okay to be always an outsider.

Once, when Gero Tripp and I were in Spain on a brief working vacation with Teresa Fijalkowski—she was editing both our books that summer and had invited us to the house she was renting near Bilbao—Gero joked that whatever country I went to, the people from that country always saw me as being of whatever brown ethnic group was most despised there. In Spain I was called moro everywhere I went. Even in Guatemala, a husky blondish drunk, in the Bar Quixote, insulted me as a morenito de mierda and took a wild swing at my head. On the Paris metro a group of working-class young thugs in tracksuits followed me off the train car imitating cartoon Arab music. Only back in November, in another bar on the outskirts of Carroll Gardens where I'm friendly with Deandra the bartender, on a night when I was the last customer, three small-time wise guy clichés right out of *Goodfellas* came in and almost right away started in on me: Hey, you Rican? You Nuyorican? Hey Rican, don't make like you don't fucking hear me. On and on like that. I was sitting down at the very end of the bar. Deandra came over and said in a lowered voice: Don't say anything, don't move, I'm going to phone the police. Like I was about to say anything. But they must have heard her say police, because they drank up and snaked right out the door.

Once, in Elaine's, that famously clubby Upper East Side celebrity bar where Teresa used to ask me to meet her sometimes—this was in the days when she was first publishing me, when I used to come up from Central America for a while, or in the years right after—I was walking back to our table from the men's room when I saw veering toward me that always-wasted Brit with hyphenated aristocratic surnames, a friend of Teresa's and her friends from that downtown New York nightlife scene she liked, I don't even know what to call him, a writer-socialite? He drunkenly grabbed me by the shirtfront and said, I hate you sweaty, swarthy immigrant people in your loud shirts. I didn't punch him, though I was still of an age when it's normal and right, I think, to punch an asshole who gets up in your face and speaks to you that way. I was too aghast and stunned to react, too intimidated by the setting of New York glamour and power. My shirt was kind of loud, I wished I hadn't worn it. He fixed me with a squinting look of pucker-faced dismissal and stumbled on. When I got back to our table, I told Teresa and her friends what had just happened. Oh, he's just like that, they said. Don't pay any attention to him. That's just his irreverent sense of humor, Jimmy loves to play the bad boy. Jimmy was what they called him. Sure, I get it, okay, yeah. Later Teresa said, I'm sorry that happened, Frank. It must be hurtful to be singled out like that. And I said, What hurts is that I didn't smash his fucking face in. I never wanted to be someone closed off and controlled by racial defensiveness, that seemed especially inappropriate for someone like me anyway, racially mixed, nothing in particular, no matter what anyone else wanted to see in me. But that insult festered inside me for years, more than other similar slurs have. Teresa doesn't come from a fancy background, though people always assume she does. She's working-class Detroit, went to Harvard, Oxford. When at a publishing house Christmas party Teresa told me that the Brit from Elaine's had been stabbed in the gut by a transsexual prostitute and was in the hospital, the words just came out: Good, I hope he dies. Teresa was horrified. Whatever else, he was her friend. I apologized, though couldn't help adding that I hoped the transsexual had a good lawyer. I'm sure she has her side of the story, I said.

On another, earlier occasion I was in that same place, Elaine's, waiting at the crowded bar because I was supposed to meet Teresa there, and an attractive woman stepped up to me, lifted her fingers up into the tangle of curls on my head, and said with alcohol-fueled merriment: Oh you black Irish mick you, you're a boxer, aren't you? So, not always whatever people most hated. Remembering her, whoever she was, I smile down into my nearly finished Spaceman IPA.

Have been subject to my share of anti-Semitism too. In Europe, my God, though usually as a sort of bystander, starting with that first-ever trip to the UK, white Brits mistaking me for Pakistani, letting it rip on the Yids. This one is my favorite, if you can call it that. At my hotel in Havana, while I lounged on a recliner trying to read by the swimming pool, a quartet of hairy male sex tourists from Spain were in the water splashing each other like children while loudly declaiming in their baritone Castilian voices, Muere, perro judio. Every "die, Jewish dog" sent angry waves of adrenaline through me. The lifeguard, afrocubano, about eighteen, lean, dark-honey skinned, went to the edge of the pool and told them: El racismo no está permitido en la piscina. If they kept it up, he calmly told them, they'd have to leave. That lifeguard and his words, so beautiful. No racism permitted in the pool.

The waitress delivers my sandwich. Of course, Natalia Ginzburg came from a loving, noisy academic and literary family, everyone a talker except for little Natalia, the youngest, a watcher and listener. Under Italian Fascist anti-Jewish rule, her father lost his university job and had to go into exile, and her brothers were imprisoned, as were many from their circle of family friends and colleagues. Natalia's Jewish husband, Leone, a hero of the anti-Fascist Resistance, was born in Odessa, in the Ukraine, the same part of the world where, incredibly, Bert Goldberg was born one year later. Leone was beaten and tortured to death in a Roman prison by Nazi SS officers. In the autobiographical *Léxico familiar*, Ginzburg hardly mentions Leone's death, the event that most marked and transformed her life, and yet you so feel her love and heartbreak that it seems somehow spread like living spiritual matter into the very ink her words are printed in. Ginzburg grew up in a secular family without any relationship to Jewish culture, much less religion. It was after Leone's death, she explained, that she began to identify persecution with Jewishness. I was rereading Natalia Ginzburg because I was curious about half-Jewish writers. I could only find a few; there must be many more. Muriel Spark was another. Both Ginzburg and Spark converted to Catholicism. Well, like my friend's lover, Sister Julia, too, whose Catholic mother had never had her baptized. Spark, too, as a girl growing up in Edinburgh, felt oppressed by the loneliness of not belonging. She had a working-class Jewish father; her mother was born a Protestant, and with her brother they were a happy, close-knit little family, a secular one, like Ginzburg's. Spark later described herself as a Gentile Jewess. In her fiction, Gentile Jewesses personify characters who are perpetual outsiders, who choose who and where they want to be, "diasporic personalities," as I recall one critic put it; they're opposed in her fiction by characters like Miss Jean Brodie who belong to one place and one identity, with fixed, even monomaniacal certainties. In her thirties, Spark went about her conversion to Catholicism in the most diligent way, holing up in her bedsit to read through thirteen volumes of Cardinal Newman's writings in preparation for her transfiguration. Almost nightly she joined her literary friends in boardinghouse sitting rooms, gardens, and pubs to discuss like apostles gathered together every aspect of Catholicism. Years later Spark's son from her first marriage claimed to have discovered a Jewish wedding certificate demonstrating that his mother's mother had been Jewish, too, not just her father; after deciding as a result that he was 100 percent Jewish himself, he so vindictively and publicly harassed his own mother for allegedly denying her own Jewishness that Spark ended up cutting him out of her will. But if I were going to convert to Catholicism, holing up to read thirteen volumes of Cardinal Newman wouldn't be my way. The only time I've experienced what I believe were strong genuinely religious feelings was at the Catholic "widows' Mass" in a sacred Maya town in the Central Highlands during the war. Possibly it was a syncretic Catholic Maya Mass; the young priest was Maya and gave the Mass in K'iche'. But it would have been suicide to publicly announce such a Mass right under the noses of an army that was still waging its scorched-earth war against the peasant Maya of Quiché and that, for symbolic effect as much as out of convenience, liked to appropriate local churches and convents and turn them into interrogation and torture centers. That priest was in fact murdered soon after. But word of the Mass must have been whispered and passed along all the surrounding mountain and forest paths because that day people came streaming in from far-flung villages and hamlets, hundreds upon hundreds of widows of men murdered in war, with their children and other relatives in their mostly worn, tattered native clothing. They packed the church shoulder to shoulder, the banner-strung air thick with the smoke of burning incense and the smells of pine boughs, candle wax, dirt, sweat, bad breath, unwashed hair; with prayers, singing, voluble exclamations of strong emotions in those strenuous and eloquent K'iche' pronunciations that seem so suited for expressing sorrow, as some would say Hebrew is, spontaneous wails, sobbing, quiet tears. In suffering you are joined to Christ in His suffering upon the Cross. Together join your suffering to Christ's and you are strengthened together. I felt it in every part of me; if I had been the kind of person truly open to that, it would have been a lastingly transfiguring moment. The image of Christ, a persecuted Jew nailed to the Cross, was often invoked by Natalia Ginzburg to explain her conversion. Also, her second husband was a Catholic. Natalia said that it was as a Jew that she felt a militant solidarity with all persecuted peoples; to her that was what it meant to be a Jew, even while she was also a Christian. You could be both at the same time. Perhaps not *always* coherently at the same time, maybe visibly one while invisibly the other and vice versa. Natalia used to say, I am fully Catholic but also fully Jewish; my father was Jewish and so was my husband. None of this half-and-half pie slicing. Just as Jesus Christ was both fully a man and fully God, rather than the Son of God dressed up as a young Jew or anything like that. Fully one, fully the other, at the same time. E pluribus unum implies a mestizo unity, neither a melting together nor an Ann Hunt library of white and a pushed-off-to-the-side infinity of separately shelved selves.

Three-quarters Jewish and three-quarters Catholic, keep a quarter secret only for myself.

HELLO? Who do you wish to speak to, please? A child's voice, a girl's, I think. I ask for Lexi. I'm sorry, you have the wrong number. No one named Lexi lives here, she says, her voice that of a confident little girl. Methodically struck piano scales in the background. So it's true, there are children. The policeman's children? And Lexi has a piano too. Well, she's always been musical.

Sorry, I mean Alexandra Goldberg. Doesn't she live there?

Yandra! she says happily.

Yandra, I repeat.

Yes, sir. Alejandra, but everyone calls her Yandra. But I don't think she can come to the phone right now.

She can't? This is Alejandra's brother, Francisco. Frank.

You're her brother? *Oh.* Yes, sir. Just one moment, please.

I hear her voice aimed away from the phone shouting: Yandraaaa! Yandraaaa! Your brother is on the phone! A moment later she's saying bossily to someone: Doogy, ve arriba y dile a Yandra que su hermano está en el teléfono. Another childish voice, whiny edge, answers: Pero Yandra tiene cel, por qué no le marca ahí?

She speaks into the phone: Why don't you try her cell phone, sir? Do you need the number?

I tried that, I respond. There was no answer. But I can try again. Are you sure Lexi's home? Yandra, I mean.

Yes, I saw her go up the stairs. Yandra has a show tonight with her band.

Her band?

Yes, sir. They have a show in Acushnet.

In Acushnet?

Yes, sir, it's a town near here.

Please don't call me sir, okay? You can call me Frank. What's your name?

Monica Tupil.

That's a pretty name.

Vos cerote sube a ver que está haciendo Yandra, I hear Monica scolding again. Pero YA! Creo que se está bañando. Into the phone: At school kids call me Tulip.

That's a nice nickname. There sure are worse ones.

I guess it's okay. I think Yandra is in the shower. I'll ask her to call you back when she gets out if you want. Does she have your number?

I'll wait. Do you mind? That way I won't miss her.

QUEEEÉ? Púchica, inútil, ni siquiera le dijiste de su hermano? Doooog! No le puedo creer.

Monica to me: Yandra is in the shower, but Doog forgot to tell her that you're waiting on the telephone. Doog has to shout that outside the door so she *hears*. Do you want me to tell Doog to go back upstairs and shout this time?

Sure, if he doesn't mind, I say. Through the phone I listen to Monica furiously unleashing this new iteration.

Okay, sir, I told him.

That's your brother you were talking to. Doug is it?

Oh God no, *please,* he's not my brother. What, do I sound retarded too? Yes, his name is Doug, but I call him Doog. But his real name is Smelly Retarded Horseshoe Crab.

Retarded Horseshoe Crab? I laugh and she does too, a mischievous childish cackle. Who is this sharp funny bilingual girl? Tupil, a Maya surname.

In the background, a stern adult female voice, this accent pronounced, interrupts: Monica, don't say retarded. We don't use that word. And Monica responds: I'm sorry, Maki. I won't say that anymore.

That's Maki, says Monica into the phone. She just got back from work. I don't know if you can hear it over the phone, sir, but Doog is upstairs shouting outside the bathroom door that you're here. Yandra will come down soon.

Okay. Well, tell Doog thank you. How old are you, Monica?

I've been ten for almost one week. You know what my birthday is? February twenty-eighth. My mother says I was born right before midnight, so if I came out a few minutes later, three out of every four years, I wouldn't have a birthday.

Wow, I'm glad you got in there just under the wire. Happy birthday, then, Monica.

Thank you, sir.

And Maki, she's your mother?

No. Maki's isn't anybody's mother. My mom is at her job. She works in a factory.

Really? What kind of factory?

They make vests for the soldiers in Iraq that bullets can't go through, you know what I mean?

Bulletproof vests, sure. For US soldiers in Iraq?

Yes, that's right. When you see the soldiers on TV wearing their bulletproof vests, my mom made them. Not just my mom, a lot of other people work there. Everyone else here works in the fish houses.

Oh sure, I say, the fish-processing houses. What about your dad? Does he work in the fish houses too?

My dad? I don't even know who he is. I mean, I've never met him. Presumably he's somewhere in this country, but he's not here in New Bedford.

Presumably?

Yes, sir, presumably. He wouldn't go back to Guatemala unless he gets deported. That's what my mom says.

You sound like you're pretty smart, Monica. Are you a good student?

Always straight A's, sir. I like to study and read and do homework, unlike some of the other retards around here who I won't mention by name. She whispers: *Doog.*

Is somebody practicing the piano there?

Yes, sir. I play piano too. But that's Brigida. She's just starting. She's Doog's sister, but she's not as stupid as he is. Their mom works in a fish house too.

And Yandra plays in a rock band?

Oh yes, that band, Monica says. They're not really a *rock* band. They're called Ahab's Hussies. It's drunk sailor music performed by crazy ladies. Sea shanties, have you heard of those? That kind of music. They won't be playing with Beyoncé at Gillette Stadium anytime soon, but I guess they have some fans around here. I told Yandra if they want to make a music video they better hire some dancers though. Right now their big move is when they all turn around and shake their butts at the audience. I don't think seeing that on a video will make a lot of people buy tickets for their shows. Monica laughs with glee.

I hear a woman's voice explode in the background. Fucking Yandra, you can't even put the fire on under the fucking frijoles! Not even that! Fuck you, Madame! Fuck you!

Oh-oh, here we go again, Monica says into the phone. Don't worry, this happens all the time around here. Oh wow, and now here comes Yandra down the stairs.

Madame? She means my sister?

In the background: Lagranputa always the same excuse. Oh I have a show. I have a rehearsal. I have to go and see my mother. Oh, I have this. I don't give a fuck, Señorita Candil de la calle, oscuridad de la casa. It was your turn to make the cena, but Madame can't even put the fire on under the frijoles.

Maki, please, just a minute, I know I know. It's my brother, please . . .
I hear my sister's pleading. Now Lexi loud in my ear: Frank! Is this really
you? What a surprise! But Maki, in the background: Give the patojos
Domino's again, eh, Madame? When all are fat diabéticos, don't blame me!

Yes, it's me, hi Lexi. Sounds like—

Maki: So fuck you, Madame!

Frankie, let me call you back—

Sure, Lexi. Sounds like you have a situation—

Maki: Not going to your fucking dyke-ass show tonight, either.

Yes, a situation, says Lexi, sounding a little panicked. Frankie, I'm
sorry, honestly, it's not so bad as I'm sure it sounds, I'll call you right back.

*Yandra?* Fuck you, Madame Yandra? What was all that? It's like
discovering a new civilization, not in the Amazon but deep inside your
own family.

I stand waiting on Tremont, near Boylston, on the sidewalk at the
edge of the Common. A Dunkin' Donuts right across the street. Every
time I see a Dunkin' Donuts, I'll be like one of those Mexico City taxi
drivers who crosses himself whenever he drives past a church, except I'll
be thinking of Lulú. The dusk is a soft, rosy brown, a pink-tinged light
that's making the hard scraps and patches of snow in the Common glow
like distant icebergs. Even though it's a Sunday evening, there are plenty
of people out on the sidewalk and in the Common, traffic moving slowly
down Tremont. The phone rings in my hand. Hi Lexi.

Hi Frank, I forgot to put the fire on under the frijoles, as I guess
you heard, says Lexi in a tone of affected, mortified culpability. Frijoles
and rice is a staple around here, she says, just like in Guatemala. Do you
remember how we always had frijoles at Abuelita's house? But it takes
hours to cook. Good thing we have tortillas, turkey hot dogs, and Kraft
macaroni and cheese in the house.

Okay, Lexi, sounds good, I say—so often this stingy brusqueness
when I talk to my sister. Stop it, I tell myself. Be sweet to her. Tell her
about the damn arrowhead.

I'm so glad you got to meet Monica, she goes on. I mean by phone, at least. Isn't she great, Frank? She was born in Guatemala but she was only one year old when her parents came here. She's going to go to Harvard, you wait and see. Lexi is making an effort to keep her voice bright, as if to compensate for all that uproar I was just listening to.

Yes, Monica seems pretty amazing, I say. But wow, Lexi, your house seems pretty lively.

Oh it sure is, says Lexi. Maki is who you heard shouting about the frijoles. Maki and I are good friends. So don't let all her fuck yous give you the wrong impression, Frank. Madame Yandra, that's just her nickname for me. Maki just talks like that, because when she first got here she heard so many people saying fuck she just thought that was English. Do you get what I mean? This is a fishing port, Frank, full of fishermen, rough guys, so you can guess how people talk around here.

I get it, I say. Hey, I have a surprise for you. But I didn't manage to pronounce that with much enthusiasm.

Maki's really been through a lot, Lexi goes on. But she's so strong. Well, she's strong and not so strong, like all of us, I guess. She's been in New Bedford twelve years. She's a bruja, you know. She has powers, so be careful, haha. Well, she isn't really, it's her abuelita who was a real Maya bruja. Maki learned from her. She can tell you all about this 2012 thing that's coming and how some of the old shamans prophesize the world is going to end in five years. Do you know about that, Frank?

I've heard of it, I say. Is this the bruja you asked to help find me a wife?

Mom told you about that, didn't she, says Lexi. I did ask her not to tell you, Frank. I'm a little upset with Yoli that she told you.

Don't be upset, Lexi, I say. I was surprised when Ma told me, but then I thought it was really nice of you.

A brief silence, followed by a little falsetto laugh. Did it work? she asks.

Well, I thought it was working, for a bit, I say. Maybe not anymore, though.

I'll ask Maki to do it again, she says. When she's in a better mood, okay? This will blow over by tomorrow, you'll see.

Okay, sure, thank you, Lexi. So what's going on, these cool kids in your house, mothers who work in factories and fish-processing houses. Are you running a boardinghouse?

No, it's not a boardinghouse, she says. It's a not-for-profit venture, she says. So no, you can't call it a boardinghouse.

A commune?

A commune? Her laugh is amused but abrupt. Oh Frank, it's such a long story. I'll have to tell you in person sometime, if you promise not to write about it.

Ha, okay. Well, I was thinking of coming out tomorrow.

You were? Why? Another nervous titter. I mean, that's wonderful, Frank, she says. But what a surprise! This is really unexpected.

I have something for you, I say.

Something for me?

Something you've been missing for a long time.

Missing for a long time?

Yeah, what have you been missing since, let's see, since you were in about the third grade?

A brother?

A moment of silence, I'm not offended, of course not, just a little taken aback. She laughs and says, Oh my God, I can't believe I said that. I was just joking.

Yeah, I get it, I say. It's okay. I haven't been around much all these years, I know that. But no, I say. I'm not the thing that was missing. When I give it to you, I'm sure it'll all come back. So, Lexi, you're in a band, too, I go on. That's so great.

Yeah, she says. You always said I could be like Mama Cass.

And I think, So this is how it's going to be. I just wanted you to be a musician like I know you really wanted to be, I tell Lexi, instead of a businessperson just to please Mom. And now, look at you. Ahab's Hussies, what a great name!

Thank you, we're proud of it, she says. We have fun, but it's just fiddling, you know. Aunt Hannah must be turning over in her grave.

Lexi, you didn't get married and not tell me, did you?

What? No, Frank, of course not.

To a policeman?

A policeman! She theatrically groans. Oh God, no. Mom means Mauricio, but that was like three years ago, right after I moved here. He was mostly just a friend, but he still comes and goes. Yes, he was a policeman, quite some time ago, in Mexico City, where you live. You must have passed each other in the street there. Anyway, Mauricio is a fascinating story, Frank. Maybe I'll tell you about him sometime.

Okay, sure, I say. A former Mexico City cop in New Bedford, love to hear his story.

You know, Yoli's memory is really starting to deteriorate, says Lexi. Yesterday when I saw the can of butter cookies in her room—gourmet cookies from Paris, oh, they're so delicious, Frank—I asked her if you'd just visited, and she didn't even remember. The nurse told me you'd been there the day before. Mom doesn't just forget. She gets fantasy mixed up with reality too. You know what she said to me? That she and Bert had a happy marriage. You hear something like that and you think, Jesus Christ, what's the point of anything if in the end you're just going to forget everything, right? But thank God most of the time Yoli's still herself, our remarkable, inspiring mother.

Yes she is, I say. And I'm glad I got to see her. But it does seem like you have a big family life of your own now.

Yes, life has many surprises, doesn't it? she says.

I can't wait to hear about it, I say. Lexi, can I ask you something else?

Sure, Frank, she says.

Do you still have that old oil painting portrait that Daddy's boyhood friend made of Mom? He was called Herb, remember? He used to come over the house sometimes when we were little.

Of course I have it, she says. It's hanging in our parlor. Herb wasn't just Daddy's boyhood friend. He was a very fashionable painter, Frank, with a studio near Newbury Street. He thought Yoli was so beautiful that he offered to make a painting of her for free as long as he could make a copy for himself. She was pregnant with you when she sat for that painting. You knew that, right? It was a few months after the wedding. She was already showing a little, but Herb hid that in the painting.

I didn't know that part. Are you sure?

Really, you didn't know that, Frankie? I've known that forever. Did you know that he was gay. In the closet though, like people had to be back then, but Daddy knew and he told Mom.

Does that have anything to do with why he stopped coming over the house?

I remember Mom saying once that he'd moved to Morocco, but I haven't heard anything about him in such a long time.

Mom told you Herb moved to Morocco, not Dad?

Well, yes, Mom and Herb were friends too. Maybe Morocco was a place where he could be himself? I doubt he's still alive, though.

He was a World War Two vet, I say. The stories he used to tell me were like episodes from that show *Combat!*

Oh yes, I do remember a little of that, she says. From *Combat!* That was your favorite show. But we always argued over which was better, *Star Trek* or *Lost in Space*. You used to make me feel like I was boring for liking *Star Trek*.

Time has proven you right, Lexi. *Star Trek* is the classic. *Lost in Space* is just another silly sitcom. But I wanted to watch *Lost in Space*, and they were on at the same time. You must also have Ma's old photo albums, right?

I do, yes, but they're put away. Don't want the kids getting ahold of them.

Do you remember her wedding photos?

I think I do, yes, says Lexi.

Is there a picture that shows Tío Memo at the wedding?

Tío Memo didn't go to the wedding, says my sister. He was against the marriage. You didn't know that, Frankie? Maybe he thought Dad was too old or because he was Jewish or both. Mom really didn't like to talk about it, you know. Uncle Memo made up with Bert later, though, for the sake of Mom and the family. Well, you know how much Mom loved her brother. You've always been close to Memo. He's never said anything to you about it?

No, he never has, I say. I kind of suspected he wasn't there, but I wasn't sure. Well, I'll call you tomorrow and tell you what time I'm coming out. Is that okay? I've always been curious to see New Bedford.

Curious to see New Bedford? That's a surprise. It's not like you've made any big effort to come here. But it's a fascinating little city, Frank. America's number one commercial seafood port, did you know that? I have a friend who says it's like a border town, except the border is the Atlantic Ocean instead of Mexico.

*The air smells so strong of codfish*
*it makes one's nose run and one's eyes water.*

Crossing the Public Garden in this cold just darkening, something of a tropical smell of cooking fire and effulgent damp turned frigid in the air. I can't believe I never knew until yesterday about Memo not coming to the wedding; it was never mentioned by anyone in the family, at least not in front me. I never knew that my mother was pregnant with me when she sat for her famous painting, either, or that Herb was gay. Felman was his last name. It's like watching a foreign-language movie without subtitles, being in my family. Flakes of snow like darting ice fleas. That first winter in New York, when I hadn't gone back to Broener—but no, maybe it was the second winter—I heard John Cheever read a short story that ended right around here, in the Back Bay, the narrator climbing up on a statue, taking off his hat, and putting it on the statue's head. The reading was at the Ninety-Second Street Y, Cheever's polished, somewhat hoarse voice, the flushed glow of his forehead. I heard Robert Lowell read at St. Mark's in the Bowery, Allen Ginsberg and Gregory Corso were there, too, that night, and the historic old church was packed. That rowdy, mostly young Lower East Side bohemian and punk crowd was taunting and shouting Lowell down as he tried to read his poems, and Ginsberg came onstage to scold them, indignant over how rudely they were treating his friend, a great poet, personally invited by him to give a reading there in the equivalent of Ginsberg's home arena. Was it just because Lowell, with his swept-back, long, white hair, was so WASP patrician and spoke in that same John Cheever, Boston Banana Brahmin voice? "Again and then again the year is born . . . To ice and death." True, not very beat or punk, more heavy metal or Jethro Tull, though that line was followed by a verse about spying through an icy window on a girl playing her French horn. Also, I heard Elisabeth Bishop read at the Guggenheim, a much more polite crowd, though I'm sure genuinely scintillated; don't think she read "At the Fishhouses"; wouldn't I remember if she had? Haven't been to a single poetry reading since moving back to New York. It's sad how you allow once pure or youthful enthusiasms to dim, but this is one I have it in my power to revive. Go to some poetry readings, Frankie Gee.

All over Guatemala, in the space of a small number of years, tens of thousands of still-young bodies were buried and hidden under the earth, the murdered young, firm supple arms embracing death and dirt for their long journeys to bone; plenty of others murdered, too, from infant to old, but mostly it was the murdered young. After the war, forensic anthropologists would spend years digging for their remains; they still are to this day. Of course, Penny and I were going around inside young bodies too. That line from the *Iliad*, "Everything is more beautiful because we are doomed." I spent long periods enthralled by that darkness, perambulating through the invisible murder clouds drifting over the sidewalks all over Guatemala City, thinking I was living close to an eternal truth. It wasn't until I was back there a decade later, beginning to look into the bishop's murder and finding the city still so terrifying and haunted, that I realized that I'd missed it, that sense of vulnerability that also makes you feel young, as if allowing you to watch yourself through the eyes of parents helpless to prevent what's coming. It's fucked up. Nobody should go near any war or killing zone if they can help it; on the other hand, you really can't learn such lessons about human insanity and depravity without being there yourself. Now Cara de Culo sends his emissaries all the way up here to wait in a parking lot outside a supermarket in order to threaten to turn poor Zoila and her relatives into invisible murder clouds; *they* come with visas, welcome, enjoy your stay.

This comes back to me now, too, from a couple of months ago, when I was reporting that story on the Abuelas de la Plaza de Mayo and their search for the children of their own disappeared sons and daughters. Most of those young mothers were already pregnant when they were abducted; some were impregnated in the Argentine military's clandestine prisons, mostly by jailors and torturers who raped them. Born in the secret birthing wards of military hospitals, weaned after a few days from mothers who would soon be put aboard death flights, those stolen infants were almost never, as they grew up, told the truth about their origins by their adoptive parents. So far, nearly a hundred of those offspring have been found and united with their grandmothers. I interviewed several, in their twenties now, and was so struck by how they idealized their true mothers and fathers, whose very existence until recently they'd been oblivious of. Though some claimed to have intuited it, to have experienced confusing sensations they interpret now as signs of mystical communion with their biological parents, with their mothers especially. A young man, sensitive and musical, now a composer, told me that he'd never understood how he could have come from parents so unlike himself, so dull and melancholy, as well as suspiciously elderly, and who'd raised him in what was then an ordinary lower-middle-class Buenos Aires neighborhood that was now a trendy one; that young man used to go on long bicycle rides far out into the industrial suburbs, compulsively returning to the same neighborhood in the same boring, ugly little suburb, even telling his baffled friends that he wanted to buy a house of his own and live out there, where no one in their right mind would want to live if they didn't have to. He couldn't really say why he wanted to live there, but he knew he wanted to. Only after he was found by the Abuelas did he learn that that marginal neighborhood, on a street lined with bleak little homes he'd slowly pedaled his bicycle down many times, had been the location of the Montonero safehouse his parents had been seized from; his father had been a guitarist, his already-pregnant mother played accordion and bandoneon. Whenever he saw a mother cuddling her child or a father playing with his baby son or daughter in a park, he told me, he cried or felt like crying, for them and for himself, for what had been lost and just over the beauty of seeing loving young parents with their children.

It's only a little past midnight. Outside it's still snowing. The dark shapes of pigeons on the sill of my hotel room window. I fell asleep with the Celtics game on. It's over, but the postgame show is still going; they won in double overtime.

The bar downstairs must be still open. I get out of bed, pull on clothing. No messages on the phone. I bring the book of Jane Bowles stories I'm rereading. It's a small bar, off the vestibule inside the front door. I'm the only customer. The bartender tonight, in a white shirt, wool vest charcoal gray with green lozenges, a black bow tie that seems to press painfully into his soft, tawny neck, wears a name tag that reads MUSTAFA. I order a double Knob Creek on the rocks and say, Thank you, Mustafa, as outgoingly as I can, though after serving me he goes back to leaning against the bar, lost in his own thoughts. The first time I went into a bar for some drinks with Lulú in Brooklyn, the bartender, a woman in her thirties with bare, thoroughly tattoo-covered, pale arms, asked Lulú for an ID. Lulú didn't have one, and so she refused to serve her. Lulú said that it was okay, she'd just have a mineral water. But I was indignant. This has never happened to us before, I insisted loudly to the bartender. She's twenty-eight, for God's sake! I bet if she were a white hipster girl you wouldn't have asked to see her ID, am I right? I'm right, aren't I? The bartender coldly told me that if I didn't lower my voice, she'd ask us both to leave. What a bitch, I said under my breath after she'd turned away but loudly enough at least for Lulú to hear. We left anyway. Out on the sidewalk, Lulú was furious. She's just doing her job, Lulú seethed at me. She doesn't deserve to be insulted for doing her job, and you have no right to call her a bitch. I defended myself: That's just a word everyone uses here, it doesn't mean anything. Not when a man uses it, she said. I only said it under my breath, I said. And I think her refusing to serve you a drink had nothing to do with just doing her job. I don't care, Lulú said, standing on the sidewalk, her eyes stormy; she looked as if she were about to turn and walk angrily away. I apologized, told her she was right. Of course she was. Lulú said that if I ever spoke with such disrespect to any person who was just doing their job, woman or man, she'd never speak to me again. She said I was no different from the rich white "bros" I was always mocking. That made me angry. I said vehemently: I'm not like them, and you know I'm not. Then don't act like them, she said. You have to respect people no matter how little money they have or what they work at. I promised never to behave like that again. Finally we were okay, and we went into another bar, where coincidentally the bartender was another white hipster woman with tattoos covering her arms, shoulders and neck, but friendly, and she served us both without any problem.

I open the Jane Bowles book to where I left off and stare blankly down at the page.

Of course, like Lexi says, our mother isn't always in touch with reality these days, I say to myself. And I don't doubt that she mixes up fantasy and reality. But what explanation could there be for Mamita suddenly having been so into *The Teachings of Don Juan* other than a mother in love, idolizing her lover's enthusiasms?

Whiskey like a glowing potbellied stove inside me, I didn't feel like getting into bed and trying to sleep, so I put on my coat and went back out to the elevator without even thinking about it. My footsteps carried me over here, to Arlington Street, along the Public Garden. The old Boston Banana Brahmin nahuales are out tonight, up there in the icy branches and treetops, hunched down inside their black feathers against the cold, lifting a claw to take a puff from an ice cigar and blowing smoke out into the drizzling ice-grained snow, if you can call it snow. It ticks and patters off the sidewalk that's more like a snow-sludged shallow river. Somewhere around here in the Back Bay, on one of these streets, Newbury, Marlborough, Beacon Street, or Commonwealth Avenue, there must have been the gentleman's club with its old New England WASP clubby décor and feel where the Banana Brahmins went to relax in the evenings, sometimes inviting their pretty young bilingual secretaries along. Hello Mr. Ambassador, hello Mr. Dulles, says Dolores Ojito. How nice to see you again. This is my friend, Yolanda, she's—Dolores lowers her voice—the secretary of the Guatemalan consul here in Boston.

Oh, I certainly do know el señor consul, says CIA chief Mr. Dulles, but please, call me Allen. And how are you enjoying Boston, Yolanda? Very much, Allen, yesterday we went to the Boston Common to feed walnuts to squirrels. Offering her a cigarette, lighting his own, Dulles, lowering his voice like a practiced spy, says through his cheerless grin: Wait until you see what we're going to do to your country, Yolanda.

The Latin American Society was here on this block, pretty sure in one of these two adjacent brownstones, but it's hard to tell at this nearly 2:00 a.m. hour, with every shop, restaurant, and business on the block shut, windows darkened. There's a realtor's sign now in the parlor-floor window of one, and next door, in a building that has been renovated so that its front window is almost at sidewalk level, there's an upscale optometrist and eyeglass shop. As I stand staring into my faint reflection in the somewhat fogged glass of that window, I see transparent hands rising from behind me to place a pair of designer specs over my eyes. They fit perfectly, and in the reflection I look transformed, even my smile looks urbane, intelligent, rakish. Over my shoulder, the transparent optometrist nods approvingly, a flirtatious curl to her smile, and she whispers: These are like the glasses Marcello Mastroianni wore in *8½*. They make you look a little bit like him. And I chortle and say, Oh yeah, just a little like Marcello, and that's when I realize who she is—Carlota Sánchez Motta—and now her eyes widen and her lips part in surprised recognition too. Ay, Carlota, long-lost adoración, of course this is what you turned out to be, a spectral Boston optometrist.

Lulú likes to say that all the young white dudes in New York look the same to her, that she can't tell one from the other. That's pretty funny, Lulú, I tell her, because I bet that's what they say about you and all the other pelicanitas, and we share a laugh over that. Let it go, man. You promised to let Lulú go. Somewhere around here, too, though on what street I also don't know, was the more comfortable rooming house for single working women that Bert convinced Mamita to leave Our Lady's Guild House for.

Heading down Exeter Street, I look down a public alley running behind businesses and residences and see a door opening. It must be connected to the TGIF on the corner, which probably closed for business about an hour ago, and a man with a short, compact build in kitchen whites comes out, dragging garbage bags that he hoists one at a time into a dumpster. Then he goes back inside without closing the door and comes out again with more garbage bags. This time I get a better look as he passes through the snow-blitzed light radiating through the door: black curly or bushy hair and maybe that's the long half-isosceles triangle of a male Maya nose. The Witness—if that's who the restaurant worker in the alley is, or wherever else he might be in the world—is thirty-three now, because it's been nine years since the night in 1998 that the bishop was murdered. He's that old if he's still alive, that is. The prosecutor in Guatemala who has the case now told me over a year ago that he and his assistants had lost all track of the Witness and that the UN refugee commission in Mexico had too. They had to accept the possibility that through their own negligence, General Cara de Culo and Capitán Psycho-Sadist's assassin, or assassins, had finally tracked the Witness down. The prosecutor said it was also possible that the Witness had crossed the border into the United States, like so many others running for their lives. For once, I'm hoping the prosecutors are hiding the truth, that they've moved the Witness to some secret place and are getting ready to launch the next round of arrests and don't want him talking to a journalist. But I've been looking out for him ever since I moved back to New York anyway. Whenever I see but don't really get a good look at any man who could be Central American, who has that

same build and thick curly hair as the Witness, a kitchen worker, a guy
selling flowers in the stall affixed to a Korean deli, that kid pushing a
peanut cart up ahead of me in Central Park who when I caught up to
him turned out to be Chilean—I bought a bag of peanuts—or even that
man I saw walking along Lower Broadway in a too-long, black winter
coat and carrying a briefcase who, despite eyeglasses, clearly possessed
those features until I drew even on the sidewalk and saw that he didn't,
every time I see someone like that I get excited and think that maybe
he's the Witness.

It was the Witness's testimony that led to the conviction of the three
military men including Capitán Psycho-Sadist and trained suspicion on
Cara de Culo. Later he became a refugee in Mexico because no other
country would grant him asylum. That was because the Witness, testi-
fying, had had to admit to having a role, however minor, in the crime,
and then to have kept secret what he knew until finally, three years later,
when the case was going to trial, he didn't. It was his confessed complic-
ity, not just his being a poor indio who'd lived on the streets, that made
him ineligible for asylum in the United States or Canada or Sweden or
anywhere else. He was a homeless ex-soldier living in the park outside
the bishop's church, supporting himself washing parked cars, when he
was first informally hired by army intelligence operatives to spy on
the bishop, and he was outside the church on the Sunday night when
Monseñor pulled his car into the parish house garage and was beaten
to death. According to what the Witness was willing to declare at the
trial, he was ordered by Capitán Psycho-Sadist and another soldier, the
sergeant, who arrived on the scene in a black Cherokee presumably
minutes after the murder, to alter the crime scene, to drag the bishop's
heavy corpse by the wrists for a few feet, painting a wide streak of blood
with his jean-clad buttocks on the cement floor, to crumple newspapers
and spread them around to make it look as if there'd been a wild struggle,
and to toss a sweater into a corner of the garage so that it would look
as if someone in the heat of homosexual passion had pulled it off and

left it behind. And then the Witness had carried in the chunk of jagged concrete and put it down on the blood-swampy floor, which allowed the first complicit prosecutor to claim that the concrete chunk was the murder weapon used in that crime of passion, rather than the steel pipes and brass knuckles that were more likely used by the killers, who afterward fled through rear exits of the church. Capitán Psycho-Sadist and the sergeant were careful to not leave behind any traces of their own presence; it would be the Witness who left a bloody sneaker print, the light brush of a bloody fingertip against a wall. But the Witness knew he only had to obey, follow orders, keep quiet, for that evidence to be ignored, and he understood what would happen if he disobeyed. He understood why murder cases like this one never had witnesses. After his army service, he'd taken a course to enter Military Intelligence, which in the end he'd flunked. But he did learn there about how the unit known as El Archivo sent its white vans out to abduct people off the streets, and he'd been taken with some other students to see, in a secret dungeon-like wing of the same military base where the intelligence course was held, the deep pits filled with rats, mud, and feces in which some of those abducted prisoners were kept. The Witness was terrified of ending up like one of those prisoners.

I wouldn't be standing here right now in Boston staring down this alley and wondering if that restaurant worker is the Witness if it hadn't been for the Witness in the first place. He's incredibly important in my life, though I've spent no more than a few hours talking to him. Maybe nobody still alive, assuming he's still alive, has had a more direct influence on how my life has turned out, recently at least. The prosecutor who'd won the convictions at the trial had had to flee with his family into exile, to a secret destination. But the prosecutor who inherited the case gave me the Witness's address because I lived in Mexico City, where the Witness was then in hiding; there were questions the prosecutor and his assistants wanted me to ask on their behalf. This was about two years ago.

We spoke in his small, windowless room in a boardinghouse for prostitutes across the street from the taco stand he worked at, a street like a forgotten neorealist film set where the same prostitutes had been standing night and day in the same doorways and on the same sidewalks for years, while the miserly trees along the curb held out the same few leaves glowing yellow green in the sun. In his halting but dogged voice, so familiar from his testimony at the trial and the videotapes of it I'd obsessively watched afterward, the Witness said, To them, I was expendable and as easy to dispose of as trash, but we all are to them, every one of us. (Me too, then, and Zoila, expendable as trash.) During a pretrial evidentiary hearing, Capitán Psycho-Sadist had managed to get close enough to the Witness to vow in a whisper that no matter what happened at the trial or wherever the Witness ended up, they would never stop looking for him. The Witness lived his life between his depressing little room and the taco stand. Even for a taquero, he seemed a little incongruous, short and foreign, a mouth full of broken teeth, with a furtive yet self-possessed, even decorous air. People on the block had seen the heavyset men in loose-fitting dark suits, Guatemalan prosecutors who'd arrived with him when he first moved in across the street from the taco stand and who, during that first year or so especially, occasionally came by to check up on him. Those neighbors kept an eye out on his behalf and knew never to answer questions from strangers such as the one who turned up one morning at the newsstand at the end of that block inquiring about a curly-haired chaparrito guatemalteco and speaking in an accent that wasn't Mexican, that sounded more like the mysterious taquero's. But it was the kind of neighborhood where nobody would ever give answers to any stranger who came around with those kinds of questions about anybody. After that, the Witness didn't leave his room for a few days. He was alone in this life, a poor indigenous man with warty hands who boasted to me that he'd been taught how to use those hands for strangling people during the military intelligence course he'd failed, and who almost never had a night of sleep that wasn't disturbed by nightmares and insomniac terrors. The problem of staying alive consumed him.

The Witness told me in his careful, slowly enunciated manner: They considered me somebody of no importance, disposable as trash, a homeless indio without worth as a human. Yes, I was poor, he said, but I was never a dirty vagrant like they said. I took care of myself. I washed myself and my clothes in the park fountain and bought new clothes and sneakers when I needed to. I deserved as much respect as a human being as any one of them. That was why he'd become a witness, I understood, to affirm that point. As a result, he'd had to come to another country to live alone in the shadows. He didn't regret any of it. He told me he'd do it again. What he'd won for himself by becoming a witness they could never take away. On his block, there were a very few people, including the taco stand's owner, who knew just a little more than the others about why he was in danger. But whenever the Witness went off that block into surrounding ones, people saw only an anonymous indigenous man. Even on his block, nobody really understood that the diminutive, quiet, boyish-looking taquero had altered the course of many lives and had even changed and made history, because his country's first-ever court-room convictions of military officers for an extrajudicial execution, one conviction among a possibly unknowable number of such executions, could never have happened without his testimony. If it hadn't been for the Witness, those military men would never even have been arrested. I wouldn't have published my book on the case. I would never have fled Mexico City to come back to New York. I never would have volunteered at the Bushwick learning sanctuary and met Lulú. María Xum wouldn't have heard me on the radio. I wouldn't be out walking in the Back Bay at this hour with an arrowhead in my pocket, in these streets full of emanations in the cold dark. Take the Witness out of my life, and who am I? It's like the Witness is my spirit guide, my soul's humble but heroic companion. But is my life fully my own if its course could be so altered by the Witness? Well, I could have *not* written the book.

Just before going back inside and closing the door, the kitchen worker looks back at me standing in the mouth of the alley, and no, his face is too narrow.


Standing on this corner under a streetlamp, I take out the arrowhead, feel the snow like icy sand pelting my palm around it. A brother is missing, not this arrowhead. Can't really deny it. Somewhere I once read about Wampanoag walking along old Newbury Street, coming in from the forests to sell huge wild turkeys to the Puritan colonists for hardly more than nothing. A dun light cast by the streetlamps and the weather fill Marlborough Street, through which the rows of facing residential Victorian brownstones on both sides of the street stand dimly outlined and sketched as if with charcoal chalk, black bay windows like black rockface protruding through the wintry murk. Walking down the street, without even any lights on in these brownstones I'm passing, I think that this can't look much different than it did when Henry James walked down it. And that's when I see, ahead and high up through the dark, the only lamp-illuminated window on the block and inside that window a geometric shape of a cerulean blue, part of a rectangle, a standing screen, a jutting wall, or maybe a portion of a large painting hanging on that wall. The same cerulean or blue-green silk background of John Singer Sargent's famous portrait of Lady Agnew of Lochnaw. Herb Felman kept a magazine reproduction of that portrait taped to the top corner of his easel when he was painting his portrait of Mamita, in which he made the backdrop an impressionistic version of the one in the Lady Agnew. Lexi has the original, so that one up there is the copy Herb made for himself, still hanging in his old painting studio. When he went to live in Morocco, Herb left the brownstone house to be looked after by his sister's daughter, Beth, a pretty girl my own age with sunken dark eyes who came with Herb, my father, and me to the Garden for a Celtics game one winter Sunday afternoon and to Durgin-Park for dinner after.

I remember how worshipful Beth was toward Herb, a war hero and a successful Boston society portrait painter in the not-yet-extinguished Sargent tradition. Haven't really thought much about Beth in ages. This was in about sixth grade, when I was still an emaciated simian boy. She wrote me a letter, but all I remember about it was how polished and sophisticated it seemed and for a while I kept the letter under my pillow. Beth lived with her family above her father's bakery in Quincy. I must have written back, but I don't recall what. Twelve sittings in all, three a week, I remember Mamita telling me, before Herb finished the portrait. To get to Herb's studio, she took the subway. The weather during any of those sittings could have been the same as tonight, icy snow lightly scratching at the window. Mamita is the same age, twenty-six, that Lady Agnew was when she sat for Sargent.

The off-the-shoulder evening gown is her own, a *Vogue* copy made by the seamstresses in Abuelita's hat and dress store. She keeps the gown at Herb's studio and changes into it behind a standing screen near the wood-burning stove in the corner. She'd rather change in the privacy of one of the other rooms, but Herb has his reason for doing it this way. He's explained: One thing the common man or woman on the street doesn't understand even one bit about portrait painting, Yolanda, is that it's a drama, like an opera or a play. Listening to the rustle of the gown's silk and lace from behind the screen as he sits on the stool in front of the easel patiently waiting to begin is the musical prologue. Often Herb puts on an opera record while he works. On the morning that Mamita turned six, her eardrum was blown out by the celebratory chain explosions of firecrackers set off too close, but her nahual, a spider monkey, caught the gossamer membrane before it hit the ground, preserved it inside the chamois eyelid of a fawn, and twenty years later changed it into a small mole on the back of her infant son's left hand; the infant now floating inside her womb without any use yet for his indispensable, directional mole. So Mamita doesn't know which operas Herb plays and doesn't enjoy orchestral or opera music anyway, too complicated a commotion for just one ear. She likes simple songs she can sing along to, tralala'ing until she reaches the words she knows: Let it snow, let it snow, let it snow. When it's her own voice inside her head, it's almost like being able to hear in both ears again.

Herb is a large, thick-necked, broad-chested, strong-looking man. Listening to opera records while he paints, he becomes very animated, puffing out cheerful baritone notes of the melody between taut lips, repeatedly bringing brush back to palette and peeking out at Mamita from behind a side of the easel. During those rousing men's choruses that Mamita described years later without knowing what they were—"like all the soldiers singing as they march," so maybe *Boris Godunov* or some such—he strides around his studio, singing along without words, suddenly coming to a stop in front of the canvas to stare at it like he's never seen it before, then launching into another extended spell of painting, vigorously jabbing, smearing, slapping paint on with his brush, his singing subsiding to soft yelps and whimpers and finally falling silent inside his tunnel of concentration, the record still spinning, stylus knocking against the last groove. He has cut-up cardboard boxes laid over the floor instead of drop cloths and often falls to his knees to draw with a charcoal pencil or chalk, rows of preliminary sketches of Mamita's hands crossing the cardboard floor. It astounds Mamita that a man can have become wealthy doing what Herb does. Even in winter, he wears a pigment-splotched white T-shirt, black horsehair shooting out through the V-neck like upholstery stuffing, and if the room feels cold, instead of encumbering his arms with sleeves, he puts on an old vest, its shaggy wool stiff as papier-mâché with paint smears from wiping and cleaning his own brushes against it. Joseph's Mastodon Fur Vest of Many Colors, he calls it.

He often makes these little joking remarks about Jewishness. Like Bert, he considers himself a secular nonbeliever. Bert rarely mentions Judaism, though whenever he does, he sounds respectful or else nostalgically affectionate, as if referring to a lunatic but beloved old relative. The priest at San Sebastián, Mamita's family church, had agreed to marry them so long as Bert vowed that their future children would be raised Catholic. But we weren't raised Catholic.

Bert is always going on about how Herb is a true war hero. Mamita has heard him brag to some of his University Club squash-playing friends: My boyhood friend Herb Felman fought in D-Day, the Shrub War to Paris, and in the Battle of the Bulge, so don't tell me he didn't have a goddamned war. Who else do you know had a war like Herb did. Bert sure didn't, he made bombs in a factory in Delaware. Bert has also told her that Herb is homosexual. Maybe it makes Bert feel a little better to evoke Herb's homosexuality in the context of his own not-so-manly war. Somebody had to make bombs and, anyway, Bert was in his mid-thirties, commonly considered too old to go to war without an officer's commission. But Herb was a thirty-four-year-old ordinary GI. With his broad face and noble nose, black hair receding over a strong forehead, thick, arched black eyebrows, and amber-brown eyes, Herb is a handsome man, he even somewhat resembles one of those broad-shouldered Aztec warriors she saw so many of in Mexico City during her honeymoon, depicted in murals and as statues. But his mouth is a little off-putting; the way his excessively rubbery lips seem nearly to turn inside out when he's excited, exposing large front teeth, reminds her of that famous comedian who only she seems to think isn't so funny. Years later, feet up in the recliner in her den, watching Carol Burnett on television performing a skit with that slapstick, doughty pathos that always brought out such gales of deeply felt laughter in Mamita, it will come back to her, and she'll look over at her son and say, I've always thought Jerry Lewis would have been funnier as a woman.

Herb begins each portrait session by arranging Mamita in a white high-backed chair, setting her bare arm on the padded armrest so that the soft inner flesh of her slender bicep and the underside of her forearm are turned toward the viewer, hand resting slightly palm up on the silvery fabrics of her lap, giving her a look of relaxed, unselfconscious summer afternoon lounging. The other arm rests conventionally bent at the elbow on the padding, fingers dangling over the whorled wooden knob, engagement ring displayed. He tucks the orchid, always a fresh one, inside her décolletage. Holding up the Lady Agnew reproduction, he says, Try to hold your head just like this, Yolanda, with your left eyebrow just slightly raised. He wants the contrast with the slight droop of her opposite eyelid. The axiom of the slight symmetry-subverting flaw that lets beauty open out from the canvas. During one of their first sittings, Herb said, Yolanda, I want you to tell me a funny story without allowing yourself even to smile, never mind laugh. She told him about Coco, her pet monkey, and how she always spoke to Coco in English. He said, That's wonderful, Yolanda. Now tell me the saddest story you know, but again, trying not to show any emotion. Mamita told how Coco had suffocated to death. Of course Mamita knew sadder stories, but this one, I think, was the one she relied on in an uncomfortable social setting to keep herself from impolitely laughing. While telling her funny Coco story, Mamita had involuntarily allowed a corner of her mouth to turn upward, and when she told the sad one, on that same side her mouth had involuntarily turned ever so slightly downward. By combining the two in a visibly invisible manner, Herb achieved the sensuous effect he was aiming for: the corner of Mamita's lips invisibly trembling, close to twitching from the tension of the two opposite impulses. Likewise, in her eyes, silent laughter rippled over their surface when she told the funny story, while their depths transparently darkened when she told the sad one. Again, he combined them.

I'm very pleased with how beautifully it's turned out, says Herb. Aren't you?

Oh yes, Herb, I am, she says happily. I think you're every little bit as good as John Singer Sargent. There's no equivalent way to say "every little bit as" in Spanish. You can say a "little bit of " or a "little pinch of." She enjoys correctly wielding this coy American idiom.

Herb has begun every session so far by saying: You know it's impossible to paint a woman's face as pretty as it really is, Yolanda. Eventually he confessed that he was quoting Sargent. Herb intensely identifies with Sargent: a successful portrait painter with Boston roots and larger artistic ambitions, who went to the World War I battlefields to paint their horrors, just as Herb went to the Second World War to both contribute to and try to end its horrors. Sargent was also a big masculine man who liked to go to rough sporting events and who never married, essentially a loner despite many friendships, including with many of the women he painted.

When Herb was only nine, his gift for artistic drawing already noted by his school art teacher, his older brother took him to see Sargent at work on his series of murals at the Boston Public Library. His older brother was a friend of the son of one of the guards, and they'd arranged to go in the morning, before the library was open but when the artist was already at work. Herb stood at one end of the hall watching through the chilly gray light as Sargent, at the opposite end, stood on a ladder painting along a seam in one of his murals. His bowler hat had so many paintbrushes sticking up out of the band, it looked like Chief Massasoit's headdress, and he wore a thoroughly splotched vest of many colors that he wiped his brushes on, though it was a tailored suit vest, not a wooly one like Herb's. The guard told Herb and his brother that when Sargent left the library to go to one of his society parties in the evening, he'd keep the vest on and come back still wearing it in the mornings. How do you like that for an anecdote, Yolanda? Isn't that wonderful?

Sargent was working on one of the last murals of his series *The Triumph of Religion*, which was supposed to be, you know, says Herb, the American Sistine Chapel. The expectations for it were very high and not just in Boston. But Sargent never finished it. Probably because of the synagogue mural that represents Judaism as kneeling, blindfolded, her scepter snapped in half, distinctly not triumphing. Yolanda, do you get my meaning? Not triumphing. In the mural at the opposite end of that same wall a radiant golden girl in a corona of light symbolizes the Christian Church, triumphant. You can see why some people were upset, not just Jews, but also taxpaying secular Americans who didn't think the public library should be used to denigrate one religion at the expense of another. Between those two murals on that wall was a larger panel, still blank, that according to Sargent's plan was going to sum up and conclude the entire series. Maybe he had in mind an allegory of varied images that was somehow going to cast a new light on the synagogue mural and absorb even Judaism into the Triumph of Religion in America. But I doubt it, says Herb. The scandal that started in Boston was reported on and argued over throughout the country. My own art teacher was one of the Jews who joined the protests at the library, Yolanda, demanding that the synagogue mural be removed. I think that even Bostonians who agreed with the protests in principal asked, Who are these bearded overwrought maniacs, shouting in their foreign and Bolshevik accents? Where did they come from?

After a pause, he continues, But poor Sargent, really, I think it was a sort of innocence that did him in. Defending himself with all that art historical baloney about medieval traditions in religious painting from Michelangelo to the Reims Cathedral. All fine if you're painting in a medieval cathedral or even a contemporary one, where I suppose you're allowed to tell your worshippers a version of their own story, but not in a democratic public institution. The library's Brahmin trustees didn't back down; they supported Sargent to the end. But I think their support embarrassed him. A fool he wasn't; he knew what was going on. He finally understood the emptiness of what he was trying to do, the vain grandiosity of what was essentially an academic imitation of a kind of art he really had no deep feeling for, however excellent the execution. So he left that culminating center panel blank and walked away. He felt exposed and knew that he had nothing of true meaning and conviction to put up there. Blaming the Jews and their protests provided an easy escape. In London, you know, Sargent was put down by the snobs as "the painter of Jews." But there was some truth to it. Somewhere he said that he far preferred the emotional and intelligent liveliness of his Jewish women to the dullness of most of the British aristocratic women whose portraits he painted. Our Lady Agnew here was an exception, but anyway, she was Scottish. Oscar Wilde was his friend. And Parliament had just made it a crime to have intimate physical relations with any person of your own sex.

A silence descends on them. This is the closest Herb has ever come to speaking about his own sexuality with Mamita. He seems more discomfited than she does. Did it just slip out? Does he think she doesn't know?

I forgot to feed the dogs, says Herb. It's horrible, Yolanda, I've been having recurring nightmares in which I'm traveling faraway, in Europe, and suddenly I remember my dogs, my cat, that they're here in Boston in a room, dead on the floor, starved to death due to my own having forgotten to feed them. What would Sigmund say about it, do you think? Please excuse me, Yolanda.

He dashes out of the room. Downstairs, somewhere, are his three dogs. She doesn't know about dog breeds. Two are quite large but extremely thin, with long noses and ears, golden brown long hair. One is small with curly whitish fur. Somewhere there is also a long, luxuriously black cat with emerald-green eyes.

There is a charcoal sketch pinned to a small easel on the floor over there in the corner, a nude man on his knees, his sinewy, perfectly proportioned torso upright but arching backward, head thrown back, mouth open in ecstasy or anguish, and between his spread thighs where his sex should be there is a smudgy blankness. I know what you must be thinking, even you, Mamita, because it doesn't look like anything else. It's as if that blankness represents the back of the head of a nebulous ghost. She can hear dogs barking downstairs, and now Herb's bellowing Red Army Choir voice is singing "Happy Birthday." A young Asian man comes a few days a week to houseclean, but there is no one to regularly feed his dogs. Herb must always worry about forgetting.

The other day I picked up this Rudolf Serkin recording of *French Suites*, says Herb when he comes back into the room, holding the record. I've been playing it in my bedroom. A quieter mood, he says, quieter but magical.

You were singing "Happy Birthday," Herb?

Yes, to Mitzy. My female borzoi. He straightens up from the record player, the music gently dancing out into the studio. Even listening with one ear, Mamita likes it.

It is magical, she says.

Reality is magical, don't you think, Yolanda? he says.

This assertion she needs to think over. How many people in Guatemala, including some she knew, who were in the Árbenz government or were even just considered sympathetic to it have been killed or imprisoned in the three years since the coup. The gringos compiled a list of suspected Communists for the new government, supposedly ten thousand people are on it. Could she be on it? Or was she considered just an ordinary young female secretary from a known anti-Communist family, not a member of the diplomatic service under Árbenz, who'd just happened to find a job in the Boston consulate. Was that why, after the coup, she hadn't wanted to return to Guatemala, because she was afraid? Worried, too, that her friendship with el joven might have cast suspicion on her? In his last letter, el joven wrote that you could get put onto the Communist list even if you'd been overheard saying or were suspected of holding the belief that "in a Democracy the people choose the government." During the months after the coup when he was taking refuge in the Mexican embassy, el joven fell seriously ill with typhoid, as did scores of others crowded together there. The United States was pressuring the ten or so foreign governments whose embassies in Guatemala were housing refugees to deny asylum to all of them because if any of those refugees were allowed into their countries they'd go on fomenting Communism there, too, and then it would all end with a giant Red stain extending from Mexico to Chile. As the months passed, those countries, exasperated with having to care for their uninvited guests, finally defied the US government, citing international asylum law as, at least, a pretext. Árbenz was allowed into Mexico, and a month later el joven followed. In his last letter el joven wrote that he'd gone to see Árbenz in Uruguay, where his exile continued, though it was destined to end in suicide after he returned to Mexico City. El joven wanted to come to Boston; he wrote that he had a new passport and identity. But we went back instead, Mamita and I, to Guatemala in 1957 or early '58. By then the government was less worried about bilingual secretaries from good capitalist families who'd married a gringo than they were about what was, so to speak, gathering on the horizon: war that was going to last for over three decades.

I'm sure Sargent, Herb is saying, wasn't even a regular churchgoer. I never set foot in any synagogue when I was a boy. My father was a Red, and we were, too, and so was your husband's old man. Bert wasn't exactly a yeshiva boy, you know. But he sure looked the part at his peddler's cart after school, selling potatoes in his wool peasant coat and pants stuffed into his black knee socks, like old Moe made him do. I used to see Bert standing there in the cold, weighing out potatoes, and, oh Yolanda, let me tell you, did he look forlorn. Who could ever have seen Bert then and imagine: There's a future University Club squash champion, master of false teeth, and the husband of a beautiful young Catholic woman from our Southern Hemisphere? The night before D-Day was the one time I ever willingly took part in a religious service, with a Christian chaplain killed the next day during the landing on Omaha. Out of a hundred and fifty men in my battalion, Yolanda, only seventeen of us survived to fight onward to Paris. Religion, schmeligion, if you ask me. Of course nowadays you have to watch your mouth; even being an ardent FDR guy is enough to make those McCarthy thugs suspect you of being a Commie fellow traveler. If these Brahmin types I've been earning my money from ever get wind of a tenth of what I really believe, you'll see me out on the sidewalk on the Common making pastel portraits of tourists. And that hoity toity University Club likes having your Bert around as long as he's winning squash championships for them, but the day they find out about old Pa Moe the Red baker, oh boy, you watch, they'll drop him like a hot potato, alright.

Mamita, you were in love with el joven before you met Daddy, is that it?

Ay, Frankie, do you see now? This is why I never want to tell you anything, because you take just a little thread of truth and pull on it and out comes a made-up story. His name wasn't el joven, it was René, and he was just a special friend. We'd grown up together. I liked him, he was intelligent, and he loved to laugh. He did have feelings for me, I know that, but I never felt that way. He was necio, very stubborn. I know Memo told you about this, because you've pestered me about it before. Do you remember that day when you were just back from your year of living in Memo's house? It was winter but you didn't own a winter coat or have any money, and I took you into Boston, to Jordan Marsh. That Beatle, John Lennon, had been murdered the night before, and in the store they were only playing his music and you couldn't stop crying. Ay chulo, there we were in the store looking for coats and you walking around crying like that, like a little boy. I used to worry, Frankie, that life, especially those difficult years you had growing up and at home with Bert, had given you a hard heart. Now I saw that you were a feeling person, and it made me happy. But I wished you'd be nicer to Lexi. Afterward, you started asking me about René, though you called him el joven, how silly, el joven, and she laughs.

Mamita, I admit it. I read that stuff about postcoup Guate and the Commie list in a history book. Please don't look at me like that, with those reveal nothing other than what's here on the canvas oil paint eyes. So whatever went wrong with your marriage during that first year had nothing to do with this René. But even if Bert was jealous because René came and visited you, that wouldn't have justified him hitting you, my God, well of course not. Something made you take me back to Guatemala with you. Most likely, Bert was already failing you as a lover, but then, what caused that? Or else, despite it being so soon in your marriage, he'd already started in on the verbal abuse. But if he was getting physically violent with you by then, during those several months of my life before we went back to Guate, it's so horrible to think we would have come back to Massachusetts anyway two years later like we did, even for the hospital. Instead of living with Daddy on Sacco Road, Mamita, we could have lived somewhere else and let him visit me in the hospital and pay the bills. That would have been so much smarter. Maybe you felt like you had no other choice, like you were a captive. Yet you at least loved him or desired him enough to make Lexi? There was still some love left in your heart, if only enough for it to be the equivalent of a heart that's deaf in one ear. Doesn't even have to have been that. That is if it was Daddy you made Lexi with.

Mamita, you were brought up keeping secrets, you know you were. Oh, your rancher grandfather was a Spaniard? You don't say, Yolanda, my, how impressive, a descendant of the conquistadors, even. But you and your brother never knew anything about his wife, your own abuela? Well, sometimes parents forget to tell their children about their own mothers, sure, very common. You were raised in a ludicrous tropical criollo society that somehow collectively realized there was a certain kind of truthfulness it was essential to do without, and so they tore it out like ripe radishes from the earth. This lack of truthfulness, twinned with secretiveness, has been passed down through the generations among the racially hyperstressed Central American petite bourgeoise, you know, all those people from "good families" without any indigenous or African blood. One look at any of us, and not just from the Montejo Hernández families, screamed out that was a lie. It was just second nature to you, Mamita, to keep things secret. Mamita, why are you suddenly huddling, grasping your elbows and shivering?

Are you okay, Yolanda? Herb's thick expressive eyebrows rise and move closer together in worry. Are you coming down with something?

I think the fire in the stove has died, she says. Can I put on the shawl?

Because she is allergic to wool, Herb bought a shawl for her that seems made of colored, thickly braided mop strings. Holding it up like an unfurled cape, he drops the shawl around her bare shoulders. He gets down on his knees in front of the stove, opens its little door and blows, picks up a magazine and fans, blows again, until new flames lift off the logs. Mamita loves coming to Herb's studio. She knows that when the sittings are over and her portrait is finished she won't see her gallant voluble artist friend so much anymore, not in this way, and a certain magic will go out of her life. Soon, though, a new magic, the one of motherhood, will be upon her.

When Herb is standing behind the easel again, he says, Your baby is due—he gives a whimsical shrug—this summer, during the sweet corn season?

In May, she says.

Is Bert impatient? Excited to be a father?

My mother seems not to hear him; her thoughts are maybe elsewhere.

I bet Bert is just beside himself.

Just beside himself? She's heard that phrase before, of course, but can't connect it meaningfully to Bert. There is Bert, and there he is standing beside himself.

Very excited and impatient to be a father, says Herb.

Oh, I think so, yes. When Mamita says that, I hear a touch of flatness in her voice, and Herb glances at her with curiosity and concern. In not quite a year's time she'll have fled home to Guatemala with her baby son, and you don't think Herb has picked up on something? Come on, Ma, tell us what it is. Sitting there, holding me in about my fourth month inside your womb, you must have some ominous sense of where your marriage is headed. Forsaken or forsaking? Look at you, Mamita, so young, just twenty-six, a pregnant niña bien from the tropics somehow marooned in Boston.

Don't you think Bert will make a good father, Yolanda?

Because the movements are so slight and discrete, the way her lips part and the way her eyes, looking a little more anxious than absent, lower their gaze to the floor, he feels rocked back by the force of her unhappiness.

Yolanda, he says. You know I'm your friend. You can tell me anything. After all this time we've spent together, I'm closer to you than I am even to Bert. Do you understand?

She looks at him as if slowly coming out of a daze. Yes, Herb? she says quietly.

Yes, he says. Yolanda . . .

That drawing over there, Mamita says, gesturing with eyes and uplifted chin toward the charcoal sketch. I haven't seen you make a drawing like that one before.

His expression deflates; it perks up again. Do you like it?

Yes, it looks like a drawing in a museum, she says. He looks so real and alive. Did somebody come here to sit for it?

I painted him from memory. But that memory sometimes does seem more alive to me, more real, than anything or anybody I can see around me.

She asks, What is his name?

Eddie Baskin, from Penn Yan, up there by Keuka Lake, in Upstate New York, says Herb. Finger Lakes country, have you heard of it? His father was a caretaker on an estate owned by a bootlegger. It was beautiful countryside, but in many ways a sordid household. Eddie was in my battalion. We were two of the seventeen who made it past D-Day. Not the bravest, not the best soldiers or most skilled, certainly not the most cowardly, it just so happens we survived Omaha Beach. That's a preliminary sketch for a large painting I'm going to make. Herb begins to explain the experience behind the painting or rather its prelude. It usually takes a long time to tell a war story. Desperate to be understood

by people who weren't there, you want to get it right and feel so obligated
to because every war story is never about just yourself but usually you
don't even know where to start.

That time in New York, when I'd run away from college and had dinner
with Tío Memo, he told me that René, el joven, came to visit my mother
in Boston. The way I see it, Mamita, that means he did. My uncle had
had a jealously tinged, disdainful obsession with el joven since you were
all teenagers. He didn't trust him, and as best as he could he kept track
of him. Memo meant it when he said he didn't think René was good
for his sister, just like he did when he felt the same way about Bert. But
did René come to Boston before or after I was born? Maybe it was three
years later, after we'd come back from Guatemala because I got TB. He
came to say goodbye, playing that classic role, the romantic who comes
to tell the woman who spurned him that he's going off to war. He was
sneaking back into Guatemala to join Luis Turcios Lima and the other
rebellious young army officers who were starting a guerrilla war in la
Sierra de las Minas. A little before or in early 1960, the year Lexi was
born, it would have been. El joven must not have survived the uprising;
not many did. It's the most credible reason for why Tío Memo never
heard anything about him again.

It happened in the forest outside the Normandy town of Saint-Céneri-
le-Gérei. Eddie and Herb had been doing some reconnaissance patrol-
ling together when they were cut off. The twelve other men from their
unit were hiding in an abandoned stone farmhouse way back there,
and now there was sporadic rifle fire coming from behind them in the
forest but also from up ahead, and they could hear the excited barking
of dogs. That's not combat, it's hunting, said Eddie. That seemed true,
says Herb. We didn't hear anything that sounded like an exchange of

fire. Hunting wild boar, probably, said Eddie. Deer, rabbit, birds. Was
it the Jerries out hunting, or was it local farmers? We didn't know, says
Herb. Maybe the Resistance, they hunted for food too. The unreturned
gunfire of hunters peppered the silence of the forest in all directions, first
over here, then over there, and some of these rifle shots now sounded
closer to them than the earlier ones. It was too dangerous to try to get
back to our unit, says Herb. It seemed safer to find someplace to hide,
at least until it was too dark to hunt, to hunt edible animals, that is. On
the path Eddie and I were walking down, we came upon a dead baby
boar, bright red guts spilling out its side where the hunter's bullet had
entered. Eddie bent over and touched the guts with his finger and said,
Still warm, Herb. This just happened, it was those shots we heard from
over there a coupl'a minutes ago. The forest terrain sloped downward
from the path, as if down into a gulch, but the underbrush was thick.
We plunged down into it, bent over, our rifles held against our ribs, says
Herb. That's when we heard trucks, the tractor sound of trucks pulling
cannon, somewhere on a road above us. Holy moly, now what was this,
Yolanda? Was it our side getting ready for an assault on the town, or
was it the Jerries bringing in their own hardware? Well, it wasn't long
before we heard the explosion of a grenade, not so near us but not that
far. That was followed by the unmistakable racket of combat. Around
us, the underbrush had thinned out. The ground was now smooth,
covered in plant mulch and some low, soft plants like ivy, and the trees
were evenly spaced. A family of boar went by, looking like big furry fish
trotting along on skinny little legs, the mom and dad with their tusks
and two little boarlets, maybe the siblings of the one we'd just seen dead.
An owl flew slowly, slowly over our heads. We heard the explosion of
artillery shells, landing in or near the town. Fighting was breaking out
over here and also over there and all along a wide circumference that
seemed to be slowly closing in on us through the forest. Eddie pulled
on my arm and said, Look, Herb, look at that. In the twilight, pecking
at the ground, was a family of woodcocks. Eddie and I sat down on

the forest floor. Honest to God, Yolanda, I've never seen anything so extraordinary as that hidden forest gulch filling up with animals, there in that dark-green glowing dusk, while the earth occasionally shook with explosions. A doe and her fawns, Yolanda, over there, and some more boars went by. I saw a mother and her boarlets calmly lay down behind some trees not twenty feet from us. There were plenty of rabbits, too, including some of those huge French hares, looking so placid. When Eddie went off to relieve himself, he saw a red fox, sitting there calmly watching him. We were in a kind of enchanted wood, Yolanda. It was where the animals came to escape the hunters and the fighting, and Eddie and I were there too. We were blessed, Yolanda, though by what divine power, I can't say. Maybe it came from the animals, maybe from what was inside Eddie and me. Do you understand?

Mamita asks, a note of wonder in her voice: Herb, this is going to be your painting?

Herb gestures at the charcoal drawing of the young man and says, Eddie and Herb together in the Normandy forest. I haven't decided yet on our postures.

Herb and Mamita stare silently at the drawing of Eddie.

We didn't expect to make it, says Herb. Especially if our side was taking the town, at any moment we were going to have crazed escaping Jerries crashing through there, into our hiding place. Eddie said, Herb, you better get rid of that dog tag. It had a little Star of David beside my name. As if it's that simple to say what a person is and what prayers or other nonsense should be said over his corpse: US ARMY PRIVATE HERBERT FELMAN, AGE 34, JEW. We're the Jerries, so we hate Jews, and it's our duty to treat them with special savagery. There must be thousands of buried Star of David dog tags everywhere in Europe the war was fought, wherever Jewish soldiers found themselves in imminent danger of capture or close-range murder. Sure, I buried mine in that dirt, it must still be there. European kids search for and collect them now, I read somewhere. Well, probably because Eddie and I thought that might be our last night, that's what made it happen, Yolanda. It was a feeling that had been growing inside us and between us since D-Day, as we made our way through the countryside to Paris. Just like it happens between young lovers in books by Chekhov, Tolstoy, or in Hemingway's *A Farewell to Arms*. Have you read it, Yolanda? Oh, you should. Like being turned inside out and emptied out and filled back up with a new feeling that seems to have no border, that just wants to flow into your lover any way it can, just as you want your lover to flow into you. Yolanda, I didn't think that was for people like me. I thought I was going to die, probably sooner than later, without experiencing young love, or let me call it, if you don't mind, the rapture of love. It was the first rapture for each of us. Like Hemingway wrote in his novel, All things of the night cannot be explained by day. But I'm not going to try to explain. I just want to paint it.

Mamita, could it ever really have been that kind of love with Daddy? Or just with the Italian. Was it like that with the Mexican Honeywell technician?

Mamita laughs with surprised delight. All the animals will be in the painting too?

Yes, of course. And that extraordinary light, Yolanda, of evening falling deep inside an ancient forest, that light somehow also infiltrated by the flash and fire of lethal artillery explosions up above, not exactly visible but that you will see somehow extrasensorially, if that's a word. I owe Eddie this painting, but I owe it to myself even more.

Oh Herb, it's going to be beautiful and famous too. I just know it. Biblical, but not like Sargent, it will show the truth because it is true, hiding with the animals saved your life.

Oh no, not biblical! exclaims Herb with a laugh. But you're absolutely right. If I ever surpass Sargent in only one painting, it will be this one.

What happened after? Where is Eddie now?

Okay, well, it was our American and Canadian troops that took that town. Eddie and I found our unit. The war went on. Eddie pretended that nothing had happened between us, Yolanda. Every day, he performed the most complete indifference and innocence. After the Liberation of Paris, he was found dead with his throat slit in a back alley in the eighteenth arrondissement. The official investigation said that he'd raped a French Moroccan girl and that her brothers had caught Eddie and killed him. I have no reason to doubt that it happened that way. And the war kept going, for me, all the way to the Ardennes. I became a very fierce soldier. If you don't mind me saying, Yolanda, I deserved a medal.

Yoli has heard Bert indignantly bellowing: We've got fellows at the University Club who got medals who didn't see a tenth of the action that Herb did. You don't think it was Herb being a thirty-four-year-old Jew with the rank of private from one end of the war to the other that kept him from getting a medal for valor?

Oh Herb, I'm so sorry, she says, such a terrible story. What else can Mamita say? She has tears in her eyes, and that's good, the only possible reaction that won't offend him.

Do people really fall in love twice, Yolanda? The way Herb asks this, it doesn't sound like a question.

All the mothers of children I know, Herb, say yes, you can, she answers. They say that when you have your first baby, you think you cannot possibly ever love any person more than this baby son. You are even scared to have another child because you might not love her as much. But when that daughter comes, you grow another heart full of love, and you love your daughter as much as the son, and if you have a third child, you grow a third heart. That's what mothers have told me. I think it's that way in romance love, too, Herb, except then maybe one heart dies and another one grows. Sometimes it takes a while.

That's very well said, Yolanda, says Herb politely. Thank you. Is that what you want, a son and a daughter?

Yes. I only had my brother, and we were very close, and he always made me feel loved and protected.

I hope you're right about that, about growing another heart. I've been waiting a long time.

Mamita has never before been called upon to find words appropriate to a moment like this. She says, Herb if you make that painting, it will be in a museum. You'll be famous. So many people will want to know you, and you'll meet somebody, you'll see.

You're right, Yolanda. Someday you'll take your son to see it here in the Museum of Fine Arts, and you'll tell him all about it. I'm a late bloomer, just like my old friend Bert. He's an inspiration to me too. Look at him, at his age, fifty not that far over the horizon, starting a family with a woman like you.

Mamita, I'm so sorry, I say. And so that you'll feel the truth of what I'm saying, I make myself stare into the seemingly transparent depth of your oil paint eyes, where nothing happens. I won't ever do that again, love with a heart that's deaf in one ear, that's a lazy, cowardly, gets-you-nowhere way to love. Still, I think I heard Gisela in stereo loud, soft, and clear, but that wasn't enough. I've never thought this before, but maybe it was *her* heart that was deaf in one ear. I'm sorry I haven't given you a grandchild, Ma, but I guess you can say I'm trying. Do any of those children who live in Lexi's house ever come to visit you? There's a ten-year-old girl, Monica. I think you'd enjoy her.

What am I doing, talking to this painting? I can do it again tomorrow if I want to, at Lexi's. Why don't I just go back to Green Meadows and try to talk to Mamita some more?

I think this copy of the painting is better than the one we had in our house growing up. Herb kept the better one for himself. I'm concentrating on the corner of Mamita's lips, trying to see that visibly invisible, if only I could think of something funny to say right now, see if I can provoke a quiver of a smile. I've always been good at getting my mother to laugh. But no words come but these: Mamita, I'm sorry I didn't save you from Bert. I'm sorry you didn't save me from Bert. I'm sorry neither of us saved Lexi from Bert, but I think you finally did, starting when she was in her late teens anyway. Ay Mamá, your Herb-painted eyes look through me in a way that makes me feel not here.

I turn and look at Beth and say, I'm keeping you up, aren't I? I'm sorry. She's sitting slumped back on an old dark-red sofa, its silken upholstery slightly shredded here and there, her knees wide apart, her long frail hands clasped over her abdomen. Besides the couch, the only other furniture is an upholstered sea-green old armchair, the wood of the arms chipped, and a couple of hard chairs pulled up to a small, round wooden table with a red-and-white checkered tablecloth on it, an empty green bottle of wine on top, and a plastic ashtray. It's like we're in an old-fashioned pizza restaurant with only one table and nothing on the walls but a portrait of Yolanda Montejo de Goldberg. An unplugged standing brass lamp in the corner, the shade missing. Grace Paley's *The Collected Stories* on the floor next to the sofa. Beth's dress fits her like a sack, hiding her very slight frame, which you can sort of make out when she's standing by the way the dress falls around her, her collarbones with their pearl-sized knobs under the taut ivory skin inside her open collar. It's a black dress, with a dense pattern of small white letters like Linotype print all over it in no discernible order, letters like hundreds of rioters milling around waiting to see what comes next. She's so small and delicate looking, Beth Alamy. You look at the bones in her wrists and think of sparrows. She still has that pretty face, eyes like lustrous prunes, and abundant dark-brown, silver-streaked hair, simply pulled back and tied in a knot. Something Emily Dickinson about her, maybe it's that impression of a small intelligent face inside an old pendant. Her teeth are a little uneven, slightly stained with nicotine or coffee in the way nearly everybody's used to be. She lives in these top two floors, rents out the bottom two. We didn't talk much before I went and stood before that painting. She did tell me that she's a lawyer. Beth sits up and looks perfectly awake, her eyes like black lamps beneath the light thrown by the naked bulb in the ceiling.

Oh really, don't worry about it. I was up anyway, she says. I would have told you to come back tomorrow if I'd really wanted to.

Herb is still alive, in Morocco, living in Marrakesh. That's what she told me even as we were climbing the stairs to come up here. I ask, How old is Herb now?

Ninety-seven years young. He has that exhausting male monster longevity. You know, like Picasso. Saul Bellow and Pinochet, one who I love and the other who I obviously don't, were born the same year and died last year, at ninety-one.

Kissinger is still going, I say. It's like that saying, Mala hierba no muere.

But good Hierba Felman no muere, either, says Beth, pleased with her pun.

Bert, too, well he made it to ninety-three. I won't say what kind of weed he was. Let Beth think good enough. Nicanor Parra, I add, because how can I not?

That sort of longevity is rarer in men than in woman, says Beth. Somehow female longevity doesn't seem to derive from that monster energy whose ideal seems to be to go on making yourself the center of the universe until no one else is left. Grace Paley. Penelope Fitzgerald. Georgia O'Keeffe. Agnes Martin. Oh my God, Louise Bourgeois. Doris Lessing. She's not that old yet, but Toni Morrison better live to be a thousand. I'll stop because I can just go on and on.

Mother Teresa, I say. Beth nods and says, Mother Teresa too. So what kind of law do you practice? I ask.

I've worked as a public defender here in the Suffolk County courts for twenty-five years and still going. This house is still Herb's. His income nowadays comes from his properties and investments; he was smart with his money. My father's old bakery gives me some income too. It's a Brazilian coffee shop now, and Herb rents the upstairs part, where our family used to live, to store his art and papers. I feel bad taking it but he insists and I do need that money. But I'm so ready to try something new. I want to write a biography of Herb Felman, Frank. Herb has had such a remarkable life, and the obscurity he lives in now makes it all seem even more, I don't know, poignant and profound.

You're going to go to Marrakesh to talk to him?

In two weeks. I'm planning to spend at least three months there.

How is Herb's memory?

Herb the Memorious, she says. I must have a slight look of surprise. She says, Upstairs, it's wall-to-wall books, and I love Borges.

I wonder what Herb remembers about my parents, I say. He spent a month painting that portrait of my mother. She sat for it three times a week. He must know what she was like back then better than anybody else who's still around.

I know Herb adored your mother, Frankie. You don't mind if I call you that, do you? It was your name when we met, it feels weird to call you Francisco. You can tell he did from the portrait, don't you think? Your mom sure does look smokin', but that's not what I mean. She has that compelling mysterious something that tugs at your heart. I find myself just wanting to stare into her eyes and, I don't know, become her friend. That portrait has hung there on that wall exactly where it is now since the day Herb finished it. That has to tell you something about how he felt about your mom.

Beth, has it really?

How many years now? Well, we're the same age. A long time. Don't be depressed. She smiles.

Fifty years, oh man. And the chair she sat in, and the screen she told me she used to change behind, are they still around?

Long gone. That stove has never moved; of course we can't use it anymore. There's a room upstairs with a skylight and views out the back window where you can see some of the river. I never really understood why Herb didn't use that room as his studio.

Maybe he just liked looking out that window down at the street.

Yes, just waiting for you to turn up at two in the morning some snowy night and see the light on and the portrait through the window and then ring the doorbell to ask the person who answers the door if you can come up and see it because it's your mother and Herb used to tell you war stories when you were a boy.

I'm amazed you let me in.

I guess I am too. But you really were convincing. It's more furnished upstairs, by the way, and there's more of Herb's work hanging, but my friend Mickey got in from London earlier tonight and she's asleep up there. I'll give you a tour the next time you want to come by.

Sure, I say.

You know, I was thinking of trying to get in touch with you anyway, now that I've decided to try to do this book. Given the obvious importance of your mother and of that portrait to Herb.

Why don't you come out with me to her nursing home sometime and we can talk to her. Her memory isn't always so reliable. Some days are better than others.

I would love that, she says. There aren't so many people still alive who had their portraits painted by Herb.

Did you know of or ever hear Herb mention a painting of a Normandy forest scene with forest animals during the war, and with himself and another soldier named Eddie?

I'd have to check in the storage. Herb has thousands of works, finished and unfinished, in there, but I don't recall hearing about that one. Forest animals? Really? Herb?

Eddie was his lover during the war, I think.

You know a story about Herb having a lover during the war? Wow. I sure don't. I was always innocent little Beth. He would never tell me stories like that, but I expect he will now. Beth's eyes in her small face are opened so wide and glow so blackly that she resembles one of those cute nocturnal jungle animals, clinging to her branch over our heads.

There was somebody important to him in Marrakesh, she says. I know that. But during the war?

You know, I don't even remember how I know about that war painting with the animals, I say.

From your mother, maybe? Please don't be offended, she says, but, you know, I really hadn't thought of you in years. Someone in my family told me that Bert Goldberg's son had become a writer, and then I sort of did connect you to some things I'd seen around by—she portentously lowers her voice—*Francisco Goldberg*. But I only really began to think of you when I decided to write about Herb.

Even apart from Herb, I say, you must have a lot to say and tell about. All those years in the Boston courts. I remember that letter you sent me, after we went with Herb and my father to the Celtics game. I remember just how impressed I was by how spooky smart but also winsome, charming, your writing was.

Oh, thanks, Frankie, she responds, her expression lighting up. I remember the letter you sent me too. She giggles, mischievously, and looks at me as if she thinks I must know what's so funny about it.

C'mon, what? I ask.

You wrote that you had an Indian arrowhead you wanted to give me.

Oh yeah, I say. I remember that arrowhead. If I pull it out of my pocket now, it'll freak her out, probably not in a good way. Anyway, I'm giving it to Lexi.

It just seemed like such a boy thing, she says. What, this kid is trying to impress me with an Indian arrowhead? She laughs and I laugh; we sit on the couch laughing. Maybe I was too mature for my age, she says. I was already into the Velvet Underground. I wanted to be Nico. I was only interested in boys who played electric guitars. I have to say, after I let you in and we came up here and I got a good look at you, I got nervous that it really wasn't you, because from when I met you back then, you just don't look anything like I would have imagined.

*Ha*, I say. Is that a good thing?

Beth laughs again, such generous jollity. Yes, it's a good thing. But don't take that the wrong way. You were very sweet. With your arrowhead. She smiles.

I really love your dress, I say. All those little letters all over it, they look like they're about to break out into a riot, you know what I mean? Hey, motherfuckers, we can spell out whatever we want. Don't even think of trying to stop us or we'll burn this whole language down!

This dress, really? says Beth. She plucks it in her fingers and holds it out over chest, looking down at it. Rioting letters, wow, really? After so many years of being a public defender, I could get down with some anarchy now. Frankie, I am having such a good time, and this has been the most fabulous and serendipitous surprise ever, but it's really late. I do have to get to sleep. You can crash here on the couch if you want. I reach into a pocket and pull out my phone. 3:43 in the morning, and there's a message from Lulú: "Panchito, I dreamed we were riding bicycles together."

June 22, 2020—CDMX

# Acknowledgments

My thanks to the directors and staff of the Radcliffe Institute for Advanced Studies, where part of this book was written during the 2018-19 fellowship year. Dr. Robert J. Kelly was a generous guide to the "science and art" of artificial tooth production. Thank you to Sandra Hernández Estrada; to Sean E. Fitzgerald for his long-ago email; to Felito (Consuelo) and Tía Babu (Barbara); to Stephen Haff for the opportunity to participate in the ongoing miracle of Still Waters in a Storm and the Kid Quixotes; to friends and colleagues who read earlier versions and provided indispensable insights and comments, Bex Brian, Dominique, Gonzalo, Chloe, Susan, and Valeria; to Lucas, Hernán and Ieva for a consequential, if hilarious, conversation at Kirkland T & T. With gratitude to Morgan, Elisabeth Schmitz, Katie Raissian, Yvonne Cha, and all the team at Grove. Amanda Urban gave staunch support from start to finish. Jovi and Azalea, and also Jovisitas during the months she spent with us, were the sun that rises every day.